# Ravens Refuge

Sojourner 4

*Catherine Gruben Smith*

*Illustrated by*
*Emilie Gruben*

*Sola Deo Gloria*

*Scan for a curated playlist of mood music!*

ISBN: 978-1-955639-95-8

All scriptures taken from the King James Version.
Cover created by Casey Webb.

"...knowing that tribulation worketh patience; and patience, experience; and experience, hope..."
-Romans 5:4

To Joshua: Thank you for all the stories. May you be a man so strong in the Lord, you inspire others to give their all. I pray you keep the vision your whole life.

Note to Readers:

Sign language is another language, not just a form of English. A signer thinks in pictures, they sign what they see, not full sentences. I translate Joe's dialogue as I would any language; making it smooth and sensible in English, just as someone would do in their mind when watching a signer.

# Contents

# Introduction

The sharpened sea shell sliced through Hamfast's collar. He felt his shirt split and his skin prickle as it buzzed past his ear and landed in the wall with a deep "thunk." The shell sunk four inches into the polished wood. A thin line of sweat congealed on Hamfast's forehead.

"What did you say about a 'suicide mission' that you *refuse*?" Ariel Athenia asked. Her voice filled the guardroom, as the team of five agents sat stone still, staring at the beautiful woman. "I hope you didn't mean the short task I'm sending you boys on this afternoon."

"I just thought going into FF headquarters after a SOLTD might be a little hard to pull off, Athenia," Hamfast said. He didn't mumble it, and his gaze stayed focused on the emerald eyes of his boss. His teammates had never respected his bravery quite as much as they did in that moment. "I didn't really mean 'refuse,' I won't do that to one of your orders."

"I'm glad to hear it, Hammy," Athenia smiled, her sweetness a cold, gilded thing. She pulled a set of building plans from under her arm and unrolled them on the table, covering the dirty playing cards and effectively ending the rummy game. "And you're not going into FF headquarters. Now the mission is closer, I'll let you in on the real plan. Listen up, boys."

The huge Hamfast and his boys listened. Gradually his face lost the guarded dislike and began to gain an expression of respect, even of wonder. This no longer sounded like a suicide mission. Ariel Athenia knew how to use her brain and resources, and she knew things about her enemies that Hamfast hoped no one knew about him. A momentary stab of fear went through him as she let the plans roll up and slid them under her arm again. What would a woman like this do to the world once she had the ability to skip anywhere in a heartbeat?

"Everything understood, Hammy?" Athenia demanded.

"Yes ma'am," he rumbled, every inch the deferential henchman.

"Be back in time and you get a pay bonus, a good one. And remember; don't hand the SOLDT to anyone but *me*." Her manicured fingers plucked a photograph from her pocket and she stared at it. Hatred twisted her pretty face. "Before that mission though, I have a side job for you, Hamfast. Someone needs to learn what happens when they double-cross Athenia."

"Then he said, 'I don't even like the color salmon!'" Peter said. The blue lines of the hologram projector reproduced his disgusted surprise to perfection, and laughter filled the day room inside the Ravens' wagon. Elizabeth's pretty, round face joined him at the projector.

"I've never seen father at such a loss for words," she grinned. "And the fish smell is still clogging our drains!"

"Oh I wish I could have been there," Anna said, clearing her eyes after the laughter.

"It's better the way I tell it, anyway," Peter said.

"You always think your stories are the best," Nehemiah grinned at him. He sat slumped comfortably at the table, cleaning his Compton laser, Hope, with slow enjoyment.

"That's because they are the best, and you know it!" Peter said. His fiancé pushed him playfully in the shoulder and turned back to Anna.

"So how are you?" Elizabeth demanded. "Besides the sudden welcome addition of a big brother again, I mean. I see new earrings. The flying ravens match your IDP[1] dove necklace very nicely."

"Why thank you," Anna smiled, fingering the new jewelry

---

[1] The International Discipleship Program, the name of the Christian underground running through most kingdoms. Because being a Christian is dangerous in most places, the IDP use a necklace for identifying brethren. Each person chooses their own personal symbol to mask the identifier, but when activated, the metal rearranges to become the universal IDP cross. Anna chose a folk-art dove with wings wide open as her mask.

accentuating her elegant neck. "Joe decided we needed trackers for when we're inside kingdoms and split up for whatever reason, and I chose one in these earrings. I like them, so I keep wearing the birds."

"What's he planning on doing that you need that kind of insurance?" Peter demanded curiously.

"Oh, don't bother asking, Joe's not the best at telling people things," Nehi said, his eyes twinkling as they turned toward his little friend in the corner of the day room. Joe sat cross-legged, eyes half closed, perfectly still, seemingly half-asleep. Nehemiah knew him better by now. He knew the mute sat analyzing each word, assessing their position through the wagon's movement. And he had chosen to lean against the wall to the night room, which probably meant he was listening to Daniel's snores through the wall, calculating how long he would stay asleep. "Guess what, somewhere (he won't tell where) Joe found journal pages from the past world that are about our ancestor. The few he had were really amazing to read. Whoever wrote them keeps mentioning a 'Lu' and we figure that's Louis Hillson."

"Wait, Louis Hillson as in the founder of the Sojourners?" Elizabeth blinked.

"Well, he didn't found it alone, he was just one of them," Anna commented.

"Oh, just a few ancient documents from the past world about a major founder," Peter shrugged, "that's all, nothing to tell people about." Nehemiah grinned and chose to move the conversation on.

"So how's Paul getting on now that the UPC have reared their head?"

"Paul can speak for himself, thank you very much," the IDP leader said, and the blue lines of the hologram changed, becoming the thin, smiling face of Paul. "We've managed to keep our head down and haven't had any more trouble yet. The Jones have settled into your old quarters in our basement for now, and the arrangement is working fine. Though I think the lack of sun may induce them to brave the tunnels again soon."

"It's a good temporary solution," Peter nodded, the lines rearranging to bring his face into focus beside Paul's.

"About that," Nehi said, sitting taller and suddenly losing his apathy, "we found a weird little country that we think will work for refugees like the Jones, until we can get the Sojourners back." Joe suddenly stood beside Nehi, his expression apologetic. He whistled to his friend to ask for translation and signed quickly.

"We'll send you instructions and coordinates to the place over your feed, it would take too long to explain it orally. At least with the way the twins tell things," Joe added with a playful elbow jab to Nehi's ribs.

"We've only been connected about fifteen minutes," Anna objected. Joe shrugged, apologetic again.

"I try not to be open to communicators for longer than that," he signed.

"Wait, you have a jammer running all the time?" Peter asked.

"Scrambler," Joe corrected, and Nehi's mouth twisted in amusement as he translated it.

"Joe's a little overcautious about some things," Anna commented in a stage whisper.

"Yes, but isn't a scrambler a little over the top?" Paul said. "Sure, it means no one can track you, but you're one small wagon in the wild lands and already pretty impossible to track. It also means no one can leave messages on your hologram, and even none of your bone plants will work–"

"We don't have plants," Anna broke in, "and Daniel says his got fried at the Tao prison."

"Joe's dealing with bad people," Nehi added. "A little extra protection when you're doing business with nasty people's crossed lovers and out Wolf hunting is a good choice." Joe's eyes flicked to Nehi, and his face went a little more bland, a little extra blank. But he didn't stop his tall friend as Nehi went on. "Which reminds me, Paul, you should know there's someone out hunting the flock. Someone with an 'in' to the IDP, I don't know who, but it's a dangerous character calling themselves the Wolf. I'm pretty sure they're the same one who had you snatched last year, and plenty of others like you."

"Great, something else to watch for," Paul said, a tight frown falling over his face. "Joe, do you think it will be as bad as when Zehn turned traitor in Story Land?"

"Worse," Joe signed, "if Wolf isn't stopped. But there are good people out Wolf hunting, and we're running their messages and helping where we can. Keep hope. God's got the end of the story."

"Do that sign again, please, for hope?" Elizabeth interrupted, the hologram's lines reforming to show her face. Joe obliged. He tapped his forehead with his first finger on his dominant hand, then keeping that hand at the same level while bringing his other up toward his chin, he flattened his fingers twice. Then he winked and crossed his first two fingers on both hands and tapped the air twice, his other fingers loosely held in a fist.

"That's 'hope' too, he gave you both kinds," Anna said, and a smile slid over Elizabeth.

"I like that. Thank you," she said. Joe's head tipped as his muscles stiffened, listening to something outside. Nehi started to quickly assemble Hope again after her cleaning. A long metallic shriek came from outside. Another joined it, and the sounds quickly grew clearer and louder as they came closer. Joe looked at the hologram feed, shrugged, waved, leapt on the table, cupped his hands around the skylight, and shot out onto the wagon top feet first.

"Phoenix are tailing us again, got to go," Nehi said, snapping his goggles over his eyes. He chinned out the skylight onto the wagon top, his feet scrabbling in the air for an instant before he found purchase.

"Next week same time?" Anna asked quickly. Elizabeth nodded, and Anna's finger tapped the button ending communications.

Hundreds of miles away from the Ravens' wagon, Peter and

Elizabeth looked at each other.

"What's a phoenix do you think?" Peter asked.

"I'm not entirely sure I want to know," his fiancé commented. She wrapped her arm through his and leaned into him, causing a brilliant goofy smile to spread over Peter. "I hope they're all right. But it was good to get to talk to them again."

Paul sat still, staring at the blank wall where the hologram projection had been. His mouth twitched, his expression dark. That call left him with a lot to think about.

"I don't understand, you want us to let the Raider keep raiding?" Freddy said. He regulated his tone very carefully, keeping it humble and confused. Frederick Masterson would be the last to challenge the Wolf. He had no intention of dying that stupidly.

"I want you to not kill the Raider, yet." The voice came from the blue lines making up the hologram picture of the wolf's head. The dead wolf circled slowly on Freddy's patio table, dim in the bright sunlight. The garden fountains tinkled gently in the background, the scent of hundreds of flowers in summer bloom filled the air. It should have been a place with families laughing over iced tea and sandwiches. "I will kill him myself, after I've gotten my use out of him."

"Simmons had him ready to fall. That worthy character is, of course, no longer an asset to us, but we still have agents able to take up where–"

"I gave you an order, Freddy." The words snapped, cold and annoyed. Freddy closed his mouth abruptly. A bead of sweat gently rolled down the back of his neck. "He has access to something I need. And he knows someone I want to find, if he dies the knowledge dies with him. That doesn't mean you have to be gentle with the Raider if he does happen to fall in with your people, you understand."

"I understand," Freddy parroted. Though he didn't, not

really. What did the Wolf need from the Black Raider? If the Wolf wanted something, the Wolf took it. Yet this Raider seemed to be dancing on the hook instead of in the Wolf's jaws. Or was the Wolf the one on the hook? It would be something about that blasted treasure, of course. The Wolf was obsessed by it. An uncomfortable sensation of uncertainty wriggled down Freddy's spine.

"Get your agents to the People's Kingdom and wait for my orders."

# Chapter One: Birding

*"For the Lord is good; His mercy is everlasting; and His truth endureth to all generations." Psalm 100:5*

The skylight thumped into the wagon as Nehemiah hopped out and crouched under the diamond glass. The hoverer's speed made the scenery a green blur around him. His goggles lay strapped over his eyes, and he clutched his Compton laser tight as he scuttled beside Joe. A long, high-pitched shriek rang over the land. The mute's green eyes shone bright and calculating as he stared at a series of red streaks behind their wagon. A sharp whistle came from him.

Cobeau dropped the accelerator stick all the way to zero and cut the steam to Prissy's wheeled shoes. The steam jets under the wagon suddenly pointed backward, driving the hoverer to a lurching stop. A thump and shout from inside the wagon told Nehi his brother's nap had just been interrupted by a sudden meeting with the floor. Seven streaks of bright fiery red shot past overhead, their rising, metallic, shriek filling even the wind bubble. Beau cut the wagon's steam and they settled to the squishy, wet ground. The three men watched the phoenix, their heads swiveling to follow the seven fiery streaks as they sped farther away into the blue sky.

Prissy squealed, an angry complaint about the sharp stop; the giant guinea pig loved traveling at high-speeds. The men's faces tightened.

Seven streaks paused in midair, turning as if summoned by Prissy's squeal. Seven creatures dropped heavily to the ground, and Nehi could see them clearly for the first time. He felt his breath catch as his chest tightened.

Orange and red plated scales covered their thin bodies and bat-like wings. The scales moved, shifting and catching the sun, as the phoenix stalked forward. The movement caught the sun and sent it glinting off in sharp beams, disorienting and blinding prey and enemies. They walked on red claws at the end of

their wings, each phoenix with eight prehensile tails whispering on the wet ground behind them, moving like snakes. A stinger projected off the end of the tails, a steady drip of poison spilling from them as they moved toward their prey. Each drop steamed on the wet grass and left a hole of burnt, bare earth where it fell. Forked tongues slid in and out of their beak like mouths. Nehi couldn't see any eyes on the things, just smooth scales sloping into a domed head. One gave their horrendous shriek again and Nehi winced, the sound so high and screeching it seemed to vibrate his brain. The creatures 'ears swiveled to face Prissy. Beaks clacked. Nehi swallowed hard, and suddenly wished the warlike Wiglaf had come with them now, instead of waiting to be picked up after their trek to Story Land.

"Echolocation?" Nehemiah asked. Joe nodded, studying the situation as his hands moved in an answer.

"And scent. They have a Jacobsen's organ like a snake, and they're sense of smell is phenomenal. We'll use that. Keep them occupied and off Prissy." The mute spun and dropped back through the skylight into the wagon.

"Oh yeah sure, just desert us to the creepy eight-tailed shriekers," Nehi yelled after him. He spun toward the driver's bench. "Beau, will they take to the air and eat us if we crack the wind bubble?"

"Takes them time to get airborne. Don't move fast on the ground," the chimera rumbled.

"Good," Nehi said, dropping onto the bench beside Beau. He could hear the muted rumbles of his siblings' quick conversation and the silent pauses of the mute's answers below him. They had better come up with something fast. His hand landed on the bubble wand. "They have scales so I'm assuming we can't kill them with lasers, but we can sure annoy them. Let's buy Joe some time for whatever he's up to." He pumped the wand once.

The clear bubble cracked open six inches. A warm breeze spun around him, carrying the scent of wet earth and wet Prissy. The lead phoenix's ear twitched, sensing the change in

# Chapter One: Birding

## Psalm 100:5

Phoenix

front of them. His beak opened and his blood red tongue flicked out again. A shriek rang from him, and Nehi gasped, almost doubling over at the pain that sliced through his brain, shaking it and fuzzing his vision. It was fingernails across a chalkboard, pots hit with metal ladles, a cat's dying yowl, mixed with a supersonic volume. Over it all a single note in a cadence at the top of his hearing pierced through his bones and muscles.

Nehi jerked Hope up and squeezed her trigger. Beside him Beau snapped his snub-nosed Brunhiem to his shoulder and fired. Through his dyed goggles Nehi saw his shot burst squarely in a phoenix's open mouth. The creature fell back in a tangle of tails and glinting scales, his wings shooting out in his distress.

A chorus of shrieks cut through the morning. Nehi curled into himself, his hands going to his ears, gasping at the pain. Beau's hand dropped on the wind bubble, snapping it closed. The noise diminished a level.

"Prissy," Nehi shouted over the ringing in his ears, "that close to the noise, it will explode her eardrums, we–"

"Deaf," Beau shouted back, shaking his head.

Seven phoenixes snaked over the land closer to Prissy as the giant pig cowered against her traces. The one Nehemiah had hit moved slower at the back of the group, his head hanging low and shaking as if it stung. One of the creatures made a quick dash, water squishing under her red claws and spraying up behind her eight tails as she moved over one of the thousands of puddles in this land. She stopped only a few yards from Prissy.

The chimera reached under his seat and pulled out a block of cheddar cheese he had apparently been saving. He broke off a piece and stuffed it in his ear, offering it to Nehi. Nehemiah followed his example, trying to ignore the way it squeaked and squished as he shoved it in. Beau dropped his leftover block beside his seat and grabbed the bubble wand. He looked at Nehi. Nehemiah nodded.

The crack in the bubble shot open and their lasers rose. Four quick shots pulsed in the wet air, and four of the phoenix

stumbled back, tails in a tangle and shrieks rising to a scream. Nehi kept firing, gritting his teeth at the way his brain shook with each metallic call from these creatures. The phoenix hissed as shot after shot burst on their shining scales, wings shooting out to menace the enemy, beaks open as their call rang through the wild lands. Beams of sunlight scattered from them in blinding flashes. Stingers rose, glinting in the wet air. Prissy cowered against the wagon.

Joe landed with a thump between the two shooters. His thin hand lobbed a ball out the crack. It landed in a puddle in the middle of the phoenix and a thick brown smoke billowed from it.

The scent of rotted watermelons and beans, dead things and skunks, wafted into the air. Nehemiah gagged, his stomach twisting. Joe's hand jerked the bubble wand, snapping their covering closed. The worst of the smell stayed outside, curling in a brown fog around the phoenix.

Terrible clacking roars filled the air, and the three men's hands clamped over their ears, cringing and writhing as the sound went on and on. But then it started to drift away. Nehemiah looked up, panting, his brain pulsing. Seven red dots soared off into the distance, the sunlight glinting off them making the creatures look like streaks of fire. Nehemiah sat up, slowly shaking his head. Joe stared at him, his green eyes twinkling and his lips curled in amusement.

"What?" Nehi asked, and wondered if he shouted it. He couldn't tell through the ringing in his head. The mute pointed at his ear, his amusement strong. Nehemiah quickly got the cheese out, grimacing at the squeak. "Well next time you run off when we have phoenix screaming like banshees outside, maybe you should at least provide hearing protection. Do you have more of those balls in the wagon?" He coughed, his hand waving in front of his nose. "Because I really, really don't want to accidently trip with a glass of water or something and ignite that."

"Made it on the spot," Joe signed. "I got D and Beauty's help

to condense the worst smells we could grab into a smoke bomb."

"Is that why you kept that dead skunk we found last week?" Nehemiah asked.

"It worked, didn't it," Joe grinned at him.

"Oh my word!" Anna ejaculated behind them. They spun to see her emerge from the skylight, one hand clamped over her nose and mouth. "That is foul. Oh, fantastic, I see a whole cloud of it has enveloped our sweet giant pig. She's already wet, that scent is going to stick to her like glue."

"Perfect, insurance against more phoenix attacks!" Nehemiah said, hopping up to his normal seat on the wagon top.

"No, she is getting a bath tonight when we stop to camp," Anna ordered. "That scent is not traveling in front of me the whole way to Story Land!"

"She is not, we need that smell," Nehemiah said. The two of them launched off in a tight argument, growing more adamant. Beau turned the steam back on, flipped the switch to Prissy's shoes, and started the wagon on their way again. Anna spun to Joe, her lips tight.

"Break the impasse," she ordered. "Do we wash the pig or not?" Joe's hands flew up, both his eyebrows rising with them.

"I'm staying out of it!" he laughed.

"Fine, coward," Anna said, her smile removing any sting. "I'll go interrupt Daniel's breakfast, he will have an opinion."

"He always has an opinion," Joe signed, his movements small and held low, in what would have been a mutter if the mute could speak. Anna already headed toward the night room and missed the signs. Nehi grinned at him and flopped back on the wagon top, rubbing his aching head and watching the multitudinous bugs of this wet land flashing by outside their bubble.

"Sisters," he sighed.

Psalm 100:5

A terrible howl rang through Nehemiah's dreams, and he started awake, gasping and disoriented. He gulped in air, the scenes from his nightmare still haunting him. Moonlight played over the grass, as bugs droned in this wet land. Joe sat rigid beside him, his breath coming in short, panicked pants and his right arm clutching his left again. The two boys looked at each other, saw the same fear, and felt the panic start to recede. Nehemiah slid closer to Joe. The ground squished underneath him as he moved, and he wished this land could manage even one dry patch of grass.

The two boys huddled together in the night, silence hovering between them. No, it wasn't silence. A bullfrog's call broke out from the pond glinting to their right, mixing with the dense insect hum that never stopped in the damp place. But that wasn't the sound Nehi noticed most. He closed his eyes, one hand rubbing his ear. That nasty howling stayed with him, clinging to his hearing even though the nightmare had fled. Joe noticed his friend's movement. A flash of understanding crossed his face, and his usual twinkle began to come into his eyes. He pointed to his ear and raised an eyebrow.

"I hear a nasty, terrible howling," Nehemiah answered shakily. "Joe, do you...is it just me?" Joe grinned.

"That's what woke us up in such a panic, brother," he signed, his white hands flashing in the moonlight. "I recognize that yelling that sounds like someone in pain. Come on, you've got to see this!" Joe motioned Nehemiah to follow and slid silently away through the tall grass. Nehemiah tagged at the mute's heels, hunching low and trying to mimic Joe's movements. The ground rose steadily, covered in a thick grass that waved and undulated like a living entity, glinting silver in the moon's radiance.

Nehemiah recognized the spot from his camp perimeter check; a small hill that dipped suddenly into a shallow, grass covered valley. The damp grass soaked the boys, and displaced bugs scattered with each movement. As they drew closer to its peak, Nehi noticed a dim yellow glow rising over the top of the

hill. The strange howling grew louder. The hill leveled as they reached the top, opening into a flat area, the grass cropped short in the uneven way that showed a herd of one horns had poured through recently. Joe dropped to his belly and began to crawl, and Nehemiah did the same, his lips pressed tight to keep from swallowing panicked little bugs. At least they hadn't run into any of the fist-sized flies that abounded out here, or the dragonflies with wingspans as long as Joe's arm. The mute stilled as he reached the opposite edge of the hill, and Nehi crawled up next to him. He carefully slid his head over the edge and looked down.

In the valley below them a large flock of birds rocked back and forth rhythmically, moving in a wide circle. They stood about three feet high, on flabby feet attached to legs so short they looked almost non-existent. Their bodies were nearly as oval as Prissy's. A smaller oval served for a head, almost as if someone had rolled two lumps of clay and slapped them together. A long curved beak stuck off their heads and two wide, gray feathered wings hung at their sides. The howling noise rose from the strange creatures' open beaks. But stranger still was their color; they glowed. A brilliant green shone off their backs, and their bellies let out an eerie yellow light. As the boys watched, the dance changed. Two birds moved out into the middle of the circle and began to hop around each other. The noise began to fade into a different song, from a howl to a high-pitched note that rose and fell suddenly. The two boys stifled a laugh at the ludicrous sound.

"They're yodeling!" Nehemiah whispered in Joe's ear. The mute nodded with a grin, and a finger went to his lips. They watched the strange courting ritual of these glowing, yodeling birds in fascinated silence. After about ten minutes, the new couple took to the air and flew away to the well-wishing yodeling of their feathered friends. The rest of the glowing birds' light began to fade. As they took slowly and awkwardly to the sky and began to travel northward in one flock, they were a deep green and dingy yellow and not a trace of a glow could be seen. Joe sat up with a smile as the flock disappeared into the starry sky.

"What were those?" Nehemiah asked, propping himself on his elbows. Joe shrugged. "You don't know? I thought you knew everything." Joe laughed and hopped to his feet. The two slid down the hill toward their encampment, disturbed bugs darting from the long grasses and buzzing away indignantly. The boys' boots landed with a squish beside the pond at the bottom of the hill.

"I've only seen them twice," Joe signed as he sludged toward their wagon. "I've never named them, don't know if anyone else has either."

"What about yodelers?" Nehemiah suggested, shaking the excess water off one foot that had gotten too close to the pond with the momentum of his slide down the hill.

"Night glows," Joe offered back.

"Not bad. Curve beaks?

"Glowers?"

"Combine it, the yodel glowers," Nehemiah said, and Joe gave his merry grin and nodded. The two made it back to camp and found everyone still in the same positions, sleeping sound.

"Are we the only two that ever wake up at night?" Nehemiah murmured as they settled back down on their blankets, shoving the annoying rubber dew protectors back. The tarps under it all crinkled with each movement.

"I guess we're the only two adventurous enough to go looking for yodel glowers," Joe signed with a wink. Nehemiah grew still. His smile faded and his eyes lifted to Joe's thin face.

"It's only been a week, Joe. Are you all right?" he asked softly. Joe's head ducked, turning away as his shoulders slumped, pulling into himself in a shy little movement. But a grateful smile hovered on his lips.

"Yes. Evil is dead. He can't plague us anymore. More than that, justice has finally caught up to him. It's…"

"What?" Nehi prodded, as Joe glanced at him uncertainly. He had seen that look quite a bit since the mute started dropping

his mask. It meant a hesitation to speak his thoughts, a person unused to having someone to talk to. Joe trusted him now. But half the time it felt like the mute still walked on eggshells around him.

"It's really, really nice to know that justice catches up, no matter what it looks like down here."

"Yes," Nehi nodded, a smile creeping over him. He settled on his back, hands sliding behind his head comfortably. "It would be hard to live without that, thinking this broken world is the only place justice could happen. I can see why some turn into vigilantes."

"Not a nice place to be," Joe nodded, his eyes distant and his smile gone. He settled in a comfortable criss-cross, his gaze going to his friend. "Knee-High, I... thank you. When I first found out the FFs were going after the Geat's book, and that whole situation, I begged God for someone to help. I knew I couldn't do it alone, and was so tired, and... It seemed like He ignored my pleading." Nehi was pretty sure he saw an "again" start to form from the mute's hands, but it was pulled back, and in the moonlight he couldn't be certain. "Then you barreled into the cabin with Hope. And you came all the way with me, and got me where I needed to go, and even picked me up again when I wasn't sure I could finish it. Thank you."

"You know, getting help might not be such a big deal if you told what you were up to more often, and let people help. You don't have to do it alone," Nehemiah drawled. *I sound like Daniel,* he realized and his eyes darted to the huddled form of his brother, snoring a few feet away. Joe's knees came up, his head laid on them, and he hunched on his blanket, perfectly still, his damp hair hanging over his eyes hiding his expression. Nehemiah wondered if the mute was pondering the strange new idea, or if something else ran behind that sudden stillness. He held back a sigh, tired of trying to guess. "I'm glad I was an answer to prayer, Joe, and I'm very thankful I was there to help when you needed it. Stick close, brother, and I'll be there whenever you need me." A smile flitted over Joe's face, hesitant and fleeting. Silence hung between them for a moment, as the bugs droned and the frogs croaked. Joe's head popped up to face his friend again, and he rocked a little, his arms tight around his knees.

"As long as we're on awkward personal topics, how goes it with you?" he signed. "Inside, I mean. You seem...strong." Nothing came from Nehemiah for a few minutes. A fly rammed into the side of Joe's head and his arms came up, beating the thing off with a splutter. The fist-sized bug buzzed away with annoyance. Joe began to assume Nehi had fallen asleep. He shifted to his knees, his tarp crinkling under the blanket.

"The six months in KAM with a settled life did something." Nehemiah's voice drifted through the night, soft and steady. Joe dropped back on his blanket, watching and listening. "I had time to think back on it all, and to what was before, to the things Mom and Dad believed and taught us. And I was able to go to church with Christian brothers on a Sunday, hear truths preached and believed by good friends...it came alongside the peace that settled in my soul last year. Just a ribbon of it then, when we were in Prophet's Peace and you told me to stop fighting it? I did. And I rested. And it worked. I mean, not right away, but... When I stopped fighting the doubts, trying to reason with them, and just clung to the cross, it's like it somehow unplugged their strength. At least most of it. Then when I was back around a real church, with brothers who had been through similar things and come out again, and... I'm resting easy with our Savior. No more questions. Except for wanting to know more about the One I love, that just seems to get stronger (not that I'm complaining). No more plaguing doubts. Trust has blossomed again, stronger than before the months of darkness. Though I...that question I asked back when we were leaving Prophet's Peace, you know, the one you said you would get back to me on? Well, the mourning still comes at unexpected times, the hole carved from Mom and Dad's death is still there. And the nightmares. But it's all been easier."

White teeth gleamed in the dark as Joe grinned at him,

allowing his pleasure to be seen. Nehemiah cleared his throat awkwardly and turned to his side, pulling the dew protector back in place and shifting his blanket over himself.

"Well, I'm not going to let a bad dream and a bunch of birds keep me up all night. You all right, or do you want to do some constellation naming?"

"I'm going to try and sketch the yodel glowers' courtship," Joe signed. "Go to sleep, Knee-High."

"Christ's peace be with you, Joe," Nehemiah muttered, curling under his blanket with a yawn. A minute later, his breath came slow and steady, his whole body relaxed. Joe still perched on his own blanket, waiting till he was sure Nehemiah was asleep. Five quiet minutes passed. The mute stood up so smoothly not even the tarp made noise. He slid to Beau, where he lay like a fallen boulder. The big man saw him coming and propped himself up on his elbow, curiosity on his simple face.

"I'll take the rest of the night watch, Glue," Joe signed, in a language he used only for Beau. "Get some sleep."

"But–" the chimera started to rumble. Joe winced and quickly put a finger to his mouth. Cobeau smiled apologetically and began to sign in the same coded language. "Dark. You may not be able to see him."

"I can't see in the dark as well as you, old friend, but I can manage if the need comes," Joe signed. "Don't worry, I'm up and I'll watch. Get some sleep finally." Cobeau nodded and rolled over, a peaceful sigh sliding from him. Another moment and a dense, grunting snore reverberated around the campsite, drowning out even the bugs' drone. Joe retrieved a pencil from his hair and a tattered brown folder filled with papers from a cubby hole in the bottom of the wagon. He picked a rock with moonlight to draw by and dropped onto it, then glanced around. Everyone was asleep, he sat alone in the night.

Joe curled on himself, his left arm cradled against his chest, a grimace wrinkling his face as he blinked and rocked. It hurt. It really hurt. By now it should be healing, the pain be lessening at least a little. But he... Joe blinked again, but this time worry scored his face. He wasn't healing as fast or as thoroughly as he should be. Harry had warned him, again and again, he had to stop getting into these messes and let himself rest, or he might just run down. Stop healing, fade away...

But then he still felt pretty worn out from the whirlwind of the past six months. Yes, that must be it. Surely.

Joe sucked in a breath, straightened up, and reached into his jacket. He pulled out a large blue paper and unfolded it silently in the night. Moonlight shone strong and silver, beaming on schematics and diagrams scrawled across the thin document. Joe studied it, his brow drawn as he worked at understanding each little intricacy.

But his gaze strayed often to the sleeping men by the wagon. His green eyes kept stopping to rest on Nehemiah's peaceful form.

# Chapter Two: Story Land

*"For thy lovingkindess is before mine eyes: and I have walked in thy truth." Psalm 26:3*

A week later, they rolled past the sign marking the border of Story Land. Humid air wrapped around them, thick and almost suffocating, as if the lush plants crowded against the road put out too much oxygen. Green waxy leaves of enormous size were everywhere the twins looked, most decorated with flowers so colorful they seemed luminous. Scattered throughout the waxy bushes and trees dangled yellow, red, even bright blue fruits, in shapes varying from ovals to five-point stars. Overshadowing it all gigantic fronds rose into the cloudy sky. The great ferns towered higher than the pines of Nehi and Anna's home forest, swaying with the slightest breeze, draping over the road and then suddenly springing the other direction to let sunlight flood in. Their intricate frond pattern mottled the company's path, as if each inch was a new work of a silhouette artist.

Joe drew the wagon to a stop and motioned to the fruit. Anna and Nehi gave a whoop and leapt off to explore. One step off the road, and they found their legs tangled and buried in thick vines and undergrowth, and their elation dimmed. Daniel started laughing as they struggled to move, calling out teasing encouragement from the top of the wagon. Joe leapt for the trees. He swung over the crowded floor like a monkey and perched in one of the trees with bright blue star fruit. He tossed one to Nehi. Daniel, still chuckling, ducked into the wagon to get a basket.

An hour later, larder full, they started on their way again. Two hours, and the green plants began to be eclipsed by brick and concrete and asphalt. A city gradually took shape; dirty buildings, cracked roads, mold spotting almost everything. After two blocks the buildings and streets surrounded them, towering over the wagon. It was hard to remember the luscious

forest existed so close to the dirty mold and graffiti.

The dirt, mold, and graffiti were all the buildings seemed to have in common. As they steamed slowly through the busy streets, Anna thought she saw examples of every architectural style she knew, and some that seemed like the builder had added things entirely at random. People wandered through the streets, laughing and talking. The twins studied the faces, and saw little signs of want, or even worry on the citizens. Most of them looked modern, peaceful, and even happy. But somehow Anna found depression stealing over her. And it was more than the incessantly overcast sky, dribbling rain, and oppressively wet air. Something about the place, the designs and minimal upkeep, the restless eyes of the people, seemed... hollow, as if they kept searching for something more. A cream colored Rocco style apartment clung to the miniscule sidewalk, the top story overhanging the wagon as Prissy pulled it down the wet road.

"Why did they put that building there?" Anna asked, watching a couple giving it cautious glances as they walked under the overhang. Joe shrugged.

"They don't need reasons here," he signed. Beau translated it automatically for Daniel's sake, his rumble wrapping around the Hillsons and Ravens. The couple made it without the fancy building falling on them, laughing in relief. But the laughter died too early to be real amusement. The woman's eyes dropped to the sidewalk, as the man's kept darting restlessly around the city.

"So why are we coming here again?" Anna asked.

"To stop some IDP trouble," Joe signed.

"I remember hearing you were in and out of the IDP," Daniel said, "but why are you rushing over here if there are problems? Are you a problem shooter; or a problem maker?"

"That depends on whose side you're on," Joe signed, his lips tight, jaw squared. His green eyes dripped ice as he stared back at Daniel. Anna and Nehemiah looked at each other and grimaced. Things hadn't smoothed out between Joe and Daniel during the two weeks traveling.

"Where do we go first?" Nehemiah broke in. Daniel muttered something inaudible and let his gaze turn to the hoverers pushing in and out of traffic around them. Joe spun to face Nehi as he signed to him.

"I go to visit a friend first. I don't think I should take all of you, not safe for him. Nowhere is safe here, though."

"Is Story Land that bad?" Nehemiah asked looking around him. "It looks moldy, and sort of..."

"Haphazard," Anna supplied.

"But not particularly dangerous," Nehemiah finished. Joe shrugged.

"It's unpredictable," he signed. "Really unpredictable. There's no truth here that stands for more than one person, nothing is the same."

"The Story Land ambassadors would come through Sojourners and pay calls on my dad," Nehemiah said. "But they were always a little cagey about their own country's belief system, you couldn't pin them down on their real philosophy. Do they actually think there is no truth? That doesn't make sense, even stating 'There is no truth,' is a truth statement."

"No it doesn't make sense, but that's what they believe," Joe signed, then grinned and shook his head at himself. "That's the kind of statement that might get you stoned here. Or hugged. It's totally unpredictable."

"I don't understand either," Anna said.

"All you need to understand right now," Joe signed, "is the only laws act as they want it to at that moment. You have no protection from anything, so watch your back while you're out. How about doing our shopping? And then Glue and I know a park nearby, want to visit there?"

"Ooh, is it fun?" Anna said.

"Yes. And beautiful," Joe signed. "Glue can show you around, if he doesn't mind. Do you mind, Glue?" Silence fell around the group as the chimera finished translating the sentence. It dragged on for ten seconds. Joe rolled his eyes with a grin and jogged his big friend's elbow. "You didn't notice anything I signed did you? Just translated it?" he asked. Beau blinked, and a bashful smile slid over his face as he nodded. A silent laugh flew from the mute, sending his green eyes twinkling like twin stars. "Can you take the Hs shopping and around our park?" Cobeau beamed and nodded at the prospect of spending the afternoon with the Hillsons. But then his brow clouded.

"You would be alone, Master," the chimera rumbled. Joe kicked his shin. "Joe."

"I'll be fine," Joe signed. Beau touched the mute's left arm, his face troubled under his thick black hair.

"Now I wonder why you're so concerned about going alone?" Daniel muttered. Joe's hands flew up and he gave him an exasperated glare.

"Fine, why don't you come along and find out?" he signed and Beau said.

"I think I will," Daniel answered with a humorless smile. "Thanks for the invitation."

"You're welcome," Joe signed with the same sort of non-smile. Anna and Nehemiah sighed. Joe leapt off the wagon, Daniel dropped heavily after him, and they walked up the street and disappeared around an apartment building painted to look like a giant cardboard box. Beau spun the wagon out of the traffic stream and pulled into a strip mall. Anna hopped off and headed for the grocers, as Nehi gratefully trotted for a hoverer supply store. He could think of hundreds of little parts in the wagon that could use replacement and touchups. Beau climbed down after them and moved steadily back and forth, offering his grunted advice, paying for purchases, and helping cart it out and stow it. In under an hour, the three found themselves steaming toward the park. But Anna's eyes kept darting down to the mute's empty seat.

"I hope they don't get into trouble," she burst out.

"I hope they can keep off each other's throats," Nehemiah responded. They watched as the chimera deftly shifted through the holographic traffic lanes, heading toward a luscious parkland. Prissy gave a piercing, delighted squeal as she caught sight of the plants.

"I can't believe our giant pig still smells–" Anna started.

"–but it kept the phoenix off." Nehemiah butted in

"Yes, yes, you got your wish despite my washing her. I never realized how futile it is to wash something that keeps bouncing in puddles. Look at the way the parkland birds are shying away from us, I bet–"

"I bet none of them have ever had to deal with a phoenix."

"Excuse me," a sophisticated male voice from the left cut in. The Hillsons quickly forgot their discussion as they spotted the speaker. A sleek 820 Barton hoverer hummed beside them, a man in one of the two leather seats. His face gleamed as though it rarely saw the sun, and his tailored clothes reeked of cologne, so strongly they could smell it even above the wet Prissy. "I'm sorry to interrupt when you were obviously having such a lovely discussion, but I must insist Rachel comes with me."

"Rachel?" the three on the wagon chorused. The man sighed and leveled a gold-plated Ruby laser.

"Now, now, let's have none of that," he said in an impatient tone. He stayed focused on Anna. "Don't you think you've kept your fiancé waiting long enough? Come on down and I won't mention I found you in the company of a handsome young man and a chimera."

"My name's not Rachel," Anna said.

"It's Anna, and I'm her brother," Nehemiah said.

"Why is your laser gold?" Cobeau asked.

"Really, this is too tiresome. If you mean to keep Len to this ridiculous promise, you have to come with me," the man said. His gaze shifted behind the threesome gathered on the wagon top. "Go on, Thomasina, she's still objecting." Nehemiah was about to say that was a ridiculously old trick and why didn't he put the laser away and they'd work through this thing, when a metal ball slammed into the back of his head. The sharp crack of it filled his world, a heavy blackness flooded his mind, and his limbs filled with lead. A hiss invaded his hearing, and a

sharp stench filled his airways. He felt a cough forming as the stench stung and tingled through him, but the tingling spread too quickly. It filled his head till it buzzed, then there was nothing.

Mottled light played over Nehemiah's closed eyelids. His stomach churned and he curled into a ball, retching as his mind spun. He knew the feeling. Memories of falling out of an oak tree as an eight-year-old played in his mind, when life was so simple and beautiful. He could hear his mother's shriek all over again as he lay on the wagon top. No, not Mom's shriek when he landed on his head... He heard the ringing in his own head, tingling and buzzing. Oh man, his head hurt.

His eyelids fluttered open and a groan slid from his parched throat. Huge, giant ferns leaned over him, waving in a slight breeze. Nehi closed his eyes and opened them again. Still the same. Had he turned tiny? Had he shrunk in size as his head grew in pain? Cobeau grunted beside him. In a flash Nehi knew the sound, the person, and everything that had happened. He jerked up, his hand scrabbling in Anna's empty seat. His stomach churned again and he doubled over the wagon's railing, retching out what he had left of breakfast.

Nehi sat still and forced himself to concentrate. His breath came in panicked, short spurts, filling his hearing. His fingernails dug into his palms as he forced himself to breathe steady and think. He felt the after effects of a knockout gas and being whalloped on the head, that was all, causing him confusion and making his stomach churn. Nothing to concern himself over if he moved slow. But as his middle clenched and burned, he knew that wasn't all.

Terror over his sister consumed him. Anna was gone. The man was gone. The park was gone. Prissy happily grazed in an empty lot in the middle of a rundown neighborhood. The shadows told him only a few minutes had passed, but he had missed so much... Cobeau sat slumped in the driver's seat of the wagon, still under the knock out effects. Nehemiah grabbed a water cup and dribbled it over Beau's head, noting the bloodied lump

under the chimera's ear. His hand shook, and he wondered whether to yell for Anna or keep quiet as he tried to figure out what had happened.

Beau came awake with a start. His big hand closed into a fist and drew back, his dark eyes unfocused. Nehemiah ducked the punch and the whistle of air darting past seemed to scream in the young man's mind. The world spun around him.

"It's me, Beau, calm down," he grunted. Beau whimpered. He curled in the seat, his eyes dim and confused, staring around him with his brow creased so hard a coin would have disappeared in the folds. A little mournful howl slid from him. Nehemiah savagely wished the chimera still lay unconscious. He dropped a hand on the big man's shoulder and told him it was ok, while everything inside him screamed it wasn't ok. His hands went to his throbbing temples, forcing himself to think.

Nehi's eyes shot open. Of course, Anna's earrings!

Nehemiah scrambled inside the wagon, darted into the night room, and ran his fingers along the wall. He felt a bump in the painted bark of an aspen, glimmering silver in the painted moonlight. Nehi jabbed it and the cabinet door swung open. Joe's direction set sat in the small recess in the wagon wall, in between the lines of canisters compressing water for the steam jets. Nehemiah's mind hiccupped and fumbled to remember the settings for the dials. Desperate pleading roared through him, eclipsing everything. Oh dear God, protect his sister! Images of evils he had seen and stories he had heard during the disintegration played in his mind despite every effort to assume the best about that foppish creature with the golden gun. Nehemiah's hand shook too hard to control the delicate dials. His strong Anna, who laughed away his fears, guided his faltering feet, lifted his head like a man, and treated him like he was strong and capable till he even believed it himself...

He dropped his head in a desperate prayer, forcing himself to breathe and remember. God is big enough to handle it all. Their Father God is always there, always with them, sovereign no matter what. Nehemiah lifted his head and forced his hands steady. He flipped the switch and programmed the set to find his sister.

Hold on, Anna!

Joe trotted down the cracked sidewalk, till it ran up the walls of an apartment house. He hopped into the street and dodged hoverers across to the next sidewalk, working steadily deeper into town. This sidewalk disappeared into a manhole. Joe hopped over the hole and trotted over the smooth grass. He hardly glanced around him, moving through the haphazard streets with the unconsciousness of someone who had walked the route a thousand times, until familiarity had turned to boredom. Joe spun off a street painted lemon yellow into a pretty, ordinary neighborhood, and his steps slowed. Daniel panted and his arm stole around his waist, grateful for the slower pace. He watched the mute's face turn to a whitewashed house, with a steep tiled roof and gingerbread crenellations, set off a few yards from the street. Joe's movements turned shuffling and hesitant, as if they longed to turn in at the picket fence and walk through the luscious yard to the blue screen door. Daniel could have sworn a mist covered the mute's green eyes as he stared over the pretty white gate.

But before he could ask about the mute's strange softening, Joe took off at a trot, turned two more corners, jogged along a seven-foot brick fence, and finally drew to a stop outside an intricate wrought iron gate. Daniel stood and panted, peering through the gate into a large walled-off square of pretty grass. A plaque bolted beside the gate read, *Doctor Harold Pablo, Surgeon.* As Joe fidgeted with the lock, Daniel studied the house inside the high spiked fence. It looked old, but well-kept and attractive. Two laden apple trees stood on either side of the door and Daniel grinned.

"Are you sure the doctor's in?" he drawled, his voice a little unsteady as he tried to catch his breath. "If the old adage is true those trees should keep him out till next year." Joe laughed, the lock clicked open, and Daniel found himself following the lock-picker in and hoping they didn't get arrested for this. As they stepped onto the covered wooden porch he took fate in his hands and rang the doorbell. A melodious note echoed through the house and died softly as the two waited. Joe swayed back and forth and whistled quietly to himself, a little smile on his face.

The oak door jerked open and a happy yell came from just inside. Two arms shot out and encased the mute in a greeting that lifted his feet six inches off the ground. The stranger plunked the mute back on his porch, and Daniel could see the man. He looked ordinary. Brown hair, medium height, clean shaven. Nose, chin, and eyes all accounted for.

"Joe, you little escapist!" the doctor chuckled in a quick, competent voice. "Where have you been, and why haven't you visited your old roost? Or this old rooster for that matter, I – Oh beg pardon, you brought company." Daniel suddenly found himself being appraised, and realized the ordinary eyes sparkled. Joe signed something. The man nodded and held out a hand.

"How do you do? I'm Harry. Joe tells me you're Daniel, and it's a great pleasure to meet you. Well, he didn't sign that, he already knows you, I meant – anyway, it's a great pleasure for him to bring me someone in decent health for once, Joe usually brings the half-dead sorts of guests to me. Come in, come in." The doctor kept talking in his quick flow, with Joe answering occasionally in his silent fashion.

Daniel followed them into the house, noting old fashioned wallpaper, oak paneling, ornate wooden furniture, and a cheerful amount of light. It was a nice, homey sort of place, Daniel decided. He cemented that opinion as he followed his guides into a bright kitchen. The noise of his feet on the enameled black and white tiling echoed a welcoming, cheery peace. He dropped into a red wooden chair at the oak kitchen table, and realized he felt very much like a tag along as he listened to half a conversation from the doctor (busy fetching water for his two guests), and tried to guess the other half from the signs shaped by the mute across from him at the table. Harry settled in a chair at the head of the table and gave Joe a smile that hinted at disappointment.

"I suppose you didn't come just to visit, did you Joe?" he asked. The mute shook his head apologetically and signed something. He suddenly looked at Daniel, flashed him a smile, and signed something else. "Oh, I'm sorry, I assumed you knew Joe's language. Allow me to translate for you," Harry said quickly to Daniel.

"As I was signing, Doctor," Joe signed and Harry said, "I really wish I didn't have to run, and I hope to come back and stay for a while soon. But now it's a business call."

"I thought so," Harry sighed. "It's always business with this fellow, Daniel, if you can make him stop for one minute I believe it's the equivalent of an act of God."

"So what's his business here?" Daniel asked.

"IDP work, as always. Feel free to raid the refrigerator, take whatever strikes your fancy. Plates are above the sink."

"Be careful, D," Joe signed with a grin. "I've been poisoned several times from that refrigerator."

"Hm. Well, I have wondered about the milk lately," Harry answered.

A smile broke over Daniel's face as he opened the refrigerator. The doctor was obviously a bachelor. Harry and Joe chatted on about various matters that didn't sound like business, and Daniel listened with interest as he rummaged in the refrigerator for something still edible. The most interesting facts seemed to be that Harry was an old friend of Joe's, and the branch leader of the Story Land IDP. After digging a little Daniel found the remains of a peach pie that was delightful, a box of beans that was fairly delightful, and a jug of very sour milk which was anything but delightful and he poured down the sink for Harry. He was working on a cold chicken sandwich and a glass of juice when Joe finally asked a business question. Harry broke off the conversation with a sigh and turned to Daniel.

"Sorry for ignoring you in the initial 'chum talk,' it isn't often Joe and I find time to exchange incidental news and old memories," he said.

"What's the problem in the IDP here?" Joe signed again.

"How you always know, I will never understand," Harry answered, "but we do have a problem that will be much larger if not dealt with soon. There's been a rage of property rearranging going on–"

"Of what?" Daniel muttered through his sandwich. "Good chicken by the way, thanks."

"You're welcome, and a property rearranger is more commonly (and rightly) known as a thief," the doctor answered. "They've been taking important things, very expensive things. The SW–"

"SW, Social Workers, the police force here right?" Daniel interrupted again. He had been hanging around Anna and Nehemiah too long, he reflected as he apologized.

"Don't mention it, and yes that's right," Harry said easily, and went on. "The SW have dubbed these thieves the Ill Trio and put their best man on getting rid of them. That's good, but now circumstances are shaping up to point to the IDP as the Ill Trio."

"You're being framed for the thefts?" Joe asked.

"It's beginning to look like it, yes. It will be a definite frame in a few days, if things keep moving as fast as they have been. Knowing you, you're here to stop the trouble." Harry said, studying his small friend. "But what do you really think you can do?"

"I'll think of something," Joe signed airily. "Problem taken care of."

"Just like that?" Daniel asked skeptically.

"Just like that," Harry smiled. "When you've been around Joe longer, you'll understand those impossible statements of his are facts, not just statements."

"What about infiltration?" Joe signed, and Harry said. Daniel got the feeling he had himself on automatic translator, like

Beau's sing-song growl.

"Oh, that's bad," Harry answered gravely. "Not as bad as when Zehn officially turned traitor to the UPC[2], but it's been decidedly uncomfortable."

"Infiltration?" Daniel asked, swallowing the last of his chicken.

"Sheep and wolves, D," Joe signed, "infiltrators are the wolves."

"That's an eerily accurate description of this thing, our people have heard of 'the Wolf' during snatches. Whoever it is has been preying on our flock, and I've had a difficult time crooking it, as I'm supposed to do as the major shepherd here. It's too vague to go after, Joe. Just something there for long enough to snatch one of us, and then it's gone again. It's like a monster lurking in the shadows."

"Efficient?" Joe signed, his sharp features serious and calculating.

"Deadly so."

"Quick?"

"Too quick to follow."

"Do the ones snatched come back?"

"Yes, at least usually."

"But a lot of repair jobs?" Jo signed, and Daniel wondered if the conversation had switched to hoverers.

"Hm. Where have you run across this before, Joe?" Harry asked, shifting positions in interest. "Yes, they always come back in a very poor condition and I have done a good many repair jobs lately, much more than I care for. But they do tend to come back. Which is decidedly better than other times. And they all have some strange story about questions and judges. Even they don't understand it. I don't suppose you, Daniel (I mean, I suppose you are that Daniel, the eldest Hillson)..."

---

[2] United Peoples Commission, a non-Christian group running under most kingdoms in the Book Base Age employing handpicked, specially trained agents to help shape the world according to their ideas and protect those they deem need it. The UPC do not approve of Christians.

"No," Daniel said, silently rearranging his ideas of this doctor. His ordinary face hid a smart mind, to automatically connect his first name and face, even scarred as it was, with a country that had fallen well over a year ago. "I don't understand it either. Why do you think it's that Judge? I mean, my father, the last Judge for the Sojourners?"

"That's what the questions seem to imply," Harry answered and looked to Joe. The mute chose to move the subject on.

"I have that particular Wolf in my sights, Doctor," he signed. "But it's still going to be a while before I can finish the hunt. Send out word through your people that you have no information or connection with judges of any sort."

"You really think that will do any good?" Harry asked skeptically.

"It might," Joe shrugged. "Especially since it's true. I'll keep working at it. Doctor, it's getting late."

"Going already?" Harry said with surprise. "Quite a short visit today. All right, Joe, you're always free to come and go at this old rooster's refuge. Let me fetch our branch's contribution to the poor." He crossed to a kitchen drawer and pulled out a wad of money. Daniel's eyebrows rose at the size of the bundle.

"You keep it there?" Joe signed with amusement as he took the bulging bag of coins.

"Same drawer I keep the nastier surgeon's tools and rat poisons in," Harry said, a smile twitching at the corner of his mouth. "It ought to deter any over eager hands. That ends our business then. Be careful. And come back sooner, Joe, will you? And bring our hirsute friend with you next time, I miss old Beau's rumble. Daniel, nice to meet you, and Joe..." Harry trailed them to the door and on out, and Daniel smiled at the way he never seemed to stop talking. He must be a lonely character. Or maybe he was always like that. They passed one of his patients coming up the porch and Harry switched his competent chatter to the patient with practiced ease. He was always like that, Daniel realized with a grin.

"So Joe, what do you do with that money Harry gave you?"

Daniel asked as he followed him down the street. "Is that how you Ravens survive, on contributions for the poor?" A pencil slid from Joe's hair to his fingers, and a note shoved into Daniel's hands.

*Knock it off, Dan, or I may not call a cab and let you walk the whole way instead.*

"No 'Dan,' don't you pick up on the bad habit. And call a cab to where?" Daniel asked. He decided not to apologize for his remark. It might still be true.

*To the leaders' place of business in Story Land, to earn that money you so cleverly noticed we Ravens need, and maybe fish up a clue to this thieving business.*

# Chapter Three: The Hernons

*"Wherefore putting away lying, speak every man truth with his neighbour: for we are members one of another."* Ephesians 4:25

A sharp "crack!" rang over the wagon. Anna spun and found Nehi and Cobeau slumping into a heap. A slim woman in a tight white suit and a hood with cat ears stood over them, a silver ball in her palm. The woman's leg shot out in a blur and sent a left kick straight into Anna's ribs. She toppled over the short railing with the force of it, her breath leaving in a woosh. Anna clawed for the wagon, just managing to grip the rail with one hand. The cat lady spun again in a showy circle and kicked her fingers off. She slammed a gas bomb between the fallen men and a brown cloud sprayed from it. The woman back flipped off the wagon, her hand hitting the wand bubble as she moved. The click of the wagon's bubble cut off the sharp hiss of the gas bomb as Anna fell into the Barton hoverer. She bounced off the cushions, and rolled onto the floor, her heart pounding and her body bruised.

Steam wooshed, and the vehicle shot off. She felt the g-force pressing into her, and knew they were moving too fast for her to leap out. Anna surged forward, her hand flattened to send a jab into this stranger's throat. The stunted, black barrel of a Brenley's stun gun pressed into her fingertips. Anna froze. Her eyes went to the stranger's pale face. He only glanced at her as he wove in and out of traffic around the sharp, haphazard turns in this city. But his face was hard and very annoyed; he would be quite happy to release the Brenley's coils. She stared down the barrel and traced the coiled wires home to their pulsing battery. Anna decided she would rather have her nervous system under her own control and not random impulses for the next three days. She sat stiffly in the passenger seat and laid her hands in her lap. The Brenley shifted just enough to point at her side. The clear wind bubble clicked in place above her, shutting off the hissing air, and she spit out a mouthful of her black hair.

The buildings fell away behind them and the lush forest zipped by outside the bubble. The stranger pushed their speed higher.

"May I know the name of my kidnaper?" Anna asked. The man shot her a frigid frown and turned back to the road. "Where are we going?" He grimaced and his thumb rubbed the trigger on the Brenley. Anna's lips pursed and she let the silence linger.

After five blurred minutes, the hover car broke through the verdant plants onto a smooth driveway running through a wide, immaculate lawn, and slowed to a crawl. A Romanesque mansion rested at the end of the drive. The man pulled the Brenley up and his sleeve down, tucking it out of sight. But Anna could still see the barrel poking out his jacket sleeve. He was ready for any move she might make, confound it. The hover car slid to a smooth stop, the wind bubble popped open, and flower-scented air and the cry of birds and insects filled the world again. The man waved at the mansion, his face set in a sort of bored anger. Anna slid over the edge of the hoverer, her boots crunched on the gravel driveway, and she walked up the large flight of stairs into the mansion. It reminded her of the Judge's house back in the Sojourner's Kingdom.

"What is this building used for?" Anna asked as she stepped through the arched doorway into a barrel vaulted, echoing entry way. A ceiling stretched several stories over their heads, with white pillars running along the sides and a fountain bubbling in the middle of the crimson tiled floor.

"Please don't act the fool, Rachel. You know it's Len's home and isn't used for anything," the man sighed. "Len may enjoy it, but I do not care for your sense of humor that runs away and has to be brought back at laserpoint a week before your wedding."

"I'm not marrying anyone," Anna said quickly. "And my name's Anna."

"Felix!" a nasal voice echoed down from somewhere over their heads. Anna looked up to see a pale young man dressed in foppish, expensive clothes (with much less taste than this Felix with the golden gun) leaning over a railing high above their heads. "I've been wondering where you've been, Rachel's been back for an hour and – But what lovely thing do you have there?" Felix stepped away from Anna as if she were a cobra and stared at her with wide eyes. Anna looked up at the foppish character leaning over the rail.

"My name is Anna and I've been mistaken for Rachel, and it really wasn't nice to knock out my brother and friend and drag me here. Can I go back now?" she called up.

"Oh dear," the young man above her whined. "Oh dear, oh dear. But you sound as much like her as Rachel does. Unless you're Rachel and she's Anna. But who is Anna and where did she come from? Felix?" the young man asked helplessly. Felix's pale nose wrinkled and his brow furrowed. He sighed, took Anna's arm, and pushed her up the stairs. Anna found herself pulled into a pretty sunlit den with poufy cushions, sumptuous couches, and seats everywhere she turned. Felix settled her on a couch.

"Stay," he ordered. Anna considered making a run for it…but she was curious. And that stun gun still peeked from Felix's sleeve. Nothing particularly bad had happened to her yet, but it might if she ran. Anna glanced around her, stared out the wall of ceiling-tall windows at the luscious gardens, and admitted it was a nice room. But she couldn't enjoy the comfort, her mind kept going back to Nehemiah and Beau slumped on the wagon, brown gas filling the bubble. And the young man in the foppish dress was annoying her. He paced the room in irregular patterns, wringing his hands and saying useless things.

"Oh dear. Oh dear, oh dear," he bleated.

"Now, Len, stop pacing and tell me what you mean by 'Rachel's here,'" Felix said as he drooped onto the loveseat across from Anna.

"You know that snoop you hired?" Len said.

"The detective? Yes."

"Well he came in a few hours ago with a young woman, very beautiful, with Rachel's trick of speech and her build and all,

and said it was her. But she's denied it, and now you come with another one–"

"I found this one in the park just at Rachel's usual time for her run, that was my main reason to assume I had found her. But now... Why don't you just give it up, Len?" Felix snorted.

"No! This was her test, we have to find her or she won't marry me!" Len cried desperately.

"But to expect a man to recognize her running loose over an entire city after she's changed her face, hair color, and even made herself look ten years younger? Don't you think that's a bit over the top for any woman?"

"Felix, I must ask you not to talk about my fiancé that way," Len said, drawing himself up and looking quite pitiful as he tried to look challenging. Felix sighed and sank further into the loveseat.

"Excuse me, sir, but Mr. Grunedike is here," a refined voice said from the doorway. Anna looked up and saw a footman there. A little man stood behind him. Beside the stranger stood a beautiful blond with the same willowy curves as Anna's build.

"Grunedike...isn't that your detective, Len?" Felix said.

"That's right, Mr. Hernon, and here is your fiancé!" the little man declared triumphantly in a nasal, squeaky voice. Len turned green, and Felix groaned as he let his head drop back on the seat. A laugh burst from Anna.

"I'm sorry," she apologized quickly, "but you both look so helpless! Now you have three Rachels, how are you going to know which one is real, Mr. Hernon?" she asked. This felt almost like a spontaneous play. If Nehemiah's desperate worry hadn't been on her mind, Anna would have been enjoying herself. Len just shook his head in despair.

"Might as well bring your other one in for comparison," Felix muttered. A few minutes later Anna found the beautiful blond on her right, a lovely brunette on her left, and two very frustrated men in front of them. Len kept asking them questions, and all three kept saying they didn't know the answers. For Anna's part it was true, but she began to sense the blond wasn't being so forthright. She shook randomly and suspiciously, and once she coughed in a way that sounded just like a cover for a laugh. After thirty minutes of getting nowhere, the two men retired to the hallway to discuss things, closing the door behind them and leaving the three ladies alone. Immediately, the blond burst out laughing. Anna looked at her indignantly.

"Oh, be quiet," she said irritably. "You do realize this other young lady–"

"Edith," the brunette supplied.

"–Edith and I have been very much inconvenienced by you, and my brother is going to be much more than that, he'll be desperate and have a rotten headache because of your joke!"

"Joke!" Rachel cried, sitting up straight and tossing her blond hair behind her. "It isn't a joke, it's very serious. I don't want the man I marry to take me for my looks, he must know me deep enough to recognize me inside too."

"How can he when you sit there and lie to him?" Anna snapped. "If you don't tell someone the truth, how can they get to know you?"

"The truth?" Rachel said with a laugh. "That's no good, his truth might be different from mine, and then where are we?"

"I suppose you did know the answers to all those questions?" Anna said, choosing to ignore the nonsensical drivel.

"Of course I did!" Rachel grinned. She slipped her arm through Anna's, smiling at her in a way that invited chummy confidences. "But do tell. What's your name, and who's your brother, and is he as handsome as you are pretty, and–"

"You really are something else," Edith broke in angrily. "I have a dinner show to go to tonight and now I probably won't even make it!"

"Oh come on, humor me," Rachel said, her large dark eyes laughing and mischievous. "After all, you want to get out of here, don't you?" Anna's jaw stayed tight as she snapped out an answer.

"My name is Anna, and my brother now has a cracked skull

after you had me kidnapped."

"I had you kidnapped? What do you think I am, a hired gunman?" Rachel's tone could have been recorded as the definition of innocence. It acted on Anna and Edith's nerves like a grater drawn over a block of cheese.

"If you don't shut up, I'm going to take your peroxide hair and strangle you with it!" Edith said furiously.

"You know you really do sound like me sometimes," Rachel smiled at Edith.

"That's not a nice thing to say," Anna commented icily.

"Well if you're going to be that way," Rachel pouted.

"My darling, I'm not the dupe you thought," Len's voice drifted to them, and Edith and Rachel both jumped. "I've been listening through the wall. I know who you are now, my dearest Rachel, and you're going to be mine next Saturday!" The door opened and Felix and Len came in. Len pointed a triumphant finger at the beautiful, blond Rachel.

"There you are! I like your new face," he declared.

"Why on earth did you go and to a plastic surgeon for a joke, Rachel?" Felix asked.

"Hands in the air, everyone!" a voice called from the other side of the room. Surprise flew over Len and Felix as they stared over the couch behind the girls. The two men's pale hands shot into the air, palms outward. Anna again had the unsettling feeling she was caught in the middle of a comedic play; one with a twist ending she wasn't sure she would like. Rachel stamped her foot moodily.

"What now?" she snapped.

"I am never going to make it to my show!" Edith cried in despair.

"Nehi!" Anna smiled, and twisted toward the voice. "You made excellent time." Nehemiah stood on the opposite end of the long room, Hope held ready in a black gloved hand and his round laser goggles pulled over his knitted mask. Cobeau slid through the window behind him with another mask and his rifle up threateningly.

"Why are you wearing masks?" Anna asked.

"I don't know, when you're sneaking into a house you're supposed to wear masks," Nehemiah answered irritably.

"He talks like me too!" Rachel said.

"Shut up!" Edith growled through gritted teeth.

"Hands up!" a nasal voice shouted behind Cobeau. The short detective Grunedike spun through a small door behind the chimera, a red Krackmen sparkling in his hands as the energy bounced against the diamond lenses; it was primed and ready, and pointed at the two intruders. "You're under arrest."

Daniel dashed across the street, the four lanes of traffic honking and complaining at him. Of course they probably complained more because their four lanes suddenly dumped into a single lane at the top of this street, in order to squeeze between a huge rocco mansion on one side, and a series of apartments built one against another out of what appeared to be packing crates painted lavender and lime.

Daniel began to remember how much he disliked this randomized country.

He hopped onto the sidewalk, blowing hard, and looked up at the skyscraper reaching fifteen stories into the lowering clouds. At least it looked normal. Then he noticed the bronze letters over the door spelling out the words, "Ducky's Pond." Daniel's hand rose slowly and he pointed at the words, his mouth forming a question he couldn't quite get his brain to spit out in words. Joe just waved him to follow and pushed through the revolving door.

Daniel shoved his way after the mute and found himself enfolded in classy comfort; deep leather chairs, a large oak information desk, black and white swirls dancing across the marbled floor. He saw people milling around the room, some in suitcoats with the austere attitudes of big shots, staring down their noses at everyone else. But most of the busy throng

moving in and out of the room dressed in as haphazard a style as the city's architecture. Except when it came to their armaments. Stun guns, truncheons, Ruby pistols, Krackmen rifles, utility belts dripping with ways to deal with humanity. Daniel looked at the weaponry and recognized it as the only uniform of the SW, the Story Land law enforcement.

What he didn't see was a skinny, blond-headed mute.

The place looked completely devoid of Joe. Daniel's gaze raked the room as he strolled forward slowly. The young woman behind the information counter looked up at him, her tailored suit an odd contrast to her violet hair sticking up in short spikes.

"Can I help you, sir?" she asked. Daniel gave her his best smile, the scarred half of his face twisting it and making him seem like a fascinating person to know.

"I certainly hope so," he said, letting his tone change to one that made her blush. He dropped his tone to be confidential as he strolled closer. "Can you explain the sign out front?"

"Everyone asks me about that, even people who have lived here their whole lives," she laughed. Her elbows went to the counter and she leaned closer, dropping her voice to match his for confidentiality. "It's the name of our book." Daniel drew back, staring at her with suspicion.

"You're just playing on my ignorance," he said. "Your pretty face will let you get away with lots of things, sweetheart, but I'm not quite that much of a dupe." She shrugged, amusement dancing over her.

"Believe what you want, tall one, but I've seen it on its pedestal in its own vacuum sealed room. A thirty-page book with more pictures than words, about a duck, titled *Ducky's Pond.* My guess is that it was written for children."

"That can't be the governing base of the whole country," Daniel said, a smile twitching at his lips again. "I know your ambassadors make it a point of pride to never discuss details about the Story Land book, but... *Ducky's Pond*?"

"What do you know about Story Land, stranger?"

"Enough to guess it doesn't really matter what the book says. In their 'own story' the politicians can state the words mean whatever they want."

"Exactly," the woman nodded, "and whatever they declare, it is true to them."

"Right. Well, I'll tell you a truth in my story. I like this country better now. Because now I know you're here," Daniel drawled, letting his smile twist his face again. She answered it with a facetious smile that said she enjoyed the flirting, but wasn't about to let it get anywhere. He had read his target right. He leaned an arm on the counter, getting a little closer so he could lower his voice. "You're the type who knows everything, and the smart women are the ones I like."

"Get on with it, tall one," she laughed. "What are you hunting for?"

"All right, Violet, I can take a hint. Who's in charge here?" he obeyed.

"Do you want to know who says they're in charge and is on the official documents?" the woman asked. A smile flickered over her face again, and she leaned forward with her chin on her hands, her voice dropping back to confidential and her face close to Daniel's. "Or who is really in charge?"

"I'm looking for the one really in charge," Daniel half whispered. "I wish it was you." The woman's finger (long purple nail glittering in the light) pointed straight up.

"Fourteenth floor, eighth door down, 'Inspector' on the label. You're looking for a man named Vern."

"Would he, I don't know, be a little upset to learn you're pointing him out to random strangers?" Daniel asked, one eyebrow going up.

"Oh no, Vern likes to know who's looking for him." The woman smiled, amusement dancing over her face. Daniel had the sudden idea he may not want to find this Vern after all.

But Joe would be visiting the one in charge.

He nodded his thanks to the woman and headed for the elevator. Gilt edging and dark wood surrounded him as he

pushed his way inside with eight other people. An SW's utility belt pressed against his side and Daniel apologized as the man stared daggers at him and squirmed a few inches away.

The man never noticed his small projectile pistol, gas pellets, and a Meslee hostage bomb went with the tall stranger.

The elevator traveled steadily up, stopping at levels along the way, creaking and jerking in the normal way. Daniel found himself wishing he had taken the stairs as it jerked to a stop on the fifth level and someone pulled the folding doors open with an effort. The floor stood three feet above the level of the elevator. This one appeared to work as well as most elevators he had found in the world; the quirks still weren't ironed out since the invention emerged two years ago. People climbed over the three-foot step, others hopped down, and the elevator squeaked upward again.

Eight minutes later Daniel stepped gratefully onto the fourteenth floor, silently wondering if Joe had already done what he came to do and was waiting for him down in the lobby. Daniel strode down the hall, counting painted doors, dodging low hanging chandeliers, and hoping the crickets pressed onto the linoleum were just a manufacturer's design.

This country was so weird.

The word "Inspector" shone off the eighth door on the right in iridescent white, set amidst paint that used to also be white. Daniel pulled his leather greatcoat sleeve over his hand before he rapped on the dingy, splattered gray door.

"Grip," someone grunted from the other side. Daniel gripped the doorknob and stepped inside.

A stocky man sat at a desk in front of a hallway. He looked up at the door and Daniel found himself staring at furry, lowering eyebrows, large ears sticking out at two different angles, heavy jowls, and eyes so deep set beneath a flat head they seemed almost like dark cavities in the man's face.

"Inspector Vern?" he asked. The man grunted. One hand sat idle on the desk, loosely gripping a pen. His other was out of sight on his lap, and Daniel knew it held a weapon ready.

Probably a strafer laser if he had to guess. Easy to conceal, able to deal with more than one enemy at a time, and almost indiscriminate in its aim. "I came to talk to you about the traffic condition outside your building."

"Green sky," Vern said, his voice a deep, gravelly growl. Daniel blinked for a second, then decided to just roll with it.

"Definitely, that's what I thought too. Listen, if you get about fifty of your SWs to head my way, we can take those packing crate apartments and push them back, rearranging them if we need to."

"Why?" Vern grunted.

A form stepped out of the dark corner behind the inspector. Daniel watched without a flicker of surprise on his face as the darkness formed into the blond-headed Joe. The mute pointed at Vern's back, then made a shooing motion. *Get him away from the desk.*

"Why? Well, that's an idiotic question," Daniel said, giving a little huff. He strode for the single window in the room. A bright breeze blew through it and Daniel found himself a little surprised it was open. He waved a hand outside. "Just look."

Vern sat for another long moment, studying his guest. Then he stood up smoothly, his movements catlike, slid his strafer pistol back into his belt and stepped up to the window next to Daniel.

"See, the traffic ponds down there," Daniel rolled on, his voice clipped and businesslike. "Give me the workers and I'll clear enough space to let the traffic stop building up like a river overrunning its banks right outside your door."

"Creaking side spawns," Vern rumbled.

"Yeah, I don't know what that means," Daniel drawled, and ran on, turning slightly to face the inspector. It put him in a position to see the desk and kept Vern's back to it. Joe glided up to the desk and his lithe fingers ran silently over papers, dipped inside drawers, every movement sure and so fast it blurred. Everything he touched with his black gloved hands went back into its exact position. If Daniel hadn't seen it for himself he would have had a hard time believing anyone had picked through the desk's contents. "Now I realize the mess down there makes the traffic move slowly, so you don't have as many speeding tickets or hit-and-runs right outside your door. But it means you have to move slowly too, when you often need to be in a rush." Joe's movements paused as he pulled a bottom drawer open, staring at something. He slid a pencil from his hair and Daniel watched it fly across a note. "I'm not just a disinterested busybody, Inspector, I'm hoping to be an investor in one of the businesses across the street. This traffic mess makes it almost impossible for anyone to stop in the area. Wouldn't it be better to take an afternoon and clear it up?"

"Back way," Vern grunted.

"What?"

"We use the back entrance. Fast. Everyone's stuck out front," Vern said. He spun toward his desk and stalked toward it. Daniel's eyes instinctively flew around the small office area. There was no Joe. Again. Had he ducked through the hallway behind the inspector's desk?

"Can you just think about it?" Daniel demanded.

"Invest somewhere else," Vern grunted. "Spaghetti and frogs good this millennium."

"Right," Daniel drawled. One shoulder rose in a shrug and he sighed melodramatically. "I'll have my people call your people." He strode for the hallway. His face smacked into painted bricks and he stepped back sharply, blinking at the wall painted like a hallway. Of course it was a wall. The inspector could use it to gauge the people who came in his office by their reactions, and to have his own private joke. Daniel wrinkled his nose at the paint job, spun on his heel, and stalked out the door he came in by. He shut it gently behind him and turned toward the elevator.

Joe leaned against the wall, his hair flying in the airflow from the vent, his expression patient. A grin flew over him as he saw Daniel, and his black gloved hand pointed at his nose.

"What would you have done if I hadn't distracted him?"

Daniel demanded, irritated by the reference to his new bruise from the wall-that-wasn't-a-hallway. Joe shrugged, an impish smile slipping over his face. His hands moved and the gloves spit out the signs in a computerized male voice.

"I manage. But now we have address we need, come on," the gloves said. The mute spun off the wall and trotted for the stairs.

"Oh, sure you wait till now to tell me you have gloves that talk for you," Daniel snorted. He broke into a jog to catch up to the little mute as Joe pushed through the door into the stark, concrete stairwell. "Wait, don't you need to earn your money?" Joe just tossed a rope to Daniel, threw his repelling box on the banister, and hopped over the edge. Daniel leaned against the banister, watching him drop the fourteen stories, his hair a blond halo waving around his head. "Of course, he got that done in the time it took me to ride the elevator. I'm beginning to wish I had let him come alone," Daniel muttered under his breath. He tossed his rope over the edge and started the long walk down.

As he finally turned the last corner into the ground floor stairwell, he found Joe leaning against the wall waiting for him. Daniel stopped to straighten his gray leather vest and greatcoat and unbuttoned his white collar as a ploy to catch his breath. Then he strode for the door leading to the lobby, his head high.

"Do not like to repel?" Joe's gloves asked.

"Down fourteen stories with a rope and gadget I don't know? No, I don't really," Daniel said. Joe shrugged and nodded, conceding that made some sense. He swung off the wall and followed Daniel into the lobby and toward the street.

# Chapter Four: Breaking and Entering

*"Let your light so shine before men, that they may see your good works, and glorify your Father which is in heaven." Matthew 5:16*

Vern watched the door close softly behind the tall, scarred stranger. A frown cut over his ugly face and his small eyes glowered.

The man's immediate realization about the not-a-hall, his silent acceptance without even a curse under his breath, showed a dangerously high intelligence. That kind of a man wouldn't have come all the way up to the fourteenth floor to talk about traffic problems.

Vern's eyes darted down as he noticed his bottom drawer cracked open. Just a hairsbreadth, but enough for Vern to know someone had been snooping. Tall Man hadn't had the opportunity to come near the desk. So who...? He slid his gas mask over his face, gripped his strafer laser in his fist, and reached for the handle. One quick move, and he jerked the drawer open.

The Shadow Spy's payroll was gone.

For six years now, information on other countries, or about people within his own country, had appeared on Vern's desk. That information had saved his life twice, and warned him of overthrows four different times, hours before it happened; just in time to get some of his SWs away before the laser bursts and screaming started. The facts were always accurate, and the Spy (always through a simple, silent note) required high prices. Though never more than Vern's department could afford. The inspector felt it well worth his money to keep the Shadow Spy supplied with what they asked.

The fee was gone again. In its place, a plain, square white piece of paper lay in the drawer, tucked between a page of Vern's black book of interesting addresses.

*Time to drive the Ill Trio out, tonight. Be at this address by two A.M. and bring noisy backup. Don't have to intervene. Just being there will do the job.*

Vern stared at the note. He stood statue-like, not even blinking, for a long minute. Slowly, gently, he pulled it from the drawer and popped the secret compartment in his desktop. He slid a plain white note from the recess, one he had received several weeks ago by a raven flying through his open window. He laid the two papers beside each other.

Same handwriting. Same paper. Same ink. Same person. His Shadow Spy used ravens on occasion, it would seem.

A pretty, raven-painted wagon rolled through Vern's memory, strains of music traveling with it as it performed two years ago at the SAMF, Story Land's annual festival. That traveling show with the chimera and the little white-blond beasty had chosen to position their show near the back alleys. Vern knew the extraordinary musician's prize money had gone to purchasing food for every denizen of those alleys. Probably the first decent meal many of them had seen in their lives. And that same day one of the rare Spy's notes appeared in his office. And then, because Vern did his job very well and liked to keep track of visitors and oddities in his home city, he knew the wagon with the ravens had parked for two weeks at a certain surgeon's in the heart of the city.

A surgeon who flung his gates open every Sunday morning, and stood by as people slipped inside, looking over their shoulders to see if their neighbor's noticed. Vern slowly pulled an old bill from another drawer and laid it beside the two notes on his desk. The surgeon hadn't actually charged for the call he made when Vern's Social Worker died. But he sent a bill to keep his records straight, and Vern kept it, as he kept anything he considered an oddity.

Vern glanced at the file always on his desk, growing thicker every day on the Ill Trio and their doings. This last two weeks had suddenly taken a turn for the nasty, and evidence of involvement with the Christian underground had cropped up.

Very conveniently cropped up. And now...

Vern's eyes flicked back to the two simple, short notes on his desk and the bill by a surgeon he knew unashamedly called himself Christian. One note left by his Shadow Spy. One brought by a–

Raven. Vern's bushy eyebrows rose, lifting like twin caterpillars, as his eyes widened. He had heard that name. It drifted down certain channels, not often, always whispered, often feared. But it was the nasty ones who feared it. The tales he heard of that name were shadowy, no one ever sure of their facts, never quite certain what part the Raven actually played. But the ones who hated the daytime, who laughed when their victims begged for mercy, they spit the Raven's name with venom in their tones.

He would be there at two A.M. and he would bring very noisy backup, lots of it.

Vern's eyes studied the three papers forming a triangle on his desktop. And maybe...maybe he would take a Sunday morning and do a reconnaissance of a certain surgeon's house. This Raven cared about preserving life, enough to spend money, time, and blood on it. He managed to preserve justice and do good, as he danced into the darkest parts of the world. So much skill, such ingenuity and craft behind every calculated move to drive back the nasties... Any belief system that could claim that kind of a person should be explored in more depth.

"Oh dear," Anna murmured. "This afternoon is moving too fast. Why are you arresting them?"

"You're under arrest too, lady," Grunedike said, a smug smile on his sallow face.

"What?" Felix and Edith chorused. "What for?"

"She recognized Bill and Will, obviously she's their elusive female operative," the detective answered.

"What?" seven voices asked. The little man sighed

theatrically. The Krackmen never shifted, the lens pointed straight at Beau's middle.

"You've heard of this property rearranging going on, surely Mr. Hernon?" he started to explain. Len Hernon nodded.

"Possibly he has," Anna broke in, "but I have no idea what you're talking about. Since I'm being arrested for it, can you please explain?"

"As if you didn't know! Well, just to humor you," the detective said in his nasal voice. "There is a group of three people rearranging property. They call themselves–"

"Wait," Nehemiah interrupted, "what do you mean rearranging property? Do they go around moving lawn furniture to different positions?"

"Most countries call it thieving," Felix supplied. "We prefer property rearranging here, it makes things clearer."

"How does that make things clearer?" Anna asked. Edith started muttering something and Rachel's toe began to tap impatiently.

"Look," Felix said quickly, "if one person says a piece of property is theirs, and another person says the same piece of property is theirs, in their own stories both facts are true. There are some–"

"Wait, I'm sorry, but their own stories?" Nehemiah asked. It had been too long since he followed his dad around with visiting ambassadors, and the Story Land ones never liked to explain anything. And, oh, he had a headache. He pulled his mask off to rub his sweaty, aching head. Edith and Rachel gave simultaneous little sighs and their shoulders slumped. They relaxed, suddenly content to sit and watch. Nehi didn't seem to notice, and Anna was thankful for his ignorance.

"You aren't from here, are you?" Edith asked. Anna and Nehemiah shook their heads. Cobeau had stopped trying to follow the conversation and just glared at Grunedike and his rifle, estimating if he could jump him without getting his belly burned out. "Then listen up so we can get this sorted out. In Story Land we realize there is no one story that connects us all, no

overarching truth if you understand that. It's whatever fits into your own story. If you think something's true, it's true, and if someone else thinks the opposite thing is true, it's just as true in their own story."

"That sounds..." Nehemiah was about to say "like some of the stupidest foolishness he had ever come across" but decided he should pick something a little milder under the circumstances. "...like it could cause quite a bit of trouble."

"There are some people who take advantage of it," Felix said. "That's where the property rearrangers come in."

"Hold on, if opposite things can be true in different stories," Nehemiah said, "then anyone could steal something and say it's theirs. And it would be just as true (in your thinking, anyway) as the person who owned it before saying it was theirs."

"Yes, you have it now," Felix said.

"So rearranging property is used instead of theft," Anna said slowly, "because if anyone can truthfully say they own it, it can't be properly said to be stolen."

"Precisely," Edith said. "Now can we please get on with this and let me go?"

"Right, well, as I was saying," Grunedike said, "there are three property rearrangers going around. They've become a real problem, and no one can say who's been doing it. There's two men, see, Bill's the leader, Will is his big henchman, and there's a girl, Jill, who does a lot of the dirty work and keeps up a front for the other two. The SW know them as the Ill Trio. And these three are them!"

"What!?" Anna and Nehemiah yelled. Beau still stood and glared and said nothing.

"Oh, well in that case, I wonder if they could do something for me?" Rachel said.

"Of course, dear," Len said patting her arm affectionately. "We will see they do whatever you want."

"Wait, how are you so sure these three are the Ill Trio?" Edith broke in, her eye on Nehemiah.

"That's right, they aren't even from this country," Felix

pointed out. He had his gold plated Compton out again, Nehi saw with exasperation.

"Well, I say they are from here," Grunedike said decisively, "and that makes it so."

"For you," Felix nodded, a small shrug lifting his shoulder. Nehemiah began to see this idea of no truth might be more trouble than just stupid.

"And then they match the description," the detective said, counting off reasons on his fingers, "they broke past all your security devices with ease, climbed to the top floor almost as easily, look at those sinister masks, and wasn't I right about Rachel?"

"Good," Rachel said, clapping her hands and looking like a spoiled child about to demand a treat. "I was just thinking this morning I needed a good rearranger and now I have three!"

"We are not thieves! We just came to get my sister back, who you stole away. If anything, he's the robber here!" Nehemiah burst out, pointing at Felix.

"Now Bill, Jill," Grunedike warned, "no getting excited. Mr. Felix or I might accidentally shoot. Now, if you really are the Ill Trio–"

"Oh who cares if they're your stupid Trio," Rachel interrupted, "they're obviously property rearrangers and that's what I need." Rachel moved to the edge of her seat, her eyes flicking back and forth between the twins. "I lost a necklace at a friends' house last night, and you're going to steal it back for me."

"What?!" The Hillsons and Hernons chorused.

"Not the one you showed me a few weeks ago, that I got insured for as much as the house?" Len said feebly.

"Yes, dear. I am sorry I left it, but it just slipped my mind completely. I was at the Simpsons last night, we were finishing a game, and I just left it on the table. You know how embarrassing it would be for us to ask for it?" Rachel's voice was sweet, but her smile was malicious, and Anna found she loathed her.

"Well," Len said to the twins, "you'll get it because my

darling wants you to. If you don't, we will turn you in to the law as property rearrangers and trespassers."

"We'll just turn you in as kidnappers," Nehemiah countered.

"Ah, but your father isn't a judge," Len said quickly, a smile cutting over his sallow face.

"Our jails here really aren't very nice," Felix sighed. "Why don't you just get Rachel's necklace, and we can all go back to normal life again."

"Just because your father is a judge here doesn't mean our side of the story won't be heard," Nehemiah said. As the words left him he remembered he wasn't in Sojourner's Kingdom anymore. Or even in KAM. Joe's warning came floating into his mind, *"...you have no protection from anything, so watch your back."* Nehemiah looked at Anna. She looked at him with the same desperation on her face. Nehemiah glanced at the cold faces in the room and bit his lip in frustration. "I suppose it really is your necklace?" he asked in a sick voice.

"Of course it is, silly," Rachel said irritably. "It was a gift. You'll wait here till it's dark, then Felix and Grunedike will drop you off at the Simpsons. If you don't have the necklace back by...oh, let's say three in the morning, your descriptions will be sent out and you wouldn't have a chance of getting away. Len does have a great many relatives, you know. It's so nice of you to do this little thing for me!" Nehemiah and Anna glared at her.

"I can't believe we're doing this," Daniel muttered as he slipped through the door behind Joe. Darkness swallowed them, seeming almost tangible to Daniel. He felt along the smooth wooden floor with his shoes, trying not to trip. Joe clicked at him to be quiet. A thin, concentrated beam of light snapped on in the mute's hands, and Daniel watched as it began to systematically sweep over the expensive room.

"Why are we doing this?" he whispered. Joe glared at him, but it was lost in the darkness. "All you're doing is looking at

things in a dark room in a big house, that you broke into illegally. I thought you were supposed to be stopping that Ill Trio! How is this helping–" Joe's hand clamped over Daniel's mouth. His other hand grabbed the back of his neck, and Daniel almost doubled over, pulled along by his head. Joe shoved him down behind something, Daniel felt the wiry mute shove in close to him, and the two hands let go. He dragged in a choking breath and turned on Joe with both hands twitching to get around his thin, white neck.

The room flooded with light. Daniel felt like someone stabbed him through the eyeballs. When he could focus on something other than the pain in his eyes and head, he realized someone's footsteps rang on the polished hardwood as they paced, muttering under their breath about jewel cuts and young fools. Joe sat stiff and still as stone, pressed against the wall. Daniel caught the mute's feeling and went rigid. Wherever they were and whatever Joe was doing here, Daniel did not want to be found as a burglar hiding behind a couch. A latch lifted and a door pushed open, swirling in humid outside air, filled with the scent of grass and exotic flowers. The muttering voice rose, accusing, quick, and angry.

"Jill, where have you been?" It was a well-toned male voice, but somehow Daniel didn't picture the speaker as kind. Of course that might have been because, just at that moment, he was imagining all the things the owner of that voice might do to an intruder he found behind his couch.

"Where do you think?" a woman answered. "Looking for someone to buy our lovely gift from last night."

"I told you not to do that! It's still too hot," the man shouted.

"Oh Bill, I was careful. Don't you know that much about me after all we've been through?" Jill said. "Besides, with the real prize already away with Will, you and I are almost free to do whatever we want. Old Will has the hard job now, making sure Wolf's precious package gets to the People's Kingdom."

"'Almost' isn't the same as free, Jill. If we slip up on the Wolf's business we'll wish we were never born." Fear rode the

man's voice. The two behind the couch could hear the sharp "tap-tap" of the girl's heels moving closer to him.

"But you never slip up, sweetie," the female cooed. "We'll be done with this and home free before you know it." Bill melted and the two moved out of the room, talking about jewels and money and fences. They left the light on. Now that he could see the mute Daniel turned to him, determined to get some answers.

"What was that all about? Where are we? And what are we doing here?" he whispered. Joe looked at him, and Daniel was surprised to see laughter in his green eyes. The mute pulled a notepad and pencil out of his pocket.

*You're a lot like A and N in some ways. We're in the Ill Trio's house, that was Bill and Jill of the Trio, and we're here to see what kind of people they are so we know what to do with them.*

Joe ran out of room on the paper, handed the note to Daniel and started on another one.

*You're the one who insisted on coming with me, so stop complaining about a little breaking and entering, stick close, stop talking, and use your eyes.*

Joe slid out from behind the couch and darted toward the door. Daniel followed at a slower, clumsier pace. The little mute was good at this kind of thing, very good. He scribbled on the back of Joe's note and stuffed it into the scarred white hand as he joined him at the door.

*I'm not as young as you, and not as used to this kind of thing. Go slower so I can stick close. And I think Harry's chicken was older than it looked.*

Joe glanced at it, grinned, and moved out the door slow enough for Daniel to keep up.

"I can't believe we're doing this," Nehemiah muttered to Anna as they struggled towards the Simpson's house. The jungle of plants and trees swaying over them hid innumerable vines and undergrowth that caught at their legs and made every step a battle. Bugs of humongous size and variety swarmed around their faces at every step. Just when Anna started to think she would scream if she had to swat another clumsy fly off her face, the tropical growth broke with the suddenness of falling off a bed onto tiled floor. Nehemiah winced as gravel crunched under his foot, and he drew back into the plants. The twins knelt in the moonlight looking up a long, winding lane flanked by perfect gardens. The corner of a mansion could just be seen around the curving lane. Felix's parting words echoed in their minds. *"You have six hours; find it and get it back to us, or the law will come find you."*

"This has been the strangest day," Anna whispered. Nehi thought back on the day, chortled, and nudged Anna in the ribs.

"Say Rachel, how does it feel to be getting married next Saturday?" he said. Anna shoved his shoulder.

"Better than being Jill, Bill!" she grinned. "I swear, it's like someone set up an elaborate comedy and stuck us in the middle of it."

"Shh," Beau whispered. The twins looked at their silent, huge companion. The chimera slid out of the trees and across the open lane to a bush trimmed like a peacock, gliding along as if he did this every night. The twins followed, running clumsily over the soft grass.

"Beau, I can hardly see you," Anna whispered as they gained the shadow of the chimera's side. "You are very good at this."

"Shh!" he answered, more urgently. Anna shut her mouth and pressed up nearer to the looming shadow of Cobeau. He stood peering through the trees at the curve in the lane, Anna and Nehemiah looked out past him and marveled.

"That house is even bigger then L-e-n's," Nehemiah signed.

"And that gardener is very close," Anna signed back. "At least I think it's a gardener?" Beau nodded, and Nehemiah was

horrified to see his short Brunheim laser out in the big, hairy hands.

"No, Glue, no hurting people!" Nehi signed urgently and pushed the laser down. "Just find the necklace and get out."

"Do you know how long it's going to take to find a little necklace in that house?" Anna signed.

"We could just leave," Nehemiah signed back doubtfully.

"And be hunted down by L's mighty relatives? I think I would rather risk this," Anna signed. Nehemiah grimaced and nodded.

"Me too," he signed. "Glue, how about you?" The big man pointed toward a covered porch that was darker than the rest of the huge mansion.

"There?" he signed.

"I guess you agree," Nehemiah signed with a grin. "Okay, let's go." They darted and tripped into the wide garden, headed toward the distant porch and trying to stay out of view of the windows and workers. The chimera took the lead, flitting from shadow to shadow, almost invisible. But when they made it to the porch he stepped aside and stood guard, waiting. Nehemiah pursed his lips and moved forward, examining the lock on the door. Anna giggled and he looked up at her, his eyebrows furrowed.

"Just wondering what Sharp Hope[3] would think if he could see us now," Anna signed, using Joe's sign name as she watched Nehemiah puzzling over the door and the Raven's lock picks.

"What about D, what would he think?" Nehemiah signed back. He decided to admit he had no idea what he was doing, and handed the lock picks to Cobeau. Eight seconds later they stood in a dark room with Beau relocking the door. A thin beam of light started up and pointed at Nehemiah's hands.

"Careful," he signed.

---

[3] Joe's sign name, given him by an old man, with the comment, "Your wits are as sharp as your nose, and your hope as strong as the sun."

"Obviously," Anna signed with her own pen light, and a grin. The three began to move through the house, looking for anything resembling the necklace Rachel had described for them. There didn't seem to be anyone on the side of the mansion they had picked. Dense darkness encased everything and made the hunt hard. A pen light has a very small radius of light, and a necklace can be curled in so many little spaces in a big room. They combed seven rooms and a hallway in three hours. Nerves were taut, and at every creak of a floorboard, Anna found her skin prickling and her heart thudding.

Nehemiah moved in the lead, sliding down the hall with the skill inspired by fear of discovery and three hours of practice. His light picked out a large wooden door on their left. Getting inside a room somehow seemed better than staying out in the open hallway, and he quickly oiled the big iron hinges. The doorknob turned smoothly and Nehi pulled it open. He jumped, and shut it, just barely keeping from slamming it, his breath panting out of him.

"What is it?" Anna squeaked, forgetting to sign. Nehemiah twisted the knob and pulled it open again slowly, leaning around it with shoulders squared. Anna noticed his hand fingering Hope. Moonlight spilled into the hallway from the door, and Anna found herself thankful for it. She spun around the door and froze, one foot still in midair. A lion stood in front of her, mouth gaping, white teeth shining in the moonlight. Almost on the instant, she realized it was stuffed; but it was an instant of throat tightening, palpitating terror.

Nehemiah walked slowly into the room, looking around him with interest. A domed glass ceiling at least two stories high glinted above them, covering enough space to fit a field inside. Statues, paintings, odd little bundles, very large bundles, stacks of papers... Mounds and mounds of miscellaneous things filled this place, from incredible jewel collections to a box full of teddy bears. Nehi had no idea what to call the room. He stopped suddenly and gave a low whistle.

"Look over here, Anna," he murmured. "It's more of those

journal pages!" Anna bounded beside him and they stared at the frames on the wall with awe.

"There are fourteen of them," she whispered as she traced the name of Hillson gently on the glass over one of the frames. "Fourteen!"

"Pretty," Beau whispered behind them, and the twins winced.

"Sign, dear," Anna signed at him with a smile. Nehemiah turned, his gaze roving over the piles stacked in this room, and his expression tightened.

"This room alone will take us all night to look through," Nehemiah signed.

"Let's start," Anna signed back. "Have you thought about Sharp Hope and D, what if they're waiting for us and desperately worried?"

"No help for it," Nehemiah signed back with a shrug. "We have our trackers if they get too worried. Come on, we can think about the journal pages later."

# Chapter Five: Swag, Fences, and Frames

*"Thou shalt not steal."* Exodus 20:15

"Joe, we've been in here for hours, have you thought about Anna and Nehemiah? What if they're worried about us?" Daniel whispered in Joe's ear as they paced down a well lit hallway. In the hours they had combed this place, Daniel had moved from worried to just worn thin and a little bored; Joe was too good at this to be caught. He wanted sleep. Joe pursed his lips and scribbled a note.

*Don't talk, please! I'm looking for something, it's got to be here somewhere.*

Daniel snatched the pencil and scribbled underneath Joe's scrawl.

*You already followed your direction set and it led us straight to something in a black jeweler's cloth in that snazzy red hoverer in the underground garage. What else are you looking for?*

Daniel started to write more on the other side of the note, his mind on the way he had watched the mute rifling through the hoverer, his movements turning almost desperate as something eluded him. But Joe's hand landed on his ribcage, shoving hard. Daniel stumbled to the left, the dark of an empty room wrapped around him, and he stood grimacing at the pencil point he had just snapped. The mute bounded in beside him, drawing the door nearly shut as he moved. Daniel could hear footsteps outside, tap-tapping down the hallway. The noise reeled to a stop and morphed into someone banging on a door.

"Bill!" the woman's voice called. "Bill, hurry up and come out!" The pounding stopped and hinges creaked as a door opened.

"What is it, for crying out loud?" Bill growled, sleep slurring the words.

"Someone's broken in, that's what," Jill hissed. Daniel and

Joe stiffened and glanced at each other. "They're here now. Who? Why?"

"No panicking," Bill ordered evenly. The tone came clipped and hard. "Meet me in the left wing. We need to think this through." Trim footsteps trotted back down the hall and the door closed. Minutes passed in tingling silence, as the two men stood unmoving in the dark room. The door down the hall opened again and heavier footsteps paced past their doorway. The steps faded into nothingness. The seconds ticked by and Joe made no move. Daniel's patience gave out and he shoved Joe's shoulder hard.

"What are you doing? Shouldn't we leave now while the coast is clear? We've been found out!" he muttered. Joe's head tilted to the side. "What do you mean, you're not sure about that?" Daniel hissed, then suddenly realized he had understood the mute's movement. He pulled back, blinking, unsure what he felt about beginning to understand the little person. Joe placed a piece of his paper in Daniel's hand, took his arm, and slid into the hallway. Daniel glanced at the paper as he followed Joe down the hall. He felt his heartbeat quicken. Joe might be good at this, but he was definitely getting overconfident if this was his plan.

*Let's go find out what's happening. After Bill we go!*

Two elegant glass chandeliers blazed into light. Nehemiah dropped to his belly and skittered behind a statue of a pig, his heart thundering and his eyes fastening on the door. A tall, handsome man in a red dressing gown stepped past the lion. He strolled into the room, his hands in his pockets and a thoughtful expression on his face. He paused in front of the box of teddy bears. A grin split his face and he showed perfect, white teeth as he laughed. One hand slid into the box and tossed a bear in the air. It landed back inside the box as the man strolled forward. He paused again at a painting of lilies in a field, the gold frame glittering in the bright light. His laugh came loud and hiccuppy. Nehemiah's brow furrowed as he watched. What amused him so much?

A wave of shock surprise drowned out his curiosity as two familiar figures slid in the door, dodging behind things to keep out of sight of the stranger. Daniel ducked behind the lion, then went to ground behind an enormous painting of cherubs. Joe slid deeper into the room, ducking behind bundles, around statues, darting on till he stopped behind a large figure of three maidens pouring something out of jars, directly across from Nehemiah. Joe mainly watched the man in the dressing gown, but his green eyes darted everywhere, studying the new room. His gaze fell on Nehemiah, staring out from behind his iron pig. Joe blinked and his face went blank in surprise.

"Hello," Nehemiah signed, amusement making his dark eyes twinkle. This situation was getting funny.

"What are you doing here? Beauty? Glue?" Joe signed, his face creased in confusion. Nehemiah pointed to where he thought they were, and started to sketch out the weird day. As the story kept going, Joe's smile grew till it broke his face in two. He started chuckling when Nehemiah got to the part of Grunedike taking them for the Ill Trio, and as Nehi finished the mute leaned against his statue with one arm around his middle, laughing uproariously. Nehemiah was about to point out the pages on the wall, when the door swung open. He ducked farther behind his pig waiting to see who came in. A beautiful dark-haired woman with a hard, chiseled expression stepped around the stuffed lion.

"So tell me about our midnight visitors, Bill," the woman said her voice ringing through the room. Nehemiah stiffened and looked at Joe. The mute shrugged.

"Yes, I do have a news flash for you," Bill answered, his hands resting easily in his pockets. "They're in this room." Nehemiah reached for Hope automatically and even Joe's humor dimmed. "Lock the door, Jill. We don't want anyone leaving before we have a chance to talk to them." Bill's hand emerged from his pocket with an old fashioned, deadly projectile pistol. The mute began to feel in his pocket for something, and Nehemiah prayed it was a very useful something as he slowly realized who these people were. "Whoever you are in here, the house isn't burglar proofed because we welcome visitors. We like to know who's curious about us."

"But you may have noticed, it's a bit difficult to get out," Jill said with a smile; it was the humorless, bared teeth smile of a predator, and a shiver ran down Anna's spine. "We Simpsons are a very powerful family in this new regime, and if we decide you shouldn't leave..." The smile spread across her pretty face as she left the thought unfinished.

"You'll be dead," Bill finished it, his smile dancing, pleasure riding the words.

"Yes, well, that's accurate if not very poetic," Jill commented. "It's usually Will who takes care of these things, but he's absent today on an errand. So what lovely ideas do you have for our visitors, Bill? Releasing the gas, perhaps? Or the snakes in the conservatory?" Nehemiah heard knuckles cracking and a low gleeful chuckle that froze his blood. He checked over Hope carefully, flipping his goggles on and slipping the safety off. He could feel the dark energy flying through the pinprick hole from one ball and agitating the other ball's dark matter, causing the gamma rays to bounce back and forth between the crystal inner lining. Hope was ready to fire, and to keep firing forever if she needed to. Nehi looked at Joe and his pounding heartbeat began to slow. Never mind. Joe held a little dart gun in his hand, old fashioned to the point of primitive; just a spring action that shot a small, drugged projectile. But it would work. Joe squirmed into range and eyed the two thieves.

Jill clamped a hand to her neck, her eyes wide and face shocked, and sank to the ground. The nothingness of sleep took over her expression and she lay still. Bill jerked toward the direction of the shot and sprinted for Joe. Sudden, graceful, quick, he moved almost as fast as the mute. Joe would never be able to get out of the way in time, and once in sight the mute would

be a dead man. Nehemiah's shoulder rammed into the iron pig. It toppled over with a ringing crash, as Nehi darted to the left. Bill spun on his heel, and a bullet ricocheted off the pig statue. It gave Joe the second he needed to rise into sight and fire. Bill's hand went limp, his eyes rolled up, knees buckled, and he folded onto the soft green carpet, a tiny piece of wood protruding from his neck.

Hillsons burst from their cover and stampeded to the middle of the room, greeting and grinning and grumping. The conversation flew fast and steady, three voices intermixing and never still, as Beau looked on and wondered.

Joe stood up on his pile of papers and surveyed the room. From here he could see the mounds of things made a deliberate, tricky maze to something in the center. Something that appeared to be a pedestal. Joe hopped down and padded his way through the maze of piled items. He pushed past a trellis dripping fake black flowers, shoved a set of china dishes to the side, and stepped into the center of the room. The stuff pulled back into towering walls of stacked items, leaving a circle about five feet wide. A marble pedestal sat in the exact middle, a velvet cloth laid gently over the top.

Nothing sat on the pedestal. Joe's heart dropped to his stomach, sickening him. He moved forward cautiously, one hand on his dart gun, and leaned over the black velvet. A white paper lay staring at the golden chandeliers, the handwriting blotchy and crude in order to mask the writer's normal style.

Too late, Raven, the Bible is gone. But don't worry, you can catch up on your reading at my place later, when I clip your wings and finally give you a home.
-Wolf

Anna noticed Joe stroll back in sight from the midst of all the weird stuff in this room, and watched him curiously as she described Len and Felix for Daniel. The mute looked pale and sober, his shoulder's slumped as if suddenly too weary to lift them. He stood for a moment staring at the window, his mouth pulled into a tight frown. He walked over to the door next and glared at it. Then he looked up, his sharp face calculating, eyes bright. He slid over to tap Cobeau on the arm, and the chimera looked at his friend.

"Can you throw me up there?" he signed, and pointed to the roof. Beau looked up. The smooth glass ceiling and gray metal crossbeams winked down at him twenty feet away. Beau looked at Joe, confusion plastered over his simple face. Joe nodded a little grimly. "I mean it," he signed.

The mute pulled a pair of gloves and galoshes out of his pockets and began to put them on. Cobeau looked back at the ceiling, gauged the distance, and picked Joe up. The mute went as stiff as a spear. Beau's muscles bunched as he pulled his arms back, then flung his master. Anna broke off mid-sentence and gaped, staring at the blond mute, spinning like an arrow over their heads. Eyes widened and breath froze in their lungs as they watched. Joe's gloved hands flailed, trying desperately to grip a crossbeam to keep from tumbling back onto the statuary. An instant, as the watchers below gaped and forgot to breathe, then two of his right fingers latched onto a metal beam. He dangled, blowing a breath out. Joe's feet rose with an easy smooth motion and fastened onto the glass.

"What's he doing that for?" Daniel asked Beau in exasperation. Beau just shrugged.

"How's he doing that?" Anna asked as she watched Joe walking upside down on the window like a gecko.

"The right gloves and shoes," Beau rumbled.

"So Daniel, these people were the famous thieves everyone's been talking about?" Nehemiah said, and his siblings glanced at him in surprise.

"Yes, but I think the show going on over our heads is more interesting," Daniel drawled. "Joe's working on cutting a hole in–"

"–the ceiling, I know. And very smart he is too, to already find a way out of this booby-trapped prison. But I was–"

"Oh, right, the burglar escape-proof house, I forgot," Anna interrupted her twin. "And a good idea, Nehi, let's get started."

"Wait a minute, I can't read minds like you two. Can you please explain?" Daniel asked as his siblings spun towards a wall. A warning whistle sounded from Joe and a large piece of round glass came tumbling down. It smashed on the head of a gray bearded statue a foot away from Anna, glass spraying. Arms shot over their heads, as everyone ducked and shouted. The four conscious on the ground looked up to see Joe crouched on the outside of the roof, leaning through a large hole in the glass.

"Sorry," he signed, then ducked back out. Anna brushed glass off her sleeve and shook her braid carefully.

"Anyway, Daniel," she said as she and Nehemiah pulled him toward the wall with the journal pages. "Nehemiah is thinking if these are famous thieves, everything in this room is almost certainly stolen."

"And if that's the case, they don't own these journal pages," Nehemiah took up, pointing. Daniel's mouth dropped open as he saw the fourteen frames. "And since they are sort of in the family, they're as much ours as anyone's, and certainly more ours than the Ill Trio's."

"So we can take them with us!" Anna concluded as she unhooked the nearest frame and flipped it over. "Oh bother, it's one of those tab frames, with all those little metal tabs you have to bend to get the picture out."

"There must be fifty of the little things!" Nehemiah said with a sour look, staring at the back of his selected frame. "Can we just break the glass?"

"And risk slicing up the ancient pages? It would probably rip open their protective sleeves, and then they would likely crumble to dust before we could even read them. I think not!" Anna scoffed. Daniel stared, his face stiff and eyes wide as they flew from page to page. He reached out and gently unhooked a frame

and turned it over.

"This is going to take a while," Daniel hissed, pulling his finger back and shaking it as one of the tabs slid under his fingernail.

"Shh," Cobeau growled, and the Hillsons looked at him. In the sudden silence a sound drifted through the hole in the ceiling, distant but getting closer. A wild wailing with a metallic ring to it, as if a host of metal cats caterwauled at the moon.

"We missed our deadline," Nehemiah said, grimly.

"What's that mean?" Daniel asked.

"It means the law of this country is coming for us," Anna said.

"What!" Daniel burst out.

"To arrest us as the Ill Trio, ironically," Nehemiah said.

"What?!" Daniel cried.

Joe zipped down into their midst, a thin, strong rope in his hands and an identical one wrapped around his waist. Nehemiah glanced up and saw it was a single rope, flung over a support beam so that both ends hung down.

"Hurry, time to leave," he signed, and handed Beau the rope he held. He quickly unwrapped the one from his waist, wrapped it around Anna, and nodded to Beau. The chimera leaned back and heaved, shifting the rope hand over hand, and Anna darted towards the roof with a strangled grunt. Two seconds later her fingers caught the edge of the cut glass. Anna pulled herself over the edge, the balmy air closing around her like a wet blanket, and dropped the rope back down through the hole. She could see for miles up here in the clear moonlight. She lay on her stomach to avoid being silhouetted against the night sky on top of the roof and watched lights moving down the road from town. Lots of lights. The caterwauling grew louder every second.

"Give me a hand will you?" Daniel grunted behind her. Anna turned to see him hanging from the rope trying to push four frames onto the roof. She grabbed the frames and dragged them over the glass, then reached for her brother. Daniel's hand

shook as he took her arm. He pulled himself laboriously over the edge and rolled to his back, gasping for breath.

"We decided we'd have to take the frames with us and get the pages out as we run." Daniel grunted, fumbling at the rope tied around his waist. He shoved it back through the hole, ran a hand over his streaming brow, rolled to his stomach, and began to pull on the infuriating little tabs again. "Running through Story Land with the SW after us and who knows who else, and we're carrying a host of frames like some delivery service! This is one of the most idiotic things I've ever..." His voice died into a mutter as Nehemiah zipped onto the roof bringing three more frames. Anna held them steady as he pulled himself over the lip of the hole and dropped the rope down again. The lights neared the long lane leading up to the house. Anna pulled her eyes away from them, and the back off a frame, and carefully lifted the yellowed page out, the plastic sleeve crinkling.

"What do I do with it now?" she said. Joe scrambled up with three more frames. He pulled a black velvet bag from his coat and tossed it to Anna. She slid her page gently into the bag, and looked up at the lights coming down the lane. The first were almost to the house. The noise pulsed in the air, and Anna wondered how those in the cars could stand it. Daniel's foot hit her and she glanced up to see her companions pulling the rope hand over hand, sweat standing on all three foreheads. Anna quickly grabbed the end of the rope to help. One long, long minute later, Cobeau's hairy hand gripped the edge of the hole and he heaved himself effortlessly out, the last four frames tucked under one arm. The cars stopped in front of the house and the caterwauling began to wind down to a dull moan.

"How many do we have left to carry?" Joe signed at Nehemiah as they crouched on the glass ceiling.

"Twelve," he answered after a quick glance.

"Twelve!?" Daniel whispered in a furious hiss. "How are we supposed to escape the SW toting twelve heavy frames with us?"

"We had better move," Anna whispered, "if we don't want to

be taken for the Ill Trio."

"They're waking up," Beau rumbled, looking through the hole.

"Great, now we're going to have the real Trio after us too!" Daniel whispered.

"And twelve frames still," Nehemiah murmured. Joe started shaking, his face pressed into his arm as he lay on the roof. Nehemiah grabbed his shoulder in alarm, wondering what fit had suddenly hit the mute. Their eyes met and Nehi realized he was laughing.

"What's so funny?" he hissed.

"I don't think I've ever been in a situation this ridiculous," Joe signed back, still laughing. He ran a hand over his eyes, and for an instant he met his friend's gaze. Nehi looked at Joe's pale, drawn face and found himself thinking those were real tears, and not from the laughter. "I needed that tonight."

A door crashed open, and the Hillsons jumped. Joe motioned them to follow. He grabbed three of the frames and carefully slipped down the roof to try and find a way to the ground that didn't lead to being caught as the burglars that were lusting for their blood. The others gathered up the remainder and followed him, listening to the thumps and shouts of the SW pouring into the big house.

# Chapter Six: Chases and Papers

*"...I am not mad...but speak forth the words of truth and soberness."* Acts 26:25

The ground seemed miles away. Nehemiah swallowed as he looked over the edge of the study roof. He took a deep breath, reminded himself it was only a little farther then jumping off the Ravens' wagon, and slid off the edge. The grass felt more like concrete as the impact jarred him to his skull, but Nehemiah ignored the pain and darted after Joe. The moon hid behind the dark clouds again, and he sent a scattered thanks to God for it as he dropped to a crouch beside his little friend and peered around a square-shaped bush.

People filled the grounds. They wandered everywhere, trampling the sumptuous flower beds, scuffing their feet until the perfect grass came up in clumps, and generally disregarding every civility. It wasn't done in a mean or spiteful way, Nehemiah felt it was more just...careless, in the true sense of the word. They didn't seem to care about much of anything, if the slumped shoulders and apathetic expressions were any sign. They wore no uniform, but every figure carried a Krackmen slung over their shoulders, a Ruby strapped to their waist, a tranquilizer pistol, a black truncheon, an electric whip, and three tasers. Laser goggles already lay strapped over their eyes; there would be no hesitation to use the tools they carried.

"What now?" Nehi murmured in Joe's ear.

"Thinking," Joe signed. Nehemiah slid his goggles on as he waited for some sort of direction from his friend and loosened Hope in her holster. Joe pointed at two sleek black hoverers about four yards in front of the boys, resting on the gravel walkway. A white stripe curved around their black ovals, almost glowing in the moonlight.

"Those, I think," Joe signed. "Two will even out our weight limit better than one."

"Wait, we're stealing them?" Nehi blinked, wondering what

the punishment might be for stealing a lawman's hoverer.

"Borrowing, always just borrowing," Joe signed back with a wink, and pulled his Black Raider mask over his face. "Cover me." The mute darted off, skimming over the ground like a shadow, his white hands tucked in his black pockets. Nehi slid Hope into his hands and pushed the safety off. An SW trotting toward the house stiffened as he caught sight of the little mute. His hand jumped suddenly for his Krackmen and his mouth opened to shout a warning. Nehemiah leveled Hope and fired. The sudden force of the laser slammed into the side of the man's head like a blow, and he crumpled to the gravel, his body traumatized by the invisible beam. But as Nehi zoomed in for a quick check, he could see the man's chest rise and fall in a breath. He would be fine in a few minutes, and just boast a new haircut. Nehi blew out a little breath of relief, glad he wasn't going around killing off the good guys in this country. But he didn't have time for the relief to sink in.

A woman about twenty yards up the drive saw the man fall, and Nehemiah dropped her quickly. Another about fifteen yards off from her gave a shout as the woman collapsed. But at least they were far enough away it would be hard to trace where the threat came from. And Joe was already in the first hoverer, doing something clever with the wiring. At least Nehi hoped it was clever as he darted back to where the rest of their group crouched behind a bush, trying desperately to get more of the pages out of the bulky frames.

"Come on," Nehi whispered, and pointed to the hoverers. A sharp hiss of steam escaped one of the big machines, and it lifted smoothly off the gravel. Daniel and Cobeau grabbed the last seven frames and darted toward the hoverer, Anna racing behind them trying to get two more of the ancient pages to slide into the black bag. Nehemiah ran beside his sister, Hope sweeping the area. He had to drop four more people before they made it to the hoverers, and another two as Daniel and Anna barreled through the steam cloud to tumble into the hoverer. Another cloud of steam billowed into the night air as Joe's tweaking managed to bring the second hoverer to hissing life. Beau trotted towards Joe's ride, his big features placid as he tossed his frames into the backseat.

A form materialized from the steam cloud in between the two hoverers. Four curled lines shot from a taser into the chimera's chest. Blue sparks lit up the darkness, the light reflecting off the white steam. Beau's eyes rolled up as his limbs jerked and twitched. Nehemiah fired Hope in an instant, but the trouble was done. Beau's knees folded. Nehi threw himself onto the big man before he could hit the ground, shoving him toward the hoverer, as Joe gripped the chimera's collar and jerked. Beau tumbled into the black oval, sprawling onto the backseat.

"Let's go," Nehi gasped, hopping backwards through the steam clouds toward his siblings' ride. Joe signed something at him, almost frantically, but Nehemiah couldn't spare the time to watch.

Eight people rushed their hoverer. Hope jerked up, Nehi's finger spasming on the trigger. All eight tumbled to the ground in four seconds, identical burn marks running down the left side of their heads, each breathing in the steady way of unconsciousness. A burly, dark-haired man froze, his ugly round face working as he stared at the people on the ground, his hands carefully held out from his body to show he held no weapon. He stood swaying at the effort it took to stop his dash for the vehicles. For an instant his eyes met Nehemiah's.

"Nice toast dogs," the stranger called in a husky growl, nodding at the heap of bodies. Nehi blinked at him. Daniel gripped Nehemiah's jacket front and jerked him into the hoverer as his other hand went to the accelerator. Nehi tumbled headfirst over the seat, his legs flailing as their black hoverer shot away, leaving a steaming wet trail. The Ravens zipped past them with a sharp hiss. Joe's ride slid past a tree with two centimeters to spare and shook dangerously as it tried to correct itself. The hoverer wobbled and sparked as the coils hit the ground, steadied, and sped away up the drive.

"That scavenger had better watch it if he wants to live

through tonight," Daniel grumbled, and pushed the accelerator wand farther toward the dashboard to catch up.

Jill staggered to the door, murderous anger on her face and a pounding headache screaming in time with the SW sirens outside their house. She hefted the Krackmen laser off the wall and grabbed for the gold-plated doorknob.

Bill caught her wrist and jerked. Jill fell back violently, gasping at the pain in her wrist.

"Don't be a little fool," Bill told her. "Don't you see His Ugliness himself out there?"

"Vern isn't going to stop me from burning a hole inside those–"

"If Inspector Vern decided to sweep us in for questioning, we wouldn't be able to finish that job for Wolf," Bill said. Jill's mouth snapped shut. Her anger drained, her face paling. Her blue eyes snapped to the windows. She could see Vern out there, with his flat head and big ears, grunting orders out the side of his mouth. His SWs almost had the house surrounded. "If we fail Wolf tonight we're going to wish we had never been born."

"It's not our fault Vern–"

"Do you think Wolf will care?" Bill snarled. "Our illustrious employer isn't exactly known for compassion."

"Hoverer?" Jill asked, her voice quivering.

"Yes, and fast," Bill nodded. "And we're not coming back. It's time to join Will." Jill's Krackmen bobbed forlornly on her shoulder as she ran, her heels clacking on the hardwood floors. The two slipped away from the door toward the sunken garage where their red hoverer waited for a quick getaway.

The two borrowed hoverers raced up the drive. The black

wrought iron gates seemed to rise out of the darkness to meet them, ten feet of twisted metal, spikes skewering the night. Nehi stared at them, wracking his brain to think of a way to get them open.

A black cone closed over the gates. Cold seemed to bite at the two hoverers, and Nehi looked quickly at the mute. Dark Ray, Joe's PUDRE, glinted in one hand, held over the edge of his ride. Fear clamped over Nehi's stomach.

"Dan, lookout, there's about to be–" A horrendous crashing drowned out the rest of his sentence as Joe flipped off his ray. Twisted and broken metal cascaded onto the drive, ripped off the gate to leave an eight foot hole in the wrought iron. A sharp expletive slid from Daniel as Anna's eyes widened and the vehicle's scanner went crazy. There was no time to dodge it.

The hoverers rushed over the debris littering their path. The steam jets hit the uneven terrain and the machines bounced and shuddered. The Ravens' nose leapt over a twisted bar of metal then came smashing down with a thundering scrunch. It shook and wobbled, but rose again and shot out the gate. Sparks spurted from the Hillsons' right side as their left pushed off twisted metal. Anna ducked, focusing on her task of getting pages out of the frames. Focusing on anything but this impossible situation. Daniel shoved the accelerator down. The hoverer shot forward, bounced over the last of the debris, and spun into the clear green grass of the road. His hand rotated the steering stick, they shifted smoothly to face the route back to town, and he hit the accelerator again. Their ride hissed off with a steady woosh of steam.

"Nicely done," Nehi breathed, glancing at his brother.

"Yeah, well, when a machine works I can usually handle it," Daniel drawled. Anna noticed his face was unnaturally pale, sweat pooling on his forehead. The Ravens' ride ran in front of them. It sped up and slowed in strange jerks, wobbling as if the steering stick kept moving back and forth.

"What's he doing?" Daniel asked. A red hoverer shot out the gate behind them, spinning with the smooth precision of an expert driver in a good machine. It hovered in place for an instant gathering itself, then shot off with a woosh that left a trail of white behind it. Nehi spun in his seat, zooming in with his goggles at this new apparition.

"Jill's behind the wheel," he reported. "I can't just take her out, she has the steering stick locked down."

"Locked down?" Daniel asked sharply. "What does she plan to do, ram us?"

"With her kind of a temperament, I expect that's her hope," Anna commented. Nehi, watching Jill's face, didn't feel so sure. He didn't see fury there, just...pale fear, a desperate need to go faster. The red hoverer drew closer with each breath. Green jungle plants hemmed in this road on both sides, growing over it, encroaching on the smooth green grass. They had nowhere to dodge.

"Let's see what this machine can do and let the scavenger know about our tail," Daniel muttered, and clicked their accelerator into a five. The wind began to cut into them, wet and warm. They sped up to Joe, giving the other hoverer a bump that took off a swath of paint. The Ravens gave a sudden leap forward and shot straight toward the wall of green trees and bushes. The steam jets shoved off the plants and the hoverer turned at an angle before bouncing back to the road in a shower of sparks. The Ravens sped off down the green path, swerving dangerously around a curve and out of sight.

"Man, I hope he lives through tonight!" Daniel gasped as he shifted to a six. Nehi looked at him in surprise, wondering if he had heard that right over the windstorm playing around their heads. Had something shifted in his suspicious dislike of the Ravens?

"Nehi, don't forget Bill," Anna ordered, trying to spit out her hair as the wind kept driving it into her face. Nehemiah spun in his seat, his stomach clenching as he realized he had forgotten the tall, nasty man. He spotted him immediately, and his heart raced. It might already be too late. Bill stood in the back of the red hoverer, behind a mini Toaster mounted on the red

machine.

A laser beam burst in white fire beside Daniel, singeing his hair as he jerked to the side with a grunt. Another shot lit up the night right between the siblings. The leather back of the seat melted, and the cotton padding underneath burst into yellow tendrils of flames. Anna dropped the frame she was working on and stomped her boots into the fire, smothering it with a fierce pounding. Nehi pivoted to one knee on the seat and leveled Hope.

The Toaster's muzzle melted, encased by laser fire hotter than it was designed for, as burst after invisible burst from Nehi slammed into it. Something inside the Toaster ignited. A sharp bang drowned out the wind as a yellow fireball wrapped around the end of the red hoverer. Bill flailed as the force hit him. He slammed into the back of Jill's seat and lay stunned.

The flames died, and Nehi could see the road back toward the mansion. A ghostly white ring whizzed closer toward the red machine. His mind swirled looking for the reason, then he remembered what rides they had "borrowed." They had that white stripe and black body too.

"SW coming up behind, probably the top brass," Nehi commented. "And Jill's still getting closer."

"Great, what other news do you have?" Daniel growled. He dropped the accelerator to zero, spun the hoverer around the sharp bend in the road, then pushed it all the way to eight. Their ride shot off in a streak of black and white. Nehi fought the wind toward the buttons and managed to hit the wind bubble. It rose smoothly, snapped closed, and the siblings sighed in relief, reorienting themselves as the force from the wind stopped. The jungle suddenly disappeared, pushed back into brown fields waiting for the planting season. Anna pulled the back off a frame and carefully, barely wrinkling the brittle yellow of the ancient paper, slid the page in its sleeve into the bag. As she finished her eyes rose to the road in front of them. Anna gave a cry and pointed ahead, outside the circle of light created by their front bulb.

A yellow hoverer zoomed toward them, moving at blurring speed. Daniel dropped to a zero, shoved the steering stick, and they jerked to the side into the field, bouncing over dirt clods and holes with their momentum. As they spun off the road, Anna caught a glimpse of the driver zipping past in that yellow ride; perfect blond hair, face chilled to stone, eyes blazing.

"Rachel's here for her necklace," she said, wrinkling her nose.

"Oh yay," Nehi commented. Daniel clicked their speed to a one, slowly working his way back toward the road as the twins spun in their seats to watch the show. The red and yellow hoverers zipped toward each other over the grassy road, white steam playing behind them. The ladies' faces were murderous, vicious hatred overriding every other thought. Or at least... Nehi zoomed in on the Trio's ride again and saw their wide eyes, the desperate hand motions, the pursed lips... Bill kept looking behind them. Something had them scared. And somehow the thought of something that could scare those two sent chills down Nehi's spine. The yards closed between the hoverers.

"If they ram and explode, we'll be caught in it," Daniel suddenly said, panic crawling under his voice. "These fields are too wet to go faster, speed will make the mud spurt up into the steam jets and clog them."

All their eyes turned back to the road. The red and yellow machines were only seconds apart. Neither woman showed any signs of swerving.

A sharp caterwauling, like hundreds of metallic cats out for a sing-along, erupted behind the red hoverer. Both drivers jumped and squirmed at the terrible sound. Their hands on the sensitive steering sticks leapt with the rest of them, and the machines veered. A black hoverer with a white stripe glowing in the moonlight shot between the two ladies. Daniel glimpsed Inspector Vern in the driver's seat.

In that moment, as the three machines lined up for an instant, the Ravens' ride shot out of the darkness.

Joe came from the side in a blurred rush, as if he had been waiting in the darkened field. Anna screamed, a raw, instinctive sound as she watched him hurtling toward three hunks of explosive engines and boiling water. It would kill them all in a massive fireball.

# Chapter Seven: Ducky's Big Pond

*"The fear of the LORD is the beginning of knowledge: but fools despise wisdom and instruction."* Proverbs 1:7

The front of the Ravens' hoverer hit a log, hidden in the dirt and darkness at the edge of the field. The steam jets pushed off the wood, caught on Rachel's yellow hoverer, and climbed it. In too short a time to blink, Joe shot over Vern's open machine, dousing him in warm, wet steam. Nehi thought he glimpsed something glinting and glittering fall from Joe's hand into the SW's lap, but it all happened too fast to be sure. Joe's ride zoomed over Jill's as the Trio veered back to the road in front of Vern, and the Ravens bounced into the muddied field. Their hoverer fishtailed, spraying mud in a fountain, covering half the Hillson's machine. The caterwauling SW rushed away after the red machine; he was moving so fast it would take time to stop. Sticky "glorp" sounds came from Joe's hoverer as it dropped on the field, doing little jumps and starts like a landed fish. Nehi popped the wind bubble.

"Get over here!" he bellowed to the Ravens. Daniel pursed his lips and pushed their speed a tiny fraction. Across from them Rachel's fancy yellow machine jumped and skidded worse than Joe's, making very sad glorping sounds. Anna could see the driver raging under her wind bubble. Rachel's face was red, her eyes wild, as she pounded at the controls. Joe's blond head popped over the console. Beau's big head rose slowly behind him like a dark monster, his beard and black hair standing straight out from the static of the stun gun. The mute hopped out, frames tucked under his arm, and steadied the wobbly chimera as Beau followed. Daniel eased onto the road and let out a long breath.

Four frames clattered on top of Anna's lap and she scooted over quickly. The Ravens leapt beside her, and Daniel admirably forbore to mention the weight limit. He shoved the stick to a six, and hoped they could wind their way back to town taking the road the opposite direction of Vern. Nehi hit the wind bubble and the two clear halves rose from the sides of the hoverer and clipped smoothly together, cutting off the balmy wind and letting the occupants draw a breath of wonderful, quiet, air-conditioned oxygen.

"See, told you going fast on mud just gets you clogged," Daniel commented. His voice shook. Anna slammed a palm into Joe's shoulder, driving him into Beau so hard the chimera grunted.

"Don't you ever scare me like that again, I was sure you were going to explode back there!" she ordered, her voice sharp with anger. Joe's face flew into innocent indignation, as he rubbed his shoulder and pouted at her. But his eyes twinkled, pleased by being lectured at.

"Joe, how are you still alive when you drive like that?" Nehemiah growled as the quiet settled around them. Anna shoved a frame at him and he started to pull at the tabs as he ran on quickly. "That maneuver of climbing *three* hoverers at once was crazy, really something dredged from an insane man's brain! The tiniest fraction of an angle off, an inch too short, and there are hundreds of ways you could have died! How are you not already dead when you drive with stunts like that?"

"I don't," Joe signed back with a shaky grin, and Beau translated a little fuzzily.

"Uh, we just watched you do it, you idjit," Daniel drawled. He shoved the stick up to speed seven, carefully watching the gauge and scanner. The machine shifted smoothly around a fallen branch in the road; they worked well. "You drive like a maniac!"

"Only his second time," Beau rumbled.

"What!" the Hillsons yelped.

"First time he drove was five years ago," Beau rumbled. "Crashed then."

"I tried to tell you," Joe signed with a chuckle, his face waxy and drawn.

"You mean..." Nehi started, and then cut it off, deciding he

really didn't want to delve into the disturbing fact Joe had been experimenting tonight. "How do we get back into town from here?" he asked instead. Joe began to point, and Daniel pushed their hoverer to an easy speed eight, settling down to a smooth hundred and forty miles an hour as they whizzed back toward town. About ten minutes later the haphazard buildings began to lean over the road. Daniel slowed down and Nehi did his best to guess where he and Beau had tethered Prissy. They got lost four times, and Daniel started muttering derogatory remarks about the road designs. After getting lost the seventh time, Nehemiah even started remarking about the haphazard city. Joe rolled his eyes and poked Beau.

"Where did you leave the wagon?" Joe signed at his big friend.

"By the palm tree," Cobeau rumbled.

"Oh that's a help. We've passed hundreds of–" Daniel started to grumble. The mute interrupted with a click that said not to be impatient. Joe leaned over the driver's seat and pointed. Daniel spun the hoverer in a neat circle and followed where Joe's thin finger told him to go. Eight minutes later, as he watched Anna throw the last of the frames out the window, Nehemiah realized he recognized the graffiti-covered street. Two minutes later their ride settled gently beside a large apartment house, built from chaotically placed planks. The jungle of plants surrounding the city loomed over the building. But there was a small clearing just behind the outstretched planks, a gigantic palm tree at the edge. The Ravens' wagon rested in the middle of the clearing's high waving grasses. Prissy squeaked happily as she saw Cobeau pull himself out of the little hoverer. The big man squeezed past the overhanging second story of the apartment and began to rub her head affectionately, a peaceful smile on his big face.

"Joe, I am never, never getting close to you when you drive again," Daniel groaned as he staggered out of the hoverer, his face pale and haggard. Joe laughed and hopped out.

"How did you find this place?" Nehemiah asked.

"Glue and I understand each other pretty well," Joe signed and Anna translated as he jogged backwards toward the wagon.

"Why are you hurrying?" Nehemiah asked, his heartbeat beginning to patter again. A horridly familiar caterwauling rose into the air. One metallic scream melded into another, until the town seemed to be alive with metal cats in a horrible mood. Joe put a hand to his ear and pointed, nodding at Nehemiah to show that was his answer.

"And we really were just borrowing the hoverers," he added with a wink. The mute motioned them to the wagon, and in the same movement grabbed Prissy's shoes and tossed two of them to Cobeau. The Ravens were back on their own territory with their wagon and giant pig. Just as Daniel finished dragging himself up the wagon, Joe flipped the switch for Prissy's motor and Beau guided her gently into an alleyway resting between the planked building and the thick, towering plants.

The wagon scraped past fronds and hanging ivy and steamed onto a peaceful little road. It wound into the trees, but they were pruned and pushed back along its pathway. Joe pushed the little engine to its full strength. The wind began to whistle too fast to allow conversation, and no one wanted to let go of their handholds long enough to sign anything. They all saw Joe's hand push on the bubble wand. Nothing happened. The mute's eyes rolled and he sat back with a huff. They turned onto smaller and smaller roads. The trees and ivy and bushes closed in closer and closer. Daniel and Nehemiah crouched on the wagon top to keep from getting the skin torn off their faces from the plants whipping by. Daniel made a move to go inside, nearly tipped off the wagon, and grabbed his hold again, hunching over with a grimace.

Another mile and Anna even had to duck. The wind rushed hot and thick and stifling. Anna found her mind drawn back to the musty prison cellars, and her one tiny dark cell far underground. She shuddered and leaned closer to Nehemiah. He draped a strong arm over her; but she felt it tremble and twitch as the ivy strands whizzed past. His mind refused to turn from the collection of whips hanging behind the door in Abid's mirrored cell. The stifling green air pressed closer. Bushes and ivies and fronds incessantly scraped the wagon's side, trying to slice into the people on top. Anna's lungs constricted. Her arm tightened over Nehi's twitching trembling one and she fought for breath. She felt she was smothering from too much oxygen given off by these swarming, menacing plants.

Silvery light rushed in, the scraping and swishing plants swept away, and clear air and space opened around them. The trees and ferns parted overhead and fell back. The moon shone through, full and bright, in all its silvery peace. A clear pathway running along the side of a small green mountain twisted off below them, in a gentle, gradual roll. The twins drew in a ragged, gasping breath and slowly sat up. Joe reached down and flipped the switch to low. The wagon slowed to a comfortable swish and everyone breathed again. There was no trace of the caterwauling SW sirens, no sound invaded the moon's glow except the countless bugs surrounding them in the jungle of giant fronds and trees growing over this mountain. The quiet was so nice. It lingered on as the wagon steamed forward. Daniel finally broke it.

"Well, that was an exhilarating day," he drawled, his voice slurred, "but I think I want it over. I'm going to bed if there are no objections." He didn't wait to listen for any and dropped heavily through the skylight.

"Did you do whatever you needed to, Joe?" Anna asked, a yawn slipping out with the words.

"I think so," Joe signed back. He turned to sign more, but Anna glanced up at the moon and let out an exclamation.

"Oh, gosh, we're supposed to check in with Elizabeth and Peter to let them know we're all right," she said, and turned toward the skylight. She paused though and patted Joe's fluffy hair. "I'm glad you're still alive after that hoverer mess. Don't drive again without lessons." A little chuckle came from Joe, he nodded, slid the scrambler's control from his jacket pocket, and clicked it off as Anna dropped through the skylight.

"I guess I'd better go join them," Nehi said, his voice quiet. He lingered in the clear moonlight, staring up at the sky. "Where are we going now?"

"Oh..." Joe signed, his expression showing he was deciding as he answered. He looked over at Cobeau, a smile on his lips. "I think our beach, what do you think old friend?" A wide smile spread over Beau's simple face and he nodded. "It's in the wild lands and will take the rest of the night to get to, especially with the wind bubble broken again. Glue and I will keep the wagon going, you go visit and go to bed."

"Are you sure?" Nehemiah asked, covering a yawn. Joe nodded and looked up at him.

"Someday you're going to teach me how to drive," he signed. Nehemiah grinned, and shuddered dramatically.

"Not me. I think you'd better stick to wheeled pigs!" he said. Joe laughed and Beau smiled happily at his master. Nehi dropped into the wagon, landing lightly on his toes. A chorus of greetings rolled around him and he smiled at the couple shaped in the blue hologram's light, peace beginning to slip into his heart again as he felt himself surrounded by friends and family.

Fifteen quick minutes passed, and Nehi hit the button to end communications. Anna's head lolled on his shoulder and she let out a sigh. Her whole body went limp. He smiled to think he could have flipped her over his shoulder and shaken her and she would have stayed asleep. Nehi swept her up, carried her into the night room, and plunked Anna on the top bunk. Daniel snored softly on the bunk below her, and the sound slid into Nehi's bones. Sleep sounded wonderful right now. Especially here, safe with his family. It was all fine with them near. He ducked back around the dividing wall to get an extra blanket, and paused.

The sound of Joe's whistles drifted to him through the skylight. A beautiful strain of music, a fast-paced delight that danced and soared, but with a slow melancholy underlying it and carrying the melody forward. A combination that twisted his heart and made him smile at the same time. It spoke of past sorrows carrying joy into the present, the two sentiments mixing so perfectly Nehi could feel the story the song played. It washed away all vestiges of the memories that hot, close air and whipping ivy had conjured up.

Joe stopped playing suddenly and started again at the beginning. Obviously it was still a work in progress. But what a work! Nehemiah grabbed his blanket, yawned, and reminded himself to have Joe play it all the way through in the morning.

The Story Land book lives on the seventh floor of Ducky's Tower. In the six floors above it, the SWs have their offices and keep the country from falling into complete anarchy. In the six floors below it, businessmen come and go, politicians claim they run the kingdom, and the world watches with interest. The book lays in the center of it all, in a shaft of light that can never go out.

Poetical, yes, but Vern Tollimé is continually annoyed by the shaft letting the skylight beam natural gray light on the book. Each new regime he sends an adamant message explaining the skylight is a terrible security risk.

The head of state always laughs at the thought, usually with the comment, "Who would dare steal a book?"

One answer to that question might have been seen tonight, if anyone had been watching. But no one saw the two black figures slip up the side of Ducky's Tower and perch on the pinnacle like ebony gargoyles. Tight black suits, skin-orienting black masks, suction gloves, they looked more like creatures from another world as they crouched there. Jill laid her hands against the three-foot glass pane. A pulse shot from her gloves, blue light sparking for an instant. The glass shattered. The shards wooshed to the left, drawn by a vacuum tube held in Bill's black glove. No shard tumbled down the six story drop through the shaft. The woman shifted, securing her rope tighter to the pinnacle. Bill looked at her.

"Good luck," he said.

"Just make sure you pull me up smart," she ordered. Jill stood in a quick, smooth movement, her arms darted in front of her, and she dove into the shaft. Bill drew his bow, his elbow crooked close to his ear, his fingers gentle on the string. As she disappeared into the darkness, he let it loose and the arrow shot forward. It sailed from the compact bow faster than Jill in her free fall. The arrow head struck the top of the clear protective shield to the book room. A pulse shot from it, an electromagnetic surge that temporarily fuzzed the security running over that sheen of diamond glass. As it landed quivering against the glass, Jill's rope tightened, drawing her to a sudden stop, and she hung suspended a foot above the clear shield. She laid her gloves on the glass.

A blue pulse, and the shards of the diamond glass showered into the small room. Jill dropped onto the ground in a crouch, her soft shoes landing without a sound. She snatched the arrow and rose smoothly to her feet, her eyes going hungrily to the pillar.

No book lay on the pedestal's smooth marble.

Jill stood frozen, staring at it. She found her eyes sweeping the ground, searching for the precious book on the glass covered floor.

A blue light shone on her face, and Jill stumbled back with a stifled curse squeaking in her throat, five throwing knives sparkling suddenly in her gloved hand. A dead wolf head spun in a blue hologram's light, projected from her shoulder pad. Jill clawed at her shoulder, her face deathly pale. She had no idea that was embedded in her suit. When had the Wolf done it? *How* had it been done, in her own private suit?!

"You should be gone already," Wolf stated. "In and out, three seconds, so security would see it as a blip of a malfunction on their machines." The voice was cold, unforgiving, hard as steel.

"It's not here," Jill hissed. She leaned over, shining the hologram on the empty pedestal. No. It wasn't empty. Jill's shaking

# Chapter Seven: Ducky's Big Pond

## Proverbs 1:7

Prophet's Peace Styles

fingers brushed a small, square note lying on the top of the marble.

*Evening, Wolf, sorry to interrupt your reading. I don't know where Ducky's Pond is. But the Hillsons have something you need, that can't be obtained through extraction. -Raven*

Jill's fingers tightened on the note as she tugged on her rope with a desperate motion. She could almost feel the crackling coming from the Wolf's anger. If she didn't get out now, she knew that monster would order Bill to leave her, just out of a furious, spiteful rage. And Bill, sentimental sap that he was, would think of his own skin first.

The harness around her chest tightened and Jill zipped back up through the shaft toward the moonlight. The Wolf head shone off the shaft wall, a centimeter from her face. Silent. It was the most terrifying silence Jill ever went through.

She shot out of the shaft and her feet came down with a light clang on the top of the building. Bill stared at her, stark terror in his eyes. They stayed frozen, the humid Story Land wind whipping around them as they perched on the pinnacle of the tallest building in town.

"Those journal pages in your swag room, I've seen one before, in a very special place..." The Wolf's voice came quiet, chewing this new twist. "It's how I know about that treasure in the Judge's family... Where did you get those pages?" the Wolf snapped, and the voice changed with the words. Black hatred dripped from him.

"A gallery in the Gaia, we were there for a vacation and knocked over a few places for fun," Bill answered, his voice shaky and quick.

"Did it have a black statuette of a lady in a toga?"

"Yes," Bill said, the word hard to get through his constricting throat. "Set apart in her own room, too priceless to be with the rest. But we had been challenged to get the papers by some old rivals and didn't really care about the rest of the collection."

Silence dripped from the hologram. The blue wolf head spun, trembling as Jill tried not to shiver.

"Get to the People's Kingdom," the wolf growled. The blue light blinked off. Jill sagged, her back going to the lightning rod rising into the night sky. Bill folded over, feeling like he might vomit. At least the Wolf still thought them necessary.

The next day the self-styled President of Story Land found himself rousted out of bed and hurried in his dressing gown up to the seventh story of Ducky's Tower. A shaky, pale SW pulled the door open, and he saw glass shards, an empty pedestal, and no book. The president staggered, his knees suddenly weak. He managed to propel himself through the door, his house slippers crunching on the shattered diamond glass.

Another crunch came behind him and he spun. Vern Tollimé's gorilla-like form filled the doorway.

"Inspector!" the president bleated. In an instant his devastation turned to burning anger. "You're in charge of security, and look what happened on your watch!"

"Said the skylight's a risk," Vern grunted. "Did my job." He walked slowly into the room, studying the scene, analyzing the method as he moved. He saw where the shape of an arrow had moved the glass shards, and knew from the size of the shards themselves what kind of pulse had been used to decimate the diamond glass. Ill Trio M.O. all over the room.

But the last two of the Trio had been reported boarding the transports out of his country at four this morning. Once those doors closed, no one came out of the transports until the end of the ride. The Ill Trio were no longer a threat to Story Land. At least not for now.

Vern slid a hand into his coat and reached into the inner pocket. He drew out a rectangular package wrapped in protective plastic that had lived with him for weeks. The president's eyes nearly popped out of his head. Vern laid the Story Land

book gently back on the pedestal.

"Goats need cereal too," he grunted.

# Chapter Eight: Holding Together

*"Happy is he that hath the God of Jacob for his help, whose hope is in the LORD his God: Which made heaven, and earth, the sea, and all that therein is: which keepeth truth for ever."*

*Psalm 146:5-6*

The stars started to fade into sunlight as Joe tweaked his song into something that satisfied him. He played it through twice to the fading moon as he and Cobeau watched Prissy roll down the road. The trees and giant ferns trickled along the road, allowing green grass to grow and room to breathe. Birches and tall pines interspersed among them, the soft breeze making them whisper about the passersby.

When the sun's fiery light pierced the sky over the treetops, hosts of flowering plants opened their blooms to its warmth and began to bathe the air with perfume. Unseen birds burst into song in an instant, adding to the ceaseless hum of the insects, and creating the morning symphony. But even the birds grew silent, listening, when Joe's song drifted to them. The beauty it carried slid into hearts and woke the hearers to its rhythmic beating, bringing bright eyes and an invigorated sense of being alive. But the undertones sang gently of sorrow traveling beside the beauty, and somehow brought the realization without the sorrow the hearers would not understand the full strength of the beauty. Joe dropped his whistles to his lap and leaned back, his eyes closing.

"Play it again?" Beau rumbled quietly. A smile twitched across Joe's scarred face. He played it again.

"You like it?" Joe signed as he put his whistles down. Beau nodded and brushed a tear from his large, dark eyes. "You like it that much?" Joe signed in surprise.

"It sounds like you."

"What does that mean?"

"You," Beau shrugged. "Strong and broken. Beautiful and shy. Happy and sad." He shrugged his big shoulders. "You."

"I think Beauty and Knee-High have been good for you too, Glue," Joe signed, studying his friend thoughtfully. He draped himself comfortably on the seat and stared at the lightening sky. "If you like it that much, I'll have to name it after you. 'Glue's Song,' doesn't work, sounds too sticky. 'Beau in the Evening'...no." Joe played the first few bars and then snapped his fingers to show that he had it. "'Holding Together.' Yes, I like that." He raised an eyebrow and tilted his head at Beau to get his opinion on the name.

"Nice," Cobeau nodded. The birds' chorus sang around them and the morning sun rose. As its fiery tendrils crept over the horizon in bright golden streams, it reflected off two green eyes staring at it unblinking. Sharp furrows dug into Joe's face, his cheeks sunken.

"Pretty?" the chimera ventured, trying to guess his friend's mood.

"Even after our disasters paint the world in black and red, the sun rises in a glorious burst of gold," Joe signed, his movements slow. "Glue, do you think God has it setup to rise automatically? Or do you think He says, 'Do it again!' every morning, just in His everlasting mercy to humanity?"

"Mercy," Beau said, a brilliant smile moving his thick beard. Joe nodded quietly. But his shoulders sagged. When his hands moved, the signs came small and tired.

"Wolf outsmarted me again, Glue. All my planning and scheming did nothing but tip off Wolf I was on my way. I didn't make it in time, the Bible is gone. Off to the People's Kingdom to land in Freddy's hands and disappear inside his headquarters, wherever that is."

"Get there first?" Beau grunted. Joe's hands flew up, a frustration so strong it translated into boiling fury cutting over his expressive face.

"No, we can't get to the People's Kingdom first, Glue! They have the SOLTD! Do you understand how big of a difference that makes, how much it cripples us in this fight? Wolf and the FFs can zip anywhere in the world in a minute, while it takes us weeks, months, to get from kingdom to kingdom! If I had a prototype of a SOLTD we could have been in Story Land a month ago, and I wouldn't have to…" His fingers stilled. His hands dropped to his lap and a deep sigh blew from him. Retrieving the Bible now meant hard, dangerous work based in the enemy's home. It would take a miracle to survive. Joe sank back against the wood and let his eyes close. The wagon wooshed on as the sun rose and the birds sang, and he poured his fears and frustrations out to the sovereign God who said, "Do it again."

Ten quiet minutes passed in the golden sunlight. Then Joe sat up and reached for the black bag with the new journal pages. Joe read as Beau watched the morning change from gold to the bright white light that let every other color shine in all its glory. After a few pages the mute's face took on the blank seriousness it got when he was thinking. He stared at the top corner on one of the pages. After a quarter of an hour of staring at the page with the same non-expression, he leaned down and pulled open a little drawer by his feet. Inside were more of the journal pages. Joe carefully placed the page he held in the drawer. He pulled a different page from the drawer, glanced over it, and slid it gently in the black bag with the others. The black bag went into the wagon through a little trapdoor, the other cubby closed tight and seamless, and Joe swiveled to face Cobeau.

"Glue, thank you. I wouldn't have survived if you hadn't stopped me from running to the FFs. You were right," the mute signed. Cobeau dropped a hairy arm around his friend and squeezed in a happy hug. The mute's hand shoved out of the embrace, flailed at Beau's beard, gripped the thick black hair, and jerked. Beau let him go and Joe reeled, gasping and laughing as he massaged his ribs. Then his green eyes caught Beau's big brown ones. His laughter died and Joe swallowed and looked away. "Look, Glue, there's no easy way to tell you this. I want you to stay behind on this next adventure. I have to go to the People's Kingdom after the SOLTD inventor, and see if maybe by some weird chance I can get a lead on the Bible. I'm

going to leave you in Geatland when we stop to pickup W-i-g-l-a-f." Cobeau's head snapped up, his big face crinkled with shocked hurt.

"Master, you want to leave me behind?" he cried, tears starting from his eyes.

"Glue, it's the People's Kingdom. You know you're in more danger there than me. I can hide, you can't. If you were caught again–"

"What if you were, Master!"

"Don't!"

"Joe," Beau corrected through his sobs. "Please don't leave me. I'll be good." His big frame shook with distress. The enormous dark eyes were so confused and hurting Joe's own softened and gave in. But the worry lines stayed creased on his face and sorrow settled deep in his green eyes as he signed his decision.

"All right, Glue, forget I mentioned it. We'll hold together as always. I'm sorry I made you sad." He took his friend's shoulder and squeezed it gently till Beau's sorrow calmed down. The two traveled on in silence, Beau content to enjoy the early morning and Joe thinking, his face dark and uneasy. He looked ahead and his troubled look disappeared into one of happy excitement. "We're here!" he signed. "I wonder what Knee-High and Beauty will think of our beach?"

"What is that delicious sound?" Anna murmured as she stepped out the wagon's door. Sand dunes surrounded her, too high to see over.

"And why do I smell rotting fish?" Nehemiah asked as he followed.

"That would be a beach," Daniel yawned from just inside the wagon. He poked his head out of the door and yawed at the balmy blue sky. A sleepy smile slid over him as he lounged down the two steps onto the soft sand beside his brother. "You two should like the ocean. Let's go see where our friendly captors have taken us now."

"'Friendly captors?'" Nehemiah prodded, plodding up a tall sand dune, each step making him sink almost as far down as he stepped up. "Are you beginning to trust the Ravens?"

"I wouldn't go that far," Daniel said. "But I don't think they're out to kill us. At least not right now." They topped the dune and a view of their surrounding area appeared. Dunes rippled away from where the siblings stood, then leveled suddenly, to create a sparkling beach of white sand. The glistening white curved away on both sides to form a horseshoe. Flowing out from the beach, a huge expanse of shining water stretched out as far as they could see. It broke over the white sand with thundering power, unrelenting, a wild untamable force that made the twin's eyes light up with thoughts of adventure. But as soon as they lifted their eyes from the breaking waves, the immense expanse created an entirely different feeling. There was vast repose and gigantic, thoughtful peace inspired by that calm, undulating water.

The thundering of the waves intermixed with a strange guttural barking, and the Hillsons quickly looked toward the sound. A large family of sea lions played on the water's edge, while seagulls dove and circled above them. The Ravens raced along the beach toward the animals, headed back toward the wagon. Cobeau's shirt was un-tucked and he was soaked to the skin, but he looked remarkably happy as he chased his little friend. Joe was laughing. His black slacks were rolled up to his knees and his habitual black turtleneck was switched for a light blue t-shirt, making him look very carefree and happy to Anna. His feet were bare as he raced along the shoreline, making seagulls take to the air in a cascade in front of him. The mute dropped suddenly to the ground next to a sea lion and started scooting along the ground in a perfect imitation of the animal's movements, and the twins burst into laughter. The sea lion seemed to think it great fun, and started racing Joe.

"He's an idiot," Daniel grinned as he watched the sea lion

shove Joe into the ocean and start barking derogatory remarks. Cobeau laughed uproariously as Joe floundered in the water, coughing and spitting.

"Well Ann, we finally get to see an ocean," Nehemiah said through his chuckles. "I knew it was pretty, but I didn't think it was this beautiful."

"Beautiful?" Anna said. "That doesn't take it in." She plopped down on the dune and pulled out her leather notebook, laid a blank page on her hard white pad, and reached for a pencil. "I'm going to try and draw it, you boys can scrounge breakfast this morning."

"That works," Nehemiah answered absently, fascinated by the view.

"I've never seen a stretch this beautiful myself," Daniel said. "And look, you can see the shore for miles from here. There's no one!"

"The sea lions and gulls aren't afraid of Joe, or even the noisy Beau," Nehemiah said. "I doubt they've ever met a human aside from the Ravens."

"Look behind us," Daniel pointed out. Nehemiah turned on his heel and a shudder ran through him. A wall of trees, dark, high, and dense, rose on the back of a small range of rocky mountains. One tiny track (it could hardly be called a road) was the only break from the forbidding green. Daniel gave an appreciative chuckle, very little humor in the sound. "There's nothing there. Just a tiny track covered by trees, then dense forest, and mountains. How did they find this place?"

"Accident," Beau panted near Daniel's ear. Daniel started, his hands coming up in a Judo stance automatically as he spun around. Joe stood in front of him, chuckling at his surprise.

"What do you mean, accident?" Daniel asked testily. "This place is a paradise, you don't just find places like this by accident." Joe shrugged, his green eyes losing a little of their joy.

"There are paradises all over this world," Joe signed and Nehemiah translated. "People don't go looking for them because the path is usually through adventures, and adventures aren't comfortable."

"That's like saying you have to get uncomfortable to get comfortable," Daniel said a little acidly.

"Yes. You won't know what comfort was if you didn't know discomfort first," Joe signed. He was withdrawn now, no longer easy and carefree, pushed back into himself at Daniel's caustic prodding.

"He's right, Dan, you have to have an adventurous soul to find the places no one else does," Nehemiah said, deciding to disperse the hovering argument. He slapped Joe on the shoulder. "Now, what does one do on a beach? Lead the way, friend!" Joe grinned and led the way, racing back toward the water with Nehemiah at his heels. Beau headed into the kitchen to find some breakfast. Daniel decided he was too tired to race and followed the chimera. Two hours later, Nehemiah and Joe came back up the dune and collapsed next to Anna, soaked in salt water, seashells in their pockets, and with the beginnings of fine sunburns. Joe sat up again, dune sand sliding off his wet shoulders in clumps, and leaned over to see Anna's picture.

"That's beautiful, Beauty. You should draw more," he signed, and pointed out a few spots that could be changed.

"Have you done any of this scene?" Anna asked, tweaking the couple of spots Joe had pointed out. He made an elusive sign that could be several things. It was a sign he used to not answer questions, and usually the twins let it be. This time Anna decided to prod. She was very good at prodding without angering. After a few minutes Joe gave in and stepped into the wagon. He came out again with a tattered brown folder. The folder itself looked like it had hundreds of fascinating stories to tell, and Anna's curiosity flew high. The mute pulled a paper out and handed it to Anna, not looking at her.

"Joe, this is fantastic," Anna breathed after a moment of staring at the paper in her hand. "It's the same scene I was drawing but...but it's more real. More alive."

"It's the same scene," Joe signed with a shrug, glancing up through lowered lids as his head hung and his feet shuffled.

Anna smiled and decided not to argue the point. It was an amazing work, and she found herself hesitant to give it back again. It was too fascinating to compare Joe's picture with what she was looking at. Joe noticed her hesitation, as he noticed everything. He started to sign something, then stopped in confusion and hastily started signing something about breakfast.

"Never mind about breakfast, what was that before?" Nehemiah asked. Joe looked everywhere but at Anna as he answered.

"You can keep it. If you want."

"Are you sure?" Anna said with delight. "Thank you, Joe!" He nodded, happy his idea had been accepted, and plopped onto the ground beside Nehemiah again. For a few minutes Anna and Nehemiah chatted about what ever came to mind. Joe listened happily and Anna finished her drawing. She decided it was as good as it would ever be, pulled it off the hard plastic pad in her drawing notebook, and handed it to Joe.

"In exchange," she said, to his obvious glee. "Joe, you've looked at my pictures, can I look at yours?" Anna asked, pointing to the tantalizing tattered brown folder. Joe froze for a moment, then handed it to her a little nervously. Before she could open it he hopped up, signed he was hungry, and disappeared into the wagon. Anna smiled as she watched the door close behind him.

"Joe may be brave when facing danger, but have you noticed he's a bit of a coward when it comes to facing everyday things, like showing his pictures, or giving people things?"

"I don't know if I would call it cowardly," Nehemiah mused as he lay on the sand and stared at the circling seagulls. "More like not used to it. You know, Ann, I think Joe's lived a lot of different lives, and never set foot in a normal one. If that makes any sense. Anna, are you listening?"

"No. Come look, Nehi, these are amazing! His paintings are very good, but these drawings..." Nehemiah sat up and leaned over his sister's shoulder. Pictures burst from the folder, the oldest dating back six years. Joe's style marked each one;

perfectly realistic, yet with a tinge of idealism and hope that lent them an air of more than reality, of the deeper reality we all know exists but can't see with our earthly vision. Looking at those pictures meant seeing the world from Joe's eyes. And everywhere he looked he saw ultimate victory and renewal. Scenes from horrible darkness to paradises, people of great cruelty and others of almost angelic goodness, despairing heartbreak, and ridiculous situations that brought hysterical laughter… The contents of that folder spoke of life as Joe had lived, and as he chose to see the world around him. Anna turned the last picture, and the twins sat still, their eyes on the papers scattered over Anna's lap.

"This world can be a dangerous, nasty place," Nehemiah said quietly, his finger gently tracing a picture. It was a scene mostly in darkness, and the shadows held hints of things; a menacing figure looming, a room in shambles and rot, vermin enjoying the chaos. One small sickly beam of light cut in from the corner, through a window the viewer couldn't see, and landed on a pencil-sketched girl, lovely, thin, ragged, with torn skin and clothes, crouched on a hard ground. But her face turned up to the light, and there was the hint of a smile, a glint in the eyes… Hope, expectation of something changing, of good plucking her out of that place; the girl's face nearly shone with it, brighter than the beam of light that allowed the viewer to see her. "Dangerous...but with beauty even in the darkness."

"Full of evil and hope," Anna murmured, her eyes on the same picture, then darting off to another. It was a self portrait, a series of Joe's scattered over a large page, folded to fit in the folder. On the bottom and ranging up the left side was Joe as a child, steadily getting older. Curled in a ball in one, hands clasped in desperate pleading in another, a frontal picture of a starved, bruised face with eyes dulled. The last in that heartbreaking collection was a Joe splayed on his side, immobile, unconscious, hopeless despair almost leaking onto the page. Then came one in the corner. It was larger than the others, and the light shone strong. Another figure joined him there, a young man of perhaps Daniel's age, a large ring on his right hand, ears too big for his head, and a button of a nose, but whose whole being spoke of strong compassion and...goodness. Anna couldn't say how she knew it, but it was goodness she saw in the stance and expression of the young man as he knelt by the immobile Joe, lifting the broken child into his arms. The top of the page was a Joe standing with his back to the viewer, but his face turned to glower over his shoulder, the shadows deep enough you could just see a pair of menacing eyes shining. The one hand in sight held a laser, dripping with a thick liquid.

The other corner, as your eye followed the pictures in a circle, had another Joe, again with his back to the viewer. But the light beamed from the page. He splayed on his knees, in an attitude that said he was too tired and worn to stand any longer, one hand clutching at the dirt, the other over his mouth as it covered his sobs. A great cross towered over that Joe. The light came from the cross, hit Joe, and didn't just cover him. It shot through the mute, the beams cutting straight through his desperate, kneeling form, and shooting out again brighter and more abundant than before. The next several Joes were mere hints and ideas of what the artist might have made them, only a few lines; a Joe laughing, one with hands uplifted, one in a field with his whistles and looking happy and comfortable. Then the shadows began to return, playing over the last few unfinished pictures so that Anna couldn't tell what they were meant to be. But one portrait lay in the center of the large page, that the others circled around. It was a simple charcoal sketch of the mute's face, a few years younger, turned just a little to the side, his GI tattoo peeking from under his unruly hair, his sharp nose in sharp relief, the corner of his mouth twisted in a smile, his eyes turned up and gleaming at something the viewer couldn't see, but something that Joe took huge delight in, and was incredibly thankful for. Thankfulness. That's what that central portrait spoke of. It was Joe expressing intense thankfulness to the heavens above his silent head.

"To be thankful for everything on that page..." Anna

murmured, her voice catching and dying away. Nehi said nothing. But his eyes flicked between the picture with the cross, and central portrait. This was Joe expressing *himself*, artwork he kept hidden, just drawn for his own need and desire. No prodding, no reason to hide the truth, or skew it out of focus. To Nehi, staring at that picture answered the nagging doubt he had tried to quiet since he met Joe. This was a young man who hadn't just been to the cross, but had been overtaken by it, overthrown in his own darkness, and forced through Jesus' light. For Nehi it proved Joe was who he said; a Christian brother, striving to make the world better while still working through old fears and scars. The worries and doubts that had hung in dark corners dissipated in that moment, evaporating like mist in the morning sun. And as Nehi's eye darted over the childhood portraits, something else stirred within him. A deep protective blaze. Pity stirred to action, fired by a friendship that had just lost the last walls holding it back. Nehi chose to welcome it and let it sink deep, replacing the doubts and frustrations over Joe's secrets.

His hand went to the papers and he pulled another one to the top, a pencil sketch of a pretty white cottage. The same two figures from the self portrait were there again. The young man with the large ears and button nose stood on the porch, legs apart, eyes studying something in the street the viewer couldn't see, his mouth open as he spoke of it; exuberance, speculation, an idea festering in his mind and about to be played out, you could see it all in him. And that goodness shone like a radiant energy from the man. A Joe, perhaps thirteen, lounged on the porch, his feet splayed over one chair arm and his hands comfortably tucked behind his head, watching the young man. The expressions on his face twisted and combined; amusement, confused wonder, and affection. You could almost feel Joe learning from the young man with the ring, soaking in everything from his protector and friend.

"But there's good people out there. Good people who change the evil and danger, step in to reclaim the world as it's

supposed to be, and lead others to start reclaiming it too. Gosh, I'm glad Josh Noble stepped in."

"It's nice to see pictures of him, isn't it? Especially through Joe's eyes. Everything in here is so... Alive with a determination to find the goodness God's planted in this world, and keep it strong! The way Joe looks at the world, there's...so much hope to be seen in everything..."

"Life everywhere you look, beauty shining around corners," Nehi nodded, flipping through the pictures gently.

"And such hope." Anna carefully closed the folder, and ran her hand over the scratched, brown front. "I feel like I've been on a long journey through looking at those."

"That's a good way to describe it," Nehemiah said. "I wonder–"

"I will have an answer Joe, or so help me I'll choke it out of you!" Daniel's voice rang out from the wagon. Nehemiah and Anna looked at each other. A grimace crossed Nehi's face. They hopped to their feet and trotted over the soft sand toward the wagon, dreading what they might find.

# Chapter Nine: Scenery and Suspicion

*"And God called the dry land Earth; and the gathering together of the waters called He seas: and God saw that it was good."* Genesis 1:10

Oh, you're back again now," Daniel said as Joe hopped through the wagon door. "Want some toast this time?" Joe smiled and nodded. He took the offered toast with a thank you and dropped into the seat across from Daniel. Cobeau sat on the floor, humming his tuneless hum as he did when he had nothing else to do, a peaceful smile on his big face.

"So, you can walk upside down on the ceiling, but you can't drive," Daniel said, as he refilled his orange juice and filled Joe's proffered cup. "Any comment?"

"Some people learn different things going through life," he signed and Beau translated mindlessly.

"Okay. Say, you have a translator now, can I ask some questions about yesterday?" Daniel said. Joe studied him through lowered lids as he lifted his orange juice to his lips. He was asking honestly, not probing for something else like usual. Joe nodded. "Thanks. So, why did we go to, heh heh, Ducky's Tower? You mentioned money. I know you Ravens don't earn enough to keep us all with your sporadic concerts."

"First off, we'll be kept even if we did just live on the money from music," Joe signed and Beau stopped humming to translate. "It's in the name."

"What?"

"Luke 12:24," Joe signed, and Daniel's Judge-trained mind automatically brought the verse up from his memory. *"Consider the ravens, for they neither sow nor reap; which neither have storehouse nor barn; and God feedeth them: how much more are ye better than the fowls?"* He nodded slowly.

"It's a good verse for a couple of traveling musicians living hand-to-mouth," he said, and let there be a dramatic pause. "But you don't really, do you?"

"Oh we do," Joe grinned at him, "you just haven't been around when we get down to foraging for roots in the woods. But you're right that we also supplement our earnings. I'm an informer. I get paid for bringing information from country to country. We went to Ducky's Tower to drop information." Joe stopped to spread honey on his toast and Daniel digested this information.

"All right," he accepted the explanation. "Next. You dropped a necklace into Inspector Vern's lap during that crazy stunt with the hoverer. When did you take the necklace, was it the same one Anna and Nehi were after, and why did you throw it in a hoverer and steam away like your work was done?"

"Lot of questions," Joe smiled and took a bite of crunchy toast.

"Only one, really," Daniel answered. "What did you do that cleared the IDP of the Ill Trio's work?"

"That's involved," Joe signed. Daniel thought that was a dodge and felt his annoyance with the secretive Joe coming on again. But to his surprise, Joe sat up straighter, sat his breakfast down, and began to sign. "While we hunted through the house, I found several of the items the IDP are being framed for. I stuffed them in the glove compartment of that snazzy red hoverer we found in the garage and took the necklace away as not IDP involved. Then after Knee-High told me his story, I decided the necklace might be a useful item to have with us and kept it. When Vern showed up it was like the perfect set up from God. I waited till Vern got close enough to get interested in Rachel and the Trio, then threw the necklace to him with a note telling him where I found it and to look in the red hoverer's glove box. Vern will do what I suggested, and will have solid proof they're the burglars. Rachel will tell him the necklace is hers and that the Trio stole it, and since she's one of the big-wigs in this regime it will basically be government sanction to lay all the thefts on the Trio. And if they're the thieves, the IDP can't be."

"You talk like you know exactly what she'll say," Daniel commented. Joe paused for a moment, studying Daniel under lowered lids again, and then decided to answer it.

"I make it my business to know about the important people in a country. Vern doesn't look like much, and sounds like less with his random words–"

"Pause, what does random words mean?" Daniel butted in. Joe sighed, looked longingly at his breakfast, and began to sign even swifter.

"There's no truth that applies to more than one person in Story Land, it's all a matter of what you want in your own personal story. If it's all a matter of personal stories, that includes words in some logical minds. Vern has a logical mind. So he can say anything, or take any word and make it be whatever he wants. Random words that mean what he wants them to in his mind at that moment."

"That's weird," Daniel said. "I mean, I knew about the truth thing, but not about the guy taking it that far into his conversation. Okay, go on."

"No matter what stories they tell, or who ends up with the necklace and stuff in the end, Vern's going to know the Trio committed the thefts now. And that they definitely are not IDP related. No matter what regime comes up, Vern is the trusted man in this kind of thing, so the IDP is off the hook thanks to a remarkably weird concatenation of events."

"Whoa, do that sign again, for concatenation," was Daniel's only comment. Joe grinned and did the sign again, then went back to eating his toast. Daniel sat still, watching him and thinking. Joe didn't take that necklace because it "might be useful." He knew Vern and Rachel were both going to be there looking for it. That meant a remarkable knowledge of how both those people worked, as well as the Ill Trio, and all the inner workings and nuances of the political structure of the country. That was a lot of knowledge. And Joe used it with remarkable skill and foresight. No, with brilliance and crazy bravery, all played together with perfection in an instant.

Daniel looked at Joe, happily pulling a hang drum from its case. The mute dropped on the ground and began to play the

hang, a peaceful smile on his sharp face. As the metallic, ringing notes flew around the little room, Daniel's misgivings awoke again. Someone with that kind of knowledge and skill was a very dangerous person to be around if they weren't really on your side. He remembered Joe's skill at acting and knew he could be anything, and look perfectly innocent and good to anyone watching him.

"Where did you find those journal pages you let Nehi look at in your bag?" Daniel asked. The music flew through the room and nothing was offered by the mute. "Could it be from the same place the Ill Trio found theirs?" Joe's eyes closed and a smile curved over his face as he leaned into his music. Daniel rolled his eyes and tried changing the topic. "So Joe, what about the conversation at the doctor's? What was all that about the Wolf snatching Christians? It sounded pretty serious," Daniel called over the music. Joe nodded and went on with his playing, the metallic notes zinging merrily around the wagon as his thumbs tapped in a blur. It was rare he found a moment just to play for fun. Daniel interrupted again. "Who do you think it might be?"

"Could be anyone in the IDP," Joe signed distractedly and went back to his music before the last note had died on the air.

"Anyone. Come on! You know who the Wolf is, Harry maybe?" Daniel asked quickly, just to keep Joe signing. Joe messed up his musical phrase, his hands skipping along the drum, then splaying over the top to stop the off-key ringing. He stared at Daniel, no humor in his green eyes.

"Hey, did I hit it on the first try?" Daniel asked, his eyebrows rising. Joe looked back at his hang drum and shrugged.

"Already told you it's just an assumption to say I know who Wolf is. I can fight the deeds and know lots of facts without knowing Wolf's identity."

"If you insist you don't know who the Wolf is, you *have* told us you know who the lover is. So how about that? Who is she? Where is she? You said you're planning things with her, what things?"

"Wolf's a problem," Joe signed after a moment. "Knows too much about everything."

"That I already knew. What are you planning to do about him? And you do know the lovers name, why won't you tell us?"

"Why do you care?" Joe asked, his eyes frozen and his face blank.

"Because I'm more than a little worried you're not actually Wolf hunting at all, that maybe this Wolf is a fiction of your own to keep us all looking the wrong way," Daniel said, his voice beginning to rise. "Joe, I want an answer now; why did you go looking for Anna and Nehemiah in the first place?" The mute's lips pursed and he shook his head. Daniel stood up, determination and anger practically radiating from him. "I will have an answer Joe, or so help me I'll choke it out of you!"

Beau shot in front of Joe protectively. His beard bristled, his eyes hard, and his rifle lay cupped in his big hands. Joe leapt to his feet, grabbing the chimera's thick arm and clicking at him to put away the gun. A metallic click came from Daniel and Joe froze, staring at the small pistol pointing at Cobeau's stomach.

"I don't think your master wants you to shoot me, Cobeau," Daniel said, his voice low. "He still wants me alive for his own purposes. Come on, Beau, what's Joe using the twins for?"

"Joe is doing good. Miss Beauty and Knee-High helping him without knowing is good," Beau rumbled. Joe dropped his hands to his side and his shoulders slumped, his face remarkably blank. A humorless smile curved on Daniel's face.

"Thank you, Beau," he said. The door opened and Nehemiah and Anna stood framed in the bright sunlight. They stopped in the doorway, staring as the sun glinted off the weapons.

"What do you think you're doing?" Nehemiah growled. "Both of you sit down!"

"Pointing guns at each other, really boys!" Anna said, her eyes flashing. "Put them away, right now. You ought to be ashamed of yourselves, two Christian brothers!" Daniel and Beau put their weapons away without protest. But they watched each other warily as they settled at the table. Anna turned to the little blond standing next to his hang drum, his green eyes on the floor. "Joe, what's this all about?"

"I'll tell you what it's all about," Daniel cut in. "Beau finally admitted what I've been worried about. Joe didn't pick you up just because you needed it, or as a favor to Dad. He was looking for you out there. And get this, he's planning on using you for something."

"We know that," Nehemiah said. Daniel and Joe gaped at him. "Oh come on, we may be young, Anna and I, but we're not quite fools."

"We've known it wasn't a spontaneous rescue from that first night," Anna put in, settling in a chair beside Daniel, as he stared at her with his mouth open. "We told you, Daniel, you just weren't listening. You don't always listen well."

"How?" Joe signed, his brow creased and eyes wide.

"You had clothes just our size," Nehemiah said, "a route already picked to get us out, you never once asked who we were and if we had anywhere to go. And once we were out, you were awfully quick to offer to keep us. It wasn't that hard to figure out, Joe."

"About that second part," Anna put in, "Daniel, we've known Joe needed us for something for a while now. Otherwise he would have set us up somewhere along the way, like he's done with others he's rescued since we've been with him. Instead he's taken us along, and he doesn't do things like that without a reason. He certainly wouldn't have come back to KAM, just to collect us, if he didn't need us."

"And you still trust him?" Daniel gaped, his voice shrill.

"That's what I was about to sign," Joe signed, looking at the twins in wonder.

"When I told you I trusted you back in Geatland I meant more than just that stunt with Daniel that you refused to explain," Nehi told his flabbergasted friend. He spun back to Daniel. "Look, if the Ravens meant to do us harm they wouldn't have risked their lives over and over again to keep us safe. You can't deny they've risked everything for us several times now, and that includes you." Daniel muttered something unintelligible and stared at the table. "And I happen to like them, and to like traveling with them. Besides, they're brothers. They've proved that in my mind. I trust them."

"We've seen at least a little of what Joe works on, and it is good things," Anna said soothingly to her older brother. "Daniel, you really shouldn't antagonize him by trying to force his hand. Of course, Joe, you should speak up and tell us what's going on, and stop antagonizing Daniel with your silence," Anna continued, swinging around and waggling a finger at Joe. Before either could reply, Nehemiah's back straightened and he clapped his hands together.

"I call a council of war!" he called.

"What war?" Anna asked.

"The war to get our book back, and defeat the evildoers overrunning our country," Nehi answered. He grabbed a folding chair off the wall and shoved it at Joe, snatched one for himself, and joined the group at the table. Joe smiled and did the same, squeezing in between Beau and Nehi.

"Here ye, this meeting has come to order," Nehemiah said in mock seriousness. Anna reached behind her, grabbed the hammer she used for cracking nuts, and handed it to Nehemiah.

"Your gavel, sir," she said with a dramatic frown. Nehemiah banged the table with his gavel. Joe hopped up and Anna followed in an instant.

"All rise!" he signed, his green eyes answering Nehemiah and Anna's laughter as he and Anna sat down in the same second. "What next, Judge Knee-High?"

"You next," Nehemiah said authoritatively. "The court hereby recognizes Joe...don't you have another name of some sort?" Joe shrugged and shook his head. "Recognizes Brother Joe. Give your statement, Brother Joe."

"What statement?" Joe asked his forehead crinkling.

"Okay, enough with the play acting, please," Daniel said. "I've got a headache and you wouldn't believe how tired I am from all that running around town yesterday. What are you trying to get at, Nehi?"

"Just what I said, a council to set our plans to get our book back and recover our country."

"That's a pretty tall order for one council, sir," Anna said.

"Oh I don't know," Nehemiah answered. "You probably have most of it already figured out don't you Joe?" The mute bit his lip and didn't answer. Nehemiah laid the hammer on the table and dropped all the playing as he stared at his friend. "Please, tell us enough to let us know we're getting somewhere." The mute stared at the table for a long minute as the others watched and waited.

"Okay," he signed finally. "But I can't tell you much."

"You mean won't," Daniel said.

"I mean both," Joe signed, with Beau still translating automatically. "I know who has the Bible. I have at least a vague idea of how to get it back, and thanks to D's input, we know it's still safe for a few more months."

"That's when the deadline's up according to the note the FFs passed to the Sojourners before the disintegration," Nehemiah interposed, "are we sure it's safe till then?" Joe nodded.

"At least as things stand it is," he signed. "It's a haphazard world, this, and it could change at any moment, but right now it's safe. I've got retrieval of the Bible under control. I hope. If the Lord wills it. And I don't die before then."

"That's really encouraging," Daniel drawled, and even Joe smiled at him.

"All right, Brother Joe has the Bible situation in hand, we'll leave it to him," Nehemiah said in a brisk, business-like way.

"Wait a minute..." Daniel started to protest and then found four pairs of eyes focused on him and realized he had no idea what objection to make. "Okay, we'll leave it to him. For now."

"What are we doing at the moment, Joe?" Nehemiah said. "Why are we going to the People's Kingdom?"

"That's part of the Bible situation, as you call it," Joe signed. "And possibly the other, getting the Sojourner's kingdom back on its feet. We need to see if we can get Quintus Leeman in our ranks."

"Wait, you've told us that name..." Anna said. She snapped her fingers in recognition. "The inventor of the SOLTD, that strange bubble thing that zaps people from place to place."

"It doesn't zap," Joe signed with a grin. "It creates a warp bubble with dark matter and dark energy, and moves you, like a hoverer or something, just incredibly faster and colder."

"Whatever it does, is that what you're thinking?" Nehemiah asked. Joe nodded. "With one of those we could go anywhere at any time, right?" Joe calculated for a moment, then nodded again. "Well that would definitely be useful."

"Useful isn't a good enough word for it," Joe signed. "How do you think all those troops appeared so suddenly in so many different parts of Sojourner's Way and swept it off its feet? How do you think the FFs are such a powerful force when they're actually a small group of agents? Why do you think it's been so hard to catch up to the Wolf these past years when it takes a wagon months to get between countries? The SOLDT is a remarkable thing, and the possibilities are almost limitless. Now that the enemy has working prototypes, it's pretty much a must for us if we want to survive and win this thing."

"So why are you just now going after it?" Daniel asked.

"We did try last year, we went to KAM first, but he had moved. But QL (the inventor) is from KAM, and now he's in the People's Kingdom," Joe and Beau answered.

"What's that got to do with anything?" Daniel yawned. Joe rolled his eyes.

"We Ravens are a GI and a chimera," he signed, and dropped his hands back in his lap like that explained everything. The others stared at him blankly. Surprise, amusement, and a hint of wistfulness shot over the mute's face with a rapidity that left Daniel wondering if he had actually seen any of it. Then the mute was signing again. "With his background he's not going to listen to anything we Ravens tell him. He wouldn't let us get close enough to tell him anything, and even if we managed to get near, he wouldn't believe we were actually communicating.

To him it would be a trick, like a well-trained dog going through its act. And I haven't exactly had time since I've had completes with me that will do my talking."

"Please don't call us completes, I don't like it," Anna said. "Asides from the horrid things it brings to mind in this world, none of us will be complete till Jesus makes us whole in heaven."

"Good point," Nehemiah interposed. "Sister Anna's motion carries, we're all a bunch of incompletes till further notice." He banged his gavel down on the table and Joe laughed. Nehemiah turned to him curiously. "Is that what you need us for? To talk to this Quintus Leeman for you? No, if that's what it was you wouldn't have told us just now. Never mind," he continued quickly as Joe's laughter died and he went back to staring at the table. "On to point two. How are we planning on getting Sojourner's Way back on its feet once Brother Joe gets our Bible back for us in a couple of months? Any ideas?" Everyone looked at everyone else and no one said anything.

"Well…" Daniel said after several silent minutes had gone by. "I guess we'll cross that bridge once we come to it."

"Good point, Brother Daniel," Nehemiah said, lifting his hammer again. Daniel snatched it and dropped it into the sink. "Oh well, motion carries anyway. Point number three, Brother Joe where are those papers we so laboriously brought with us last night? Let's have a look at them and see if there's anything useful." Joe hopped up and got the black bag he had pushed into the night room early that morning. He popped open a cubby in the floor and the others glimpsed a familiar black bag in the recess. Joe's hand dived into it, pulled out his black notebook, and pushed the cubby closed. Joe laid the fruits of last night's hunt and his notebook on the table. The Hillsons reached for them, excitement radiating. Each carefully, almost reverently, drew a yellowed page and started to read. Joe spread the remaining ones on the table, to be examined when ready. Time ticked on, and Beau's peculiar hum covered the scene as the others studied the journal pages in fascinated silence. Joe whistled and pointed at his. Everyone leaned over to see what he had found.

"So this treasure is an 'it,'" Anna said. "Not a lot of 'its.' If that makes any sense."

"It does to me," Nehemiah murmured as he looked thoughtfully at the page. "And it's fairly small, Lou could carry it around on his own."

"That doesn't mean much," Daniel put in. "Haven't you been around mothers enough to know they still talk about their children like they're three when they're thirty?" Nehemiah shrugged and nodded. Joe pointed to the last sentence and Nehemiah quickly began to dig through the rest of the papers. Anna and Daniel leaned farther over Joe's shoulder to see what their brother was frantically looking for.

"*This really is a treasure, this-*" the sentence said, and then the page ended.

"It's not here," Nehemiah said, dropping heavily to his seat. "She was about to name it, to say right out what this annoying, mysterious thing is that's cost us so much, and she ran out of room."

"And we don't have the next page?" Anna said, her voice soft. Nehemiah shook his head and Daniel slumped in his chair with a grunt of frustration. Joe's face creased in disappointment and his shoulders slumped as he laid the page with the others. After a moment Nehemiah stirred and assumed his earlier air of mock seriousness.

"This meeting of the mighty Vision Keepers is coming to a close–"

"The what?" Daniel asked, a yawn taking him over. When he focused again he saw Anna and Nehi were smiling; but it was a half smile with a sad crinkle to the eye and a deep well far down in the depth of the pupil... He knew they were about to take him back to their parents before the words were out.

"Don't you remember the speech, Dan?" Nehi said, his voice a queer combination of soft and amused. "Always keep your eyes focused on heaven where we're going to end up, through Jesus' blood, no matter how the ground shakes under us as we run the race. He's waiting for us there."

"As long as we keep that vision burning in front of our eyes," Anna took up, "Jesus, waiting to welcome us in the end, all of life takes on meaning, all worries are defused, and the joy of that certainty permeates everything."

"Keep the vision burning." Daniel's voice finished it, firm and strong, filling the room. He nodded, his scars making his smile lopsided. "It's a good name."

"Right," Nehemiah said, his shoulders squaring and his mind working hard to come back to the point. "So this meeting of the VK's is ended, and here's the summation of the things covered; Joe's in charge of getting our book back and whatever other mysterious things he has up his sleeve (and may the Lord protect you in them, Brother), and the rest of us ought to be thinking over what to do once we have the book. At the moment, the plan of attack is through Geatland to pick up a Warrior Hero, then to the People's Kingdom to try and pick up an inventor."

"The Battle Kingdom comes in between," Joe signed and the others looked at him. "We have to cross through that kingdom to get to the People's Kingdom. At least if we want to avoid months of travel, and we do."

"Okay," Nehemiah amended, giving the mute an encouraging smile. He had actually volunteered something, if only a small detail of traveling. That was a big step forward. "The plan of attack is through Geatland, then the Battle Kingdom, to get to the People's Kingdom, to try and enlist an inventor. What comes after that, and between it, and before it, is in God's able hands. Brothers and Sister, how about closing our council in prayer?"

Nehemiah's motion carried unanimously, and for a long while the little wagon filled with praises and pleas, thanks and supplications to the Lord of life and time. As is usual when God's saints cast their cares on their Father, they rose refreshed and hopeful. Nehi sprang to his feet and grabbed his water cup, lifting it high. The others reached for theirs, even though Daniel

grimaced and moved slowly.

"VKs, here's to whatever comes next."

Five glasses raised, the toast pledged with a solemnity belied by the twinkle in the twins and Joe's eyes, the sharp twist to their lips; it spoke of the unshakable hope settled in their Savior, in the joy of the adventure knowing He walked with them wherever life went.

Daniel took a sip, groaned, and went to bed to try and relieve his growing headache. Beau drained his cup and opted to stay in the wagon and hum. But the other three darted to the beach. They played hard the rest of the day and had horrendous sunburns that night.

"It was worth it!" Anna declared rapturously as they steamed back towards Geatland the next day. Joe and Nehemiah agreed.

Don Mackenzie put a protective arm around his wife's waist as they walked toward the door. Amie hurried beside her husband, but kept throwing glances over her shoulder, worry on her pretty, middle-aged face. The Green Back Inn was not the place either of them had expected. Don had only been looking for a little black-market wine for a thrill and knew nothing about the town of Maybe; he should never have listened to that creepy salesman in the alley. Stupid, stupid to bring them to this seedy, dangerous place!

A giant form stepped in front of them and the door, and Don decided he was going to take a hammer and smash his informant when they got out of here. A massive hand reached out and shoved into the chubby little man's chest, and Don stumbled back, losing his hold on his wife. *If* they got out of here, he corrected, his throat constricting. Amie's hands went to her hips and her chin lifted.

"I'm sure someone taught you better than to push your elders," Amie said, every inch the mother. The giant of a man

paused, watching her in surprise. Then he smiled. It was not a nice smile. Even Amie shrank back, stepping beside her husband as fear ran through her. The giant of a man reached toward her, his smile turning into a leer.

In that moment of panic, Don and Amie would have been greatly comforted to know of the small team of men gathered at a booth near the back. Atif and his four agents waited in the depths of the market, and it was all that saved the Mackenzies that day.

Strong, slim fingers wrapped around the giant's wrist and twisted. A howl came from the man, and the slim hand twisted again.

"Quiet now," a lugubrious voice spoke in the giant's ear. "We don't wish to bother the other drinkers, now do we?" The big man whimpered and shook his head. Taban released the man's wrist and looked at the Mackenzies. The chubby, middle-aged couple stared at him with wide eyes. "I think you are in the wrong part of town. It would be a wise choice to return to the surface, perhaps?" He held a hand out, motioning politely to the door. The couple scurried out, murmuring thanks as they went. Taban turned away, swept up the five dirty, metal mugs from the bar, and began to weave his way through the laughing, drunken crowd. He pivoted around a chair as it crashed backward in his path, hopped over a dark red-brown stain on the wooden floor, danced around a cackling woman holding a battered man's wallet over her head, and reached his booth at the back of the room. The metal mugs plunked onto the table and were quickly distributed among the team. Atif leaned back in the corner, his eyes on a distant point on the roof and no interest in the company or the drink.

"Shareef, you know well how to disappear," Taban commented as he slid in beside Otar.

"I know good doctors too, eh?" Shareef smiled at him.

"I will be the first to agree to that," Taban said, just managing to stop his eye from twitching at the reminder of his first two days here. The nightmares from his drug-induced sleep

still plagued him. "We are safe and well, and I am grateful. But I will be glad to see the sun again."

"Two weeks," Otar complained. "We have been two weeks under the dirt and tar and evil of Maybe."

"Under the evil?" Taban scoffed and moved his hand in a quick sweeping gesture around the inn. "Have you been paying any attention? We are in the midst of it. More robberies than sales happen in the underground markets here, and usually the robberies become a murder before the deed is done. I have seen more bodies dumped in the sewer system than I would dare count since we have been walking these dark tunnels."

"Do not drink Maybe's water," Naqi murmured, his face still turned to the boxy gadget on the table. A little smile played over his face, lit from the blue light of the screen. Taban snorted and turned back to his drink. Shareef had managed to get tech gear that was unavailable, even unknown, in the upper world. Naqi stayed oblivious to everything else.

"Only one more day," Shareef soothed. "My contact comes through tomorrow."

"Are you sure you can get us out again?" Taban murmured darkly. Everyone's mind flew to the night two weeks ago that had led them into the depths of the earth. The seedy club, the back room, the twelve friskings, and fifty armored goons Shareef had fast talked, all watching them disappear through the time-locked door into the depth of the Night Market. A visible shiver went over Naqi at the memory of that door slamming behind them, and even he looked up. Shareef shrugged, a smile on his face.

"I can get us out. My father–"

"–he knew some people, yes, yes," Taban broke in testily, and the rest of the team grinned, even Atif. So he was paying attention. Shareef turned to him.

"Boss, why did you veer toward the forest?" the supplier asked. Atif blinked, as if he were coming back from a long way off, and his eyes flicked down to his teammates. "You handled that henbrau 300 with an expert's skill. But you pretended to

be out of control when we first started."

"There was blood on the grass," Atif answered. His team stared blankly at him. Atif's legs moved, sliding off the bench and under the table, as he finally reached for his drink. "The black one we set out to rescue got to the trees himself. But there were blood drops on the ground, showing where he fled into the forest. The steam from the hoverer washed them out, and kept all eyes on us, so the wicked Simmons would not be able to get a DNA match or follow with dogs."

"But it would do no good if Simmons had guessed what you were doing, he would still have known the direction to start his hunt," Shareef nodded slowly. "You are very good at pretending to be bad with a hoverer, boss."

"Atif," the boss corrected mildly. He slammed his mug back down and grimaced. "What is this horrible concoction? I am not drinking this." Atif hopped abruptly out of the booth and disappeared into the raucous crowd, carrying his mug.

"He isn't really going to complain, is he?" Naqi gaped. "The manager beat the brains out of the last man who complained. Literally. I couldn't eat my dinner after that."

"Shouldn't you go with him, Taban?" Shareef asked, his words quick and laced with worry. The grim fighter laughed, no humor in the sound.

"I was cornered when Atif found me," Taban said. The others tried not to show their surprise. Taban never mentioned his past. Ever. They didn't even know his last name. "I was known as a convert, and the Wazir's black team had pinned me down after three days of a fighting run. I hadn't been able to shake them, or beat them. I was seconds from being immobilized and dragged to the Wazir. Then Atif showed up, young, quiet, grim, and steady. In thirty minutes we two walked away, with no one else alive. No, Shareef, I do not need to go with him." Silence rested at the back booth as the others contemplated it. Otar raised his mug and drained the contents in a noisy gulp.

"Why are we waiting here?" the big man rumbled.

"A D30 tracker," Shareef answered.

"It is the smallest and most adept tracker in the world," Naqi took up with enthusiasm, and rattled off a series of unintelligible specs about the gadget, till Shareef interrupted with a laugh.

"English, my young specialist, English!"

"Sorry," Naqi said, a sheepish smile creeping over his thin face. "It is undetectable, and can be traced anywhere, even underwater or down here in the midst of these tunnels. No one has yet succeeded in blocking the signal."

"I know *what* we are waiting for," Otar rumbled. "*Why*, why have we waited so long for this particular piece?"

"Atif is putting it on the hoverer," Shareef explained. The team looked at each other.

"Well." Taban raised his dirty metal mug. "Bring the hoverer to the surface and let Simmons have it back, and we have a sure way of finding the head of the snake." He gagged behind the pewter mug and a muddy colored liquid sloshed out the top as he pulled it away. "Oh, that really is terrible." Taban slid from the booth, drink in hand and headed into the brawling crowd. The other three watched him go with incredulity. They turned back to their drinks and pretended it wasn't terrible.

# Chapter Ten: Overman City

*"Who can find a virtuous woman? For her price is far above rubies."* Proverbs 31:10

The ground shook as three-hundred pounds of lizard tail slammed into it again. The wagon's wheels (clicked on to reserve water in this dry land) wobbled dangerously. A deep, grating roar burst from the stumpy tail lizard.

"Beware the rush!" Wiglaf shouted, crouching on the wagon, his sword drawn. Nehi didn't answer. He lay on his stomach, steadying Hope on the wagon's edge, aiming for the inside of the monster's mouth as he roared his challenge. Nehi saw his shot land, then another and another in quick succession. The stumpy tail writhed, welts rising in his poison filled mouth. The lizard fell back flailing, his thick tail slamming into the ground. Yellow dust rose with each movement of the giant black lizard. The dust coated the scene. His mouth clamped closed, and his two beady eyes blazed. His claws dug into the desert ground and the stumpy tail rushed toward them.

The monster shot forward, speeding toward the wagon like a ravenous bullet. Prissy screamed in her traces, as her wheeled shoes pulled them on in a cloud of yellow dust. Cobeau strained at the steering stick trying to keep her on the bumpy, dried track that made up the road. Wiglaf roared out an unintelligible challenge, his muscles bunching and his eyes alight as he waited for the clash. Nehi shoved Hope back in her holster and snatched the long dirk Daniel held out for him. He leapt to his feet and his shoulder pressed against his brother's.

"Aim for the eyes," Daniel said, his voice grim. "It's our best shot." Nehi could see those eyes clearly now, two small bright black beads, maddened with hunger and anger, rolling in the lizard's head. He was almost to them. Nehi's sweaty hand tightened on the dirk handle as he ground his teeth together.

The door flew open below them, banging into the wagon side. Joe and Anna heaved out the one horn carcass they had

painstakingly hunted down and cleaned yesterday. The meat thumped into the ground in front of the stumpy tail.

A cloud of dust rushed into the air as the lizard screeched to a halt. His rows of sharp teeth dug into the meat as a happy rumble echoed up from his throat.

"Fine, if you wish to take the easy way..." Wiglaf huffed, plopping down on the wagon top, his long legs trailing over the edge. Nehi's shoulder's slumped in relief. He chuckled at the Geatish warrior's disappointment as the feeding stumpy tail dropped farther and farther behind them. The skylight flew open and Joe scampered out. As a wash of cooler air spilt up from the wagon's interior, Nehi couldn't help thinking Anna was the smartest one among them. She had taken to "spring cleaning" after a few days in the desert; Nehi wished he had the same excuse to stay inside and didn't feel the urge to pretend the heat wasn't intense out here with the other men.

"You disappointed poor little Wiglaf," Daniel teased the mute. Joe ignored him and dropped down to the bench beside Beau. His white arms glinted in the sun and Nehi grinned at his sleeveless black turtleneck. Daniel's eyes lit up. "You finally listened to me and ditched the habitual high-collared jacket. What did it, throwing up from the heat yesterday?"

"No, it was your constant heckling, the enraged fashion expert who won't shut up," Joe signed, rolling his eyes. Nehi knew it had been a migraine the mute tried to ignore yesterday, not just the heat; that would linger today at least as a headache. It would make tempers thin. He stepped in quickly before it could turn to a real argument. In the back of his mind the memory of Joe-the-mad-fox kept popping up when his brother started to push the mute, and a cold niggle of fear slid into Nehi. If Daniel woke the mad fox, he would be certain he had found the real Joe, and it wouldn't be pretty.

"Where do we find more meat?" Nehi blurted.

"Yonder stumpy tail would have yielded much meat, if I had been allowed to bring my boar spear," Wiglaf commented, and Daniel's crooked smile shot over his face in amusement. The warrior hadn't stopped complaining about having to leave half his weapons behind in Geatland.

"Too much," Cobeau grunted.

"We couldn't store all that," Nehi agreed.

"It dries out here," Joe signed, almost listlessly, his head very still as he lay propped against Beau's thick side. "Cut meat in strips, lay it on the wagon top with salt, and in a few days good enough for storing indefinitely."

"Tastes bad," the chimera frowned.

"Well, there is that drawback about stumpy tails," Joe agreed.

"I don't think we'll have to worry about finding meat out here," Daniel drawled. "I'm more concerned about keeping from being meat. Are all the animals fiercer because of the heat?"

"Not the heat," Joe signed and Beau rumbled. "It's the hunger." The three men on top the wagon paused and looked around them again, studying the terrain. Spiky bushes stuck out of the dry, cracked dirt, and a few spiny plants rose like giant trees in the far distance. But nothing else. No water. No vast herds of one horns, or flocks of birds to bring down and feast on. Nehi spotted something else. He sat up a little straighter and pointed. A sign stood beside the road, off in the distance. The wagon jolted forward over the cracked road, and it drew steadily nearer.

"Do all countries have such signs?" Wiglaf demanded. "Of what are they made? Do they have a purpose other than informing travelers of the border?"

"Yes, depends, and usually that's about it," Nehi said, suppressing a sigh at more questions from the Geatlander. But as they rumbled past the sign, Nehi knew that wasn't just it. The way each sign was fashioned, the upkeep, what they chose to place on their signs, all of it told about the people in a country. This sign was a dust-covered, carved plank of wood. A serpent and an eagle circled around a golden staff, carved above two simple words.

They jolted past and left the wild lands.

Nothing changed. For two days of steady travel, the rough, hot, dangerous wild lands stayed unchallenged. Four times they passed collapsed huts, each set stark and alone, the only signs of human activity in the region. The roofs were rotted and caved in. One of them had obviously been burned before it collapsed.

On the evening of the second day a town finally appeared on the horizon, very faint and far away, but there. Nehemiah sat up straighter, relieved and excited to see signs of humanity. Beside him he saw Anna's eyes shine with the same thoughts, and behind him Wiglaf and Daniel started talking again, their words animated instead of the listless murmurs they had been. Joe slowed the wagon, his eye on the smudge of a town and his face blank. The hoverer drew to a hissing stop and settled on the dusty ground.

"We camp here tonight," Joe signed and Beau rumbled.

"What? But we're so close!" Nehi whined. Joe didn't smile at his friend's childish excitement. He hadn't smiled in two days; Anna had been watching, and knew. The others began to protest. Anna spun to Nehi, poking and teasing him relentlessly for his curiosity. It put an end to the complaints, no one else wanted to draw her comments. No word escaped the Ravens that evening. Joe hardly even looked up from his dinner, and the two Ravens turned in early. But Anna, watching as the stars came out to blaze in brilliant clarity, could see Joe's shoulders still tense, his breathing shallow. He wasn't asleep, just trying

to get away from the rest of them. She leaned against Nehi's side, her legs tucked up beside her on the dry tree they were using as a bench, and stared at the dancing fire. Should she go ask him what was wrong? Or send Nehi? Or ignore it?

*"But I always carry the key with me..."* Joe's signed words echoed in her memory, as the mute huddled sick and worn back in Geatland. She glanced at his tense form again. The fact he always carried the key to remove Simmons' tools meant Joe lived in constant fear of the pain returning. Anna sighed and slumped farther onto the log. She was too tired to decide how to help tonight. Too tired of the sorrow and brokenness in the world. Her eyes fluttered closed as her brother's conversation wrapped around her like a soft blanket. Tomorrow she would do what she could to cheer up her little friend.

But the next day, Joe dug a toe into Nehemiah's ribs as the first burning sliver of daylight cracked over the flat horizon and got them started on their way in record time.

By midmorning, the city seemed to loom in front of them. Some of the stark square buildings could be made out through the burning heat. As the day wore on Prissy's wheels turned, dust rose in a tireless cloud around her, and the unremitting sun sliced straight through the dry air till the travelers felt baked. Conversation was scarce. They sat and sweated in taciturn silence. They sighted no other living thing.

The noon sun shone bright and relentless through the wind bubble when Anna started shoving trays onto the top of the wagon. Cold mint tea, sandwiches, and cool crunchy cucumbers invigorated the little group, and they felt more alive after lunch. Nehemiah looked up from the last cucumber and realized the city stood only a mile away. The shimmering haze peculiar to the desert dissipated as they drew closer, and he could make out the individual buildings. Most of them were cave-style dugouts rising out of the desert ground like bubbles in the earth. A few buildings of sticks and trees stood out amongst the rest, all of them scattered and far from each other. Nehi's mind flew to the broken huts far out in the wilderness. It appeared these people prized their solitude.

The wheels spun on, dirt rose in the same brown cloud, and the city grew in his vision. The huts and dugouts grew fewer, overtaken by square simple buildings. Anna found herself thinking they were created of necessity, as if the builders hated every stone, and kept it ugly out of spite. It was a large city, bigger than the twins had expected after having traveled three days through this kingdom without seeing a soul. A gigantic concrete structure loomed in the midst of all the ugly squares and dugouts. Nehi couldn't decide what it was, and the structure was lost to sight as the wagon rolled into the middle of the stark square buildings. The wagon jerked off the dirt onto a cracked asphalt road and rumbled past the second official sign spotted in this kingdom. "Overman City," was all it said.

"I have never heard this word," Wiglaf spoke up. "What does 'overman' mean?" Neither Raven moved to answer. Joe sat stiff, his face hard, staring straight ahead as the others looked about them with interest, his jacket back on.

"I heard an ambassador use it once, but never understood what he meant by it," Anna answered as she noted the rough concrete and wood houses had no yards, or even porches to relieve their appearance. Everything looked dusty and uncared for, and she felt that spite again, that dislike of the buildings creating the city itself.

"I don't know it either, Wiglaf," Nehemiah answered the repeated question with a smothered sigh. "Do you notice the way the men walk alone–"

"And their noses are all in the air," Anna interrupted.

"I wonder how they see where they're going with their noses turned up like that?" Daniel asked.

"By looking down them at everything," Wiglaf replied. It was so in tune with the expressions of the people they passed the three Hillsons looked at the warrior in surprise. A dirty boy ran down the street grinning at the travelers. A crowd of boys soon gathered behind their wagon, whooping and hollering. At least they looked cheerful, Anna thought. She glanced toward

the houses and saw a few girls had ventured out. But they stayed in the background and watched silently as Prissy pulled the wagon down the dusty street. They didn't look happy.

"So Joe," Nehemiah said, prodding his solemn friend in the shoulder, "I'm as curious as Wiglaf over this one. What does overman mean?"

"It's the goal here," Joe signed absently, Cobeau translating automatically. "It's a sort of super person."

"That tells us next to nothing," Daniel drawled.

"A super person?" Wiglaf asked in confusion. "But you have been telling me, Ravenswing Ashe-Maker, that we are all one people, descended from Adam created from dust by God."

"Don't mention God here!" Joe signed fiercely, his green eyes snapping with urgency as he turned on the group on the wagon. "Or anything to do with our religion!"

"Okay, no mentioning that, got it," Daniel said, impressed into not arguing the point by Joe's ferocious look. "But you still haven't told us much. What's the book base here?"

"A strange, sad book called *Thus Spoke Zarathustra*. Overman is the goal of humanity," Joe signed, dropping back into his watchful seriousness. "Men now are just a bridge between animal and overman. He is the great overcomer. The one who has overcome all superstitions, moralities, weaknesses; he creates his own purposes, standards, even reason. What it really creates is a man of merciless pride..." Joe trailed off and Beau tensed as he looked at him. The mute stared to their left, down a little alleyway. A wince cut across his face. They passed it in a second and none of the others managed to see what caught Joe's attention.

The mute suddenly began to sign to Beau, and Nehi couldn't catch any of it. He wondered if it was the speed or if something else was...different about those signs. Beau pulled to a stop on the side of the road so quickly one of the boys chasing the wagon ran into it with a thud and rebounded reeling into the street. Joe leapt off and disappeared down the alleyway, too quickly for any questions. When the wagon stopped, a soft,

breathy sobbing could be heard from the alley. And a steady thudding, like a stick coming down on something. That noise prickled down Nehi's spine and Anna felt him stiffen. Beau's big hands wrapped around his rifle as he sat still on the wagon seat, waiting. The crowd of boys scattered remarkably quickly when they saw the little snub nosed laser cupped in the big, hairy hands. Everyone else in the street ignored them.

Nehemiah stirred, readying to go see what was going on, when a woman's voice cut out of the alleyway. It was a hot, fiery tone, angry enough the phrase was nearly incoherent. What was coherent Anna rather wished wasn't for the language. The voice was cut short by a rough male voice. At the first word Nehi stiffened and his eyes shot to Anna, his expression highly annoyed that she'd heard it. She decided not to admit she had no idea what it was and put a sticky-note in her brain never to use it. Half a second later, the voice rose to a higher pitch, a note of fear crept in it, and then it suddenly stopped. Silence and dust drifted on the air. Joe strolled out of the alley, his hands in his pockets and his face thoughtful. His green eyes looked up, fell on Anna, and rested there.

"What?" she asked.

"I was wondering if I should ask you to help a couple of your fellow women," he signed a little reluctantly.

"I'd love to help, if I'm needed," Anna said, and clambered quickly down the wagon. Joe gave her half a smile that said 'good girl.' It didn't reach his eyes. He hopped in and out of the wagon and handed her a first aid kit.

"What am I doing?" she asked as she took it. "And why just me, Joe?"

"A man won't work," Joe signed. "Beauty, this is a bad country. I just want to pass through and fill our water cylinders, but filling up gives you about an hour. Be careful. Yell if you need us. I think we'll do a concert out here to cover you after we've started the cylinders filling."

That was all the information he gave her. Anna found herself walking down a dark alleyway with a first aid kit and no

idea what to do next. The square buildings hemmed her in, managing to block out the bright sun's rays. The sudden darkness felt refreshingly cool, but a little hard on the nerves. Her foot caught on something soft and heavy and she pitched forward, stumbling over a body, her hand slamming into a concrete house to keep her upright. Anna spun and dropped to her knee beside an overweight man sprawled on his back in the middle of the dust. A snore rattled from him. She couldn't see anything wrong with him. Anna stood up and listened for a moment. Voices came from the left. She picked out the angry-woman's voice, drifting muffled through a door set beside her. The dirt of the desert covered it, she had mistaken it for part of the wall. Anna stepped over to it and knocked on the heavy planks, dust spurting up under her knuckles and creating a fine brown cloud around her head. The voices stopped abruptly. After waiting a moment Anna decided she had better say something.

"I was sent with a first aid kit by the blond young man," she called through the door, and put her ear to the rough planks.

"Don't open it Natalie," a timid woman's voice said, the tone a pleading whine. "Didn't you see what he did to Willie?"

"Yes I did, and that's why I'm opening it," the angry voice answered. Anna quickly took a step back. The door flung open, banging against the wall with a dusty "smack." A pretty woman in her mid-thirties stood in the doorway, brown hair cropped short to frame her face, and her brown eyes hard. Her clothes were stylish and didn't match the loose, unadorned cotton styles Anna had seen in this country.

"Hello," Anna smiled at her. The brown eyes softened and the woman even smiled back. Everyone softened to Anna's smile. Natalie stepped aside and held the door open. Anna stepped into the dim opening and glanced around. Dingy, simple, but fairly clean. Another woman sat in a roughly hewn rocker by the empty fireplace, dabbing at a gash across her forehead with a rag. She looked...worn, Anna decided as she smiled at her, introduced herself, and opened up the first aid kit. The strains of Joe's "Holding Together" began to drift into the little room from the Ravens concert, and it scattered Anna's sense of being alone in this situation.

As she skillfully cleaned and bandaged the wound, Anna began to talk in her friendly way, introducing herself, complimenting the décor and asking questions. She learned the two women were sisters, Natalie was an immigrant to KAM, and the other, Lena, was the wife of the man in the alley. When Anna asked why he was sleeping in the street, Natalie promptly said it was drink. But Lena explained he had been displeased with her and then a little blond boy had suddenly appeared and held a small bottle under his nose, and he had fallen down in that stupor.

"If Joe used his bottle, he'll probably be asleep till tomorrow morning," Anna said as she put the finishing touches to Lena's bandage and began to put salve on the bruises beginning to show through the woman's dark coloring.

"Joe, is that the name of your man?" Lena asked.

"I don't have 'a man,' in the way you mean that phrase," Anna smiled.

"Good for you," Natalie said explosively, "and don't you ever get one! All they want is domination, to be the 'overcomers' over us. We're their equals, just as smart and capable as they are. We don't need them, Anna, and never fall into thinking you do."

"As you can see, my sister doesn't hold with a woman being under a man," Lena said uncomfortably. "That's why she immigrated."

"And you're coming back with me, Lena, this afternoon. You are not his property," Natalie spat out.

"But that's what we are, dear," Lena said with a faint smile, "you would know that if you had stayed. And it's not such a bad thing to have a man's protection."

"You're awfully silent suddenly, what do you have to say?" Natalie snapped, spinning on Anna, a leftover of her annoyance at her sister's timidity. Anna finished packing up the kit and

didn't look up, Joe's warning ringing in her ears. Usually she would have just told them the gospel. She chose a middle ground. Stating the truth and not explaining how she knew it would have to do.

"You're both right, and wrong," Anna said. Even without being able to say them she kept ticking off verses to support her statements in her mind, and Anna found herself thanking God again for how her dear parents had faithfully made her learn the Bible. "Natalie, you're right in that we are men's equals in brains and competency and humanity[4], but Lena's right to say that, in a way, we are under our men folk[5]."

"That makes no sense," Natalie said quickly. "If we can do things just as well, no, if we can do things better than men, why shouldn't we? You know we can!"

"Just because we can do it, doesn't mean we should," Anna shrugged. "We were made to help men do their jobs better[6], to help them take truth and use it well, not to take over their job and put them in our position."

"See, Natalie, that's what I've been telling you–" Lena started to say, but Anna interrupted out of habit.

"No not really, dear. You see, while we are under our men's protection and leadership, we aren't owned by them. We are not only free, but bound by duty to protect ourselves if our situation becomes dangerous[7]. Our welfare is important, and men are supposed to protect, and even cherish those under their care[8]."

"'Under their care,'" Natalie scoffed, almost trembling in her anger, "why do you put us down like that, Anna, we don't need men's protection!"

"Sometimes we do, if only to protect against other men,"

---

[4] Genesis 1:29; Ephesians 5:25; 1 Peter 3:7

[5] Genesis 3:16; Titus 2:5; (a lament) Isaiah 3:12; 1 Peter 3:1-5; Eph. 5:23

[6] Genesis 2:18

[7] Exodus 20:13; 1 Cor. 3:16-17

[8] Ephesians 5:25 and 33; Col. 3:19

Anna said. "We're built differently, and they're physically stronger. Deny it all you want, it can't change the facts. Oh, we women are stronger than men in many ways, certainly, but..." Anna paused trying to put her heart into words. She had met many like Natalie in KAM and it always made her sad to look into their faces. They were so unhappy, and hard, and searching. Maybe she could at least explain to one of these misguided females what it was she was missing by her folly of misplaced strength.

"In the country I came from, women were, in a large way, the ones who kept things running straight. They didn't do it by running the country, the men did that. They did it by standing behind the men, holding a standard up to them. By gently helping them when they were weak, and by training the next generation truth and goodness, by not approving bad mannerisms and habits. A woman in her proper sphere is the one with a finger on the heartbeat of the nation. She's the one that makes or breaks a kingdom in the long run. How she influences 'her man,' how she teaches her sons and daughters (or nieces, or siblings), the way she keeps a house neat and peaceful, all of it has an impact deeper than you can see. A woman is the heart of the family, and the family is the heart of a nation. Our influence can be great enough to sway the world our way. But it's not by overrunning the men, or by letting ourselves be trampled."

"Oh come on," Natalie scoffed, "I don't work in the home, I work in the political realm of KAM. I do just as much shaping of nations as someone you describe, only I do it more certainly and immediately."

"And are you happy?" Anna asked. Natalie suddenly stopped and looked at her in surprise. "I don't think it's possible to be happy while ignoring what you're made for. And more importantly, will your work last for generations?" Natalie made no answer and looked away after a moment. "A woman in the family, whether sister, aunt, friend, or mother, has an influence that lasts so much longer than her lifetime."

"I have a home to keep," Lena said quietly, "but I don't have that heartbeat of a nation you describe. There's something different in that description then what I've seen here. What is it?"

"Honor, respect," Anna said. "Real protection and *loving* leadership from men[9]. A home is broken if a man won't accept his job and do it right. And a woman's not helping her man if she lets him abdicate his role of protector and fall into oppressor." Lena looked at her hands, her bruised face thoughtful.

In the sudden silence Anna realized the Ravens' music had stopped, and hadn't been going for some time. Alarm spread over her. She muttered a quick goodbye, grabbed her first aid kit, and ran down the alley. Anna burst into the street, one hand rising automatically against the sudden glare of the sunshine, dust from her run filling her nose and mouth and stinging her eyes. Her gaze swept the street, her heartbeat steadily accelerating. She saw dust blowing down an empty street. The wagon was gone. The Ravens and all their passengers were gone too, the street stood utterly empty. She shouldn't have stayed talking! What had happened, and where on earth were they now? A hand took her arm, and Anna spun around to find Natalie at her side. She looked concerned, and that made Anna's worry flutter into full fear.

"What's wrong?" Natalie asked.

"My two brothers, Wiglaf, Cobeau, Joe, they're all gone, wagon and all. They were doing a concert right here, and now they're just gone," Anna said, her eyes sweeping the empty street again, looking for some clue.

"Concert?" Natalie glanced around and bit her lip. "That wouldn't include dancing would it?"

"Yes. Very strange, but very talented dancing," Anna answered, her alarm rising.

"Oh dear."

"What's 'oh dear'? What does dancing have to do with the fact that they're gone?"

"It's part of their stupid overman idea," Natalie answered

---

[9] 1 Peter 3:7; 1 Cor. 7:3; Eph. 5:33

quickly, "he's supposed to be able to dance, it's a sign of inner joy or something like that. They probably snagged them as overmen candidates."

"What does that mean?" Anna broke in, her voice a sharp demand.

"The people here aren't really a cohesive unit, it's not like governments in most kingdoms, going against the stream is such a big deal that here there's a million separate streams and no river. But they all like to watch fights. It's a part of the book, sort of, but what it translates to in this kingdom is the men always being willing to grab people off the street, and anyone near will happily lend a hand in the grabbing. They throw them into the arena to see how they overcome whatever opponent is tossed their way."

"That doesn't sound good," Anna found herself saying. A harsh laugh came from Natalie.

"No, it's not good. When the street's this empty it means something interesting is happening somewhere else. I'd try the square or the arena, do you know where they are?" Anna shook her head and Natalie began to give her a list of street names and corners that were very confusing to someone who had just ridden into town that morning. Natalie realized it, stopped talking, and started to walk down the street.

"Thank you," Anna said gratefully as she ran to follow. Every step she took, the feeling of danger kept growing in Anna, and with it a desperate need for hurry. She said nothing, but her mood was catching. Soon the two women ran through the streets, kicking up dust as they turned corner after corner. They met very few people. Large squares that made up stores, offices, and factories, flashed past Anna's vision. The street ended suddenly, and so did the concrete and wood squares. They stood at the top of a wide open place in the center of the town, where the ground suddenly dipped into a concrete theater, filled with benches and seats. Natalie stopped and stood panting as they gazed at the empty seats around them.

"This is...the square," Natalie panted.

“And it’s empty,” Anna said. “Is that good?”

“I don’t think so. No, it’s not good. Who are you people? To suddenly show up and knock out a stranger, and come with a first aid kit and advice, then empty the town like this? There’s something extraordinary about you.”

“Oh please! Where is that arena you were talking about?” Anna pleaded. Natalie nodded, and the two started to run again. Up one street, down another, then another, and another. Anna thoroughly lost all sense of direction. Natalie’s breath came in heavy gasps. A couple appeared in the street ahead of them. As they spun around the next corner, a party of eight men came into view, laughing and joking about something. More and more people began to appear. Three streets later the crowds forced them to a walk. A few more streets and they had to join hands to keep from being jostled apart. They turned another corner and Anna’s mouth dropped with her heart. A huge building made of heartless steel and cold concrete towered over them and stretched out farther then she could see. This newest street was a wide thoroughfare and people filled it, all of them moving toward the building. Natalie stopped in the shadow of a square grocery and pointed at the rising structure.

“Yes, there’s the arena,” Anna said for the gasping Natalie. “And there’s something more interesting to me,” Anna said, pointing across the fluctuating sea of people. The Ravens’ wagon pressed against the side of the concrete wall across from the ladies, abandoned in the flood of strangers.

# Chapter Eleven: The Cages

*"A righteous man regardeth the life of his beast: but the tender mercies of the wicked are cruel." Proverbs 12:10*

Anna took Natalie's hand and plunged into the crowded street. The hot sun streamed into the throng. Sweat, dust, heat, and too many people crowded Anna's senses. She shoved her way through, bursting into the cool shadow of the towering building beside the Ravens' wagon. Only a frightened Prissy greeted her. Anna calmed the pig, and ducked inside. Natalie laid her hand on the giant guinea pig, moving with the slow deliberate motions of awe, and walked around the wagon studying the paintings before following Anna through the thin, pointed door. She found her new acquaintance in slacks instead of her skirt, with her hair hanging in a long braid down her back. And digging into a drawer of highly dangerous gadgets. Natalie watched in shock as Anna slid an extra clip for a pistol into a black utility belt and strapped it around her waist.

"What do you think you're doing?" Natalie gaped. "It's too dangerous to go in there! Even if you made it in, there's nothing you can do alone."

"I don't know what I'm going to do," Anna answered honestly as she slipped things in her belt and tried to decide what sort of a laser she should take. "That's why I'm taking all this stuff. Natalie, I need to know what this place is and what is going on in there."

"That's the arena, it's where they decide things here. How much do you know about this country?"

"Nothing."

"Nothing. And you're plunging into the middle of it for a group of men." Natalie studied Anna, her lips pressed together. Then she gave a shake and launched into it. "Well, for starters nothing is solid here. Everything comes under question, the 'will to create' is one of the strongest things in the kingdom and applies to each individual's values and truths. Which ultimately

means that there's no real agreement, they're supposed to clash with each other, going against the values of the crowd is prized as being courageous. But to have a kingdom, they have to agree on some things. The main one is what this arena runs on; stronger wins all and weaker dies. The only thing that does matter is winning over yourself and other's weaknesses. Being an overcomer. So they decide things by battles, against combatants, against wild beasts...however they set it up it's usually ugly. Whoever lives gets honor, whoever dies isn't pitied. Anna, there's nothing you can do. That blond kid I saw in the alley is too small and frail to cope with what he'll be set up against in there. It's probably too late already."

"Joe is stronger than he looks," Anna said, quickly slipping the strap of a luttle rifle, a class 5 dye laser, over her shoulder and drawing it in place to rest against her back. She slid a pair of copper goggles over her eyes, then pushed them up to rest on her black hair, and turned back to Joe's drawer, trying to decide if there was anything else she might need. "Also, Joe's not the only one in there. I'm the one outside, and that might make the difference between life and death. I'm not going to just leave them to face it alone. Thank you for bringing me here, Natalie. If it won't endanger you, will you show me how to get in?"

"You know, Anna, you're not the wimp I thought you were," Natalie commented. Anna laughed.

"Living as you're designed to tends to make you strong," she grinned. "How do I get in?"

"Well...Willie, that horrible excuse for a man asleep in the alley, is one of the keepers for the cages here. I know a few back ways. If you have to try them." Anna insisted and Natalie led the way out of the wagon.

A few minutes later Anna found herself alone in a dark, dusty passageway, the scent of large hot animals and worse hanging in the air. The dirt floor remembered what else had traveled this way. It soaked up the smells, the remains, the refuse, and sent it back up into the hot, close air. A fresh pool of fluids Anna refused to name loomed in the gloomy light. She

gagged and her hand went over her mouth as she hurried around it. The air grew closer and darker as the passage went steadily down. Things were making noises farther on in that passage, deeper in the darkness. There were wails and squeals and growls and noises she couldn't even give a name. No, she could give it a name. The place stank of fear, despair, and pain.

A large form that must once have been a gigantic monster appeared in the gloom in front of her, huge flies hovering around the rotting carcass. There were other things crawling on it, but Anna looked away before she could see more. The flies buzzing around their feast thrummed in her mind in their low, inhuman pitch. Dark blood stains, dried and fresh, covered the dirt passageway for yards around it and stained her shoes as she moved quickly past. Anna shuddered, knowing she would never hear a fly again without thinking of this stench of despair and death. She broke into a trot, pleas for her family and friends spilling from her. After a moment she was surprised to find her prayers had turned from Nehemiah and the others to Natalie and Lena. They were so mistaken, so very lost and sad. And so much like the other women Anna had met on her travels. Always on one side or the other, miserable rulers or playthings. How lost the lost really were!

A sharp pain wrenched the back of her scalp as something caught her braid. Anna twisted, adrenaline singing through her veins, her braid flipping over her shoulder, the laser swinging up in her hands. A one claw hunched in a filthy iron barred cage. His giant black claw glimmered where it hung through the bars, the tip hooked in her braid. The huge beast grinned at her, and Anna gaped at it. She had never seen anything as hideous as that blubbery, hairless thing, steaming in the heat, and grinning out of the darkness of his cage.

A roar, not from a single man, but from a thousand, a million throats slithered up the passageway to Anna. Her hot skin suddenly went clammy. Whatever those people were excited about, it was not good. She couldn't stand here staring as if she was at leisure in a zoo. She knew from experience in the wild lands not to get closer to that claw, and whipped out a dagger. Sweat from her palm made the handle slippery, and Anna suddenly realized just how ferociously hot it was down here. The blade sliced through the braid, her hair tumbled down to frame her stunning face. Her head felt suddenly very light. The shortened black strands whipped her face as she raced down the passageway, swinging the luttle around as she ran. That yelling crowd boded something terrible, and Anna had to be ready for it.

The filthy, hot metal dug into his cheek as Joe pressed himself against the bars. His knees pulled up to his heaving chest, his bare arms hugged them close, as if by scrunching himself into a tighter ball he could disappear and leave the nightmare behind. The cages stood shadowy in the gloom around his own. Vast shapes prowled or slumped or beat madly against the iron. None of it did any good. They would never get out.

*Oh dear God, why again? Why are You making me do it again?* Joe's face pressed harder into his knees and he fought the oppressive heat for every breath he managed to drag into his constricted lungs. Past the panic. Past the terror. Past the memories.

Four years. It had been four years. It seemed like a blink. And a lifetime. And now another imprisonment. More days and long, long, long nights of fighting off the despair. Beating constantly at the hopelessness and anger that tried with each breath to eclipse everything human in him.

And that last time.

Diamond's mangled body shot through Joe's mind and he shuddered as if an electric wire pushed through him. His face pressed harder into his knees, cowering into the corner farthest from any living thing. Cowering so hard the iron bar began to cut a red line down his cheek. Joe didn't even notice. He was alone. All alone. Forever now. The heat was a ferocious,

meddling monster that ate even your mind down in the cages. Joe was already giddy with it, too far gone to realize he was gone. Four years ago muddled with the time two years ago and all of it collided with the realities facing him now.

Betrayed. Alone. Why had he let him into his heart? It hurt more than the overseer's punishments. It hurt inside where Joe couldn't reach to lick it clean. It broke and twisted him, and no splint could fix it. *Betrayed for a bag of coins, for love of a hover board. A used board. Friend. That's what I called him. I was such an idiot!* Joe rocked, the bar steadily taking off a patch of skin. *Josh! Oh Diamond, why do you trust? Why do you always, always have to trust people? I told you it would kill you!* The rocking picked up and the patch started to grow on the mute's face. *Too late. I was too late!* His fingernails bit into his legs till they tore holes in his pants and dug into the skin. But it wasn't in the terror or frustration of the cage. It was anger. An old, unforgiving anger based in a sorrow that would never leave him alone. *I was too late! For the one person who ever really loved me. Who I ever dared to really love back. He called me brother. And meant more than just Christian. Oh God, why did You let me come if You knew I was going to be too late?*

Joe's head snapped up, mouth open in a silent, furious scream, green eyes wild, and face flushed with the heat. His skull rammed into the bars behind him. The force jarred through him and woke him from the past. The gloom, fetid indescribable smell of the stifling air, the monsters sharing the huge room in their own cages, the dousing station, punishment block, all of it closed around him like a dark cloud. This was his reality. Again. Joe snapped his mouth closed and sucked in air through his nose.

This was his reality. He had to deal with it, now. Joe eased his legs out, forcing himself to uncurl. The tighter he held himself the hotter he would stay. He had to cool himself down, as best as he could. His mouth became a tight line as his eyes burned. He wasn't betrayed. Not this time. Nehi and good old Beau and the others were up there in that blasted, dratted overseer's room, and only Joe could keep them alive. He wasn't betrayed. He wasn't alone. They really were there. His mind revolved on it, sucking in the memory of his friends in the same way he forced himself to pull in the fetid, burning air. In and out, in and out, just keep it coming. He had to do this. He had to win. If he died, they died.

The cage was big for him. But he didn't waste the energy it would take to stand. Joe sat waiting, but no longer curled. He would have loved to strip down to practically nothing, get rid of everything he possibly could while still retaining any decency. But Joe had been in the arena. He knew out there the sun didn't broil, it toasted. It took bare skin and turned it into red bubbling blisters, then toasted those, and made a blackened heap of a man. That was, of course, only the skin that managed to stay on after being raked across the cactus covered ground over, and over. No, he was already sleeveless after they had stripped his jacket off him, and that was all he could dare to lose.

Voices drifted down the outer tunnel. A familiar pause came in the pacing, the roaring, whimpering, flailing, whatever the heat and fear crazed monsters were doing. Each beast slunk down, crouching into their corner farthest from the walkway. A grim smile cut across Joe's face. They were old hats at this. They knew nothing good ever happened when a human came down that tunnel. But this time the animals were safe enough. Those animals at least, he reflected bitterly. These men came for Joe. His eyes turned softly to his hands as they lay flaccid in his lap.

*Jesus, I'm sorry. I'm sorry for doubting Your goodness, even for a moment. For letting the anger take me. I can bring nothing but thankfulness to You, and no accusations. You're the Sovereign of all the universe, for crying out loud, and You died for me! What else could You do to prove Your goodness? Forgive me. Forgive me for doubting that You know what's best for me. Stay with me now. Please. I need You.*

"This one?" The growling voice came right in front of Joe.

The man gave a harsh laugh. "I wondered why we came to the cages and not the dormitory."

*Because the dormitory is where the humans are kept,* Joe silently supplied. He didn't lift his eyes from his hands. Never look a complete in the face. If you meet their eyes, even accidentally, they see you. They see *you*. And something in them knows it's just like them. Shock can turn to fear, and fear can turn nasty, all in the blink of an eye.

A sharp crack came from the side of his cage. A pair of big, calloused hands shot in and closed around Joe's neck. His air shut off and he was jerked up and past the bars. The hands kept dragging him. Other hands jerked his arms behind him. Metallic fibers, interwoven and crawling with electric impulses, slid onto Joe's thumbs. The cuff cinched four times harder than it needed to, and the muscles in his hands cringed and began to jump and pull against each other. He couldn't see who did it, his vision blurred. The world started to go dark. *Air. Please, just air. So little to ask. Just air.* Blackness, sparking with searing white-hot stars, closed over his vision.

The hands swung, and Joe's body snapped like a whip, rammed into something hard, and dropped helpless to a concrete ground, gagging and unable to even try to catch himself with the thumb cuffs. Cold water flooded him as he tried to suck in a breath. He sucked in half water half air and gagged harder. But he was silently gasping out thanks instead of insults. Not that these two would have tried to understand either.

The cold water plunged over him again, a hard, painful force, stinging his skin even through his clothes. Joe closed his eyes, curled so as much of him could get in the stream as possible, and sucked in what he could from the filthy ground as the water gurgled away through a rusted drain. It was all he was going to get for the next long hours. And he would need every drop. The stream stopped. Joe opened his eyes, forcing himself to ignore the muscles and nerves trembling and jumping through his hands. Two burley men stood over him, almost identical with every other keeper of the cage he had ever seen.

Mutt and Jeff he would call them. Didn't matter. Beau. Nehi. Anna. They mattered. Joe controlled his breathing. He lay still on the concrete, his body shaking as it tried to regulate his temperature against the extremes it had just been handed. Joe controlled his body. He eased his legs, stretching out like a luxurious feline waking from a nap, and rolled his shoulders. He had to win. He had to. If he died, they died. And they were here. He wasn't betrayed, he wasn't alone. Not this time.

"What an ugly, weird little beast," Jeff grunted.

*Thank you,* Joe thought sarcastically, running mentally through scenarios, trying to prepare himself for what he might meet out there.

"Well, to the weapon's shelf," Mutt said, grabbing Joe by a fistful of hair and jerking him up.

"No, Emeric says to send him out as he is," Jeff said, studying Joe with an inhuman scrutiny; like an entomologist watching his enemy's best specimen.

"Really?" Mutt asked in surprise.

*Really?* Joe thought, trying to decide if that was good or bad. No weapon, bad. Not being shot full of performance drugs that hurt like crazy and clouded his judgment, good. But no weapon, bad. Very bad.

"He says he wants to see this one dance." The two men chortled, staring down at Joe, on his knees, suspended from Mutt's fist. Jeff turned and began to lazily stroll for the far wall. Only it wasn't really a wall, Joe knew. It was a series of tunnels, all controlled by that dratted overseer, and all leading to that blasted arena. Mutt jerked, and Joe silently cursed him, roundly and completely, forgetting the decencies he had picked up from Anna and Nehi. The heat had brought on a headache. The headache had grown to a near migraine, and Jeff's choking grip and now Mutt's big hand were close to making it a full blown attack. That would not help matters.

Mutt's hand jerked and Joe scrambled to get his feet under him. The hand didn't let go and it was heavy. Joe stayed slumped, bent almost double, and loped along like a good dog at the man's heels. Metal screeched, and Joe's aching brain cringed and jumped. Dust blew over them as a burning breeze played through the open tunnel. It carried the sound of a crowd roaring. Joe's mouth went dry and he felt his throat trying to close.

That horrible, familiar, deadly sound, of so many entities making up one enormous, thousand-throated monster that screamed for death and violence and pain and blood. The teeming mass of humanity searching for entertainment. One man might intervene when the fights got so vicious boys and ladies started vomiting under their seats. Thousands of men just cheered louder. The swaying, vibrating multitude in the stands, screaming, laughing, pulsing with the energy of a huge living mass, and all of it baying for blood. Those who tout true democracy have never stood in the arena.

The hand jerked. Joe's feet flew from him as white sparks seared into his brain. He dragged for two long strides before he managed to get his footing. He stumbled on behind Mutt over the dirt. His stomach churned, just waiting for it to come again. Because it would, Mutt was that kind. The hand jerked. Joe stumbled, the world sparked, but he managed to keep his feet. Mutt didn't look back. It was an unconscious cruelty, an ingrained habit. The mute's stomach tumbled and tossed in dread, just waiting for that hand to do it again, the crowd's noise pulsing around him.

Joe closed his eyes and started to pray. Letting his feet stumble up that metal, dusty tunnel to the desperate fight and burning sun, while his mind went home. The roar of the crowd grew distant. His stomach settled. The blowing dust seemed to disappear. Even the meaty hand on his scalp seemed to lessen in its intensity. Joe's heart beat in time with a gentle, loving, good voice from somewhere deep within himself; and yet not of himself. He soaked in the sweet, wordless presence and let himself be strengthened. He would win today. He had to. For Christ's own.

The hand jerked. But this time, it meant it. Joe flung forward,

his body slamming into a concrete wall. The world spun into a gray blur and he scraped down concrete. Someone slid the thumb cuff off. A boot rammed into his ribs and he rolled, out into the full sunlight of the arena.

# Chapter Twelve: To Win

*"...lo, I am with you alway..." Matthew 28:20*

The roar of the crowd soared as Joe hit the dirt. His body arched and sent him leaping to his feet, and he found he had his back to the wall, massaging his hands into working condition, his eyes slits against the white sun as his gaze devoured the arena.

Nothing rushed to kill him yet. The tunnel slammed shut behind him with a metallic screech. Joe ignored it, that wasn't the sound he needed. He listened to the pulsing roar from the stands, but with a purpose now. The crowd was expectant. It waited. Joe's opponent hadn't been released. The mute closed his eyes, took one long, slow breath, and just stood, adrenaline slamming through his veins. He wasn't alone. Jesus was always with him. And he wasn't betrayed. Not this time. *I have to win. If I die, they die. I have to win.* Joe's eyes opened. They were deadly hard and his face held nothing of the merry, kind musician Anna and Nehi knew so well.

Dust eddied behind him as he strolled, lithe as a jungle cat, into the midst of the short cactuses and spiny bushes. The arena was just a large oval of enclosed desert. Nothing fancy. Nothing comfortable. He scanned the oval with an expert's eye as he walked slowly to a position where he could see any tunnel open. Not a single bush or cactus stood higher than his waist. This overseer was more meticulous than the last. Great. Joe absently glanced up, high above him to the top of the arena. The clear room of the overseer perched there, where the man watched every move of his combatants, his slaves till death took them. Joe stopped in mid stride. Daniel, Wiglaf, Nehi, and Beau stood caged in one half of the overseer's room, where they could watch their friend die. Joe only saw two. Cobeau's face pressed into the clear wall, his nose smashed against it. Nehi stood beside the big man, his hand on the chimera's shoulder as he watched his friend. Joe stared at those two forms. They

were here. A warm ribbon of comfort began to niggle its way through the pumping adrenaline and quiet terror.

"I'm praying," Nehi suddenly signed. The words were clear, even from such a distance. Joe could see their stance, the way both of them stood tensed, rigid, furiously longing to be down here with him. To help. A smile crept over the mute's face. He only nodded up at Nehi. But inside the last of the maddened nightmares and insecurities flitted back to just being scars and bad memories, raging in their cage, walled back in the corner of his mind. He could focus again, inside and out. And Joe knew that mattered most in a fight like this.

Another figure in the room caught his eye, outside the cage, a guest of the overseer. A hulk of a man, nearly as big and tall as Beau. But this was no chimera. Hamfast Georgina, soldier for hire, smart operator who still held a few scruples even with his choice of business. Joe knew who employed him right now. He remembered the three Battle Kingdom dignitaries turning the corner to watch his concert. The way they came ready to sweep in, snatching his companions to make certain Joe came quietly. With all the right tools to keep any of them from fighting back. How they knew to take his jacket and fling it away before sending him to the cages... It would seem the crossed lover had a grudge against the Raven.

Beau banged his fist against the glass of the cage, desperate to get to his master. Joe woke from his thoughts and remembered his business. He turned in a slow circle, watching. He had to win.

The crowd's noise gradually changed as Joe walked forward. At first it was a tiny ripple by his tunnel entrance. Then it spread out as more and more people caught sight of the small, inconsequential figure in the black clothes. Laughter drifted through the crowd. Cat-calls. Insults. Disappointment and anger, from those who came for a good show and were offered this instead. There was another reason Joe had walked on to the center of the arena. It would take a good arm for trash missiles and smuggled-in rocks to hit him out here. The humans

were always worse than the mere animal monsters. The adrenaline pumped faster as he stood there waiting, trying to guess what the overseer would set against him.

A metallic crack boomed through the arena. Joe spun on his heel and faced it before the first spectator in the stands had even connected what the sound meant. A heavy, rusty red door slowly lifted. He could see nothing yet in the blackness beyond. The crowd grew silent, watching and waiting in delight. Again the metallic boom shot around them, and the door slammed open.

A mass of black, bald flesh, rippling and folding on itself with each movement, a huge round simian face, the single central eye blazing red, four massive tree-trunk sized legs, and one glimmering black claw on the right front arm. A one claw, of a size and strength Joe had never even seen. That claw was nearly as tall as Joe. The simian stood twice as tall as the wagon, and could have fit four Prissy's inside its reeking, rippling skin. The ape pounded into the sunlight, his great fists closed and slamming into the ground as he moved in an earth-shaking run. The great claw decapitated bush after bush, and Joe's heartbeat paused in a deadly realization. They had sharpened the whole length of that enormous claw. It wasn't just a skewer and a club now. It was a simitar, ten feet curled on itself, wielded by an angry simian with power that could easily knock over a skyscraper with two blows.

Then there was Joe. Four-foot eleven. A hundred and two pounds. And unarmed.

The great red eye focused on him. A mouth full of incisor teeth opened as the thick neck turned in its rolls of fat. A roar of pure, furious, animal rage rose into the bright sky. The one claw began to pound toward its prey. The dust under Joe's boots vibrated and shook, getting more violent by the second. The mute stood still, staring. Another great roar broke from the thing, shattering through the hot air, and new heat lines danced along the feted breath, as the war-cry rebounded off the walls and swirled around the arena. Joe was vaguely aware of Nehi

and Beau, Wiglaf and Daniel, all at the window frantically screaming at him to move. Of the crowds yelling and leaping in the stands. Of the overseer casually watching at his instrument panel. Of Hamfast gone, his work done. But all that, even the toasting sunlight and rising dust, were things relegated to a tiny spot on the fringe of his brain.

The rest of him, every square inch of his viral person, focused on the rushing monster. Analyzing each movement, every ripple of the hideous bald skin, watching the way the eye rolled in terror at the crowd, the way the left front fist twitched with an old injury. Then the moment passed. The one claw reached him. The dust swirled, the heat waves danced, bushes and cacti flew up as the simian's feet plowed into the ground, and every hot throat in the arena gasped.

The simian's claw darted forward, all hundred pounds of rock hard cartilage aimed with an inhuman speed at the enemy. But Joe had been given time to calculate his move. He swung under the claw, gripped the hairless skin flap just behind it, and jerked himself up. In an instant he ran up the one claw's arm, deftly balancing with each movement of the monstrous beast. His hand shot up and found the nubby skin flap the thing called an ear. Joe grabbed it and swung off, both his legs slamming into the thing's jaw. It was an educated kick, not just a random desperate punch.

The huge simian reeled, dazed with the impact, its jaw hanging loose as an agonized, confused moan rumbled from its belly. Joe still swung upward with his momentum. He let go, using the one claw's own movements to sail up over the creature's head, twist in midair, and slam down directly behind the enemy's head. The mute's legs shot out and clamped around the thick neck, sliding between the grooves of fat to find a purchase. Joe's hands went to the creature's mouth, as it still reeled from his attack. Four of the ninety-two teeth had been knocked loose. Joe jerked two out. The simian screamed, a sharp animal screech intermixed with a rumbling bellow from deep inside its belly. Joe's ears rang, and his pounding head sparked again. But

he flipped the teeth in his hand, leaned around this thing, and plunged them toward the single eye.

Every spectator leapt to their feet. The overseer half rose from his chair, craning to see. Eight seconds. It had been eight seconds since the two combatants met, and in that teeming dust cloud, the small black-clothed figure who moved like a shooting star was hard to keep separate from the black bulk of the one claw. One thing was certain, as the one claw let out a second scream, louder and more agonized than the last. The dancer hadn't been killed at first impact as expected. The one claw scrabbled desperately for its neck. The overseer leant closer, training his glasses on the area. Gore dripped from the central eye. The simian only had his two close-vision pinpricks now.

The dancer clung around the monster's neck. He pulled his hold tighter, trying to cut off the one claw's air as the simian scrabbled and reached to get him off. Two white teeth moved in the dancer's hands. They flashed in the sunlight as he jabbed and swung like a sword fighter, beating back the simian's attacks. As the overseer watched, the great claw came down on the dancer. Sparks flew. Little yellow dots of light, sparking as the teeth and claw met. But there wasn't enough strength in the dancer's arms to keep off the claw. The legs unlocked. The small black form tumbled down the back of the huge bulbous simian, and was gone. Emeric, overseer of the games, pulled his glasses back and blinked. Where had he disappeared to? Emeric swiveled in his chair and flicked on his heat sensor, watching as it found the distinctive heat signatures of the life forms on the arena grounds and formed a picture. There he was. Emeric actually laughed.

Joe crouched on his hands and toes, the dust choking him as it rose in reams and clouds around him. But he stayed down and danced. The one claw's huge form towered over him. The great simian spun and shook, trembling in rage, pain, and physical shock. Looking for the little stinging thing that took his teeth and put out his eye. Joe danced under the monster's huge

belly.

He could hear the fluids shaking and rumbling in the great, wobbling stomach over his head. The heart beat thundered like an infernal drum. Even the monster's flaring nostrils, as it tried to scent its enemy, could be heard over the ground-shaking slamming of the thing's paws. Joe mimicked every move, spinning and running, stopping and twisting, even the writhing. He aped the ape. And it let him go invisible. It was a temporary solution, he knew, but he was back in his moment-by-moment lifestyle. If he could just survive this moment, he would be alive to deal with what came next. The great ape shifted around the arena, searching for the mute that danced under its thick hide. Over cactus and bushes, over the hard packed ground. They circled the great oval contained in the massive concrete walls.

A sharp hiss, of rushing, whistling air came from somewhere out there. A curse flew from Joe's silent lips and he shot forward. The overseer had grown tired of Joe's game. He wanted action, and knew the best way was to shoot the one claw with one of his power darts. Who knew what the bullet contained. Maybe just an electric node, to shock the great ape into changing its game. Maybe a plunger needle full of a maddening agent. Whatever it was, Joe knew what the response would be. The one claw reared up, screaming at whatever had hit it, its backside hitting the dirt just millimeters from Joe's boot as the mute darted out. Whatever the overseer had used, it didn't stop the simian from seeing what it had been looking for. The two close-sight pinprick eyes found him.

Joe saw the shadow coming. He flung himself to the side as a fist almost as wide as he was tall, rammed into the ground. The earth shook under him, wobbling like the simian's stomach. He couldn't gain his feet. Both enormous fists rose, and rammed down again in the same second. Rose and rammed, rose and rammed, a little closer to the desperately rolling mute each time. The one claw roared in triumph. The noise around him was indescribable, as Joe desperately fought for purchase on a ground that shook like a sheet in a wind. His head pulsed

and his vision shimmered with a migraine. But the only way he knew it in that nightmare world of adrenaline-pumped terror and action, is that it was annoyingly difficult to focus on anything.

The world shook and fuzzed and the simian above him roared in deafening triumph. But Joe didn't panic. He never panicked when it was important. He had to win. If he died, they died. He watched the fists. Raise, bang, raise, bang, raise, bang. Joe drew a breath in, blew it out, and watched as the bang happened again. His boot slammed into the only solid thing as the earth shook and cracked under him and the fists rose again.

The one claw hardly noticed the miniscule little boots that rammed into its wrist bone, pushed off, and slid over its other wrist. But it noticed its prey no longer rolled under its pounding fists. The nostrils flared, reverting to smell. He caught the sent. The smell of sweat and cruelty and starvation and everything evil in its life; its enemy was human. An animal is not as easily fooled as a man, and the simian knew the truth. And it would hunt it down and rip its head off and use it to feed more life into itself, so that it could eat more of the puny things that plagued it. The nostrils flared again, jerking the heavy head around as it followed the scent. The prey ran scared. The simian's mouth split open with a great howl of pleasure.

Joe scrabbled over the arena grounds, his heart laboring and his head trying to shut down to deal with the ceaseless searing sparks going off inside it. The dust kicked up around him and swirled. A rumbling note, lifting quickly into a singing howl that shook his poor brain with its volume, reverberated around him. The one claw, hunting.

It knew where he was, and it was coming.

Joe stopped running, forcing himself to turn and watch. Weariness and hopelessness dragged at his limbs and made him sluggish. But he turned. Over the dry ground, the one claw came thundering. It focused on him, its huge, dripping nostrils flaring. Now it had Joe's scent. He couldn't outrun it. Couldn't hide. Couldn't get out of this dratted, dratted concrete arena.

Could never match that strength. He had to outthink it.

Joe shut the pain in his mind into a corner. He pushed thoughts of Anna, Nehi, Beau and the others to another corner, but let it keep a pulsing link with his brain to give him strength. Visions of used hover boards and broken bloody heaps that used to be a Diamond he caged in a recess he refused to let out. The dancer's thoughts began to spin. The one claw's fists rammed into the earth, pulling it closer with each revolving second. The dancer stood riveted and his thoughts spun and flipped, collided with each other and pirouetted onto new threads, drawing it all into a desperate tapestry as he watched and analyzed and planned. The howl sang from the rushing, triumphant, ground-shaking simian. The answer lay bound up in the name. Joe's eyes focused on the glimmering claw shining black in the dazzling sunlight. He had to engage the claw.

Noise, dust, fetid breath, shaking ground, and hot rippling black flesh collided into the mute. He moved, two leaps to the side. The claw rammed into the ground, one leap too slow, biting a hole into the hardened desert. A backflip, and again the claw came too slow. Four bounding jumps to the left, always a little backward, dancing over the cacti and bushes. The claw followed, jabbing, scoring the ground, and kicking up huge clods of dirt that fell back down and exploded into dust clouds. Joe gave two more backflips. The claw followed.

To the crowd in the stands, it looked like a game of cat and mouse. The giant one claw kept ramming its claw down, inches from the little GI beast, as the black-clothed incomplete danced backward, inching toward the concrete wall of the arena. Emeric knew that isn't how a one claw played. A one claw played by batting at the skulls of its decapitated, regurgitated enemies. The GI beast led the simian on. Maybe he was proud of his skill, showing off how close he could get to the monster without dying. Whatever the reasoning, the dance was about to end. The mute reached the wall.

Joe's back rammed against the burning concrete. The hunting howl rose to a triumphant, high-pitched yowling cadence

# Chapter Twelve: To Win

*Matthew 28:20*

*One Claw*

and the claw lifted. Joe watched and waited, as everything seemed to slow in time. The claw rose a little higher. Joe leapt, his boots shot into the wall, and he rocketed across the air between him and the simian. His shoulder slammed into the great claw with every ounce of power he had. His move came so fast, so furious, and so unexpected, the simian didn't react. The claw rammed backward. Right into the chest of the great monster. Joe slammed head first into the pulpy, steaming flesh. He grabbed handfuls of the skin, hung on, and kicked with both legs together, driving the claw deeper home, kicking and kicking. The simian stumbled backward, too shocked and mortally wounded to even realize what had happened.

Its own weapon pierced its heart.

A hushed silence gripped the thousand-throated monster in the stands. The simian's back claws scrabbled another four yards. The great arm wrenched free, dripping, and letting a gushing stream loose from itself. Joe clung where he was in self preservation, the monster swaying under him. The paws gave way. The one claw fell backward. Its arm fell with it, the hundred-pound claw headed straight down where a winded, heat-struck mute clung in a daze.

The bang shook the ground even in the back stands as the one claw landed. Every person leapt to their feet. Even Emeric, his chair clattering to its side. No movement came from the arena. Monster and beast, neither moved.

Joe lay under the great claw, his mind dim with the heat, the stress of the arm pressing his face into the black flesh, and the wound in his back. White sparks pulsed in his mind and seared, but there was something else pulsing there too. Names. Faces. Nehi. Beau. Beautiful Anna. They needed him. He had to win.

He had to *win*.

Ten seconds. He had to move, to stand, in ten seconds or both contestants were declared out. It didn't matter who survived; except heaven help you if they got you back into the cages alive after an unclaimed win. What mattered was who stood up and pleased the crowd. He had to win. Joe's arms moved, driving his shoulders up. A scream, silent and agonized, came from him. But he pushed up anyway. Shoving the claw deeper in its furrow on his back, but driving himself up, pulling toward the sunlight, the burning heat and living air. He had to *win*.

The simian's arm trembled. The crowd held its breath. The arm slid, slowly, so slowly, off the great black belly and down toward the dirt. The thump of the great claw landing on the desert rang in that stillness. The GI beast staggered upright, off the huge monster, two steps away from the hulking corpse. His head lowered, blond hair plastered to him with sweat and blood and grime, and his hands clenched in effort. The crowd held its breath. Would he stay upright? The black boots bit into the ground. For an instant he swayed.

Then one fist shot into the air. The universal token for a win.

Cheering thundered down around him. Joe stood still, his breath coming in gasps, his mind still reeling. His eyes focused on the fist clenched at his side. The roaring, cheering, wild crowd sparked in his head and made the searing stars dance and his fear wake again, from where it always slumbered just under his skin. But his eyes stayed focused on that clenched fist. Blood dripped from it onto the hot desert ground. The simian's blood and his own. Joe's eyes saw Diamond's blood mix with it. Horror coursed through him. He stood stunned. Only partially conscious, even upright in the burning heat. Then mentally, that quiet, inner self that wasn't Joe spoke to him from the crack opening in the dry ground to soak up the blood.

*"I am with you always."*

The mute sank gently to his knees. He knelt there in the dazzling light. Still, in body and soul, his mind a blessed blank. Just breathing, as the workers began the grueling work of dragging the one claw's body away. Whatever came next, Jesus walked it with him.

# Chapter Thirteen: Behind the Glass

*"For he shall have judgment without mercy who hath shewed no mercy; and mercy rejoiceth against judgment." James 2:13*

When people spoke of Emeric the Overseer's steely eyes, they didn't mean their bright blue color. Unbending, merciless hardness marked his features, radiating from his soul. Nehemiah understood it as he watched the man, his muscled form draped on the metal chair and his gaze focused out the clear wall of the Observation Room.

The room perched on the top of the arena and stretched out past the concrete and steel. Three clear walls and floor gave the room a perfect view of everything below, while the white ceiling and west wall gave it protection from the burning sun. The hard gaze of the overseer of the games could scrape over every centimeter of the arena's oval desert. Bone chips and microphones connected him with workers surrounding the enclosed desert, and gave him instant access to any area. Someone trapped in that burning oval had no chance of getting free, or sitting out a fight. And heaven help them if they stepped out of the bounds of the Battle Kingdom's opinions.

"Our little overman contestant is doing better than I expected," Emeric commented watching the workers drag the dead one claw out. Twelve burley men strained and sweated, digging furrows in the hard earth as they tugged its huge body. The overseer's steely eyes glanced to his left, to the clear cage sealing off the prisoners from the rest of the room. Nehemiah stood beside Daniel and Wiglaf and looked around their cell again, desperately hoping to find some way out to help his friend. Nothing breakable, only the same sickeningly strong clear material that made up this floor, the walls, and the partition into the rest of the room. No holes, not even an air vent in their cell. No chink or weak point to exploit in the cage that held them at the end of the Observation Room. Nehi looked down again.

Joe knelt, quiet and still on the dusty ground, waiting for what might come next. His bloodied hands lay on his lap, his shoulders hunched, head bowed so far strands of sweat-soaked hair brushed his fingers. Nehi's lip tucked under his teeth and he gnawed, helplessness eating at him. Cobeau stood with his face plastered against the glass, his breath coming quick and desperate.

"Why is he down there?" the chimera rumbled for the hundredth time. "And why can't I go to him?"

"I swear, if he asks that again I'm going to–" Emeric growled, but Nehemiah held up a hand and laid his other on Beau's shoulder.

"Listen very closely, Beau," he told the chimera slowly. "They liked Joe's dancing and wanted to see how he fights. Joe had to go to keep us alive, and their electric prods and tasers got us all before we could get out. We can't go down to him because we can't get out of this cell. Prayer is all we can give Joe now, and he needs it. Be quiet and pray." The chimera nodded, his face creased and eyes wet. He slid back to the far corner and slumped there, his back against the single white wall. The chimera's lips moved in a passionate, soundless prayer. Nehemiah turned to Emeric. "I think he'll be quiet now."

"Prayer," spat Emeric as he glared at Cobeau. "His kind can never get out of that narcotic of a God! They will never be strong enough to face reality and realize God is dead. Only so could he embrace the task of creating himself, he will always be amongst the animals and rabble."

"I do not understand," Wiglaf frowned.

"Look, I don't think we should ask questions right now, let's just ride it out," Daniel murmured to the warrior.

"Ride it out?" Wiglaf asked. Daniel rolled his eyes to heaven, his lips pressed together. The door in the white wall flung open, and four people strode in. Nehemiah recognized three of them too well; they had suddenly announced they were taking Joe, and then grabbed them all to ensure Joe's cooperation. Tasers flying without warning, electric whips wrapping around their convulsing bodies before they could even start to fight. Everyone in the street had happily lent a hand. There were too many to fight back, it had been Natropia all over again. Natropia with a well-armed enemy. At the sight of those three, fury began to boil in Nehemiah. He was a hostage, being made to watch Joe kill himself down there to keep them safe, and the frustration rolled and bubbled and boiled in his guts. He swallowed hard and forced his mind away to something else.

He let his eye stray to the men finding seats around the observation room and ticked them off in his mind as they got situated. The scarred one with the wizened, wiry look was Talon, and the name fit him. He looked like a bird of prey. The huge one with the melancholy air was Harb, not a very nice looking character, and his name didn't fit at all. Then there was the incredibly handsome proud one...Collen, that was his name. And the new one, tall and as well-built as Emeric, but as somber as Harb, and as energetic as Talon. The others called him Gor and seemed to have great respect for him. No, more a fear of him. Gor's eyes flicked from the preparations happening below to the group of captives near him. His gaze fell on the chimera in the corner of the cell. His eyes narrowed and he uncurled from his chair.

"I know that one," Gor commented in a deep, gravelly voice. He strode for the front wall and stuck a hand on it, leaning forward for a better look at the contestant. "And I know that one too. You remember Talon, they've been here before. Several years ago, they were the ones that just kept surviving through the summer games. They wouldn't die. And then they disappeared during the uprising against Bakstun."

"Of course, that's when Emeric took over," Talon nodded, recognition scoring his sharp face, "since we got rid of the old overseer. We couldn't keep the one who let our favorite contestants out. They had an amazing will to live I remember, and a strength of mind and body that was remarkable. Especially the little one, being a GI. Even the strongest GIs go crazy after a month in the cages, but not him. I thought he looked familiar!"

A metallic screech interrupted the talk, and every eye turned to the arena. A great red gate swept open, taking four bushes with it, the massive hinges squealing. A hoarse screech rent the air, but it wasn't metallic. Nehemiah's heart leapt into his throat, his mouth parting as his prayers turned desperate again. Surely it wasn't... A yellow beak loomed into the sunlight. It was as long as Joe, and ten feet in the air. The bright eyes of a green back followed the beak, and a huge feathered bird stalked into the burning sunlight. His neck stretched up to reach twenty-five feet into the bright air, and the yellow beak opened in a screech that shot through Nehemiah's skull and made his brain vibrate. A sick weight fell into his stomach as another beak pushed out into the sun.

Two giant green backs.

With each step into the arena, their clawed feet left indentions a man could sprain an ankle in. Their sharp bird eyes flashed everywhere, searching for their prey, and their beaks opened to let out the hideous hiss of the hunt. The glaring sun glinted off the black and white pattern of their feathers. But the brilliant green running down their backs shone, almost blinding. Nehemiah's gaze flitted to Joe. The little mute gathered his legs under him and pushed himself off the ground, moving slow and weary. His shoulders slumped, his bare arms scratched, bleeding, and bright red from the sun. Nehi mentally chalked up his chances. Unarmed, spent, dehydrated, and alone? There was no chance. Nehemiah's hand splayed against the glass, feeling the heat through it, begging, pleading for some miracle. Daniel's hand landed on his shoulder and Nehi glanced to the side, his eyes haunted. Daniel didn't try to give him an encouraging smile, say it would all be ok, or anything else ridiculous.

"Keep the vision burning, Nehi," Daniel murmured, his face sad as he watched the mute. "Joe's still in His hands and headed home." Nehemiah blinked rapidly, trying to clear away the mist that would cover his eyes, and just nodded. It was the best comfort (the only comfort) he could take right now. Good old, grumpy Daniel. For all his complaints and frowns, he understood, and always knew what to say when it counted. Talon's voice cut into his thoughts and he glanced at him distractedly.

"You should have seen him dance, Gor, no one can dance like that and not at least know about overman! Even if he was mistaken several years ago–"

"Mistaken?" Gor cut in, his voice ringing with disdain. "He was a member of the Way, and merciful too, like most of that kind. No one can be called strong with those two on their record. Pity is the great, the last sin. Remember how the chimera and GI would help each other in the games, and even endangered themselves to help other contestants? Multiple times? No. I saw pity in his eyes back then, even mercy when he would step aside and not kill, and it persisted though we kept raising the punishments in the cages. And the way he came meekly along here to avoid hurt to his companions' shows me he hasn't changed. Still, this should be interesting. Back then he was only a child, not yet at his full potential. Now he must be… How old is he?" Nehemiah found Gor's hard, bright eyes fixed on him.

"Eighteen. I think," Nehemiah answered.

"See, he's practically at his full strength now," Gor said. "I wish I had seen the first phase, it must have been fascinating."

"It was," Emeric commented. "Fascinating enough to make me think he might know one to overthrow you, Gor. I've never seen such original and skilled fighting. As you say, he was a child when he was here before, sometimes when a boy comes to manhood his ideas grow with him. Maybe his old pity and religion died with his childhood and he will lead us to a real overman to guide us. Whoever trained him must be phenomenal."

"Phooey," Gor spat. "Whoever trained him allowed the beast to cultivate pity, the kind that offers 'love' and service to the ugliest man. Once merciful, always one of the weak rabble."

"He's doing all right now, even with two green backs instead of the usual one," Collen commented. "You might just be replaced, Gor."

"Replaced as what?" Nehemiah found himself asking, fascinated by this strange conversation. And trying desperately not to think too much about how helpless he was to help Joe. His stomach roiled with it, his head pounding with his own pulse.

"Our guide, the prophet who leads the way," Emeric answered absently, his eyes on the arena below.

"You pick your leaders by feats of strength?" Nehemiah asked incredulously.

"What else is there to pick from? Nothing will last past the end of the world, and nothing is as almost real as the survival of the fittest," Talon answered with a shrug.

"There is one way to find out if he holds the same weaknesses," Gor broke in. "Harb, go find a girl and throw her in there." The huge man rose and left. Nehi glanced at Daniel and saw the same shocked disbelief in his face. A green back's hideous shriek sounded from the arena below, and all eyes fastened on the dusty battle. The fight moved directly below the Observation Room.

Joe clung to one of the giant beaks, his arms wrapped around it, desperately trying to keep it closed as his legs scrabbled for a hold on the feathered, serpentine neck. Nehemiah dropped to his knees on the hard transparent floor, cold sweat frozen on his spine as he watched. The bird snapped its neck like a whip, and Joe shot off into the sky. The second bird snapped at the air as the tasty bit of warm flesh hurtled toward him. Joe twisted in midair and his hand closed on the animal's tongue as he sailed past. The long, black tongue jerked out of the bird's mouth with the mute's weight. He used his momentum to sweep up and drop onto the green back's head. Joe's boots shoved off, flinging himself head first toward the dirt. The tongue came with him. The bird's head jerked, wings flailed, and it tumbled to the ground in a dusty heap of clawing legs and flapping feathers, its neck twisted unnaturally and a strangled squawk rasping from it. If Joe had an ounce more strength left in his sweat soaked body, the neck would have broken.

Dust spurted up in a sharp cloud; the second green back,

clawing at the ground as it pounced on Joe before he could scrabble off. The mute flung himself back as the snap of the razor sharp beak filled Nehi's mind. It snapped on air. But the bird's foot caught the mute. Blond hair, dust-drenched clothes, bleeding arms, white face pinched with pain and fear, for an instant the sight seared into Nehi's vision as the mute sailed through the heat waves. His friend slammed into the concrete wall. Nehemiah could hear the sickening thump of his impact even from the thirty-eight feet separating them. Joe slid to the ground and lay dazed, bruised, winded, probably broken. The two birds stalked closer, hissing, wings half raised, razor beaks open.

They had cornered their prey, and they knew it. They could move slowly.

The first green back hopped closer, a pleased squawk lifting from it. The ground vibrated as it landed. The mute twitched. The bird's eyes glinted, and it jabbed down at its feast. Joe rolled, staggered to his feet, and threw himself into a bush. The move came fast, unexpected, a blur, and the bird missed as it snapped after its prey. But the mute was getting weaker. Nehi could see it in his movements. One of the green backs lunged. Joe leaped aside and rolled under one of the spiny bushes, missing the pecking beak by a fraction of an inch. The green back gave a pleased squawk and hopped closer to the bush. The huge bird reached down for its meal and Nehi felt his throat constrict in helpless despair.

The animal jerked its head up, shrieking and flapping in pain. Joe seized the moment to stagger away, disappearing into another part of the arena. Emeric picked up a pair of binoculars and focused in on the shrieking bird.

"One of the leaves of the razor bush is in his eye," the overseer murmured. "A clever move on the dancer's part." A new shriek joined the bird's. A terrible high pitched, terror-laden scream. A little girl, of about seven years old Nehemiah guessed, blue dress fluttering around her, dropped past the short railings of the stands into the arena. She screamed for her

mother, tears and terror in the little voice.

"They did it," Daniel muttered beside him, his dark eyes wide. Nehemiah's jaw clamped with the roiling fury and frustration playing through his rigid body. He stared at the weeping girl, clawing at the concrete wall of the arena, vainly trying to climb up to her mother. Bile rose in his throat. The uninjured green back tipped its head on one side, wings lifted again, and it hopped closer to the little spot of trembling blue. It began to circle the girl. Her frantic sobs and cries filled the dry air.

Joe darted in front of the bird.

His boots dug a dusty furrow in the ground as he slid to a stop. Head high, spine straight, one arm already pushing the girl behind his back as he stared a challenge at the monstrous hunter. Tensed, watching, everything about him bristling with a dangerous anger. Bristling with the urge to shield. The little girl threw herself at him, clinging to his waist, her cries stilled as she found a protector. The mute swept her up, his cut, sunburned arms cradling the child, his eyes burning into the circling bird.

The green-back struck out, with the lightning reflexes of a hunter.

Joe leapt on its head, with the faster-than-lightning reflexes of the survivor.

A screech of fury and surprise rent through the air, cutting through the vents in the observation room, and the bird jerked up, wings flapping. Joe flew up with it. He used the momentum. The mute curled around the girl, and sailed off like a black cannon ball with a streak of fluttering blue. He arched through the air as the bird spun in an earth-shaking circle, looking for its prey. The second bird lunged upright, screeching and flapping, and drew every eye by his sudden noise. No one noticed Joe land.

Silence sparkled in the Observation Room. No one spoke as they raked the arena with their eyes. Had he been crushed by the landing? Did he take the easy way out, choosing to break both their necks instead of watching the birds peck them to death? Or was Joe still out there, protecting a stranger because he was the only one who could. Emeric's scanner picked up two small heat signatures, and a shimmering outline of two people crouched under a bush came alive on his screen. A collective breath filled the room, and Nehi absently noted it; for all their mercilessness, they wanted him to win. They all stirred, easing tight muscles and sinking back in chairs as they watched the birds began to circle the arena looking for their prey.

"Verily, I have spoken a truth," Gor said smugly. "I told you he was still just as weak." Disgust wrinkled the others faces as they watched the mute crouching with his little charge. "He could have used the distraction of the girl to bring down the weakened bird, but instead he dove into trouble and only just got out with his life. And why? Because he pitied. He saw a helpless thing and chose mercy instead of overcoming. It always makes men weaker, and it will kill him yet."

"I do not see what you see." Wiglaf's voice rang clear and strong. Every eye in the room turned to the tall, bulky warrior with his arms crossed over his chest, watching the scene below his feet. The birds had found the scent. "In my country some hold to what you say. But I have watched the world, watched the warriors and the true heroes, and I have seen the truth. You say having pity on the helpless makes a man weak, but even here that is not what happened. It makes him strong. Look. See how he knocks over the bird, at the least three times as large as himself, before it can snap up the child! That is not weakness. Before he had someone to protect, Ravenswing moved with a warrior's will to survive, and even to win; but now he is a hero, his skill and metal and wit renewed to ten times their power. His strength waned before. Now it has returned tenfold and brought with it a clarity and strength of mind enough to defeat ten such animals."

"He's right," Nehemiah said. "Pity and mercy make a man strong, and protecting those who need it sharpens every skill he has. They make him what he's supposed to be. You can say the opposite all you want, but that doesn't make it true. Joe's proving you wrong down there right now."

"You seem awfully certain of his success," Collen said, strolling languidly over to the translucent screen cutting off the prisoners from the others. "Could it be you hold to his ideas of mercy? And even religion? Perhaps you do not think God is dead?"

A burst of sudden, bright laser light split the hot desert air. A bird screamed, a huge, screeching shriek of anger and pain.

# Chapter Fourteen: A Black Slit

*"The merciful man doeth good to his own soul: but he that is cruel troubleth his own flesh." Proverbs 11:17*

Everyone spun to the arena, craning to see what had happened. A burst of white laser light burned a hole just in front of a green back chasing Joe as he spun, dragging the screaming girl out of its way. It took a talon off the bird's foot. Another burst of laser light cut off the bird's shriek as its lithe neck reached for the girl again. The green back fell, a burning hole in its head. It gave one convulsion, and lay still. The screaming crowd suddenly quieted. A dead silence fell on the arena. Three more burst broke into the sunshine in quick succession, and the other bird fell dead. Emeric pointed at one of the tunnels leading into the arena.

"It's open," he grunted, his voice hoarse in his anger, and fear. Nehemiah squinted, but couldn't see what the overseer did. But Joe must have seen it. He swept the girl into his arms and ran, for both their lives, a black streak cutting through the hot desert air. Emeric grabbed for his controls, raking every channel open.

"Block and clear tunnel number four," he called into it. "Block and clear tunnel number four!" Keepers and other workers began to flood the arena, racing to cut off Joe from the delicious darkness of the opening. The mute's body craned forward as his feet seemed to fly over the ground, straining every ounce of strength to reach that one dark line that meant hope. Now Nehemiah could see the open tunnel. It stood cracked, only a thin line of blackness. But it was enough for Joe. He flung himself down, under the arms of a grasping worker, shoving the girl under the crack in front of him like a hockey puck, and sliding in a dusty cloud. The crack snapped shut and two keepers slammed into it with a bang.

"Emeric," Gor said, his voice slow, a dripping, dangerous tone, "I suggest you don't lose that little dancer like your

predecessor did." Sweat stood on Emeric's brow as he began to pull levers and give orders. The rest of the room was still, watching the overseer. Relief so intense it made him nauseous and giddy flooded Nehemiah, and he slumped against the white wall.

After ten minutes of no sign of the escapees or the mysterious shooter, he could watch Emeric growing frantic. The crowd in the stands began to leave in disgust. Trash and insults and threats hurtled from them into the arena. Fifteen minutes passed, and Gor stood up and stretched.

"Well, we might as well take care of his security, since the little dancer ran off and left them with us," he said, and walked over to the partition. The man leaned against the clear wall and looked speculatively at the four men contained like an exhibit at a zoo. Goosebumps crept over Nehemiah, a cold shudder running through him. Visions of cages and wild fights and merciless captors filled his mind. But he wasn't there yet. He stood before a man who thought throwing a girl out to be eaten was not only acceptable, but good.

"Do you really believe nothing but fighting is real?" Nehemiah blurted out.

"When you're fighting, everything is more real," Gor shrugged. "Surely you've felt the rush of life through you as you've stood in pitched battle. Death is never so far away as at that moment. And death is always shining around us to sap our happiness. In this revolving time, I want more of the real times to relive. 'Oh, how I love eternity!' I seem eternal when the rush of battle, of *feeling* myself overcoming, runs through me. Why do you ask, boy? Are you seeing how inadequate your own lifestyle is?" A snort of amusement at the thought of his one solid hope in life being replaced for *that* slipped from Nehi before he could pull it back. Gor's eyebrows went up. A slow wicked smile lifted the corners of his mouth. But before he could give any orders, a clatter interrupted him.

The grate to the single air vent shoved out and bounced on the clear flooring. Two canisters flew into the room, and a dense white smoke billowed up in a hissing cloud that filled the room in a moment. Gor and his men folded up, eyes rolling. Emeric clawed at his instrument panel, holding himself up for an instant, his eyes wild and throat constricting on his cries. His muscles relaxed and the overseer crumpled to the floor, splaying over Collen.

"You know, I'm kind of glad that partition's solid now," Daniel drawled as he watched the acrid smoke swirling around the room.

"I am of the same mind," Wiglaf answered. Beau bounded beside them, hopping up and down in his excitement.

"Joe, Joe, Joe," the chimera repeated the name over and over. Thirty seconds ticked by with infinite slowness, as they watched the white smoke swallowed by clean air. The last wisp curled on itself and disappeared. A dusty, booted foot appeared through the grate, became a dangling leg, then two dangling legs. Joe dropped through the air vent into the observation room, staggering as he landed. His arm shot up, hand held toward the vent. A slim, olive hand took it, and their miracle rescuer slid into the room.

"Anna!" Nehi and Daniel yelped. Nehi found himself grinning in pride and relief at seeing her here, safe and rescuing them all. She turned a dust-smeared face to him, framed by dirty close cropped hair, and waved. Joe fished the keys out of Emeric's pocket and stepped to the partition, fumbling the right key into his grip. His hand shook too hard to slip it in the lock. Anna's hand closed over his as she took the key, inserted it, and turned it. The click rang through the room. Daniel and Wiglaf shoved into the partition, and rebounded back, cursing under their breath. Nehi had been paying closer attention when they were pushed in here. His hand found the bottom of the partition and he flung it up. It rattled into the ceiling and he bounded to Anna.

"Nice haircut. Do you know where the wagon is, and how to get out?"

"Well thank you, I call it the claw cut. I know where the

wagon is, and I think if I go back through the vents and shoot a couple of pistol shots as distractions, it will draw enough people that direction for us to leave from here," she answered. Joe quickly began to sign he'd be the one to go back through. He shook so hard his signs were almost unintelligible. Anna grabbed Nehemiah and pushed him into position as a ladder back up to the vent.

"Joe, that vent scared you more than anything I've seen you face," she answered as she scrambled up. "I don't think you have the strength to go back through it, and no one but you and I fit."

"You'll be all right, Anna?" Nehemiah asked.

"Don't worry," her voice echoed out of the vent, "we stretched a ball of orange twine as we went so I can't get lost, it will be much faster coming back, and I'll be fine."

"Be careful and hurry," Nehemiah smiled, but Anna had already slipped away. Beau and Wiglaf started piling the unconscious forms in the cell. Daniel fiddled with the keys, trying to figure out the partition's lock, and Nehemiah crossed to Joe. The mute leaned against the white wall, smearing it with muddy sweat, shaking weakly. Nehi leaned beside him and blew out a breath. He couldn't think of anything to say. Joe's green eyes lifted slowly, and the mute smiled at him. It looked like the face from his self-portrait ringed with self-portraits. A beautifying thankfulness radiated from the mute, even through the grime and exhaustion. Nehi knew he didn't have to say anything; and he felt a little embarrassed at the intensity of Joe's response, he couldn't think of anything he had done to explain it.

A click came from the partition as Daniel finally got the lock to work. A cloud of dust billowed from the vent into the room. Anna's sharp, short cough drifted out of the woman-shaped cloud, and Nehi wondered how she breathed in all that.

"Can we go now?" she coughed, her voice scratchy.

"Beau, check and see if it's clear enough for us to leave," Nehemiah ordered, sweeping Hope up from Emeric's desk and checking her over. His hand hovered near her as they filed out of the room. But he didn't need to grab his Compton as they trotted out of the arena and followed Anna back to the wagon.

The group pushed in and out of milling people, quick, forceful, and competent. No one gave them a second glance. The only one the crowd might recognize shuffled in the group's center, dwarfed and shadowed by even Anna. The whole city murmured and milled outside, mystified by the lack of directions coming from the Observation Room. A careful door jamming job by the chimera kept them that way. Dissatisfaction and unease grew in the crowd. Murmurs of "replace him," and "new governing," moved openly among them.

Everyone was too distracted to notice six strangers. The group clambered up their wagon, quietly pushed Prissy's wheeled shoes to the fastest they could in town, and rolled away. The streets began to clear. Five more minutes, and there was no one on the dusty, cracked pavement. Joe's trembling hand pushed down on the accelerator, the hot wind slammed into them, and everyone held on. Nehemiah kicked the wind bubble stick hard, and pumped it. A little squeal rang from it, but the bubble lifted and clicked in place, cutting off the wind. Beau pushed the pig to a better pace. Five more minutes and they sped along a silent, dusty road through the desert, leaving Overman City farther behind them with each revolution of Prissy's wheels, the world around them a blur. Anna dropped to the bench between Joe and Beau, popped the first aid kit open on her lap, and handed Joe water. The sun began to set in a brilliant bath of color. The beauty of it, and the town growing so small it was almost out of sight, finally began to relax the company. Beau kept the pig racing, her fur rippling behind her, head lifting to snuffle the wind. Anna finished cleaning the last of the cuts on Joe's face, and gently pressed a bandage smeared with ointment onto the patch of missing skin on his cheek. She nodded once for a job done, clicked the kit closed and slid back to the wagon top.

"Are all towns in this country that...venturesome?" Wiglaf

broke the silence. Joe shrugged.

"It depends on the day," he signed.

"You've stopped shaking," Anna commented quietly. "Was it that bad?"

"It was that stupid vent that did it," Joe signed with a grimace. "I don't like vents."

"You were awfully good at finding your way through them, for hating them that much," Anna said, curiosity tinging her voice.

"You faced an angry mob, a one claw, and two green backs. And it was the air vent that scared you?" Daniel drawled. Joe gave a weak laugh.

"I'm a strange character like that," he signed.

"A fear of air vents and stickiness," Nehemiah speculated teasingly. "I wonder if there's a name for that disorder?" Joe just smiled and didn't offer a reply.

"What happened to the child?" Wiglaf asked.

"Elsie's mother was crying for her outside the arena wall. We were able to drop her down to her mother before we came after you," Anna answered.

"Elsie, that's her name?" Nehemiah asked. "I hope she and her mother run as far as they can from that town."

"From the whole country, Nehi," Anna grimaced.

"Were you and Joe really kept here for a whole summer?" Daniel asked Cobeau, knowing an answer was more probable from the big hairy Raven than the mute. The chimera shrugged. "I find it hard to believe you could have survived a whole summer of what I just saw in that arena. How many years ago was it?"

"Daniel..." Nehemiah interrupted quietly; Joe probably didn't want to talk about it just now, he knew he wouldn't if the positions were swapped. Joe waved his concern away, giving him a thankful look for the thought as he did so. But Nehi also saw he had absented himself, a masked Joe answered. As he signed, the real him, with what he actually felt, lay somewhere tucked away far down inside the mute. Nehi was a little surprised he could recognize the mood in his friend. Nehemiah put his qualms away and let Joe the Detached answer whatever he wanted.

"Four years ago," he signed. "You remember, Glue. We went in after Tibble and ended up caged for three months. The cage keepers were worse than any of the contestants." Beau nodded slowly, his brow creased in his effort to remember.

"Never gave us water. And hot," he frowned after a moment.

"That's an understatement," Joe signed with a wry twist to his expressive face. "You almost died of the heat with all that hair of yours. Several times."

"No, it's not possible you could have survived, not that young," Daniel decided.

"It wasn't I guess, but I didn't know it at the time," Joe smiled, a tight look that didn't reach his eyes. "Still, one of the longest summers I ever went through."

"Only one of, Ravenswing?" Wiglaf asked, shock strong in the words.

"Well it seems like you would have learned from that not to dance today–" Daniel began caustically, but Joe clicked irritably and interrupted.

"I'm not that much of an idiot, D! I didn't know about that quirk, it wasn't dancing that got us into trouble that time." Inside he remembered watching Gor's three special companions stride around the corner toward their show, saw Hamfast in the overseer's room, and felt the hot conviction rush through him. She had set them on the Raven, on purpose. Those three didn't just show up at a concert together. Joe stared at the blurred yellow landscape outside their bubble, his aching mind whirling, searching for the meaning behind it.

"What happened then, that time?" Anna asked. Joe didn't move, his eyes bright as he watched the world. Beau jogged his elbow. The mute snapped toward Anna blinking hard.

"I'm sorry, you said something," he signed, every inch of him apologetic. Daniel's eyes narrowed.

"I just asked about the last time. If it wasn't dancing, what happened?" she repeated. Joe's face went blank and he turned it away from the others so they couldn't see his eyes. The answer ran too deep through the mute's blood and marrow for the detached state to compensate for.

"A family we thought were Christian friends turned us in," he signed. Another puzzle piece slid neatly into the picture forming his little friend, and Nehi just caught himself from nodding. Beau shook his head sadly.

"Poor sad, evil people. Dead now," the big man commented.

"Did you kill them?" Wiglaf asked curiously. Nehemiah punched him in the arm, not gently.

"Not us," Joe signed, his green eyes hurt and angry as they flashed at the warrior. Wiglaf stammered out an apology, a very sincere one. In his world, given certain circumstances tracking down an enemy might be a matter of honor. He hadn't considered it insulting.

"How far do we have to go to get out of this kingdom?" Nehemiah interrupted quickly to change the subject.

"We picked a short road through," Cobeau said. "Not far now."

"And no more towns," Joe signed, slumping down in his seat. He sat up sharply again, a hiss of pain sliding through clenched teeth as his back hit the wood of the wagon. A dark smear splayed over the wagon seat behind him.

"Joe, you should have said something!" Anna complained.

"Are you all right?" Nehemiah asked.

"Seriously?" Daniel laughed, jogging his brother's shoulder. "You saw his afternoon, no he's not all right. Come on Joe, stop signing, drop inside and get doctored. I'll keep an eye on things with Beau out here."

"You should have said something without prompting," Anna said, her voice a little sharp as she shifted toward the skylight.

"It's not that bad," Joe signed bashfully.

"'Not bad' is still bad enough to mention," Nehemiah said as Beau grabbed Joe around the waist and hefted him onto the

wagon top, and Nehi pushed him toward the skylight.

"You're one to talk!" Anna's voice drifted back up from the day room as she began to assemble the bathtub. "What about that splinter you let fester for weeks before you asked me to get it out?"

"That was a splinter," Nehemiah argued as he landed beside her, "not wounds from battling ferocious monsters all day, there is a difference. You have that piece wrong, would you like me to?"

"Fine, you put the bath together, but you're not listening to me," Anna said as she moved to find the bandages and liniment.

"Yes I am," Nehemiah said. "It was a splinter."

"That you let fester," Anna prodded.

"A splinter's not something you have to worry about–"

"Till you let it sit there for weeks on end–"

"Do splinters sit?"

"Oh, you're not listening again!"

Joe sat perched on the rim of the skylight, dangling his legs through, slumped, pale, and looking ready to collapse. But a smile broke over his face at the growing argument. It turned into a regular quarrel as the bath filled. Joe turned to the three men still on top the wagon. He pointed at the arguing twins and grinned, his eyes twinkling.

"Aren't we funny the way God has us wired?" he signed. The mute disappeared, dropping down to let himself be doctored and help make peace. Daniel watched him go with a thoughtful frown. Why had Joe lost the conversation just when it rolled to their being nabbed today? The little mute had been thinking about something, hard enough he missed Anna's comment, and Daniel knew Joe always paid attention to Anna's comments. So what distracted the mute? It had been awfully convenient for the ones who basically ran the kingdom to round that corner just as Joe went into his rhythm dance... What if it hadn't been an accident? What if someone had sent them?

But who?

Daniel turned his eyes to the darkening desert sky, and the

frown stayed on his face as they rolled on.

"Out already?" Daniel asked in surprise, as Anna walked toward the campfire. They were settled in a sheltered indention under a knoll, inside a dead forest. Twisted gray skeletons of trees rose around them, scattered evenly over a half mile of ground. It made an eerie landscape. But plentiful firewood. The desert dropped to twenty degrees or lower at night, sometimes even reaching the negatives, and the burning pile of branches made a welcome friend for the little company. Daniel and Wiglaf had handled dinner tonight, roasting piles of meat the warrior had hunted down, and vegetables and potatoes wrapped in tin-foil and then slathered in butter.

Anna was too busy doctoring Joe. The repair work had been longer and harder than anyone suspected from the mute's easy conversation after the wild flight from Overman City. The wound on his back needed close stitching, and with Joe that meant an ordeal. He refused to take anything for the pain, and usually moaned and writhed in a very dramatic and unnerving way. From Nehi's reports (after Anna had kicked him out when her twin kept trying to give her and the patient "good advice") the rest of the company had expected it would take several hours.

"He was quiet about it once we actually got started," Anna said. She settled on a log beside Daniel, her hands rubbing compulsively even though she had washed them well. "Then he said he wanted sleep and asked me politely to leave him be."

"Sounds like he finally decided to take his doctoring like a man," Daniel commented in approval, and handed Anna a skewer with the remains of some sort of animal on it. "Try it before you judge the way it looks," Daniel commented, and ran on telling his sister all about the cooking method and what they might change next time. Anna's eyes rose and locked onto Nehi's. Their expressions held the same concern. Polite and quiet? That wasn't a good response after the day Joe just experienced. A sharp snort came from Cobeau as he practically inhaled his meat, starting to stand. Nehemiah beat him to it, waving him back down and absently wiping the meat grease on his pants. Beau sank back to his log, chewing again, and watching Nehi as he strolled for the wagon. A happy smile covered the chimera's simple face.

The light spilled over the fold out table as Nehi slipped into the wagon. But darkness overtook everything as he pushed carefully through into the night room. For a moment he couldn't even see the glowing stars on the ceiling as his eyes adjusted. Then he spotted a small ball curled by the pillow on the bottom bunk. Not an easy, comfortable curl while he slept, but a tight protective ball. A desperate defense against the whole world.

"You sure you don't want more light?" Nehi murmured, unsure what to say. The ball shifted, and Joe's bright blond hair and white face fairly gleamed in what little light came through the cracked door. He moved slowly, reached beside him and slid his gloves on.

"Headache," the mute signed. The word was stinted and staccato as the gloves spoke it in their computerized voice. "Rather sleep." Nehemiah let the door close and dropped to the ground beside the bunk.

"I'm sure you would," Nehi said. He stayed where he was. The minute ticked into five minutes and he still just sat. A confused click came from Joe. It was answered by a wry chuckle from Nehi.

"You and I both know you're not going to sleep, even though you want to. Migraines, pulsing open wounds, and reawakened nightmares aren't exactly conducive to a decent rest. You're clicking instead of signing."

"Hands hurt," Joe signed.

"Thumb cuff?" Nehi asked. Joe nodded, strangely comforted to have someone near who knew enough to assume that. Then immediately regretted the nod as his hand came up to his head, his glove spouting random gibberish. Nehi's bulk loomed in the blackness beside the mute, and he stepped out of the room. The slit of light from the day room grew, then slimmed again, and Nehi knelt beside him, laying one of Joe's compresses across the mute's forehead. It was deliciously cold.

"Ice?" Joe signed.

"The last," Nehi nodded as he settled comfortably in his spot again. "We'll have to refill when we have the chance. At least the water tanks nearly filled before we were interrupted." The two stayed in quiet, companionable silence.

"You do not have to sit in the dark," Joe finally signed, the words disjointed as the gloves spouted them. Did Nehi imagine it, or was there hesitation in that offer of freedom?

"I know," he said, and stayed. The minutes ticked on. Nehemiah finally broke it again.

"You know, my dad used to surprise people with his theories about life. Sometimes after a hard day judging all the nasty things people had been up to in the kingdom, a visiting dignitary would notice his mood and comment on it smugly. Something like, 'It's surprising isn't it, to find your God has let all that in His world if He's as loving and powerful as you say.'" Nehi paused, a ribbon of shame burning through him as he knew he had thought those words before. A sniffle came from the little curled ball on the bunk. "Dad would look at them with his clear eyes that never backed down from a fight, and say, 'What really surprises me is how much goodness we see every day, even after we've broken the world.'" Another pause drifted into the room. Joe lay still, stiff and thinking. "The more I live, the more I see, the more I realize he's right. The evil seems so strong and so wicked sometimes. But then I realize it's because it stands out from the sweetness and goodness of most of life like a gangrenous finger. God's mercies are so bountiful around us, we forget that's what they are. The sun rising, our body's healing from trauma, minds that can understand beauty, wildflowers and clean springs, soft fur and laughter... There are so many things everywhere that we forget are gifts given only from

God's mercy."

"To a murderous, traitorous people," Joe's gloves added. Nehi nodded in the dark.

"There's more good than evil, even with the world so broken by our sin. Even when we're so broken." The blond hair shifted in the dim glow from the stars, a fractional nod. Nehi leaned his head back against the bunk and let the silence linger. It stretched on. But Joe's thoughts had been turned to remember the good things around them. Slowly, the ball uncurled. The hard, defensive set to the mute's shoulders changed, as his tight muscles relaxed. Another few minutes of quiet companionship, and a little smile rested on Joe's face as he lay relaxed. No fear or plaguing nightmares tightened his expression, and Nehi silently blessed God for it.

"Too quiet. Story?" Joe signed. A smile spread over Nehemiah. He stretched his long legs out into the blackness and began one of the bedtime stories his father used to offer the twins, about a naughty, lion-hearted sheep named Eric. There were many Eric the Sheep stories. Joe's smile grew and he lay still, listening, as time kept spinning on.

Nehi had no idea, with each minute he stayed in the dark, how many wounds he was binding up in the soul of the tattered, battle-weary mute.

# Chapter Fifteen: Voice from the Dark

*"Dearly beloved, avenge not yourselves, but rather give place unto wrath: for it is written, Vengeance is mine; I will repay, saith the Lord." Romans 12:19*

The street lamps didn't glitter. They gloomed, reluctantly letting yellow light pool, illuminating round patches of cracked concrete covered in mud and tendrils of fog. Some of the gloomy lights stretched far enough to illumine the old-fashioned brick houses lining the street. It seemed an unlikely place to leave a hoverer as fancy as the one they had taken from Simmons, Shareef considered as he lounged in a doorway across from the vehicle. But then, it was an opulent portion of the Kingdom of the Wise. Considering the hoverer had been parked here for over a month and no one had tried to drag it off, maybe it was a decent spot to leave it. Shareef slouched, letting himself sigh into the gloomy night. Boredom ate at his mind during these long night watches.

White fog inched and undulated up and down the street. It snaked up the first step in the little porch, trying to claw at Shareef's boots, and he watched it idly. Footsteps rang on the asphalt, and the young man looked up quickly, snapping his goggles back over his eyes. The world turned green, and things that had been hidden came alive in his vision. Two mangy cats prowled at a garbage bin in the alleyway across from him, while rats crept under the fog, scurrying to their nightly work. Shareef turned the goggles up the street, a hand adjusting the reach as he faced the sound of footsteps. His tense shoulders slumped again and he leaned back in the alcove, a petulant grimace cutting across his face. A man and woman paced up the road, arms entwined and faces close. Their heads drew closer, low laughter came from the woman, and Shareef shoved his goggles back up onto his forehead. That certainly wasn't what he was looking for. He sighed again and shifted his weight, his muscles aching from standing here for hours. For a few minutes he amused himself by estimating how long till Otar showed up to relieve him. But it wasn't a cheery calculation, and he didn't stick to it long. He ran a hand through his thick red hair and realized it was damp from the clinging humidity of the night.

Footsteps thudded on the street again. Shareef lowered his goggles and adjusted the focus. His hand froze, poised on the side of his goggles. A man paced up the street. He was of medium build, straight brown hair, ordinary features, blunt nose. Nothing remarkable about him, except what he carried. The man held a jar loosely in his hands, letting it swing as he walked easily along. Shareef's goggles lit the interior of the jar a macabre glowing red, identifying the undulating liquid. Blood. Shareef's face steeled and he stood still, watching. Slowly his hand shifted down till it rested on his jaw.

"Atif, you there?" Shareef said softly. The sound, like the light, was absorbed by the thick humidity that seemed to wrap the world in its grip.

"'Agent Two, reporting,' is what I should hear," Atif's dry voice vibrated up Shareef's jawline to his hearing, and the supply man rolled his eyes.

"Reporting sighting of interesting subject," Shareef said, keeping his voice low as he watched. The man reached the hoverer. He walked around it, a little smile on his face as he admired the symmetry. "Not Simmons. He has a jar of blood." Nothing came over his feed.

The door behind Shareef cracked open, swirling the fog away and letting a whiff of cool air into the night. The supplier glanced behind him, even though he knew who he would see. Atif's black leather greatcoat was absent and his feet were bare. But that was the only sign he had come from bed. His Healy laser pistols still hung at his side. He stopped beside Shareef, staring from the shadows of their doorway. The man finished pacing around the hoverer. His finger pushed the button and the clear protective bubble slid smoothly into its grooves, leaving the vehicle's interior accessible. He dropped into the driver's seat, an appreciative smile still on his face.

"Do you know him?" Shareef murmured.

"Nicklaus Tarter," Atif answered. "Underling to Simmons. Usually called Nicky." The two stood silent in the shadows, watching the man in the hoverer. Nicky ran a hand over the starter, checking the water levels and eyeing the machinery visible through the clear sheeting. Atif's hand went to his pocket, sliding around the tracker. His finger pushed the little gadget on. It began to vibrate, ever so softly in his palm, sensing even the slight movements Nicky's weight made in the vehicle. Nicky reached into his coat and came out again with a latex glove on one hand. He reached for the jar by his side.

"That's a really big sample to use for the DNA starter," Shareef muttered as the hoverer flickered to life, headlights piercing through the fog and coils softly humming as they heated. Atif just nodded. The hoverer's heating coils only turned on when it sensed its owner's DNA pushing the starter; it would seem Simmons was no longer a threat. The vehicle rose, hissing gently, spun in a neat 180, and shot off. Atif drew the tracker from his pocket. Its screen lit the alcove with white light as a map congealed in front of his face. A single red dot pulsed rhythmically in the middle of the gridded map, flying toward the edges of the city. Atif allowed himself a smile. Nicky hadn't noticed the tracker as he retrieved the property of a man who was no longer alive, making certain there were no loose ends for people to start wondering and investigating. The sleek, expensive hoverer would be going to the head of the snake. And they could follow it.

Anna's voice wove through the crowd like a breath of joy over a funeral march. Slumped shoulders straightened and dull eyes brightened. The lyrics spoke of hope, a folk song of the Sojourners dealing with mountains and travelers and late returns. But hope moved through every word. Anna reached the end of the second verse, the songspinner waiting for news of the travelers, and let her voice falter. The crowd gathered around the wagon stood still and hushed, waiting to hear if the hoped for return would be dashed or joy would come.

Joe launched into his rhythm dance. The mute spun and kicked in the midst of the wood and metal, his boots scraping over gravel and singing against drumheads. Energy burst from the sounds, exploding into the hushed crowed. Every eye grew wide and jaws dropped to their thin chests. Anna picked up the song, her voice strong and joy lacing it with the sweetness of honey on dry toast. The songspinner's travelers made it back to hearth and home.

Nehemiah stood at the back of the makeshift stage and his fingers flew over the violin's fingerboard, his bow darting over the strings. But his eyes watched the people, analyzing the Kingdom of Walden through its citizens. He decided he was glad this was a small country. He laid his violin gently against the wagon and hopped into the rhythm makers to join Joe in a duet. The two boys spun and kicked around each other, blurs of blond hair and black curls. The crowd surged into wild enthusiasm, the cheers almost drowning out the rhythm.

Song followed song, ringing through the outskirts of town, and more people flowed out to join the crowd. By the time the last note ended, it looked as if the whole city gathered on the plain around them. Joe and Nehi took Anna's hands and dipped into a theatrical bow. The volume of the applause rose to deafening, drowning out Beau's final words as announcer for the troupe. Daniel grimaced at the volume as he dumped his third collection bag into the bowl at the edge of the stage. Only a few coins clinked into the bowl, a very small amount for this many people. But then the citizens looked like they barely had enough for supper.

The noise changed to a dull roar as the people began to slowly unpack themselves, grudgingly accepting the end to the concert. Joe hopped off the stage and reached for the bowl. He stuffed a handful of coins in one pocket and trotted for the wagon.

"Hey," Daniel called, "we should be splitting that." Joe paused and blinked at him, obviously considering the idea.

"Your concerts are our best means of income, Joseph Music-Maker–" Nehi started, but Joe cut him off.

"Don't call me that!" His hands cut through the air, his face pale and eyes burning. Nehi stopped midsentence, his mouth slightly open in surprise. Joe's eyes closed, he spun with his back to the others to grab up the violin, and then spun back again. His expression was bland and normal, his color back as he tucked the instrument under his arm and signed again. "D, that makes sense. Right now I'm going to do some shopping for all of us, so I'll take that handful as joint funds. Count the rest of the takings and split it. Even portion for each musician? You decide." The mute spun back to the wagon and stepped inside to put the instrument away.

"Take my grocery list off the counter!" Anna called after him. The mute gave a whistle to show he heard and hopped out the door, flipping his hoverboard under his feet as he moved. Joe wooshed off toward town, white steam trailing behind him.

"Verily, he waits for no companion," Wiglaf commented, watching the mute disappear into the dirty streets.

"Of course not," Daniel said, "because he's doing more than just grocery shopping, and he doesn't want any of us along to find out what."

"Help," Beau rumbled, his head jerking toward the rhythm makers. Nehi hopped down to help him clean up, carefully silent. Curiosity burned through him and he longed to be behind Joe on that board. But he didn't want to give Daniel the satisfaction of gloating over it.

Joe shifted through the quiet streets, keeping his speed high. Their concert had emptied most of the buildings, he knew, but there were always people ready to ambush you here. Ready to cut your throat for a single coin. His board took him steadily higher up the central hill. The opulent houses rested at the top of the city, staring down at the derelict buildings massed below. His errand today lay at the very top.

In the most expensive house in the city, Ariel Athenia sat at her desk, bent over a magnifying glass. Sill air and complete silence rested around her, the heavy velvet curtains drawn to keep the stink of the city from drifting through the cracks. She touched the delicate yellowed page under the magnifying glass with a gloved finger, shifting it to a better position.

"It was not nice to turn me over to the Battle Kingdom."

The voice came from the darkness behind her, deep, mechanical, and inhuman. Ariel sat up slowly, her spine straight. She didn't turn around. Her smooth hand casually flicked a photograph over her shoulder. It settled on the carpet, in easy view of the darkened corner.

"You changed our plans," she said, each word slow, cold iron. "And I know you have seen Wolf, my agents are equipped with the latest technologies to bring me information. You thought you could play me, Raven, and you are wrong. I meant you to die in an agony of memory and mangled blood. It was not nice of you to escape alive."

"Your anger against Wolf poisons you to all other thoughts," the automated voice said from the darkness. "There are other ways to be true to our alliance then to bring death."

"Death is better than the Wolf deserves!" Ariel snarled, spinning in her chair, her long blond hair flashing behind her like gold in the dim lighting. She could see nothing in the darkness of the corner. Not even a vague form. "That monster dumped me, after promising everything! Me!"

"I sent you word of other things besides vengeance," the Raven's automated voice came from the shadows. Ariel froze, her jaw tightening, and her expression suddenly uncertain. "There is more at stake. You and I alone know about the treasure. We kill now, we lose that. All of that."

"You are certain of your facts?"

"I am."

"It would be easy for me to assume you are creating this to draw me along with your own plans."

"You cannot be drawn anywhere against your own desires. I know you have double checked my facts."

"And gained only rumors and vague hints!" Frustration creased Ariel's perfect face, drawing lines over her features. Silence fell around the room, deep and complete. It dragged on into a minute, then two. Manicured fingernails clicked against the desktop in impatience.

"You offer me nothing, Raven."

"You know what I have to offer. I need not add to it."

"Why are you here?"

"Stop trying to kill me." Was it her imagination, or did those stinted, automatic words come quickly; as if the Raven spoke in frustration, anger even? A smile twitched over Ariel's face. She had a way of getting under powerful people's skin. And for all his shadows and secrets, the Raven wielded more power than most world leaders ever dreamed of. "If we work together we have a chance at vengeance and the treasure."

"We had a plan earlier." Her perfect hand waved at the photograph, lying on the carpet. "You changed it, why should I listen to you now?"

"We both grew impatient. I learned facts I did not know before, and now we need to move slowly. We must have the coordinates only Wolf holds. We cannot get that without a powerful lever."

"And what kind of 'lever' do you think the Wolf will listen to?" Ariel scoffed, a little snort of laughter lacing the words. "Wolf needs nothing, heeds nothing, except his own pleasure."

"So we use the Wolf as our lever."

Silence fell again in the room. Ariel sat rigid, her beautiful mouth in a tight frown, her brow knit as she considered the words. A cube an inch square, clattered onto the desk beside her hand.

"A token of my trust," the Raven's automated voice said. "Now you can know where I am, anywhere in the world."

“And if it vibrates?” Ariel said, pushing the cube with a perfect finger. “I know what this was made for. A distress signal for a special agent; discontinued because it only sent word, it could not bring help in time.”

“A pity the inventor of that cube could not move at the speed of light.”

Again Ariel froze, her gaze riveted on the black cube. She thought she alone outside Wolf's picked few knew of the SOLTD. Did the Raven know she had agents occupied with the theft of a SOLTD, right now? Of course he did. This cube held no importance, it was just an excuse to ease into the conversation. He wanted her to remember he knew every action she took, and could snuff out her life from the shadows in a second if he chose.

"Work with me," the automatic words came from the darkness. “We will trap a Wolf, and gain a treasure like our world has never seen.”

# Chapter Sixteen: Flour and Slugs

*"Wherefore we receiving a kingdom which cannot be moved, let us have grace, whereby we may serve God acceptably with reverence and godly fear: For our God is a consuming fire."*
*Hebrew 12:28-29*

Nehemiah trotted over the short grass, glad to get away from Wiglaf's ceaseless questions for a little while. He glanced up from the blueprint of the wagon, trying to decide how to prove to Joe that there were better ways to fix a wind bubble than banging on it with a hammer. Black curls blew into his face and he staggered to a stop. Nehemiah stepped back, spitting out hair. Anna spun toward him, her mass of curls bobbing around her, two locks sticking straight up from her head. The claw cut would look nice enough after it had a month or two to grow into itself. Right now, on a humid day it seemed to have a life independent of Anna.

"Shh!" Anna hissed. She spun and leaned around the back of the wagon. The hammering started again from above them. Nehemiah leaned around his sister's shoulder and tried to see around her hair. There was nothing there.

"What are you watching?" he whispered.

"Joe," Anna hissed back. "Now shush!"

"He's on the wagon top, can't you hear the hammering?"

"I know! But he always jumps off right there!" Anna pointed, and Nehemiah saw a bulge in the grass. A week from the battle kingdom had brought them into a land of short grass and stunted trees. The grass came up in clump-fulls when you touched it, perfect stuff for hiding things.

"I don't get it," he whispered. Anna's hands flew up and she spun on him in exasperation.

"He bought me four times the flour I asked for, all right, and then left in midsentence when I was trying to tell him. Now shut up, you'll give us away!"

"But..." Nehemiah caught Anna's glare and shut up. The

hammering stopped overhead. Anna leaned around the corner, tense with anticipation. A mute sized shadow fell over the bulge in the grass, and Joe dropped off the wagon.

A soft, "poof" lifted into the air, and with it a cloud of fine white dust. A hacking cough spilled from Joe, and kept going, coughing and coughing, as he staggered away covered in fine flour. Anna gave a shout of triumph and Nehemiah started laughing. White covered the mute, only his blinking eyes showing any color. Every step left a white boot print, as he reeled and hacked.

He spun toward Anna, flicking his hands at her. She squealed and ducked, leaving her brother exposed. Nehi just glimpsed white, and the cloud from Joe's hands spurted into his face. Flour sailed up his nose and down his throat. A cough rent from him, and he pulled back, laughing and sneezing. Joe darted forward and Anna leapt away, shrieking in fun and scampering over the grass, her skirts flaring in the sunlight and curls bouncing. Joe sped off after her, trailing flour.

The next night, Nehemiah turned the corner of the wagon, rubbing his hands on his pants to get the last of the grease off. A warning click came from above him, and Nehi froze, his head jerking up. Joe perched on the wagon top, his legs hanging off as he leaned precariously forward. A bucket hung from his hands. A trail of green, algae infested water dribbled over the side as he tried to balance it on the raven peg right above the door. The mute pulled his hands away, staring at the bucket. It jiggled, but stayed. He turned to Nehi, a brilliant grin on his face.

"Anna!" Daniel bellowed from by the campfire, in front of the wagon. "Where are the potatoes, the coals are ready!" The wagon door flew open and Anna stepped onto the stair, her arms full of potatoes.

The wagon shifted with her movement.

Green, sludgy water cascaded over Anna. Nehi just caught a

glimpse of her face, tightening in shock, horror, and anger. The silver bucket clanged over her head, green water spraying. She staggered off the step, slipping in algae, potatoes rolling everywhere.

"Joe!" she roared, her voice muffled and echoing from the bucket. Nehemiah's guffaw covered Joe's huffing, breathy laugh as his legs disappeared over the wagon top, removing himself from the scene. Anna shoved at the bucket, growling out threats, and Nehemiah did his best to swallow his laughter.

"It's Nehi," he chuckled as he stepped up next to her and tried to grab the slimy bucket. "Don't hit me."

"Oh, I'm not going to hit him," her voice came muffled and furious. The bucket slid off with a wet slurping sound. Anna straightened up, algae sailing into the air as she flicked her wet hair out of blazing eyes "That's much too simple, no, Joe gets something very special for this one. This means war!" She spun on her heel and stomped into the wagon, a strand of slimy green trailing from one foot. Nehemiah grinned and turned to gather up the potatoes.

"Anna!" Daniel bellowed again. "The coals are ready!" Nehemiah put the bucket under the tap on the outdoor cylinder, sloughed it relatively clean, dumped the potatoes in, sprayed in more water, and trotted around the wagon. The last few rays of the setting sun cut into his face, and he smiled, his eyes tracing the deep gold, reds, and purples painted on the sky. "Where's Anna?" Daniel grunted, interrupting Wiglaf's question about the shape of the continents, and Nehi pulled his eyes back down from the horizon. A bright campfire twinkled, holding back the night. Four pairs of eyes turned to him, Joe's just as innocent as the others. Nehemiah didn't bother to hold back his grin.

"She'll be a while," he answered, and plunked the bucket beside his brother.

"They're all wet!" Daniel complained.

"Better than green," Nehi shrugged. A snort came from Joe, and Daniel spun to look at him suspiciously. But the mute just stared innocently at the fire, slumped and relaxed, his blond

hair tousled. Nehemiah walked around the fire and dropped onto the soft grass beside his friend, watching the sparks trail into the sky. "You're in for it now," he murmured to the mute. "Anna's declared war."

"Oh, she already started the war," Joe signed at him, his motions cutting sharp lines in the air, "what do you think the bucket was for? That was just my first offensive move." Nehemiah groaned and slumped back.

"Booby-traps are going to start popping up everywhere!" he complained, laughter lacing the words. Joe grinned at him and turned back to watching the coals sparkle.

Anna strolled toward the campfire as Wiglaf and Cobeau were busily rolling the steaming potatoes out of the coals, their sticks glowing as they poked and prodded, and Wiglaf asking if you could start a fire with a laser beam. Daniel glanced up as he sat out the butter and spices. Nehemiah was the only one that tensed, his eyes darting from the mute to his sister and back again.

"You're all wet too," Daniel commented. "What is this, a water epidemic?"

"Just a mistake," Anna said, smiling sweetly; but fire still sparkled in her eyes. "It will be dealt with soon." She settled on the log beside Daniel and began to help divvy out dinner, cheerily answering Wiglaf's question about water compression and ignoring Joe. The mute stared at the fire, watching the way it danced and dived and hissed and spun. Dinner was uneventful and yummy. The cleanup happened mostly by the licking flames, as darkness spread around them. Gradually the company broke up, Anna drifting off to bed, Beau, Daniel, and Wiglaf gathering their blankets and settling on the more even ground on the far side of the wagon.

Joe and Nehemiah stayed beside the fire. The dark deepened. Night insects and animals slowly invaded the air. Stars began to twinkle out of the heavens. Nehemiah slumped off the log and leaned against it, staring up at the sky, a smile on his face. The wood settled with a hiss and a pop, and the fire

spluttered. Joe tossed on another log. The two boys just sat, silent and easy with the quiet company. No, more than easy. It felt good. The fire danced, the stars twinkled, and neither considered leaving. A low hum drifted from Nehemiah, a hymn about God's creation of the world. Joe's face softened into a smile. He listened for a while, then his finger flicked at the flames.

"I think I have them now," he signed, sitting back and easing his shoulders.

"What?" Nehi blinked, bringing his thoughts back with difficulty. Joe gave him a look, and he grinned at the mute. Then paused, because he had understood it. That look said, *"You've been off in your head someplace like you always do, it's really annoying to have to wait for you to come back."* He and Joe had gotten pretty tight for a look to mean that.

"I've been studying the fire, the way it moves and seems to live and die at the same time," Joe signed. "I think I can draw it now. But I don't know what I would name the picture."

"'Consuming fire,'" Nehemiah supplied. Joe's head tilted, asking why, and Nehemiah gave him the whole quote. "'For our God is a consuming fire[10].'"

"Oh. It says that?"

"Yes."

"Not very comfortable."

"Depends on what God consumes. After He's done with us, we're more like we should be, which makes us more comfortable."

"True," Joe signed, nodding. Silence drifted companionably back between them. The two boys sat on, watching the stars twinkle and the fire dance. Gradually the flames died out, and only the coals glowed red in the darkness. Nehemiah turned on his side on the clumpy grass and let out a long yawn.

"You're going into the wagon first in the morning," he murmured, and Joe's teeth showed in the darkness as he grinned.

---

[10] Hebrews 12:29

"I'm keeping out of this war if I can manage it."

"So, Joe..." Daniel drawled, glancing down at the wagon seat. Joe's back was towards him, and he didn't see the mute's eyes close, his mouth tightening. By now the mute knew the mood those words portended. "We're only a few days from the People's Kingdom, how about you tell us something about it? Maybe, you know, explaining beforehand for once instead of waiting till we're in the middle of it with no chance of backing out."

"What's to explain?" Joe signed with a shrug, pivoting on the wagon seat to look up at the eldest Hillson. His blank, defensive mask lay over his face like a blanket. It covered the mute every time Daniel spoke to him. Beau's translating rumble rolled around the little group, filling the wind bubble. "You've traveled, you even trained for the judgeship, why are you asking me about it?"

The two glared, Daniel's eyes narrowed and Joe blank. Nehi and Anna glanced at each other as Wiglaf's eyes turned to the sky, attempting to ignore it politely, again. Daniel's question and not-answer sessions cropped up a lot during these three weeks of travel.

"Most people, if they say they trust someone," Daniel drawled, "don't worry about telling them things. What are we doing here really? Is it about that crossed lover you've mentioned, surely you have to meet with them to stay coordinated in this Wolf hunt?"

"Most people, if they travel over the world with someone, don't keep assuming they're the devil incarnate," Joe signed, apparently at ease. But Anna saw a muscle twitch on his jaw. Memories of Nehemiah's hurt fuming after he prodded the angry fox Joe alive swarmed into her mind, and her imagination had no problems inserting Daniel's reaction into the slot. The air in their wind bubble seemed suddenly cold.

"Dan, why don't you come help me with a trifle?" she burst out. "The wild strawberries Wiglaf found for us yesterday aren't going to slice themselves!"

"Why don't you two see anything suspicious in his silence?" Daniel asked, spinning on the twins.

"Suspicious, or just infuriated by your caustic grumpiness?" Nehi yawned, splayed over the back of the wagon top with his eyes closed. He could almost feel Daniel bristle, and he smiled. "No offense of course. We wouldn't have you any other way. You wouldn't be our Danny if you were warm and cuddly."

"And you are our Dan," Anna cut in, slipping her arm through her older brother's and giving it a squeeze. "We're your family, we've learned to like your grumpiness, you old goat."

"We grew up with it, Joe and Co and Wiglaf haven't," Nehemiah said and let it turn into another lazy yawn. "Life would be missing something without your barbed comments."

"I like that," Daniel complained, "I'm just trying to save your oblivious skins from this nasty little scavenger and all I get are insults!"

"Because you never make barbed comments or insults," Nehemiah grinned, his eyes still closed. Daniel's finger waggled at him as he growled.

"If you insist on hanging around these Ravens–"

"Oh stop," Anna interrupted, and tugged on his arm. "Come on, help me with the strawberries like a good old goat and leave Joe alone for a while."

"'Old goat,'" Daniel snorted, shifting to his hands and knees and scuttling after Anna. He spun back to the general company and shook another finger at them. "I am not old!" Daniel let a little smile quirk over his face as he listened to the chuckles, and dropped through the skylight, muttering to himself. "I still trust him less every time he doesn't answer my questions."

"No wonder you think he's a horrid character then," Anna commented as she pulled out the paring knives, "you get after him five times a day."

"Do not," Daniel said, and one shoulder lifted in a shrug.

"Only three or four times. I want the blue handled one, it works best for me. Where are these strawberries that we're trifling?" Anna pulled a cracked blue crock from under the single counter, a faded yellow dish cloth flapping at the movement as it lay over the old dish. The wagon's movement changed, beginning to slow down, and she braced herself absently.

"We need to use the cream so–" Anna's words cut off into a stifled shriek and Daniel spun around, the blue handled knife twisting into an underarm hold, his arm going up ready to stab into someone's throat. Anna's hand covered her mouth, her face pale under her olive skin, as she stared in the crock. Daniel leaned over her shoulder.

A slug oozed and sludged in the dish. It curled around itself, its own gel squishing and splashing up the sides of the crock.

"Dang. That thing must be two feet if it stretched out," Daniel commented. Anna made a noise and backed away. "I take it we're not trifling the slug." Another incoherent noise came from his sister, and Daniel grinned. Whatever else that little mute was, he was pretty good at practical jokes.

The artificial light in the night room spluttered and frittzed. Daniel leaned around the partition and glanced into the room, studying the light fixtures. A guffaw rang from Nehemiah, drifting through the open skylight. Wiglaf and Cobeau's laugh melded with it, and Daniel looked back at Anna. One hand was over her stomach, but her color was back again.

"There, I already got him back for it," she said.

"What did you do?" Daniel asked.

"Just a little rewiring job, on the wind bubble stick. I expected him to use it this evening though, not already."

"You know how to rewire a stick?" Daniel blinked.

"I can read a blueprint too, thank you very much. Now take that hideous thing out of here while I find out where Joe put the strawberries and see how marvelous his hair looks after his little shock." Daniel grabbed the crock and headed for the door, grumbling about how hard it was to stay out of trouble in this wagon; but as he turned his back to Anna he let another smile onto his face and glanced back at the slug. He turned to his sister, scrambling through the skylight. "Send Nehi down here!"

"I hear you, Dan," Nehemiah's voice drifted to him. The light dimmed, then cleared, and a heavy thump rang beside Daniel as Nehi dropped down. Daniel tipped the crock toward him. "Whoa, that's a big slug," Nehemiah said. His eyes lit up. "Hey, we're headed toward a pond for the campsite tonight!"

"Perfect. I'll take half, you take the other foot, and we'll see who gets the biggest fish."

"You're on!"

"Does your little suspicious friend need a hunk of this thing?"

"No, Joe doesn't like fishing," Nehi said. A grin cut over him, and he poked at the giant bug oozing in the dish. "But you do. Which means I get you to myself for a while, and for a few hours don't have to try to defuse arguments or watch for trip wires. Believe me, I'm looking forward to that."

"Ok, little brother," Daniel nodded, "it's been over a month since we went fishing. I'll let you jabber to your heart's content. But if you get eaten by your catch with this sucker, I might just let the fish swim off with you, to enjoy the quiet."

Nehemiah laughed and headed to go find their equipment.

# Chapter Seventeen: Chimera Keepers

*"They shall not build, and another inhabit; they shall not plant, and another eat...and mine elect shall long enjoy the work of their hands."* Isaiah 65:22

When they crossed into the People's Kingdom, the land became a place of swamps and dark pines. Not the Story Land swamps of cypresses and tropical flowers the size of a grown man, these were dark oozing pools that bubbled and smelled foul. The pines stood alone, with very little growth around the vast trunks. No stately beeches, soft aspens, or graceful willows eased the stark straight trunks. It was only towering, dark pines. They were thick trunked and straight, rising sometimes two hundred feet, with bark so dark it looked almost black. Their outspread needles were hard and deep, deep green. Menace seemed to drip from the forest. The bubbling, sucking swamps underneath the dark boughs made the menace a reality. A misstep in this forest could easily be fatal.

But in the night the dark trees swayed with the slight wind, allowing glimpses of the silvery sky to shine down, and in the quiet Nehi could hear the hard needles tinkling like thousands of tiny windchimes. It wasn't so bad at night, he decided as he lay on his back, staring up at the stars. Joe sat a few feet away hugging his knees, his eyes on the sky. They sat still, enjoying a constellation party, a little ways from the wagon so as not to wake Wiglaf, Beau, and Daniel; and to escape the medley of snoring. They rarely had one for the old reasons. Tonight it was an hour stolen before they turned in with the others, a breath of quiet after another busy day.

Joe didn't think Nehi knew his extra reason. The pain still kept him awake. The wound on his back healed, but slowly, more slowly than it should. His bone-deep bruises from the arena still persisted and ached hardest when he laid down to sleep. Joe tried not to think about it, especially about the weakness that clung to his limbs, intertwined with his aches and

pains from the desperate fighting. It was easier not to think about it with Nehi near. And it was really nice to just stop for a moment, to sit still and breathe, with a friend to keep his mind off it and give him company through the night hours.

But the quiet didn't last.

A piercing, yowling shriek rent the summer night. It hung on the air, enfolding them in a creepy, fear-stricken sound. Nehi's back arched as his arms shoved against the damp grass, vaulting him to his feet. He stood rigid beside Joe, staring into the darkness to their left, and Nehemiah found he had Hope in his hands. Footsteps pounded over the needle covered ground from the wagon, and Nehemiah heard Daniel's quick pant just before his brother's hand landed on his shoulder.

"What was that?" Daniel muttered. Wiglaf stepped beside him, his sharp eyes slitted as he tried to stare through the blackness under the trees. The sound came again, piercing through the dark. The four men drew closer, huddling together under the trees, spines crawling. The yowl lasted longer this time, long enough for Nehi to notice it had an eerie mix of a woman's scream and a creature's terrified wail.

"A runner caught," Joe signed, Nehi translating. The mute's hands cut through the air in swift, almost vicious movements, his face stiff, hard, eyes bright and calculating. He looked over at Cobeau, showing against the darkness in a black hump, snoring rhythmically. The mute clicked contemplatively, trying to decide what to do. The shriek sounded again, even louder than before.

"I know not what that is," Wiglaf said, his face pale and determined, "but I own it is a creature in need of succor. I will not stand idle and let them suffer when I have breath in my body and a strong sword!" Joe sighed, his eyes still on Cobeau, and nodded.

"Let's go quickly then," Nehemiah said, flicking his goggles over his eyes and flipping the safety off Hope. Joe shook his head adamantly.

"You Hillsons stay here," he signed to Nehemiah, and Nehi

translated for Daniel. “If it comes this way we need someone awake at our wagon, Glue and Beauty aren’t stirring. Harness up Prissy so we’re ready to leave.”

“And you don’t want us with you,” Daniel growled. The yowl sounded again. A desperate, hopeless scream of terror. Joe grabbed Wiglaf’s arm and the two disappeared into the trees surrounding their camp. Daniel strode after them, his face angry and suspicious, but Nehemiah grabbed the back of his greatcoat and began to tug him toward the wagon.

“There’s a lot of sense in what he says,” Nehemiah reasoned. “Anna and Beau don’t wake up for anything. And if I’m going to be on guard I want you here too, with whatever that is wandering the forest. Besides I’m not sure I want to see what’s causing that shrieking sound.” Daniel pulled away and glared at his brother.

“And what were you two talking about all by yourselves in the dead of night?” he growled. Nehemiah began to get Prissy’s harness together as he answered calmly.

“Stars, Daniel. Nothing but stars and the Lord that made them.”

“Are you sure?”

“I don’t keep things back from my brother, and I don’t lie either!” Nehemiah snapped.

“I’m sorry, I shouldn’t have suggested that.” The words came fast, and the tone held none of Daniel’s usual causticness; it was embarrassed, apologetic, humble even. “I didn’t mean it, honest. But you have to admit, it’s just a little weird you two sneaking off into your own clearing. Again. It’s not like this is the only time, I’ve noticed.”

“Even you snore like a sick pig after your allergies kick in,” Nehi grimaced. “And have you heard Beau and Wiglaf? They sound like caterwauling lions with nasal issues.”

“Ok, ok.” A deep sigh flew from the eldest Hillson as he dug for Prissy’s wheeled shoes under the seat. He paused, leaned over the giant pig, and looked at his brother in the dim moonlight. “It’s just that I…thunderation, I like you Nehemiah Hillson,

and I'm worried that little mute is getting to you. I'm afraid you're going to be heartbroken by him one day. And Anna! You know, I've caught a look in her eyes during this idiotic prank battle of theirs. I'm afraid he's getting to her even worse than to you."

"Is that such a bad thing Dan, honestly?" Nehemiah burst out, throwing the harness over Prissy and getting it straightened out. "Joe might not tell us much, but he's saved all of our lives by now, and is a strong Christian brother. You know how brave he's been fighting for the IDP."

"I know what I've heard from Joe about how brave he's been fighting for the IDP," Daniel answered as they strapped the harness onto the giant pig. "How do you know any of it is true? How do you know what he really does in that Black Raider outfit of his? Has he ever taken you along? All right, yes, there was the time in the Prophet's Peace. But one time out of so many? It could have easily been setup for your benefit. You know, I wouldn't be too surprised to see him come back alone with a story about how Wiglaf ended his life bravely out there in the woods." The piercing shriek sounded again and Nehemiah jumped and dropped the buckle he was handling. A form shot out of the trees. In the darkness all they could tell was that it was alone.

"Ravenswing has sent me back for the Great-Chested one, we need his strength," Wiglaf called. Nehemiah breathed again and darted toward the chimera.

"Wait, Wiglaf, waking up Beau is dangerous." Nehemiah swept up a tall weed, using it to tickle the large flapping ear of the chimera. Beau swiped at his ear. The weed kept on, and he stirred and mumbled for 'master to let him sleep.' The shriek sounded again, farther away this time, and Wiglaf hissed at him to hurry. Nehemiah dropped the plant and kicked Cobeau in the shin, leaping back in almost the same move, and just barely getting out of range of the chimera's huge sweeping arms as he reached for whatever unknown danger woke him up. The shriek came and Cobeau stood up, his tousled hair making his grim face a thing out of a horror story.

"Joe's gone after it, Beau," Nehemiah told him, knowing a mention of Joe would be the quickest way to get the fuzzy headed man moving. "He needs you to go with Wiglaf." A moment later the two men were gone, melting into the trees as if they were a part of the blackness of the night. Daniel and Nehemiah finished hooking up Prissy and climbed into the wagon seat to wait, their earlier conversation dismissed by silent consent. Two long minutes ticked by.

"I miss them." Nehemiah's voice came small, the sorrow it carried more than a passing thing. It rolled out of him from an empty place in his soul, carved out by the ones gone. Daniel didn't move for a long moment.

"Me too," he murmured. It drifted out like an echo, bouncing from Nehi's own well of mourning for his parents, and Nehi drew in a deep breath. It was comforting just to know someone else still felt that, even after two years. Daniel stirred, easing his position on the wagon seat. "But God is still good." Nehemiah's head snapped up. He turned slowly, watching his brother, his face working with something, Daniel couldn't quite decide what.

"Did you struggle with... I mean, that's kind of a telling response," Nehemiah said lamely, his courage deserting him. Joe had found him in his weakest, with everything still raw and bleeding. Now, with time and growth behind him, Nehemiah found it hard to talk about the doubts and brokenness even with his brother. A smile twitched over Daniel's face. But it wasn't humor.

"I know what you mean," he drawled, and leaned back, staring at something high up in the trees. "It was when Uncle Adam died. I was about your age, a little younger I guess. We were pretty close. And it was so senseless!"

"Boating accident, right?" Nehemiah asked quietly.

"Ever wondered why Dad never liked fishing with you?" Daniel said. A tingle ran through Nehemiah. Of course, how could he have been so stupid never to see it? He suddenly

wondered what else he didn't know about his parents. What else he would never know, now they weren't here to ask. He drew in a breath again, forcing it to fill his lungs, reminding himself he would have the chance to ask later, when he met Jesus face to face. His eyes darted back to Daniel. His brother shrugged. "Oh, I think you know the way it goes. 'How could God let it happen?' 'Can He really be good?' 'Does any of it really matter, is it actually true?' 'Why did he have to die?' That's the real one that revolves and revolves, right?" Nehemiah just nodded, his throat tight, finding it hard to reply. "Dad kept spouting that vision speech of his. That was when it evolved, really, you and Anna grew up with it, but it sprouted out of Uncle Adam's death. Dad never had to work through it. Everything was just the way it was for him. Suffering was here because of sin, but sin didn't have the victory, and we are all going to win out in the end and get to Jesus' side. Faith that never wavered, that was Dad. And Mom."

"And Anna," Nehemiah sighed. A snort of laughter, with no humor in it, burst from Daniel; a noise only he could give and not make Nehi bridle and want to punch him. From Daniel it was just...Daniel.

"That's sure true! But it's sometimes a blessing to let the doubts come."

"Really?"

"I bet you learned a lot through the process. Oh, I can tell you're through it. Probably have been since before you found me, right?"

"Yes. But it...sometimes in the dark, I remember the questions. I don't really give them much thought anymore, but..."

"They hover in the back of your mind, and break out at nasty moments, and you're left going, 'Where did that come from?'"

"Exactly!"

"Deal with it, brother. It doesn't leave."

"Some comfort you are," Nehemiah grumbled, slumping back.

"If you want comfort go to someone soft and cuddly," Daniel

grinned at him. Nehemiah punched his arm and Daniel gave a dramatic groan. But his voice came low and serious when he took up the conversation again. "I'm not saying it's easy. But useful things can sprout from the questions. For those of us who have to work through things... Well, I've decided it's not a bad way to be."

"Just don't let the doubts win. It felt like they did, at one point," Nehemiah admitted. "But even in the darkest moments, I wasn't alone. He never left me alone, even when I couldn't feel Him there. Nothing can trump that comfort."

"Yeah," Daniel said, his voice soft and a half smile quirked over his face. "Like a rebellious son, there may be times when the strictness seems overwhelming, but a few years later (with any luck) you see the love behind it."

"And suddenly that love shines like Jesus' hope revealed in the flesh."

Silence fell between the two as they sat waiting in the quiet, thinking. Daniel stirred and turned to face his brother.

"Did Mom and Dad ever give you anything particularly special growing up? I mean, something–"

A twig snapped to their left, and a tree limb rustled. Hope spun and leveled as Daniel's Brunhiem hummed red in the night. Four forms came flying out of the trees, one a dark blotch in Cobeau's arms. Nehi just had time to recognize the silhouette of Joe's tousled hair and Beau's huge form, then the Ravens rushed past his line of sight, the wagon blocking them out. Nehi leaned forward, trying to see. Joe wrenched open the cubby hole under the driver's seat where the Ravens hid Anna and Nehemiah the first night they met. Cobeau shoved his burden at the hole. It was so quick, neither of the Hillsons were able to see anything of the person, but when the door began to close a smooth feminine voice cried out.

"No smothering!" she whimpered.

"They are coming, Ravenswing," Wiglaf called, standing stiff by the trees. Joe jerked something from a pocket. Nehemiah heard a cork come out of a bottle, and suddenly felt nauseous and dizzy as he leaned over the wagon seat, trying to see into the cubby hole. Joe threw the bottle into the cubby and latched the door shut.

"I wouldn't want to be in a small place with that smell," Nehemiah commented. Joe shushed him with a quick, urgent motion, his can of anise spraying up a cloud, covering any scent of their guest. At the same moment he grabbed Cobeau and shoved him inside the wagon, signing something so quickly Nehi couldn't catch it in the moonlight. The mute scrambled onto the seat with Nehemiah and Daniel, shoved the primer down, and pushed the starter to release the water into the heating coils. The wagon spluttered, but hissed and rose steadily. Joe jerked their ride out of the damp grass, and they hovered down the road, Prissy's wheeled shoes rotating steadily and blowing out steam as the boilers heated. It took Nehemiah a moment to realize Wiglaf wasn't among them. He spun to look behind them, searching for the Geatish warrior.

A piercing white light shone on the wagon, powerful, painful, almost paralyzing. Prissy squealed in terror and hunched down on the road, her huge eyes wide with fright, and her chubby belly blocking her wheels. A wisp of white smoke curled into the night from her shoes rubbing frantically against her belly, and boiling water spluttered out of the boilers. Daniel hit the emergency cutoff to the pig's wheeled shoes.

"Hold, strangers!" someone ordered from behind the light. The voice rang through a megaphone, unnatural and metallic. "We are the Chimera Keepers, workers for the People's Kingdom. We have reason to suspect you have an escaped worker among you. Explain yourselves."

"Translate, Knee-High, make it good!" Joe signed, turning so his signs were made to the wagon back, making it look like he was just squirming to get the cutting light out of his face. As he glanced at him, Nehemiah saw fear shining through Joe's foolish blank look. It terrified him to see Joe scared. Joe began to sign secretly as he huddled in the driver's seat. Nehemiah swallowed and translated, allowing himself to seem to be the leader.

"We just entered your borders today. We are traveling musicians come to spread our happy sounds to our brothers here in the People's Kingdom. Are you looking for someone?" The white light held them in its blinding, unwavering glare, and Nehemiah closed his eyes to slits and turned his head.

"A happy worker has decided to move from her station without filing the proper papers," the voice said.

"I'll bet!" Joe signed viciously, then his green eyes darted up to Nehemiah, warning him not to translate that. *No kidding,* Nehi thought.

"Some of our CK's believe she is with you, and that you have another chimera in your company. An undeclared chimera."

"We have none such as you describe with us," Joe signed and Nehemiah translated. "We are all tired and wish to get our sleep for our first show to our brothers here. We would appreciate it if we could move on to our camp."

"You cannot move on till we are satisfied you are not deterrents to society's evolution," the metallic voice rattled. Joe's hands moved in a sign Nehemiah and Anna had carefully never asked the meaning of, but both understood the feeling behind just fine. Joe began to warily finger the laser rifle he and Cobeau kept beside the wagon's seat. Nehemiah tensed, hoping he could get to Hope in time to help their dash away. Then Joe's eyes fell on the quivering pig in the road. His fingers pulled away from the rifle, curling into fists so tight his knuckles turned white. They couldn't run for it, not with Prissy scared out of her wits by that blinding light.

"You will be searched, strangers, so we know you are brothers before you come farther into our borders." Soldiers in blue uniforms emerged from the light, as if spawned by the merciless, hurting glare. They strode toward the wagon, tall green hats making them seem misshapen, a gross parody of a human. A round badge stood out in the center of the hats, an illustration of a face, half a man's and half a vicious, snarling hog's. Joe's face stayed blank, as he blinked foolishly at the people. But Nehemiah knew him well enough now to see the desperation just

under the vacant veneer. Joe squirmed again, turning his back to the light as his head ducked, wincing. As soon as he faced the wagon his hands moved.

"Brothers, would we be coming into your borders if we were harboring this runaway?" Nehemiah translated as adamantly as he could. It still sounded fake; he needed to learn how to act better. "We would be trying to make a dash away from your borders, back into the wild lands." The metallic voice laughed.

"Dash? With that round, hairy creature?" it scoffed. Joe saw his point, and stopped trying to sign anything. Nehemiah felt a familiar clarity overtaking his mind as adrenaline started to pump through him. Whatever these efficient soldiers with the creepy insignia were up to, he didn't like it. He prayed fervently these blue uniformed soldiers wouldn't find the secret cubby hole. And especially wouldn't find Beau. They reached the back of the wagon and stared at the painted trees trying to figure out how to get the door open. Joe dropped to the ground, moved around to the back of the wagon, and pushed on the catch. The door swung out, almost hitting one. Four soldiers filed in without a glance at Joe.

Nehemiah shifted to the skylight, and he and Daniel peered into the day room at the soldiers prowling inside. Daniel's mouth moved in a humorless smile as he watched them sweep the few dishes that hadn't fit in the cupboard off the counter, smashing them into pieces and grinding them into the polished wood floor as they tromped about their business. The four soldiers began to pound their rifles into walls to look for secret compartments, heedless of the damage to the paintings. They found the icebox. They found the cupboard in the elm where they kept the dishes. They even found the tiny hole where Joe kept his spare pencils and notebooks. Nehemiah winced as he saw the hoarded papers (often Joe's only means of communication) rifled through, knocked out, and ground under heavy booted feet. They even found a cubby Nehemiah had never seen, filled with raven snacks and strange looking pouches.

Anna stepped out of the night room, the banging and clunking loud enough to even wake her up. Several of the soldiers looked at the pretty girl brushing her tangled hair out of her eyes, but they were too good at their work to do more than glance. They came to the little table underneath the oak. Joe tensed, his eyes shining in the darkness as he stared through the door. Nehemiah's fingers brushed Hope. A rifle swung down, ramming into the wall just above the first chair. A solid thunk sounded from the hardwood, ringing against the filled water cylinder resting inside the walls. The rifle swung back for another try, shifting farther under the table.

Joe stood rigid at the door, his knuckles white, nails digging into his palms. His face was blank, but inside he felt himself screaming. *Oh God, help!*

# Chapter Eighteen: Wara

*"But Jesus said, Suffer little children, and forbid them not, to come unto me: for of such is the kingdom of heaven."*

*Matthew 19:14*

Brothers, hold!" a voice bellowed from outside. The rifle paused in mid swing as the soldier looked up, staring past Joe as if the mute didn't exist. Nehemiah jerked up, searching the dark forest fringe for the speaker. A group of blue uniformed soldiers trotted out of the woods, a thickset man a little in the lead.

"We were wrong, brothers," the one in the lead called. "We have found her track, headed to the border. Move, we need speed." The soldiers obeyed with efficient skill. The wagon emptied in seconds, and blue-uniformed soldiers trotted in loose formation for the woods. The blinding light swept past the wagon, following the soldiers. The light switched off, and natural night fell around the Ravens wagon, the hum of the soldier's engine growing faint. Joe darted to Prissy, clicking to her comfortingly, getting her back on her tiny legs and flipping her shoes on again to start the water heating. He kept glancing at the dark trees surrounding them, and Nehemiah found he was doing the same. Where was Wiglaf? Joe clambered back onto the wagon's seat as Prissy started to roll. He looked at Nehi and signed, his movements small, still turned to the wagon seat.

"Tell Beauty to let him out, but he has to stay in the wagon."

Nehemiah moved quickly to the skylight and gave Anna Joe's message. Anna reached under the table and fingered a tiny knot on the oak painting. A click sounded, and Cobeau tumbled out onto Anna, nearly crushing her. She scrambled from underneath him, half gasping for breath and half laughing, and reached up for Nehemiah. Nehi pulled her up next to him, and Beau reached for the skylight too. Nehemiah shook his head.

"Joe says to stay inside, Beau," he told him. The cover for the skylight felt heavy and rough to Nehi as he closed it, and the

snap of the painted sun falling in place seemed to echo around them. His heart still raced, his senses sharpened. The twins scuttled over the wagon top toward Joe and Daniel, Nehemiah dropping into Beau's usual place on the seat beside the mute.

"Who were those people?" Anna asked.

"And who do we have underneath us?" Nehemiah added.

"Where's Wiglaf?" Anna asked.

"Here, my lady," Wiglaf panted behind them. They spun in their seats, Hope glinting as she sprang into Nehi's hand. Wiglaf heaved himself over the back of the moving wagon, blowing with exertion. Joe grinned at him, his face shining with the expression. He shoved the steering stick at Nehemiah and began to pump Wiglaf's hand up and down.

"It was no more then what you or Cobeau would have done, Ravenswing Ashe-Maker, if you had thought of it," the warrior said in embarrassment. In his quick way Joe pushed their speed up to three, slid the wind bubble up, and poked Anna's knee, requesting translation.

"I didn't think of it, you did. And your warrior-hunting skills were perfect for it, I wouldn't have been able to make a reliable track, especially that quick! Your swift thought and action saved my Glue tonight, and I will never forget it. You've earned yourself a sign, hero of the Geats, you are now Track-Maker." Wiglaf beamed and his shoulders squared. Homesickness flooded him at the simple speech. It reminded him of all the tales of great deeds that flitted from mouth to mouth in his country. If he were home it would have been second nature to stroll into the local thain's hall and casually tell the tale of how his wits saved the day. Joe gave his hand one final pump and turned back to the road.

"Well that was one question answered," Anna said, sliding over to allow the warrior room to sit beside her and Daniel. "Now what about the others, Joe?"

"Those were a group of the Chimera Keepers," Joe signed, his nose wrinkling and mouth twisting down, as if he had swallowed something nasty.

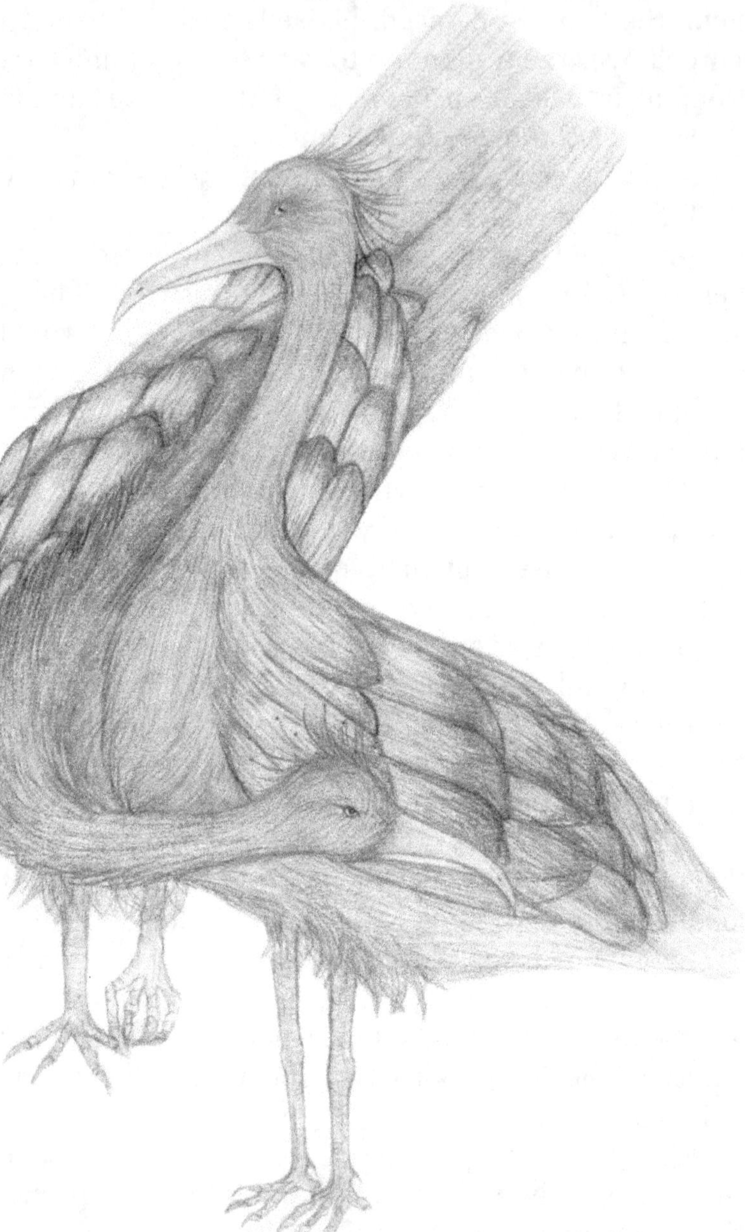

## *Chapter Eighteen: Wara*

*Matthew 19:14*

*Chapter Eighteen: Wara*
*Matthew 19:14*

*Green Backs*

"That tells us next to nothing," Nehemiah prodded. "This is one of the major countries, I know the book here states society is going to evolve into a classless utopia where everything is shared equally. A place where everyone lives like one big family, and no one is put down or raised up, and all work for the others' good. They're determined they've reached that point. (Except it just makes everyone but the ruling Brotherhood poor in reality because the sharing isn't equal no matter what they say.) I also know their little unofficial slogan, 'Blood will flow and society evolve'! But I haven't heard of these Chimera Keepers. Explain please?" Joe nodded, to Daniel's open-mouthed astonishment, and began to sign quickly, Anna translating for Daniel and Wiglaf.

"Everything has a use-value here. It's all valued by how well it can produce a profit. Classes are what drive evolution, the revolution of one class against another is what make society evolve, and economics is what drives the change in classes. So at the base it's economics making society evolve."

"What's this got to do with those soldiers?" Daniel interrupted. Anna shoved him in the shoulder and told him to be quiet and listen because Joe was explaining it to them. Joe ignored the interruption.

"Look," Joe signed, his eyes never still as he scanned the trees beside them, his body tense, "if everything you worked toward and everything you sweated for was immediately taken away from you, would you be motivated to work?" Four heads shook in the negative. "Neither are the citizens here. But the state needs work done. They could have solved the problem by forcing their citizens to work at gunpoint, and I hear they've done that in the past, but now they have a different method. They raise chimeras, and they grab the suitable genetic incompletes from the Advancers in KAM. They have what they call 'work stations' where they use them. The GIs don't usually last very long, the stations aren't exactly suited to a healthy life. Especially just starting out life as most of them are–"

"Were you grabbed like that? Is this where you started?"

Anna interrupted. Joe nodded.

"I was 903 in a station here, before I managed to run," he signed.

"Wait, 903," Nehi blinked, "'Joe?'"

"I wanted a name after I got out, and since that's what I had, that's what I used," Joe said, one shoulder rising in a shrug. "They don't care quite so much about an incomplete making a run for it, especially before they're old enough to be of real use. But the chimeras are sturdier, and being simpler they don't object to the slave labor as much. The bits of animal in them, I think, automatically makes them more willing servants. So the state here mainly relies on chimeras to get their work done. The Chimera Keepers are there to see their charges work as much as they can and don't leave. They do a pretty good job, and are not pleasant people. A few chimeras still have the guts to run, even with the CK always on the watch, but if they're caught they're made a good example for the others at the work station." Joe looked away suddenly, a steely blankness over him that spoke of deep trouble raging inside.

"And the lady we have underneath us is one of these brave few who run from these stations?" Wiglaf prompted. Joe looked up at him and nodded.

"And the first of your refugees, Track-Maker. As soon as the hunt has died down, I'm sending you back home with her," he signed. Wiglaf opened his mouth to say something, then closed it and sat back on the top of the wagon, staring at nothing, his forehead creased.

"And Beau?" Anna asked quietly.

"Glue wasn't a runner, not for himself. He was helping his brother and sister-in-law out. None of them made it. I was able to save him after the CK's got them back, but not the other two. I don't think Glue remembers any of it. I hope he doesn't. It would kill him to remember his brother."

"They said something about an undeclared chimera, what does that mean?" Nehemiah asked.

"It means they're always on the lookout for new workers,

theirs wear out pretty frequently. Glue's not really one because he was declared earlier in life. But if they find Glue, as a chimera he automatically gets reassigned to a station."

"Wait, if they have GI stations too are you in the same danger?" asked Nehi.

"Yes, but incompletes aren't as easily spotted as chimeras, and aren't as highly coveted," Joe signed.

"You mean you were out here signing in front of all those people and could have been...whatever you said, if they had noticed?" Anna broke in, her face a study of shocked horror.

"You should have mentioned that without prompting, Joe. It's sort of important to know we have to watch out for you too," Daniel said, anger underlying the words. Joe just shrugged, but he glanced back at Daniel through half-raised lids, as if he were trying to decide what lay behind the comment. Nehi couldn't really blame him. Silence came on the wagon. Dark trees loomed over them as they sped along the road, boggy mist drifting in tendrils from between black trunks.

"I still can't comprehend how one human being can be so evil to another," Nehemiah burst out. Joe's eyes snapped at him and Nehi was surprised to see frustrated anger taking him over, almost writhing in an inner flame of wrath as his hands moved in vicious, chopped signs.

"We aren't part of the human race, Knee-High, Chimeras and GIs aren't human. Haven't all your travels with us taught you that much?" he snapped.

"No," Nehemiah said. Joe's anger faded as suddenly as it had come. He slumped back and his head dropped against the wood of the wagon, his tense features melting into intense weariness.

"Me either," he signed, his movements small. If it had been words, Anna thought, it would have been a whisper.

"I do not understand," Wiglaf's deep voice rolled out and filled the air in the bubble. "You have told me that, contrary to what some of my countrymen believe, Cobeau Monster-Slayer is not one of the descendants of Cain, creatures of immense strength and questionable siring. Why do you speak of doubt in

the matter of his kinship to our race?" Joe looked away from the group quickly. Anna's position allowed her to see his face; he was fighting a snippy comeback, hot irritation and amusement colliding in him. She decided she should answer and let him alone for a few minutes.

"What Joe means, Wiglaf, is that most of the world believes in a fiction called evolution, which lets the people who believe it do a great deal of evil."

"It says humans are just animals, really, just smarter than most. That we changed over time from various things," Nehemiah picked up the thread, "including rocks and monkeys, to become what we are today. They think that humans are still changing, and many are trying to get us to rise to a higher state. Here, the concept is also applied to society. They believe incompletes–" Nehemiah stopped suddenly and began to murmur something about the world slipping up behind him and putting its terms into his mouth, and Anna finished the sentence for the confused Wiglaf.

"They believe those who are not physically perfect, especially who might have children that are not perfect, and people like Cobeau, are holding the race back from climbing to the next step. With the proper group of people, according to evolution, you should be able to hop forward to another race of beings that are greater than humans now."

"It means that anything lower than men, such as animals and anything they choose to classify as an animal, is both an inferior and an ancestor," Daniel took up. "And it says there is no Creator, God doesn't exist, which ultimately means there's no morals and you can declare what's right and wrong."

"Which of course denies Genesis 1:1," Anna put in, "and lots of other passages in the Bible too."

"Of your courtesy, my lady, what other passages?" Wiglaf asked, always ready to hear more of the Bible.

"Well... 'For by Him were all things created, that are in heaven, and that are in earth, visible and invisible–'"

"'–whether they be thrones, or dominions, or principalities, or powers: all things were created by Him, and for Him,'" Daniel interrupted.

"'And He is before all things, and by Him all things consist.' [11]" Nehemiah finished. "That's only one of many, but you get the idea."

"That is a wondrous strange thought, this evolution," Wiglaf said. "And I see that it fashions great harm in this world and is contrary to the very words of the great God." The conversation died into quiet as everyone dealt with their own thoughts.

"What were all those shrieks we heard earlier tonight?" Daniel asked.

"They weren't anything yet, just terror," Joe signed and Nehemiah said. "The CKs had just caught whoever we have underneath us and were beginning to drag her away."

"Pretty loud terror," Daniel said.

"You would be pretty loud too if you were headed to what she was. Besides, she's a chimera," Joe answered with a sudden smile. "Glue doesn't say much, but you've probably noticed he's loud when he does."

A groan sounded from underneath the seat, and it began to grow in volume and desperation as their newly acquired passenger came slowly to her senses in an unknown, cramped place. They heard a click and a deep thump, as Beau pushed the button to open the hidden compartment. Joe increased their speed, his eyes on the side of the road, his manner suddenly urgent again. A deep rumble of voices came from below them. A side track veered off the road, a thin rutted break in the great trees. Joe pushed the stick, shifting Prissy onto the track.

"No, you aren't," the feminine voice drifted from inside the wagon. It was smooth and slow, as if the speaker had to think about each word. Fear clawed through it.

"Yes we are," Beau rumbled back.

"No you aren't!" the woman said, her voice rising and anger beginning to lace it.

---

[11] Colossians 1:16-17

"Yes we are!" Beau's voice rose with hers, frustration matching her anger. The two voices turned to shouts, shaking the wagon's walls with their volume. Joe pulled the wagon to a stop in a small clearing under the dark pine trees, the smell of the bogs thick around it. Nehi and Daniel exchanged a worried glance as the shouts thundered through the trees. Someone would hear this... Nehi looked at Joe and felt his worries dropping away.

The mute laughed, his twinkle back in his green eyes. He dropped Prissy's stick and scuttled toward the skylight. The rest of the company followed, letting their curiosity carry them. They slipped up to the door to the night room and peeked inside, wincing at the volume of the shouted argument.

Beau stood nose to nose with a woman in tattered rags of a tan dress, thick orange hair flowing down over her shoulders to her waist. Her nails grew into points, Anna noticed, and her eyes were deep violet ovals, pointed at the top and bottom. Joe stepped up to the two screaming chimeras, whistled, and held up two of Anna's chocolate chip cookies. Silence came on the room so suddenly it felt almost as deafening as the argument. The woman and Cobeau looked at Joe and held out their hands. He handed them a cookie and pushed the woman gently to sit on the bed.

"What are we?" Joe signed at Beau, his eyes twinkling. Cobeau looked at his little friend blankly, obviously having forgotten what the argument was about. To the others surprise, the woman answered Joe's signed question.

"They aren't, friends," she said, motioning toward the four crowded in the doorway. "They're complete. You're not. And you have cookies. You're a friend."

"Yes I am, good deduction," Joe grinned at her. The woman looked a little confused and he went on quickly. "But you're wrong about the others." He motioned Anna toward him and laid a hand on her shoulder. "This is one of the finest friends you could ever have. What's your name?"

"Wara. And..." She pinched her thumb and first two fingers

together by her nose, and drew them out.

"'Cat,'" Joe gave her sign name back. "Now, to prove Beauty is a friend, she's going to go and get you dinner, one like you've never had before in your life, I bet." Wara's eyes lit up in eager expectation, and Anna quickly slipped out to try and justify the look. She filled one of Cobeau's huge bowls with the remains of last night's casserole, added on a large slice of bread and butter, another bowl full of leafy salad, and grabbed a pitcher of milk. As she was finishing, Wiglaf and her brothers shuffled through the day room.

"We've been shooed out by Joe, seems we were worrying Wara," Nehemiah told her as they walked out. Anna nodded, and moved back into the night room balancing the food carefully. Wara grabbed it as soon as she stepped through the door. The big woman hunched over the food, stuffing in huge mouthfuls and snorting and grunting, her eyes unnaturally bright. Cobeau crouched on the floor, watching the newcomer with interest, and Joe shifted to a corner to wait. Anna moved to the corner with him, not sure what to do with herself. Joe's laughter was gone. Pity and a tired sorrow had taken him over as he watched Wara disposing of her dinner; as if he had seen too much of the same heartbreak and was weary with the hurts. Anna opened her mouth to say something, but Joe signed her to be quiet.

"She knows your language. Do all chimeras?" Anna signed back.

"The incomplete and chimera work stations are often in the same spot," Joe signed back. "The Chimera Keepers and Incomplete Keepers (I know, not very creative about names here), don't mind if their groups mix on their rare off duty hours. Sometimes a friendship strikes up."

"She and Glue have names..." Anna's signed words trailed off.

"But I just had a number?" Joe finished for her. "A name defines you. It's something given by someone who at least notices you, usually who loves you enough to grant you something they consider beautiful. The state here raises chimeras, remember. That requires families. Families name each other. The Incompletes are given numbers, and that defines you too. A small part of a machine, alone, and thrown away when you don't work anymore. Numbers help the IK do their job." He waved at Wara, abruptly changing the subject before Anna could comment. "Do you mind sharing your room with her while she's here?"

"Of course not," Anna signed. But she didn't let him dodge. "Sharp Hope, you aren't alone anymore, and God's given you His own family. Remember it. Knee-High and I are here, and we will never throw you away." A smile flitted over Joe's face, a delicate, easily broken thing like a bubble drifting in the sun or a butterfly in a field of hawks. He didn't look at her. Wara held out her empty bowl.

"That was good," she commented in her smooth voice. Joe moved forward taking Anna with him.

"You're going to share this room with Beauty," Joe signed at Wara as Anna took her bowl.

"I don't think I want to. Share a room," she said, backing against the wall, worry clear on her big face.

"Oh come now, Cat," Joe responded. "You'll like Beauty once you get to know her, and besides, I expect she'll like the company."

"Yes," Anna quickly said, taking the hint, "you know, Wara, it's only me here with five men." Wara's eyes opened wider and she looked incredulous. "Yes it is. I'm the only woman here, and I am delighted to have some female companionship."

"Five of them..." Wara mused. "And one's him." Her nose wrinkled at Cobeau, and he lifted his head off his knees in confusion. Wara clamped her teeth together, opened her lips, and blew air, hissing through her teeth. Cobeau's mouth dropped open and his large brown eyes flew wide in astonishment. Anna had to clamp her lips together to keep from laughing at his shock, and felt Joe doing the same beside her.

"We'll leave you two ladies now," Joe signed, and shoved the astonished Cobeau out the door. As they left Beau's rumble

drifted back in.

"She hissed at me. She hissed at me, Master! Ow. I mean Joe." The click of the door sounded, and Anna smothered another giggle. She composed her face and turned around, frowning at Wara.

"You really shouldn't have done that. Beau's a lovely person, and you upset him."

"He has flapping ears," Wara said, but she looked up from lowered eyes, obviously ashamed of herself.

"Well, you have pointed ears, and I have round ones," Anna said. Wara's eyes suddenly filled with tears. A sobbing wail broke from her as she rocked on the bunk.

"I've done it!" she sobbed. "God likes us to be nice to people, and now I've made Him sad!" Anna sat down on the bed next to her and put a hand on Wara's shoulder.

"Now, now, if you tell God you're sorry and ask Him, He'll forgive you. You should tell Beau you're sorry tomorrow, too."

"I'll tell God, but I don't know if I'll tell him," Wara said, her sobs calming down to a sniffle. She leaned her big head on Anna's shoulder. After a moment, even her sniffling stopped. "You feel nice," Wara said. "Soft. And kind. And safe. And you smell good. Like garlic." Anna grinned and told herself to wash her hands better after she made spaghetti. She settled Wara on the bottom bunk, tucked the blanket over her, and turned to get an extra blanket off the shelf. Wara grabbed her hand and held it, eyes wide, mouth a little parted, fear almost shining from her.

"I'll be right here, Wara, all night," Anna told her, sitting back down on the bed and allowing her hand to stay in the chimera's. Wara nodded and the fear melted into a smile.

"Can I go to sleep now?" she asked.

"Yes, dear, you can go to sleep now," Anna answered, and left her hand in Wara's as the stranger began to fall asleep. Images of little Hannah, and the other young ones she had worked with flew through her mind, and Anna tried to decide what mental age to classify this woman. Anna yawned. It must be

very late. Joe and Nehi were the ones who enjoyed the night watches, not her. And she had stayed up too late last night getting her retaliation to Joe's latest prank ready. His switching the chocolate for mud had been good, she would think before she poured next time.

Anna smiled as she leaned against the bed post. It had been funny to see Joe's shocked expression as his bare foot hit his rhythm makers and stuck there today. The glue had been a good idea, but no more stickiness. It actually worried Joe. No, scared him would be more accurate. Anna closed her eyes, reminding herself to watch out for Joe's retribution tomorrow.

Sunlight cut into her face, and a sharp ache shot along her spine. Anna groaned and stretched, blinking hard. Morning poured into the room. Wara still slept on the bunk, her large, wasted face calm and still. Anna stretched again and stifled another groan as she got her feet under her. Great, she had spent the whole night leaning against the bedpost. What a backache she had this morning.

Joe's eyes shot open, focusing on the dull embers of last night's campfire. A bulky figure crouched in the darkness, moving toward him. Joe lay frozen, his ear still pressed against the ground, his breathing pattern unchanged, his muscles limp. He heard the figure's heavy boots, the cadence of his steps, watched the swing of his shoulders in the darkness, and knew him. Joe sat up as Wiglaf drew near, pivoting to sit cross-legged. Joe's head tipped, asking why the warrior was up and dressed this early.

"I go to see the work stations for myself, Ravenswing," Wiglaf murmured. He knew a whisper carried more than a rumble in the darkness. Joe stiffened. "I ought to be able to tell my king what I have seen, not only what I have heard." Joe quickly pointed to himself and reached for the laser under his blanket. "Nay, do not come, it endangers you too much and you are needed here to protect the others." Joe's hand flung out toward Nehi, his expression suddenly pleading. "I will take no one, for I will move swifter and safer alone. I think you, of all those here, know how that can be true." Joe's arm dropped to his lap, slowly, reluctantly. "Which direction do I start?" Joe stared at him, his lips tight and eyes worried. "I *will* go, Ravenswing. And the better start I have, the swifter may be my return." Joe's hand lifted and waved toward the east. "For this I thank you. Do not fret, I will return." The warrior stood and stole toward the dark trees.

Joe ghosted up beside him, and Wiglaf's brow furrowed, his hand going automatically to his sword hilt.

"I said I would go alone," the warrior growled. Joe pushed a piece of white paper into his hand, and slid away into the darkness back toward the campsite. Wiglaf turned the paper to the moonlight filtering through the trees.

*We will wait for you here for three days. That's all the time I can spare.*

They stayed in the same little meadow for three more days, letting the outcry for Wara die down and waiting for Wiglaf. The second day, they were searched again. Through the Lord's mercy and His providing thick trees and time to prepare, the CK declared them clean and handed Nehi a slip to prove it. After the coast cleared, Joe summersaulted out of the tree, ecstatic over the little blue slip. When Anna asked why, he explained it let them out of all other searches, all they had to do was show the slip and they were clean. Daniel asked why Joe never answered his questions like he did Anna and Nehemiah's, and Joe said the twins weren't as obnoxious when they asked. Wara became a part of the group during the three days. Anna realized she would miss the big woman. Joe and Daniel managed to stay out of each other's way enough to get along. Altogether, it was a pleasant three days.

The sun went down on the third night, and no one said anything. The campfire crackled and popped. Everyone stared at it, quiet, dealing with their own thoughts, and praying Wiglaf would find them that night. The dark pine trees swayed in a wind that brought the stench of rotting bogs. The moon looked like the sliver of a fingernail, and the clouds hung low and glowering; no starlight made it through to cheer the camp. The only light came from the shifting fire, casting fiendish shadows in strange places with its capricious dance. The smoke twisted and shifted as if there was a mischievous mind behind it, darting into the eyes of one of the companions, then another, and coating them all with its dense smell and woody grease. A drop of sap fell into the fire from a tortured piece of burning wood, and its sharp sizzle sounded like a scream to Anna in the ominous quiet of these glowering woods. She looked over at Joe, searching for a glint of hope.

The mute sat crosslegged, staring at the chocolate chip cookie in his hand. The little disc of sugar and chocolate clicked over his knuckles, then back the other way, and rested on his palm. He stared at it, his face lined and sad and ageless.

"Not your favorite flavor?" Anna asked. He had been staring at that cookie for half an hour now. The mute's head shot up, his eyes darting to hers. An embarrassed little smile flitted over his face and the cookie popped into his mouth whole.

"I like it, honest. Chocolate chip are…" his eyes dropped and his expressive face showed a struggle for the right words as he chewed. "They have memories. Mostly good. Yours are really good, and keep making better memories every time you make it. Don't stop. How come some are big and soft and some are like yours, smaller and yummier?"

"Different flour to butter ratio," Daniel muttered. Joe nodded quickly as if that made perfect sense to him and the silence drifted over the campsite again. The wood popped and sap screamed.

A noise, soft and distant, floated into the quiet. Through the woods drifted the sound of a child singing a snatch of a song.

# Chapter Nineteen: Runners in the Woods

*"I cried unto thee, O LORD: I said, Thou art my refuge and my portion in the land of the living."* Psalm 142:5

The voice came nearer through the darkness, drifting past the glowering trees. A young voice, soft and sing-song, as if the singer was half asleep. Joe's eyes suddenly lit with excitement. He leapt to his feet, his silent laugh breaking from his lips.

"I know those words, that's the Ballad of Grendel's Mother!" he signed, stiff with delight, and Beau's translation rumble wrapped it around the campfire scene. The others looked at him in bewilderment and he had to explain his excitement. "It's Track-Maker!" A tree branch creaked as it swung outward, and the Geatish warrior pushed through into their meadow.

A little boy clung to his back, one arm (bone-thin, with torn, reddened skin) wrapped around Wiglaf's neck. The boy's head rested on his protector's shoulder, black hair hanging in stringy strands as he sang gently. A girl lay in Wiglaf's arms, of the same emaciated, torn, raggedness as the boy. A pair of cornflower blue eyes stared about her, and a look of perpetual fear seemed to radiate from her face, framed with filthy, stringy brown hair. She shrank into Wiglaf's arms at the sight of so many strange people, her wide eyes huge in her gaunt face. A wild shriek of delight ripped from Wara as she saw them.

"3940 and 3941!" she yelped. The girl didn't look around at the sound, but the boy stopped singing and turned a pair of blind eyes toward the big chimera, a smile splitting his bruised face.

"Wara?" he asked. Wiglaf dropped to one knee to let him off, and sat the girl on the ground. The two were in Wara's arms in a moment, laughing, signing, and talking as the chimera held them close, her simple face beaming. Wara pulled Anna and Nehemiah to her and began to explain all about her little friends, introducing the boy as 3940 and the girl as 3941. The boy spoke up, and pointed happily at where he remembered Wiglaf stood

by the fire.

"We have names now, Wara," he explained, fairly bursting with pride. "I'm Halbred, and 3941 is Finlia, and isn't that better than numbers?" Wara nodded happily, not quite following the train of thought.

"Pretty One, 3940 can't see, but he has a lovely voice doesn't he? And 3941 doesn't have a voice at all, and can't hear 3940's lovely songs, but aren't her eyes perfect?" She ran on about the children as they huddled against her and watched the campsite. The twins nodded to all of it and tried to decide how old the two emaciated children were. It was hard to tell. Age clung to them, a wary, sly wisdom in their gaunt faces that spoke reams. Anna moved off to the day room trying to decide how to stretch the dinner she had been keeping warm for Wiglaf into three helpings. When she came back out again, Anna found Wara sitting on the ground with the two children perched on her knees and Cobeau in front of them happily teaching Finlia how to shake hands. Nehemiah knelt near Halbred, talking with him about something. Anna noticed her brother's eyes were moist though a smile hung on his lips.

She needn't have worried about stretching the dinner, Wiglaf waved it away. He looked worn and somber as he stood by the fire watching Wara and the children. Daniel still sat on his log. He kept having to sweep the Geat's cloak away from the flames as Wiglaf stood oblivious. Another fetid breeze blew through the campsite, catching up the cloak and driving it into the flaring flames. A cinder caught the edge as Daniel swept it out again, muttering under his breath. His hand slammed into the burning material, beating it out. Wiglaf's face turned and he blinked down at his smoldering cloak and Daniel complaining and blowing on his hand. He stepped away from the fire.

Joe had disappeared.

Relieved of cloak watch, Daniel stood up and moved toward the children, walking slowly, his face softening with a smile. He stopped when still out of arms reach and knelt down to talk to the boy, every move slow and calculated to be unthreatening as

Finlia stared at him warily. Daniel's drawl drifted to the Geat and he recognized the tone from countless hours around the campfire; an amusing tale spun from Daniel, an expert story-spinner. Halbred laughed, his whole face changing with the expression, his tight muscles relaxing. Wiglaf's eyebrow rose, studying Daniel as he moved slowly closer to the boy, still talking. The Geat had been around the child for two days, and never heard that sound from him. Daniel Hillson had skill indeed to draw out such a reaction so quickly and Wiglaf found himself pleased he would take such careful thought to his mannerisms. Nehemiah stood up to help his sister with the dishes, as the children's heads snapped toward the smell of Anna's braided meat loaf.

"They're both seven, they think," he whispered to her. "They've never been away from the work stations."

"Just like Wara," Anna nodded, her heart twisted as she stepped toward them. Daniel and the boy were in the midst of a cheerful conversation about sunshine. Nehemiah moved over to the girl, where she perched on Wara's knee.

"Do you like your new name, little one?" he signed with a smile. She smiled back shyly, the fear still strong on her, and lifted her arms to Wiglaf. He stepped forward quickly and picked her up. A smile broke over his haggard face as she wrapped her thin arms around his neck.

"Be still," Wiglaf murmured to her, not caring that she didn't hear him. "You are among friends here, small one. You are safe now." He glanced toward the dark woods as he said it, and Nehemiah suddenly wondered if the Geat's statement was true. As the thought occurred to him, Joe came strolling from the trees. He moved with his hands in his pockets, smooth, cool, and easy. But under it, a supple tightness hardened his muscles and brightened his green eyes.

Nehemiah tensed, and wondered why Daniel just sat there chatting, so calm. Nehi suddenly realized he, Anna, and Cobeau were the only ones who knew Joe well enough to recognize the danger signs. His gaze flew to his older brother, a revelation

breaking through to him. Daniel didn't really know Joe. Not Joe on the inside, the mute underneath the layers he wore. Dan had never even met the real mute.

Joe strolled quickly up to Wiglaf and laid his hand gently on Finlia's head. Nehi stood as casually as he could and strolled over. She shrank into Wiglaf, but her blue eyes looked out with interest at the newcomer. Joe smiled at her and signed hello. Then he looked up at Wiglaf.

"They're right behind you," he signed, keeping it low and small, and Nehemiah translated quietly. The girl caught the signs. Her eyes dilated, terror shining from her. She scrambled out of Wiglaf's arms and darted to Halbred. Wiglaf followed quickly, but Joe's movements were too quick to follow. In an instant he knelt beside them, took the boy's hands, and began to sign with them, swiftly and gently, so that Halbred could understand his words. The boy let his hands and fingers go limp, and Anna knew he was used to this kind of communication. Curiosity sprang into her, realizing all the things she didn't know. A whole culture had formed around these people forced away from normal society.

"We're going to put you two and Cat in a small place, but don't be afraid. Do you trust Track-Maker?" Joe signed with Halbred's hands. The boy nodded, his face tight with fear. "Do you trust Cat?" Both children nodded. Joe took the girl's hand and put it in Halbred's. He looked her in the eye and signed deliberately. "Do you trust me?" Finlia searched Joe's vibrant green eyes for only a moment.

"I trust you," she signed with Halbred's hands, so he knew her answer. A competent smile flashed over Joe, he winked at the girl, swept her up, grabbed Halbred's hand, and trotted to the wagon. One slim finger slid into the tiny hidden hole behind the driver's seat, and the square door of the cubby underneath the seat swung open with a creak. Joe shot a glance over his shoulder at Wara and jerked his head toward the hole. She backed away shaking her head. Anna and Nehemiah grabbed her and hurried her to the wagon.

"They need, you Wara," Anna told her. Wara looked at the two children and slipped into the dark hole. Joe and Wiglaf slid the trembling children in, and Joe closed the door. His manner and movements went back to blurring speed as he pulled his can of anise spray and spun in a quick circle, dousing all of them. His fingers shifted, his face hard and green eyes urgent as he signed Cobeau to his own cubby. Nehemiah grabbed Joe's shoulder and shoved him after Beau.

"Go with him," he said. "Quick, we'll handle it out here." Joe looked at him, his brow furrowed, hesitating even though his eyes snapped and his body was as tense as a bowstring. Every instinct screamed at him to run, Nehi could even see it in him. Wiglaf turned to the trees, listening.

"They are almost here," he murmured. Nehemiah pushed Joe toward the wagon, and Joe let him. The mute pulled the blue slip out as he reached the pointed door. His boots suddenly planted themselves on the wet grass, stopping Nehi's shoving.

Joe spun around and pushed the slip into Daniel's hands. Everyone paused for a moment, just staring. Night noises and the fire crackling took over as Daniel met Joe's intense gaze, the flickering firelight turning the scene surreal.

"Sure," Daniel said. "I'll take care of it, you go on." Joe gave a curt nod and disappeared into the wagon after Cobeau. Daniel shooed the rest of the group back to the campfire.

"You two can't lie to save your lives, let me do the talking," he murmured to the twins.

"I think I like it better when Joe says were rotten actors," Anna whispered as they scrambled to get to the fire and settle around it in an attitude that said they had been there all night. Nehi dropped to the grass, stretched his legs out, and leaned back against a log. Anna sat on the log beside him, straightening her skirt. Nehemiah forced his breathing to be normal, and his gaze settled on the fire instead of searching the trees. A twig snapped in the woods to the left of the wagon, and Nehi felt Anna twitch. A long branch with needles nearly sweeping the forest floor shoved upward suddenly, the needles bouncing and swinging wildly, and a glimpse of blue showed in the firelight. For an instant, Nehi saw the glint of metal, recognized it as rifles, and had an overwhelming desire to snatch up Hope.

Soldiers in green uniforms with tall blue hats stepped out of the trees, marching in what seemed at first a haphazard pattern. But after a second look he realized they were spread out in such a way that every inch of ground was swept by their competent gaze. Nehi sat up in surprise, letting his breathing speed up. Normal people would be alarmed to have their campsite suddenly invaded. In ten seconds the tramping soldiers had the little company efficiently surrounded. They stopped as one entity, their old-fashioned projectile rifles held ready, their faces hard, set, and unresponsive. The blue felt hats bore a badge with what was almost a child's face, but it had something bestial about it. Anna glanced at one of the insignias, shuddered, and stared at the fire. The officer in charge stepped toward the group, an iron competency radiating from him, as if he had already decided this group was guilty. Daniel stood up slowly to meet the oncoming officer, exasperation and outrage written all over him.

"Not again, brothers!" he burst out. The officer looked at Daniel, towering a head above him, his scarred face stiff with indignant wrath, and hesitated. "Don't tell me. You're looking for a happy worker that's managed to slip out without filing his papers," Daniel drawled, his voice dripping contempt.

"Two of them, actually," the officer said reluctantly. "I'm afraid you will have to be searched. They were definitely headed this way."

"We will not be searched," Daniel snapped. "We have already been searched." He pulled out the blue slip and dangled it in front of the officer's nose. His eyes blazed and the scars showed in pale relief as his face suffused in fury. "I thought this country was one of free and happy brotherhood. We've met with nothing but insults, claiming that we are harboring enemies of the state! Ha! What a state, you can't even keep up with a few incompletes!" Daniel launched out with all his caustic

humor, biting into the soldier, insinuating more than he actually insulted, his wit searing. The officer listened in astonished dismay. Wiglaf sat still, staring at Daniel as if seeing him for the first time. But Daniel knew how far he could go and didn't keep up the barrage for more than a few blistering sentences before launching into what he really had to say. "We are here on good business, to cheer our brothers. Our friends of KAM and my especial friend Margaret of the Gaia assured me we would be welcomed on our mission. But if we have one more of your insulting, incompetent, ill-worded, inappropriate interruptions, so help me we'll complain to the Brotherhood and leave!" The officer had glanced at the blue slip, but had barely taken his eyes off the tall, fuming man in front of him. At the mention of the name from Gaia the man trembled. At the Brotherhood he blanched. The officer quickly handed Daniel back the slip.

"It is all in order," the officer stated, his voice gruff. He spun on one heel, his voice raised to a shout at his men. "They are not here. Deploy southward, brothers!" A few efficient minutes later the troops had tramped away, and the night noises and tendrils of stinking fog wrapped around them. Daniel sank down on the log, easing tight shoulders, and grinning at his chuckling siblings. Wiglaf dashed to the wagon's seat, and his coarse hands began to run along the painted wood, trying to get the cubby open. Nehi and Daniel's lips pursed. It was too soon, much too soon. Even an easily cowed soldier might be smart enough to have someone stay behind watching. Anna stood up, brushed the dirt off her skirt, and trotted toward the warrior.

"We fixed that crack," she said, her voice raised just enough she knew it reached the trees around them. "Come inside the wagon if you want to see the work." She pulled him through the pointed door, into the night room, squirmed onto the lower bunk, and fumbled for the right knot painted on the aspen tree. Her fingers brushed it and she shoved the button down. A sharp click sounded, and the cubby flew open, spilling Wara and the two children out onto the bed. Wiglaf was swamped by all three, tight voices hushed in fear as they asked for news. Anna

left him to deal with them and moved to the oak tree in the day room. Her thumb found the latch easily, but it stuck. She grabbed the nut-hammer off the counter, reversed it to stick the handle on the button, and slammed her fist down on the top. A sharp click sounded as the button shoved home.

Joe and Co spilled out, gasping for air, flushed with heat, hair and clothes damp with sweat. Nehemiah and Daniel stepped inside, and the twins started laughingly telling Joe about how their brother handled it. As the twins' swift talk flew on, Daniel handed Joe back the blue slip. The mute's fingers closed over it and Joe looked up at him. A smile slid over him; it was so clear a thank you, Daniel said you're welcome before he realized it. Daniel turned his eyes to the wall, an ill-tempered frown cutting across him. This was bad, he was starting to understand enough to answer the mute.

The little group flowed into the night room and found the children half asleep and Wara little better. The minutes turned flurried as the group worked on getting over the children's fear and getting them to bed. Anna shooed the rest out as a crowd and began to work on it alone. After a few minutes she had Wara, Halbred, and Finlia settled in the night room. She slipped out quietly to join the men around the campfire. Weariness pulled at her eyelids, but she wanted Nehemiah's reassuring company more than sleep. Anna's heart felt heavy and bloated, and she longed for someone steady and strong and good.

As she opened the door and stepped down the two stairs to the squishy ground, she could hear Wiglaf speaking near the fire. She stood still for a moment, letting the breeze blow her flurry away. The tall trees swayed and rustled, and seemed suddenly friendly allies shutting out the sight of this horrible country. She turned to the fire and noticed it looked warm, and no longer evil, now that Wiglaf had made it back. The Geat was nearing the end of the tale of his adventures. It must have been quite a story judging from the way Nehemiah and Daniel stared at him open mouthed. Anna slipped up and sat down beside Nehemiah. He shifted to make more room for her and she

swiveled, tucked her feet up beside her, leaned against his side, and let the comfort of his safe, steady, presence sink in. A soft sigh slid from her into the night and her heart quieted.

"We traveled on as quick as we might without leaving a large track for the IKs to follow," Wiglaf continued his tale. "And yet they tracked us here. I am sorry, Ravenswing. I know that I should not have brought danger on you, but I could not leave them. I could not go my way with the knowledge that those brave children–" His voice caught and he stopped, staring at the fire.

"Never apologize for a good action, Track-Maker," Joe said through his big friend. "You rescued two defenseless children who could do nothing for themselves. You've already given them more love than they've ever felt. Never apologize for something like that. Especially to me. You've done as our Lord would have you do." Across the dancing fire, Anna saw Wiglaf as a black silhouette, shifting and changing as the shadows moved with the firelight. His shadowy shoulders rose a little at the words, regaining some of their usual broadness; but his voice came hesitant and doubtful.

"I do not understand completely what you mean. What does the Great Creator have to say of this matter? Does He deign to care over what most would see as trifling, the fate of two unwanted children?"

"'Pure religion and undefiled before God and the Father is this,'" Nehi quoted, "'to visit the widow and the fatherless in their affliction and to keep himself unspotted from the world.[12]'" A prodigious yawn from Daniel broke in and he blinked blearily at the campfire.

"'And oppress not the widow, nor the fatherless, the stranger, nor the poor,[13]'" Anna added. "There's a lot more like those. God cares very much what we do with orphans and the defenseless."

---

[12] James 1:27
[13] Zechariah 7:10 a

"I understand," Wiglaf said, nodding slowly. Joe spoke up again, through Cobeau's deep rumble.

"You understand, Track-Maker, but have you made it your own?" Anna saw the black shadowed head swivel, turning toward the mute. Joe sat scrunched on the ground, his chin on his knees and his hands moving in his swift signs. She could see the sparkle of the fire dancing in his eyes as he challenged the Geat. "Jesus is not just a King to serve, though He is that. He is a personal savior and friend. Have you accepted Him as your own?"

"I have not dared," Wiglaf murmured, wonder in the tone. "I am not worthy of such an honor and have not the strength to gain such worth!" He was surprised to see everyone around him smile.

"Of course you're not!" Nehi laughed. "None of us are. But, '...when we were yet without strength, in due time Christ died for the ungodly[14].' He wants you now, as you are, Wiglaf. Jesus will work on changing you as life goes on. Come on, kneel with me." Nehemiah dropped on his knees in front of the dying campfire, and Wiglaf slipped beside him. "Just repeat after me, if you're sure you're ready to serve God above all others." Wiglaf nodded, his eyes wide. Nehemiah laid a hand on the other man's shoulder and prayed. Wiglaf echoed the words, at first hardly above a whisper, but gaining in confidence and joy.

"Lord Jesus, the Creator and King above all kings; I kneel before you now, a sinner, one who has been a traitor to Your kingdom. I believe Your Son, Jesus Christ, died for my sins. I acknowledge I have defied Your laws, and I beg for Your merciful forgiveness, through the blood of Your Son upon the cross. I have no virtue of my own, but I ask You now to clothe me in the righteousness of Jesus Christ. Make me Yours, Lord. Claim me as Yours. Thank You for calling me, for choosing me. Cause me to love and serve You more every day, my Savior. Amen."

As Wiglaf's eyes opened he found the rest of the group kneeling around him, smiles dancing in the firelight. Daniel

---

[14] Romans 5:6

thumped the Geat on the back, grinning a welcome into the family. Beau threw his arms around Wiglaf and squeezed him tight. Joe grabbed the chimera's arm, laughing and pulling on it, signing him to let their new brother breathe. Beau let go, looking bashful, and a sharp gasp came from Wiglaf, a hissing, sucking breath. Joe grinned at him, knowing the sensation. But then his face dropped into a frown and his green eyes went serious.

"It's probably safest for you to get out now, Track-Maker," Joe signed. "You can follow behind the searchers and slip out when the IK turn back." Anna silently thought it would have been nice to know that before she got the children asleep. Daniel slid onto the ground and let his head rest against the log, blinking hard at the flames. Wiglaf went to go fetch his charges. A new light filled his eyes, and he had a lift to his head that hadn't been there before. Halbred and Finlia recognized it and felt new confidence from his sudden joy. When Wiglaf came out, he found Daniel fast asleep by the dying campfire, Joe and Cobeau swathed in dark clothes, and Nehemiah checking over Hope. Anna stepped forward and wrapped him in a quick, tight hug.

"Be safe, Wiglaf, and go with God!" she said. Whatever she said next was smothered by Wara, as the chimera grabbed her in a hug. Joe tapped her on the shoulder, and the big chimera let go. Anna staggered out of her grasp with a breathless laugh, caught her foot on the log, and ended sprawled on the ground. She crawled up against it, murmuring something about the night and her eyes fluttered closed.

"The Ravens are going to see you on your way," Nehemiah said. He handed Wiglaf one of Joe's black velvet bags. "Here's enough money to get whatever you might need on your trip back, along with a Ruby pistol, a charger, and an extra battery. Now remember what I taught you about lasers, you have to–" Joe's hurry up whistle interrupted him and Nehemiah dropped his earlier sentence and started another one. "There's a map in here too with your route plotted on it. It's a longer way than we came, but safer according to the Ravens. I'm staying as watchdog over the two sleepers and the wagon. Goodbye, brother. God go with you!" Wiglaf murmured a goodbye, Beau and Joe herded them toward the dark trees, and Nehemiah watched them disappear behind the waving branches and the blackness of the forest. He let himself grimace, and settled down between Anna and Daniel to wait and watch.

"This cannot be true!" Wiglaf rumbled, his entire body tense with agitation and fury. Joe's signs were smooth, his face blank. He flitted under the dark trees, swiftly leading the way around the treacherous, stinking bogs. Cobeau translated the signs in a whispered growl. Joe's hands dropped to his side and they walked in silence. Wiglaf's dark head bowed, his face strained. After two minutes, Joe reached out tentatively and prodded the Geat in the shoulder, a quick jab, almost as if afraid of what he might wake. A deep sigh flew from the man.

"It is quite a tale you tell, Ravenswing Ashe-Maker. One that saddens me greatly," Wiglaf murmured as he marched under the trees on the heels of those searching for him. "I do not like to hear of such treachery and evil even amongst Christ's own! And I do not understand why you come to me for counsel, Ravenswing. Or perhaps you would prefer Joe?" The mute gave a lopsided smile at the man walking beside him. A sliver of moon shone down on the strange company stealing their quiet way through woods, with Wara carrying the children, and Joe, Wiglaf, and Cobeau walking a little ahead.

"I think I prefer Ravenswing from you, Track-Maker, Shield-Bearer to the king," Joe signed.

"I will always be Shield-Bearer to my king, and honored by the title," Wiglaf broke in quickly. "But I am more now. If I may adapt the words of the wise Nehemiah, I am now Wiglaf, God-Beloved. And it is more noble a title than any I could have gained on my own prowess. But even as a saint loved of God, I do not understand why you would come to me for council in

this marvelous tale you have told me tonight. It is of much greater import than I feel adequate to address."

"*You* don't feel adequate!" Joe signed with a sudden outburst of vehemence, his face working, and his hands moving in exaggerated patterns. "I'm only eighteen, and a GI, just for that I'm forced to move in secret, and have the death sentence on me in–" Joe controlled himself with an effort, the blank veneer falling back over him; but he let a little of his real self be seen through the mask. His green eyes begged as he looked back at the man walking beside him. "I'm too deep in this, Track-Maker. I need advice. You've always been wise, and as I've watched you give up false ideas and shoulder right ones so quickly, I've realized your wisdom is even deeper than I thought. I desperately need it tonight. I can't go to anyone else, I have a very limited circle of trusted friends and the ones who would accept the idea about the books wouldn't about the Wolf. Please, I need to know what you think I should do." They walked on in silence as Wiglaf weighed his answer. Birds twittered in the dark, rustling trees. A twig snapped like a rifle shot, a quarter mile ahead of them, as one of the sweeping soldiers broke it.

"You have done right, Ravenswing," Wiglaf said finally. "I think you must continue on the path you have started. You have shouldered a very large burden, one that I could not bear. But you have proved yourself very able."

"No," Joe signed, no expression betraying his thoughts. "I am not able, but Jesus is. You think I ought to keep it quiet still?"

"You mean, should you tell the Hillsons the whole truth?" Wiglaf asked. "No. I say it again, you have done well, and you have done the only thing you can. You must assume the Wolf believes you do not know who they are, and wait until the time is right and we are strong enough to draw the net tight about him for the catch. If you tell of it too soon, or too late, all will be lost. This evil one would destroy us with joy, and cares nothing for the good the books could do. We must not let the Wolf win. Joe Ravenswing, you have placed yourself in the breech and are the one thing holding back the flood of death that would come

on the Way. If you break, or let yourself be bowed under by the weight of the undertaking, the IDP will be destroyed and untold numbers of its members will die. You must hold the breech." Joe nodded. Wiglaf watched him a few steps, the shifting moonlight filtered through the swaying trees playing over his small form. The mute's shoulders hunched, and his head drooped, as if he was simply too weary to lift it. "I would that I could remove some of this burden from you, my friend."

"You just did. Thank you for your counsel. I am very deep in this, and am getting deeper. I needed someone else to tell me if I'm on the right track, or completely off. I trust your judgment. I will stay the course I've started, and I will hold the breech," Joe said through Cobeau's deep rumble. Wiglaf nodded, but he stared at him with sorrow mingled with undisguised wonder.

"I have never heard of such a hero as you, Joe Ravenswing. To have come from such evil…to have lived such nightmares! I have seen only a part of what you have survived, of the evils you have been put through when so young. I cannot grasp how you could not only still live, but love… Love so strongly, and give of yourself constantly; continually give up of your own life and happiness for other's safety and so that others may keep their peace. And never to speak of it, always to go your way unthanked and unknown. You have been fighting with more strength than you ought to have, to keep a hope alive and growing for this world that has hated and harmed you since birth." Wiglaf's bearded face lined with sorrow as he looked at the hunched form beside him, and a helpless shrug lifted his shoulders. "I would the world knew of your great love. It would bring many to our Savior only to see what you are willing to do in His service."

"You talk like I'm an amazing someone," Joe signed, a smile trying to break over his blank face and not quite making it. "I'm just a man, Track-Maker, and what good I do is only from our Savior's strength."

"I know this, Joe Ravenswing. It is through our Savior that you are granted strength, but there is a part of you that must be

willing to accept and use His might. You have chosen this path for your life, laying yourself down in service to our King, and for love of His own. I know of none other who would have dared the path you have trodden for years." He laid a hand on Joe's shoulder and his words took on a sudden earnestness. "Do not give up hope, my friend. You may still find joy, even from this. The young Hillsons are not fools and they love the right and despise the wrong. They will not condemn you, and they will not desert you." Joe looked up at him, and Wiglaf was shocked to see tears in his green eyes. He had never seen Joe's mask slip so far. One spilled over and slid down his scarred cheek, leaving a salty wet line that glinted in the moonlight.

"I wish I could be so certain, Track-Maker!" Joe signed, a sniffle escaping the mute. A sob ripped from Beau, big and blubbery (though he had no idea what the conversation was about) and he shifted, wanting to fold Joe in one of his crushing embraces. Wiglaf quickly held out a hand to stop Beau, swinging to a halt as he turned to the young man beside him.

"Joe, you have earned a place in their hearts as more than just another brother in Christ. I say you have earned it, and I mean those words. You have spilled more sorrow and pain and blood for their welfare than any other. You have fought their war long before they knew a war was happening, creating a chance for them and keeping a hope alive, ignoring the pain it brought on yourself. No, embracing the pain and trouble, and fighting to keep it from spreading beyond you. They are not fools, Joe Ravenswing, and they will not overlook this service and love, and they will not forget it. Even when they learn what you have been keeping from them, and why you have had to keep it. Be comforted, my friend, and remember it in your doubts!" Joe nodded, running a hand quickly over his eyes.

Wara stopped beside them, and put a hand on Halbred's mouth to stop his quiet singing. Joe suddenly turned sharp and lithe again, his focus on something ahead. They had reached the border of the People's Kingdom. The tall pines grew staggered and stunted as they straggled to the edge of the fetid swamp land. In the light from the new moon and the shifting, dark boughs they saw a line of green uniformed soldiers stretching out in front of them. They moved in competent silence.

"Here's where we part," Wiglaf said. "God be with you, and always look to Him for your refuge. Be strong and hold the breech. Know that I am in constant prayer for your succor and success, brother!" Wiglaf held out his hand in farewell. Two wiry arms shot around him, and the mute squeezed. Wiglaf's burly grip fell around the mute's thin shoulders, and defiance ran through the warrior. His arms tightened; he didn't want to let go and allow this young man to plunge back into his fight alone. Joe pulled away as he heard the soldiers beginning to turn from the border. The black bag with the map and extra funds dangled from his fingers, slipped silently from Wiglaf's belt. A mischievous, prankster's smile flitted over Joe's face and his twinkle sprung into his eyes.

"You're not using the map," he signed and Beau rumbled. "I have a better way to get you home."

"Hooray, you're back!" Nehemiah grinned, hopping up to greet the Ravens as they walked out of the woods. Cobeau nodded happily and moved toward the fire. A shiver ran over him and he paused for a moment, warming himself by the flames. Nehi noticed his hair bristled, as if trying to compensate for an intense cold. Before he could ask about it, the chimera turned, kicked his blanket out for sleep, and plopped down on it, his big face unconcerned and cheerful. Nehemiah turned to Joe, eyes laughing, to tell him he had sprung Anna's last prank by accident. He stopped, the laugh dying when he saw his friend's red eyes and tired expression.

"Are you all right?" he asked. Joe nodded a little too quickly.

"Are you really happy to see me?" he signed in his half serious half humorous way he had. Nehemiah was getting used to these fits of insecurity from his small friend. He smiled and

threw an arm over Joe's shoulders.

"I've hardly ever been happier to see anyone," he said honestly, and was gratified to see a real smile cross Joe's face. "Come on, it's turning into a cold night, let's gather more wood before we turn in."

"Okay, but watch out for wild people flying from trees," Joe signed.

"I'll watch for them, you watch for the dreaded sap," Nehemiah said.

"That sap can be dangerous, I know it!" Joe signed, and Nehemiah laughed as Joe began to describe the fiendish substance. He started to throw in a few descriptions of his own, and soon the two boys were laughingly creating a vicious monster out of the thing called sap as they gathered firewood.

Joe paused as he followed Nehemiah back to the wagon, their arms full of their gleanings. The black trees shifted and creaked in a breeze somewhere too high to be felt, and it seemed as if they moved on their own, leering and laughing at him. But something had changed. This forest had suddenly lost the terror it had held over him for fourteen years, ever since he had fled through it with the IK at his heels, alone and homeless. Because of a friend's teasing and a strange sticky substance God chose to put in trees. A grateful smile slid over Joe as he watched Nehemiah's retreating figure, and he thanked God for him, even if...even if. Joe's face went blank and he stood still in the darkness.

A prickle along Nehemiah's spine told him he was alone. He spun on one heel, searching the trees, and managed to pick out a black patch among the thick trunks.

"Are you coming, or are you going to stand there till that despicable, purple, bubbling villain gets you?" Nehemiah called. Joe grinned and trotted through the woods of the People's Kingdom back toward his wagon. The last stretch of this long battle drew near, and it felt wonderful to have a friend here with him. Tomorrow they would head toward the capitol and it would all begin. He had to track down Quintus Leeman and gain his help,

even if it came to kidnapping and making his argument at laserpoint. And stop the Wolf from stealing the kingdom's book, no matter what the cost. And try to track down a lead to the Bible, though that was unlikely. The Bible situation would take finding FF headquarters and getting inside, and that would mean… A chill played across Joe's skin as he dumped his wood on their pile and his arms stole around his chest.

"Hey Joe, look at this!" Nehemiah said, and Joe looked over at him. He sat cross-legged by the flames, the firelight playing over him. He inhaled a lungful of smoke and then blew it out again, making it look as if he was the one generating the billowing white clouds. "I'm a fire breathing behemoth!"

"Go to sleep, Knee-High, you've been up too long!" Joe laughed. The mute dropped to the grass between Nehemiah and Cobeau, rolled to one side as his arm pillowed his head, and let his heavy lids fall over his eyes. A hacking cough rent the night and Joe smiled as Nehemiah tried to control his breathing. Whatever came in this last stage of the battle, it had been a wonderful ride with Anna and Nehemiah. He would always be thankful for the time with their friendship. If they dumped him after they found out, the fallout would be worth that. And even then, his great God would be with him.

A word Wiglaf had chosen flitted into Joe's mind and burned like a fire in the dark. *Refuge…* Joe lay on the grass, the dark woods rustling, feeling almost as homeless as he had fourteen years ago. The Wolf's note played through his memory, and he acknowledged the enemy had driven a dagger into a nerve, and knew it. But a doctor's laughter and his Lord's love invaded the insecurity and drove even the Wolf's looming threat into nothing. Joe had a refuge. Here on earth, and forever in his Father's arms. Jesus sat beside him, right here, and always stayed near, protecting and listening. The memory of that wordless presence in the arena, the voice from the ground, welled up in the mute. Suddenly he found himself grateful even for that day; God had spoken through it, giving Joe a tangible memory of His God with him. Joe sent his fears and plans and sorrows swirling to

his Lord, and let himself rest in the comfort of knowing he served a truly sovereign God. Jesus wove the paths of men into a dance of His own design, always for their good. All would be well in the end. God had promised him that. Joe's mind went blank and he drifted off into sleep. It claimed him in a few minutes, all his fears and insecurities quieted by the certainty of his faithful God.

The clouds crept over the stars again and the night grew darker as the wood burned down. But high above the shadows, above the gathering clouds, the Lion of Judah watched over the sleeping campsite.

Ariel zipped her mer suit, and moved into a quick stretch. She felt the scales shift with her, every one capable of sending a laser blast ricocheting back on the shooter, and turning any knife blade. She ran a gloved hand over the utility belt strapped around her hips, silently counting the sharpened shells and loosening her laser in the holster. She flicked her long blond hair behind her and strode for the door, her lips in a tight frown and her emerald eyes bright.

Hamfast hadn't come to deliver.

Ariel Athenia had no qualms over selling out an enemy, or even something as impersonal as a state. But she carefully cultivated an aura of being true to those who stayed true to her. It was the only way to keep from being murdered in her own bed.

And Hamfast hadn't come back.

She strode down the darkened hallway, her scaled boots silent but dancing with reflective colors from every shred of light. She would not desert her agents without at least finding out their fate.

In the back of her mind the metallic voice from the darkened corner of her office kept revolving, filling her with questions. Could the Raven have something to do with Hamfast's delay? It might have been that nagging thought that sent her first to the

ending rendezvous, where Hamfast and his boys were supposed to have landed to deliver her goods four hours ago. Ariel shifted her hoverboard carefully through town, fully aware every dark doorway stared after her glittering scaled suit with envy.

The hill outside of town loomed tall and dark in the evening sky. Ariel's board swished around it, almost silent in its precision, the best that money could purchase. Her heel hit the off button as she rounded the hill and the board dropped to the ground, skidding to a halt.

Twenty-eight beady, malicious eyes spun to look at the woman in the glittering suit. The fourteen scavengers shifted, turning on her. She could see her team at the heart of the group, lying face down and still. Their gear hung from the scavengers' hands. A woman near the front hissed, rotting teeth showing in her wasted face. Ariel smiled.

"Really, children, those aren't your playthings," the mer woman said. Her voice rang like hard iron. "Drop them now and go play somewhere else."

A concerted rush of bodies charged at her. Ariel spun, her board sailing into the front rank and taking out five, bleeding hard from head wounds. Shells shot from one of her webbed gloved hands, and more fell screaming. Her other glove moved, and electric pulses flew from each finger. More screams filled the darkening air. Ariel spun and twisted, her gloves shooting out, each movement a cold calculation that brought death to those who did not listen to her commands.

The air grew still and quiet around her. Ariel's scaled suit caught the last rays of the sinking sun and sparkled in greens, blues, purples, pinks, and oranges as she picked her way through the bodies littering the plain. She reached her agents and knelt beside Hamfast's hulking form. His chest rose and fell steadily. He lived. Ariel's eyes flew to the others, watching for signs. Each one breathed, lying flat and still... but with no marks except those made by the scavengers dragging their goods from their bodies. Her eyes fell on a white canister on the ground in

the middle of the boys. A raven in flight lay stamped on the canister's side. A sharp curse spilled from Ariel.

The Raven had her SOLDT.

*Next is*

# Ravens Raid

*penultimate book of the epic!*

# Appendices

# 903

***March 234:*** *Born in KAM, marked as GI, "adopted" by the Incomplete Keepers of the People's Kingdom.*
***April 238:*** *Successfully ran from the IK Station.*
***August 238:*** *Picked up by Geego Thomle's slaver caravan.*
***January 239:*** *Sold to Bart Meilson as a pet for his ninth birthday present.*
***February 240:*** *Acquired by the Advancers of KAM for testing.*
***March 241:*** *Bought by Jarl Furt, the Music Maker, traveling musician and cat burglar.*

*The tool sat hunched against the porch's support post. The rough wood pressed against his face, and he welcomed it. The sensation gave him somewhere to focus his mind past the biting pain and gnawing hunger. Always so hungry. So tired. The bone plant fused to his mandible seemed heavy and pinching, warning him he mustn't move. The Music Maker set his radius on this porch in a three foot box, the tool knew, and setting finger outside it meant pain. More pain.*

*Drunken voices rose in louder guffaws from inside and the tool hunched a little closer into himself. He knew what the hours spent here today would mean for him tomorrow. The dread clawing at his empty stomach was his most familiar companion these days.*

*Other voices invaded the air around him and the tool's eyes fluttered open. Young voices. Happy voices. A blue ball sailed through the skies and his green eyes tracked it, noting its bright beauty, the joyful color. It landed with a bounce in the street and ten children chased after it, screaming and laughing. The tool blinked at them. Something almost alive enough to be called longing moved deep inside him. But the hunger clawed and his eyes began to close again.*

*A smell drifted into his invisible box. Rich, sweet, intense. The tool's eyes flew open and his spine straightened, his green eyes searching for the source, his pinched face tight with the hunger.*

*A woman had stepped out of a house across the street*

*from the bar. She held a plate with round, brown somethings on it, steam lifting off it in tendrils into the cold Tao country air. The children crowded around her, greedy hands reaching for the plate. The tool stared, stiff and still. The crowd of children rushed off again, holding the round food, chasing the bright blue ball. The woman turned, her straight dress accenting her pretty form. Her brown eyes found his green ones.*

*The tool dropped his gaze, his arms tightening around his skinned knees. His gray-green hair fell in foul-smelling clumps over his face as he laid his head on his arms.*

*The sweet smell grew stronger. The hunger clawed at his insides like a wild bear trying to get out, tearing, biting, hurting.*

*"Would you like a cookie?"*

*The voice came soft, sweet, rich. Gentle.*

*The tool lifted his head, slowly, his senses swimming. The woman was in front of him. Leaning down, smiling. Holding the plate toward him. The tool blinked at her. Had he slipped into a hallucination again? The plate moved a little closer, gently, slowly. Her smile grew a little wider. His green eyes rose, wonderingly meeting hers. Tears sparkled behind her smile.*

*"Go on," she said, softly. Gently. It had been so long since anyone had spoken to him like that. Minnie, with her wrinkled skin and her cackling laughter in the kennel across from him, had been the last. The memory of the three months of conversation between tests, joking and teasing, bubbled in him for an instant, like hot lava lurking under the deadness inside him. Bringing warmth. Memories of human interaction. Reawakening things he had forgotten. Giving him back his name.*

*"Go on!" she whispered again, pushing the plate a little closer. It moved into his three-foot radius. Joe's hand shot out, scooping the cookies into his lap, all that was left. His eyes rose to meet hers again. A smile twitched at the corners of his filthy, broken lips.*

*She nodded, her eyes still glistening behind her smile,*

*straightened and walked back to her house. She didn't give him a second look. Joe watched to see if she would look back, until the door closed behind her. Then he lifted one of the warm round...what had she called them? Cookies?*

*It tasted like sugar and chocolate.*

*It tasted gentle and good.*

*It tasted like joy and sunshine.*

*Joe ate one, letting it tame the clawing beast inside him. Letting it wake him up, remind him of his name, kindle the tiny spark that spoke of goodness living somewhere outside the Music Maker's caravan. He hid the other six, slipping them under the loose floorboard in his tiny radius marked out by the bone plant in the wagon. Those cookies lasted him seven months of hoarded nibbles.*

*Each stolen bite gave him back his name, even if just for an instant. Reminding him there were other people out there, other people unlike his master. That somewhere, in some people, something good still survived.*

*It tasted like hope.*

***April 243:*** *Upon the death of Furt, able to slip off into the streets of Hurn in the Kingdom of the Wise.*

***June 244:*** *Captured by Gretta Netters, Purveyor of Inferior Peoples.*

***September 244:*** *Sold to Valus, pawn shop owner in Kallipolis, for odd-jobbing, renting out, and venting anger.*

***February 245:*** *Freedom purchased and home established by Joshua Noble.*

***October 246:*** *Rescued the chimera Cobeau in the People's Kingdom.*

***November 248:*** *Joshua Noble betrayed and slaughtered in the arena of the Battle Kingdom.*

***December 250:*** *Met Nehemiah and Anna Hillson.*

# *Chimeras*

**Report: Chimera Handler Carl Savenberg, Camp 24**

Orders have arrived to prepare the pack, Shadowfangs, for operation Dark Horse. I will instigate the preparations according to the schedule placed in my hands.

*-Carl Savenburg*

Calla and Ydara stood tall, the sunlight glistening off their sleek hair. She slumped closer to her new mate, yielding to let her head fall on his chest. A warm tingle ran through her as his arm slid around her. She had never felt anything like the protection and love that strong arm carried with it. For the first time in her life, Ydara felt there might be a future to look forward to. Calla's arm tightened gently, his face radiating joy. His feet moved, and he shuffled slowly toward the bunkhouse, never shifting his hold around his mate.

Cobeau watched silently, as he crouched with the rest of the team outside, leaning against the Gritbiters bunkhouse. The brown fog began to thicken and curl around the pack. They would be covered with the sticky mud when they woke tomorrow. But none of them begrudged Calla his night alone, the first night for he and Ydara.

The door closed behind Calla and a sense of utter loneliness slid into Cobeau. He felt like howling, his whole being wrapped in a sorrow too profound to just be the loss of "how things were." He would have howled, long and dismal, a mourning for all that was, and mostly all he knew would come; but Calla would know his voice, and he would not mar his brother's happiness with his own grim vision of the future.

Mates meant someone else to care for. And that brought a change in how a man reacted. And change would kill them all.

# *Lasers and Gadgets*

In the early days of research, the main problems with using lasers as a weapon were the source of energy and the heat emitted by the process. It takes so much power to create a weaponized laser, the apparatus used to excite the atoms was too heavy for even a tank to carry, and handheld weapons were out of the question. Also, most of a laser's energy burns off as heat, before the laser light becomes strong enough to be useful. One more problem with the practicality of lasers was atmospheric interference. A high concentration of dust or water in the air might tamper with a laser's accuracy, bending the beam, or causing it to reflect off the atmospheric conditions.

The first two problems were finally solved by the Pylum battery. A man named Ralph Pylum, in the year 20 of the Book Base Age, discovered a battery powered by heat. It is the perfect solution for a laser weapon energy source. The Pylum battery requires an initial charge, which it uses to start the lasing process in a weapon. The laser passes through its chosen medium and begins to bounce between a complicated series of mirrors, increasing the atoms' excitement and thus the power of the laser. This is called priming. Some take more time than others to reach a weaponized level of energy, it depends on many factors, including the size of the battery and the medium chosen. But as it primes, the laser is giving off wave after wave of heat. The Pylum battery absorbs it and uses the energy. This creates a weapon which basically powers itself. If allowed to sit unused for some time the battery loses its charge and needs a "jump start" of external heat to start the lasing process. But if kept in proper order, a Pylum battery laser will provide its own energy indefinitely.

Atmospheric conditions are still an issue with some lasers, throwing off the accuracy. The lens of a laser (what the beam is finally sent through, after the energy has climbed to useful levels) as well as the lasing medium affect the accuracy. It is possible for the beams to be reflected back, or even scattered. This kind of reflection would be too weak to cause much damage, unless they landed in a person's fragile eyes. Because of this danger lasers are never to be fired without safety-dyed goggles.

**Brunhiem**

The laser of choice for the Sojourner Guards, the Brunhiem is a compact liquid fiber laser. The lasing medium is optical fibers, coiled to pack more power into a weapon that is smaller, lighter, and more easily maneuverable than most of its contemporaries. The Brunhiem employs three separate packets of carefully coiled optical fibers. The packets each have access to the Pylum battery, a relatively small affair for a laser. Because of the smaller size, the Pylum does not consume all the heat created by the lasing process, and so is surround-ed by a liquid coolant, running through tubes wrapped around the battery. The separate beams from the three packets combine in the reflective chamber as the weapon primes.

Priming: 3 seconds
Health Length Without Charging: 2 weeks
Weight: 9.27 pounds
Accuracy: Excellent

**Toaster**

A large optic laser employing several stages of photon conversions for optimum interaction with the target. The Toaster starts in the first chamber as infrared beams, travels through special optics to become green light, then converts to ultraviolet in a third chamber. By the time it releases from the third chamber, the Toaster beam is one of the more powerful laser weapons employed. The three different phases of the photons however make it too large for a handheld weapon, and most used in the field are from KAM's design of a truck-mounted version.

Priming: 15 seconds
Health Length Without Charging: 10 days
Weight: 208.6 pounds
Accuracy: Tolerable
Strength: Decimating

**Ruby**

A mass market weapon, the Ruby is a solid-state laser found in most kingdoms during the Book Base Age. It employs a synthetic ruby rod as a medium and is prized for its small size. Because of the single-handed size, the battery is necessarily smaller, making the power less effective. It creates a lethal laser shot, but only at a range of up to six feet. A popular choice for personal defense, but not optimal as an army weapon.

Priming: 4 seconds
Health Length Without Charging: 5 days
Weight: 6.3 pounds
Accuracy: Average

**Strafer**

Setup very like a Ruby laser, this is a close range weapon used for personal defense. It is small enough even for concealment upon a person, a rare thing with a weaponized laser. The strafer varies from the Ruby in the makeup of its lenses. The strafer has a combination of five lenses, carefully overlaid with one another, capable of being aligned into one stronger beam, or shifted to create up to eight different beams. In a close quarters fight it can be used to take down multiple enemies, making it ideal for self defense.

Priming: 4 seconds
Health Length Without Charging: 5 days
Weight: 6.5 pounds
Accuracy: Average

**Krackmen**

The Krackmen is a prepossessing weapon with its intricately crafted red carbon stock. It is a dye laser utilizing rhodamine, and the accuracy is legendary, though the priming time is a serious drawback to the weapon.

Priming: 7 seconds
Health Length Without Charging: 1 week
Weight: 15.9 pounds
Accuracy: Exceptional

**Luttle**

A dye laser, the luttle uses a gain medium of organic dye that can be switched out according to the type of beam desired. It is a fairly small, light rifle, designed to be adaptable to the particular skills and preferences of a shooter. Often the choice for young learners, as the dye can be adapted to less dangerous options. Some object to the luttle on the grounds the aiming mechanism is not as advanced as others, such as the Krackmen, but many prefer it for the size and flexibility.

Priming: 3 seconds
Healthy Length Without Charging: 3 weeks
Weight: 7.2 pounds
Accuracy: Moderate

**Healy**

Termed by some a variation of a Brunhiem, the Healy laser is a liquid fiber laser, with the battery wrapped in liquid coolant, as the heat from the lasing process is not fully consumed by the Pylum. It contains four chambers of optical fibers. With the smaller size, and the four chambers placed directly against the Pylum battery, the priming time is excessively short, and the energy impressive especially with being emitted almost immediately.

Priming: 1.5 seconds
Health Length Without Charging: 2 weeks
Weight: 9.47 pounds
Accuracy: Excellent

**Compton**

A revolutionary weapon, the Compton laser is the first to utilize dark energy and matter as an energy source. Two balls of carefully fashioned Z shielding are bound next to each other in a copper fitting. Inside one is a ball of dark matter, inside the other dark energy; they are small enough as to be almost trace amounts. But when activated, a "window" is cracked between the two. Dark matter and dark energy excite each other when combined, and create what science currently sees as an inexhaustible source of

energy. The gun then utilizes Compton scattering between the two balls to harvest gamma rays. The rays are fired through a crystal lens fashioned after the Krackmens' excellent design. Gamma rays are invisible to the human eye, and so most Compton guns are sold with specially dyed goggles to allow the shooter to see where his rays land. Currently thought inexhaustible, nearly unbreakable, and as small as a Ruby laser (though considerably heavier), a Compton is viewed as the best weapons breakthrough since the Pylum battery.

Priming: 0 seconds
Health Length Without Charging: Unknown
Weight: 9.4 pounds
Accuracy: Very Exceptional

**PUDRE Dark Ray**

The Pulsating Ultrasonic Dark Ray Emitter, or PUDRE, came on the market ten years after the invention of the first Compton laser pistol. Observing the interaction between the dark matter and dark energy, the inventor of the PUDRE foresaw a different use than the laser; through careful experimentation he discovered how to form a localized, directed black hole effect. The ray beams a concentrated black hole, sucking anything it hits into the devastating dark force. It is capable of twisting steel and titanium, breaking diamond glass, generally wrecking anything it hits. The distance and concentration of the beam can be adjusted, its range being between six yards to twelve yards.

**Speed of Light Transportation Device - SOLTD**

A foray into new technology during the mid-200s of the Book Age, the SOLTD utilizes dark matter and dark energy to form what the inventor, Quintus Leeman, terms a space-warp bubble. Originally he was searching for a method of time travel, and speculated on the possibility of creating a time-warp bubble by the use of the black hole. Through careful experimentation he discovered there is a calm at the center of the massive force caused by mixing dark

matter and energy, and it is possible to be enclosed safely in the midst of the swirling mass of a black hole by intentionally causing it. The bioelectricity of living beings is "felt out" by the black hole as it forms, and it molds itself around it. The SOLTD makes it possible to move large amounts of living things at the speed of light, if there is no break in the chain of bioelectricity within the center of the hole.

The inventor admits it was an accident that set him in history as the first SOLTD traveler. During an experiment his assistant entered, opening the specially-reinforced door. The black hole currently formed in his lab sensed a small source of other dark matter and energy and the inventor found himself displaced, suddenly in the Kingdom of the Wise quite literally crashing in on the inventor of the PUDRE, as Hyram Grange completed his work on that gadget. Leeman did not travel through time as he had originally hoped, instead he found he had moved kingdoms with almost no time involved. He was quick to see the possibilities of the SOLTD as a transportation device.

The method of programming the direction of travel took him two years to perfect, and to this day only those specially licensed to build the SOLTDs are allowed to know the intricacies of the method involved. We do know it employs small bits of dark matter and dark energy, attracted to particular places through the peculiarities of the earth's magnetism. The smaller pieces are carefully introduced to the larger pieces contained in each individual SOLTD's Z shielding balls. Through this they come to "know" each other, thus eliminating the possibility of multiple SOLTDs detecting the same pieces of matter and energy and intersecting.

The SOLTD changed the course of the Book Age, allowing those kingdoms and peoples who first attained proficiency in the gadget to gain a solid foothold over those slower to acknowledge the incredible usefulness of being able to "zap" people anywhere on the planet. To this day it marks a turning point in the technologies of mankind.

# *Kingdom Worldviews*

## *The Battle Kingdom*

***Book Base***

*Thus Spoke Zarathustra*

Nietzsche, Friedrich, *Thus Spoke Zarathustra*. Translated by Walter Kaufmann, Viking Penguin, 1966.

***Government Structure***

> *"I teach you the overman. Man is something that shall be overcome. What have you done to overcome him?... What is ape to man? A laughingstock or a painful embarrassment. And man shall be just that for the overman: a laughingstock or a painful embarrassment... Once the sin against God was the greatest sin; but God died, and these sinners died with him. To sin against the earth is now the most dreadful thing, and to esteem the entrails of the unknowable higher than the meaning of the earth." (Pg. 12-13)*
>
> *"All-to-many are born: for the superfluous the state was invented... Only where the state ends, there begins the human being who is not superfluous: there begins the song of necessity, the unique and inimitable tune. Where the state* ends *– look there, my brothers! Do you not see it, the rainbow and the bridges of the overman?" (Pg 49, 59)*

The goal of the Battle Kingdom is to overcome humanness. They desire to create something new, something more than what man is now. Throughout their book contempt for the rabble, the crowds, the common people, runs alongside the elevation of a greater, stronger, pride-filled man.

> *"Companions, the creator seeks, not corpses, not herds and believers. Fellow creators, the creator seeks – those who*

*write new values on new tablets." (Pg. 24)*

When the reader first meets Zarathustra (the narrator and hero of the book), he has been ten years on a mountain with the eagles and sun for company. He flees down to the people because he must burst if he does not tell others of the wisdom he has discovered in his solitude. At the end of the book, Zarathustra is once more in solitude, and the very end he is striding off alone into the wilderness to find the overman, the greater-than-human.

Solitude and a huge emphasis on going against the throng, standing above and outside the rabble, are major themes playing throughout the Battle Kingdom. It makes it difficult to have a cohesive government. Many leave the cities in an effort to have true solitude. But the Battle Kingdom sits in a desert, with little water, extreme changes in temperature, and very hungry animals. Those who seek true solitude there rarely last longer than a few weeks. Many travel through the desert to places more able to sustain a solitary lifestyle. It is almost commonplace to find citizens of the Battle Kingdom in caves and huts scattered throughout the mountains of the world, regardless of what border they actually inhabit. Because of this wholesale searching for solitude in which to create their own values and wisdom, the Battle Kingdom is necessarily smaller than some others in the BB age.

Even Zarathustra realized there must be some sort of state wherever humans inhabit the world. But another difficulty with creating a cohesive government is that values of good and evil are to be created by the individual, and must not be applied to a whole kingdom.

*"All names of good and evil are parables: they do not define, they merely hint." (Pg 75)*

The only definitions of "good" given in the book are for the creation of the overman, the great overcoming. Most of the emphasis is upon personal overcoming. Each man is to create their own overman, it isn't really meant to be a social construct. But in order to survive, they found the few passages in the book that do speak in generality instead of individualism.

*"You say it is the good cause that hallows even war? I say to you: it is a good war that hallows any cause. War and courage have accomplished more great things than love of the neighbor. Not your pity but your courage has so far saved the unfortunate." (Pg 47)*

*"Men should be educated for war, and women for the recreation of the warrior; all else is folly." (Pg. 66)*

*"Your love of life shall be love of your highest hope; and your highest hope shall be the highest thought of life. Your highest thought, however, you should receive as a command from me – and it is: man is something that shall be overcome." (Pg. 48)*

It is logical in their book to extrapolate a leader above the rest. The method of choosing that leader becomes difficult, however, when everyone has different values of what is highest. What developed naturally from the book, over the course of several generations, was trial by strength; those who overcame everything placed in their path became the leader of the Battle Kingdom, holding the title of Overman. It is a position that overturns fairly regularly, as new challengers rise. The Overman does little more than be the face of the kingdom to the outside world, the Battle Kingdom citizens do not look kindly on another's values imposed upon them.

Those within the kingdom exist as individuals highly independent of one another, but often grouped into informal brotherhoods of those with common ideals. (Zarathustra speaks of his "friends" fairly often throughout the book.) There is a small circle of inner elite holding more influence and power than the others, as friends of the Overman. This is the extent of the governing in the nation.

There are no laws, as such. To place laws over those seeking overman would be to make more rabble, to cow the spirit of those striving to create. Zarathustra gives a railing speech (Pgs. 36-40) against judges who condemn murderers as "evil" and "sinners;" the evil of today, he says, wasn't always considered evil in other

times and cultures. It is up to the individual to cultivate their own values. There are a few tempering agents in the kingdom, such as Zarathustra's comment, *"And there is nobody from whom I want beauty as much as from you who are powerful: let your kindness be your final self-conquest. Of all evil I deem you capable: therefore I want the good from you." (Pg. 118)* "The good" is left to each individual to define, but there is supposed to be a specific goal to each value created.

There are a few ideals held in common in the kingdom, mostly stemming from common loathing by the citizens. They do not allow any form of religion in their kingdom. It will bring capital punishment: either in the form of a mob lynching or being thrown into the arena for entertainment. Much of the book is a pounding home of the fact that God is dead, and those who look outside the world to otherworldly things, are sick and deceivers even of themselves, people who corrupt everything they come in contact with. *"Many sick people have always been among the poetizers and God-cravers;" (Pg. 33)*

There are no national charities, and healthcare is difficult to find and not of an advanced kind. *"If I must pity, at least I do not want it known; and if I do pity, it is preferably from a distance." (Pg. 88)*

Schools are not prized, what a boy learns is usually only what is passed on from their father. *"That everyone may learn to read, in the long run corrupts not only writing but also thinking. Once the spirit was God, then he became man, and now he even becomes rabble. Whoever writes in blood and aphorisms does not want to read but to be learned by heart." (Pg. 40)*

The Battle Kingdom desires overcoming. It is, as has been stated, mostly an inner overcoming, a striving to overcome yourself and create something higher. But that is hard to measure, and frankly, in a kingdom of strong men constantly talking of battle and overcoming, rather dull. Also, if the leader desires to remain the leader it is wise to turn the citizen's eyes to overcoming something besides himself. The kingdom often strikes out and attacks

other kingdoms. The citizens did not name themselves. In the first two generations of the BB age, they attacked almost everyone. The rest of the world dubbed them The Battle Kingdom, and it remains their name to this day.

### *Incompletes and Chimeras*

*"Life is a well of joy; but where the rabble drinks too, all wells are poisoned." (Pg. 96)*

*"And he whom you cannot teach to fly, teach to fall faster!" (Pg. 209)*

*"Behold the superfluous! They steal the works of the inventors and the treasures of the sages for themselves; 'education' they call their theft – and everything turns to sickness and misfortune for them. Behold the superfluous! They are always sick; they vomit their gall and call it a newspaper." (Pg. 50)*

Evolution is a part of the belief system for the Battle Kingdom. If evolution is not true, man cannot evolve into the overman. If it is true, the philosophy propounded by KAM about the incompletes and chimeras makes perfect sense. The Battle Kingdom views incompletes and chimeras as lower animals, they are not humans.

### *Art and Music*

*"I would believe only in a god who could dance. And when I saw my devil I found him serious, thorough, profound, and solemn..." (Pg. 41)*

*"Only in the dance do I know how to tell the parable of the highest things: and now my highest parable remained unspoken in my limbs." (Pg. 112)*

*[Several passages have Zarathustra singing, for instance, The Seven Seals on Pg. 228]*

Somewhat surprisingly for a book that fosters prideful warriors, dancing and creating your own poetic songs is encouraged,

and considered a sign that the overman draws nearer. Because reading is not encouraged the songs are never written down, and as the individual is exalted and the past is of no interest, word-of-mouth songs do not last more than one generation. While in the Battle Kingdom you may hear many songs, and sometimes you will even find Battle Kingdom contestants entered in the Seal Annual Music Festival (one of the most renowned artistic endeavors of the BB age). But the songs rarely last longer than a few years, and because solitude is so encouraged, it is rare they are carried to other kingdoms.

### *Science and Advancements*

*"God is a conjecture; but I desire that your conjectures should be limited by what is thinkable. Could you* think *a God? But this is what the will to truth should mean to you: that everything be changed into what is thinkable for man, visible for man, feelable by man. You should think through your own senses to their consequences.*

*"And what you have called world, that shall be created only by you: your reason, your image, your will, your love shall thus be realized. And verily, for your own bliss, you lovers of knowledge." (Pg. 86)*

*"Alongside the bad conscience, all science has grown so far. Break, break, you lovers of knowledge, the old tablets!" (Pg. 200)*

Science is welcomed in the Battle Kingdom. "Lovers of knowledge" are applauded by Zarathustra in the book. Anything is allowed in the pursuit of science. However, the sections speaking of science and the lovers of knowledge are short and not seen often in the book. The pursuit of scientific advancement is not something many people aspire to in the Battle Kingdom, as the emphasis lies elsewhere.

### *Army*

*"To die this is best; second to this, however, is to die fighting*

*and to squander a great soul. But equally hateful to the fighter and the victor is your grinning death, which creeps up like a thief – and yet comes as the master." (Pg. 72)*

*"On a thousand bridges and paths they shall throng to the future, and ever more war and inequalities shall divide them: thus does my great love make me speak...arms shall they be and clattering signs that life must overcome itself again and again." (Pg. 101)*

Like the government structure, there is no cohesive army in the Battle Kingdom. But as entering a war provides many tangible expressions of overcoming, the citizens are willing to join in when needed. The book has many statements about enemies and conquering throughout it, the citizens feel closer to Zarathustra when engaged in the rush of battle. *"And when I want to mount my wildest horse, it is always my spear that helps me up best, as the ever-ready servant of my foot: the spear that I hurl against my enemies. How grateful I am to my enemies that I may finally hurl it!" (Pg. 84)*

There is no standing army in the kingdom, but the people there come together to fight willingly.

***Social Structure***

*"The happiness of man is: I will. The happiness of woman is: he wills." (Pg. 67)*

*"A real man wants two things: danger and play. Therefore he wants woman as the most dangerous plaything." (Pg. 66)*

*"You are going to women? Do not forget the whip!" (Pg 67)*

*"...and verily, I did not feed them bloating vegetables, but warriors' nourishment, conquerors' nourishment... Such nourishment, to be sure, may not be suitable for children or for nostalgic old and young little females. Their entrails are persuaded in a different way; I am not their physician and teacher." (Pg. 311)*

A woman is not a part of the dream of overman, unless it be that she can give birth to one. In the creation of new overman (i.e. birthing new babies) she is to be a partner to the men of the kingdom. In other things, she is a recreation and a snare. Marriages

that last a lifetime are not necessarily encouraged:

*"Therefore I would have those who are honest say to each other, 'We love each other; let us see to it that we remain in love. Or shall our promise be a mistake?'*

*"'Give us a probation and a little marriage, so that we may see whether we are fit for a big marriage. It is a big thing always to be two.'*

*"Thus I counsel all who are honest; and what would my love for the overman and for all who shall yet come amount to if I counseled and spoke differently? Not merely to reproduce, but to produce something* higher - *toward that, my brothers, the garden of marriage should help you." (Pg. 211)*

All this put together means the family structure in the Battle Kingdom is shaky, at best. The family unit is one of the things that helps to bring cohesivity to a kingdom. The lack of it is one more thing that makes the Battle Kingdom always on the verge of straight anarchy.

Thinking is encouraged, learning is not.

Strong bodies are nurtured. The sick or weak are not pitied, and usually not helped.

The ideas propounded by *Zarathustra* are individualistic. When a kingdom attempts to employ them it devolves into men attempting to gain physical and mental superiority over each other. The only time cohesiveness comes to the nation is in periods of warring with other states; this creates a joint enemy, instead of seeing each other constantly as the enemy, especially those in a place of authority above you. No matter who the Overman, this philosophy brings about a practical effect. Ten-thousand men who view him as a personal enemy naturally causes the Overman to desire a common enemy that is not himself. The Battle Kingdom is almost always at war. This of course means there is little time for trade or agriculture to flourish. What the Battle Kingdom does have mostly comes from spoils of war.

When too impoverished of either money or manpower to make war practical, the Overman usually attempts to distract his people by fights in the arena. There are no wild beasts left alive in a radius of a hundred miles around Overman City. "Enemies and spies" are found disturbingly often and end in the arena, and everyone watches for the hated few who might still cling to the old dead God. However, many contestants enter the arena willingly, as it offers a clear, physical way to overcome both yourself and outside enemies.

The women stand in the background and watch, only pulled into the light as playthings and procreators.

---

## *Story Land*

### *Book Base*

*Ducky's Big Pond*

Vlanderbelt, Vera, *Ducky's Big Pond*. Illustrated by Laura Moler, Penguin Random House, 3466.

### *Government Structure*

*"I will go for a walk today. Perhaps I will find something to do." (Pg. 1)*

Let me tell you a story. There once was a man named Jarrod Talum. As he traveled along the coastline, he came to realize that people understood things differently according to their own experiences and interpretation of the world. And why not? Why should there be one thing that's true for everyone, instead of each individual having their own truths? The more he spoke to people, the more he realized that none of them really understood what he meant.[15] This confirmed his theory that truth could only be grasped by the individual, and that it changes from person to person.

It was about this time *Ducky's Big Pond* came into Talum's hands. He flipped through the book and enjoyed the bright illustrations. Gradually he came to see the small duck's journey to find something to do as an allegorical expression of life. We are all, according to Talum, on a journey to find something to do. And the

---

[15] It never occurred to Talum their confused expressions might stem from their thinking his ideas nonsense.

answer comes differently for each of us. Each individual sees life through their own lens. Sharing viewpoints, or "truth" as most of the world call it, is practically impossible. Even the duck in the book came under Talum's own interpretation. When the duck said, "Quack, quack," to the cat did he mean, "Chase me," or "Please look at the blue sky." The cat heard, "Chase me," but Talum heard, "Look at the blue sky." Both were true according to the different individuals who heard it.

Talum settled along the coast. Gradually others settled around him, those who either agreed with his assumption that truth changes according to each person's perception, and those who simply preferred the tropical flowers and unrestrictive kingdom.

It didn't form into an actual kingdom until a woman named Beria approached Talum with a desperate plea for help to recover her three-year-old son from her husband-turned-nasty. Talum turned to his best friend, a man named Greg. History has lost his last name, it seems everyone knew him as Greg. They also knew him for being just and brave. He listened to Beria, immediately declared that interpretation went only so far as the single individual, when it invaded other individual's lives to their hurt, intervention became necessary. He formed a posse and restored Beria's son to his mother in less than an hour.

For most, that day marks the formal creation of Story Land. Of course there are some who interpret it as other days, that is in the nature of the kingdom. But for most, Story Land formed the day the one law came into being: If one individual's interpretation causes harm to another individual, there is just cause to intervene. Of course there are thousands of interpretations of that one law, but in the history of the kingdom we find people who are willing to draw a line and step in: those are the people keeping the kingdom functioning as a kingdom. Because of their work, social interactions are possible within Story Land. They gradually became known as the Social Workers, and they have a strict hierarchy and long work hours.

Those who term themselves in charge of Story Land, the government, change frequently. When anyone can extrapolate their own meaning from the kingdom's book, anyone can claim their own form of leadership. Usually the overthrows come by

employing mercenaries from outside and the seedier elements within the kingdom. (A kingdom with only one law naturally caters to those who prefer not to follow laws.) But after the dust clears and a new form of governing comes into play, the SW is still there, and still keeps the kingdom's general structure.

### *Incompletes and Chimeras*

*"'What's your name?' Ducky asked the frog. But the frog just stared." (Pg. 20)*

Once there was a governor named Janet Grange. She admired KAM very much, and declared incompletes and chimeras not wholly human, and therefore not entitled to full rights. But one day she was overthrown by the Neil Family. The Neils, like the other governors of Story Land, took this portion of the book, and the strong leaning toward individualism throughout the kingdom, and choose to see incompletes and chimeras as the same as anyone else.

### *Art and Music*

*"When the leaf fell from the tree, it danced. Ducky watched as it swirled and spun. 'It needs music to dance to,' thought Ducky. She began to sing." (Pg. 11)*

Let me tell you about Ben Carson. Here is a man who loves music. Ben Carson lived in Story Land in the year 100 of the Book Base Age. It seemed a very significant number to him, and somehow needed marked and celebrated. His interpretation for marking the 100th year turned into the Seal Annual Music Festival, so named after his favorite animal (at that time abundant in great herds on the beaches of Story Land). Let me tell you of another individual, Ben's wife Henrietta Carson. Thanks to Henrietta's exceptional organizational and promotional skills, the SAMF quickly became a worldwide sensation. Any band stamped with the label, "SAMF Champion," can be assured of their future popularity.

Naturally, as the home of the SAMF, musicians and artists abound within the kingdom. Most of them also appreciate the "anything goes" attitude of the Story Land, and settle happily within the borders.

***Science and Advancements***

*"Ducky waddled on, leaving the frog, and the cat, and the leaf. The pond seemed to stretch out forever in front of her. 'Maybe it does go on forever! How do I find out?' she wondered." (Pg. 21)*

Violeta Yin loved science. She grew up longing for nothing so much as to be a scientist and help the people around her by finding new things. Story Land welcomed her ambitions, and others like her, and she enjoyed a long career in the Niel Science Hall. Some of her interpretation of the world, however, other kingdoms find it hard to agree with. Violeta loved the color violet. She loved it so much, she placed violet dye in her permanent contacts, and thereafter declared the world could only be observed in shades of purple. Another time, she published a widely read paper stating popcorn balls were overgrown atoms humans felt compelled to create, because of outside influence from the stars.

There are many similar storylines of scientists within Story Land. If a scientist has a desire for worldwide recognition, emigration to KAM or the Sojourners is the most often sought course.

***Army***

*"The dog ran at Ducky, and his teeth looked very sharp. Ducky fluttered her wings and landed gently in the pond. The dog slid to a stop at the edge and stared at her. 'There you war hound,' Ducky quacked as she paddled, 'you will not eat me today.'" (Pg. 13)*

Once a Story Land governor named Wilt Umtern chose to see the world in red. The export fees had been high that season, the coffers of the kingdom full. He used it to outfit a great army, and marched off to war. They overthrew two kingdoms before Umtern met his death at the hands of a Battle Kingdom spear, and the army dispersed with their kits.

During his lifetime Wilt Umtern expressed a great loneliness, because no one in the past or present of his kingdom seemed to adhere to his truth. It is a kindness he did not know the future. The coming governors, like those in the past, looked at the dog section of the book, and their own personal stories, and decided being the attacker is not wisdom.

There was another man named Vergal the Vicious, Wazir of the Prophet's Peace, who saw overrunning new kingdoms as his main truth. The year 92 of the BB Age saw his black army ranged against the Story Land border. The citizens decided they did not like the idea of Vergal the Vicious, and raided a local munitions plant. Vergal the Vicious was forced into retreat with only a quarter of his army left alive.

### *Social Structure*

*"And so Ducky arrived back at her nest. She fluffed the downy feathers and settled in for a rest, suddenly very tired. 'I suppose "having an adventure" was what I did today,' she said to herself. 'But I am glad I'm home.'" (Pg. 22)*

There are some interpretations which state Talum lived on the verge of insanity, and just happened on good friends and good luck. Other interpretations place him as one of the smartest leaders in history, who used a philosophy to his advantage. Whichever story you choose, Story Land sits on the best coastland for trading known to the Book Base Age. The import and export fees are usually kept low, which facilitates a great deal of movement back and forth. The busy port creates revenue for the kingdom, and lots of jobs. The high turn-around of governments combined with the heavy emphasis on individual stories fosters factories with almost no government regulations, and medium to low tax rates.

Like Frank and Myra Yeals, makers of personalized bone plants, most of the people of story land enjoy prosperity. This allows them leisure to enjoy each other, and find time to foster the things they love. Architects find a great deal of work around the country, as the citizens enjoy expressing their personal stories through their building styles.

It would take much too long to tell all the stories of the living styles, work ethics, school tactics, and religious preferences of Story Land. Just so long as no serious harm comes to someone against their will, anything is allowed. Some things are quite unpopular, such as holding to a truth that tells others their stories are untrue, or believing there is only actually one truth which ought to be applied to everyone. Usually any who do hold to viewpoints of that nature (completely at odds with the basic Story

Land premise) merely face extreme peer pressure and dislike from their fellow citizens. But there are times the dislike becomes hatred. The lack of laws and government oversight tends to foster a criminal element in Story Land, which are always for hire: those holding fast to the belief there is only one real truth sometimes find their neighbors' hatred flare into violent action against them.

But on the whole, the social structure of Story Land can be summed up in the words, "eclectic and individualistic."

# *Recipes*

## Chocolate Chip Cookies

1 ½ cup Crisco*
2 ½ cups brown sugar
4 Tbs milk
2 eggs
4 cups flour
2 tsp vanilla
2 cups chocolate chips

*Crisco can be substituted for butter. If you do substitute, omit the milk.

Cream the butter and sugar. Add the milk and eggs. Mix in the flour a cup at a time. Stir in the vanilla and chocolate chips.
Roll into 1-2 inch balls and place on a cookie sheet. Bake at 375 for 8-10 minutes, and enjoy.

## Lemon Chicken and Asparagus

### Makes 4 Campfire Foil Packs

4 chicken breasts
Two lemons
1 pound asparagus
4 Tbs butter
1 tsp black pepper
1 tsp rosemary
2 garlic cloves
Salt to taste

Make four 12x12 foil "plates" and lay them on the counter. (Remember you can use more than one sheet if you need to layer.) Slice a lemon in half and squeeze some of the juice onto each plate. Slice the rest of the lemons.
Place one of the pieces of chicken onto each foil plate.
Slice the tough ends off the asparagus and discard, then divide the

pound between the four plates.
Melt the butter. Mix the spices into the butter, then drizzle over the asparagus and chicken.
Arrange the lemon slices on top and around the chicken and asparagus.
Carefully fold the foil over to create a packet. At this point you can either place the packet directly on your campfire coals, or place in Ziplock bags and refrigerate until ready to cook.
To cook, place the packet on an area of the campfire where the fire has recently died out; not on direct flames, but on hot coals. Allow to cook for fifteen minutes, then turn to the other side, and cook for another fifteen minutes. Puncture the foil, allow to rest for five minutes, then unwrap and enjoy.
(If you feel like being boring, or have no access to a campfire, you are allowed to put the packets on the grill.)

# *Sign Language Alphabet*

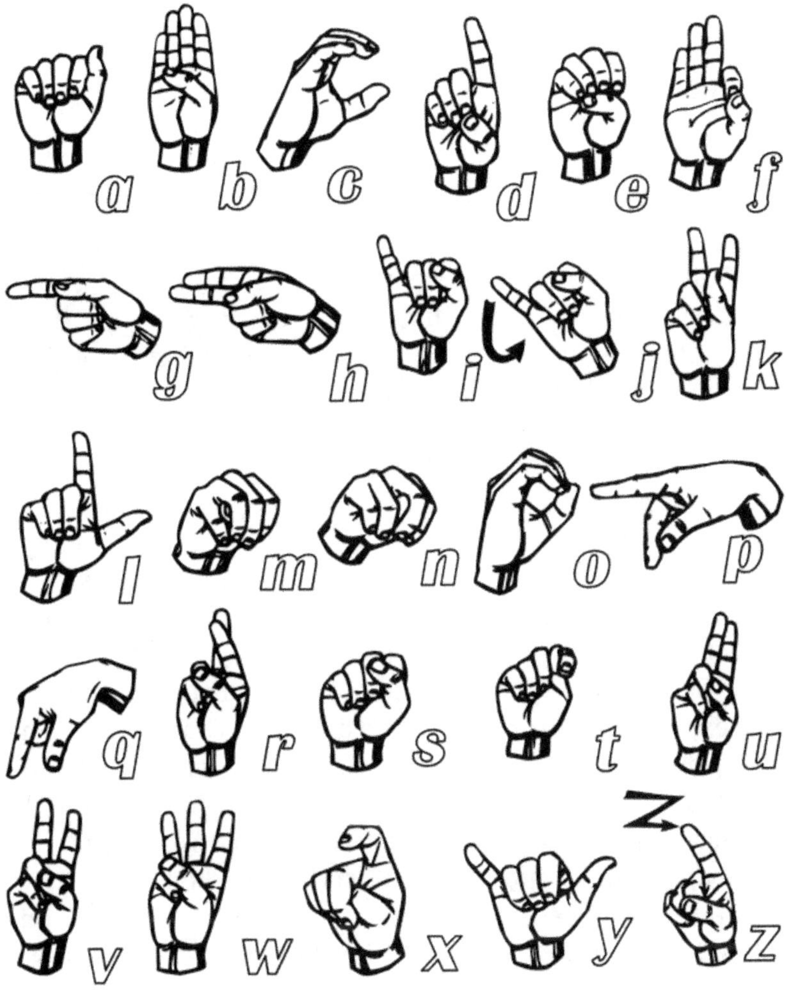

a b c d e f

g h i j k

l m n o p

q r s t u

v w x y z

# *Author Bio*

Catherine Gruben Smith lives in the middle of Texas, which she begrudgingly admits is probably better than a magical tower. She grew up mostly in a dusty town in the southern New Mexican desert and will always carry the quirks. (Yes, New Mexico is a part of the United States, and no, she was not a missionary, and yes, you can drink the water.) It is her delight and privilege to be a housewife, mother, and an Earl Gray connoisseur. Another of her constant activities is trying to keep her dogs from terrorizing the house and neighborhood with their determination to be always underfoot and hungry. (The work of a dog lover is never done.) She has always been fascinated by the written word, philosophical reasoning, and good stories of bravery and honor. When not writing, reading, chasing children or dogs, Catherine can be found board-gaming, baking, hiking, or possibly broad sword fighting with her older brother. If you want a fuller explanation of Catherine, go and read Psalm 30. The heart and purpose of her life can be found there, especially in the last two verses.

Catherine prays reading her books will help her readers find the urge to get up off the couch and serve. The Lord of all life calls us to the battlefield, to mop up the enemy after He has won the war. Don't sit on the side-lines. We have the tools to fix this broken world.

**Where to find more information, or contact Catherine:**

catherinegrubensmith.com

catherinegrubensmith@gmail.com

posttenebrasluxbooks.com

Books by Catherine Gruben Smith

***Sojourners:***
*Ravens Ruins*
*Ravens Rescue*
*Ravens Return*
*Ravens Refuge*
*Ravens Raid*
*Ravens Rebirth*

***Parabaloni Series:***
*The Parabaloni*
*The Slingshot Effect*
*As the Eagle Flies*
*Solitaire*
*Adele Angst*
*Blind Leader*
*Gathering Shadows*
*Black Out*

***Dreaded King Saga:***
*A Son Rises*
*Reign Falls*
*Knight Duty*
*Heir Raising*
*Splitting Heirs*
***Knight Job Series:***
*Wail of the Wyrm*

***Faerytales of Deweot:***
*How to Unmake a Dragon*
*Faery Wings and Pirate Things*

www.ingramcontent.com/pod-product-compliance
Lightning Source LLC
LaVergne TN
LVHW020705110826
845149LV00012B/2121